Smitten with the Orthopedic Surgeon

Daphne Dyer

Skyway Creative Endeavors

Copyright © 2024 by Daphne Dyer, Skyway Creative Endeavors

All rights reserved.

No part of this publication may be reproduced, distributed, or transmitted in any form or by any means, including photocopying, recording, or other electronic or mechanical methods, without the prior written permission of the publisher, except as permitted by U.S. copyright law except in brief quotations in a book review. For permission requests, contact daphne@daphnedyer.com.

The story, all names, characters, and incidents portrayed in this production are fictitious and products of the author's imagination. Any resemblance to actual people, places, or events is entirely coincidental.

Book Cover by Daniel at thebookbrander.com

Editing by Emily Shelton Poole at Midnight Owl Editors

NO AI Training: Without in anyway limiting the author's exclusive rights under copyright, any use of this publication to "train" generative artificial intelligence (AI) technologies to generate text is expressly prohibited. The author reserves all rights to license uses of this work for generative AI training and development of machine learning language models.

Other Titles

Emerald Bay Chefs Romances

Road Trip Bestie

Restaurant Wars

The Puppy Bribe

The Football Bargain

Third Coast Medical Romances

Road Trip Ruin

Smitten with the Orthopedic Surgeon

Hating the Emergency Physician, part of the *Sweet and Swoony Holiday Anthology*

Stuck with the Anesthesiologist

For everyone who has ever been told they are "Too Much,"
Be You! Don't let anyone hold you back or try to make you small because of their insecurities.
You are exactly who you were created to be.
Love, Daphne

Contents

1. Chapter 1 — 1
2. Chapter 2 — 10
3. Chapter 3 — 17
4. Chapter 4 — 24
5. Chapter 5 — 33
6. Chapter 6 — 45
7. Chapter 7 — 57
8. Chapter 8 — 68
9. Chapter 9 — 76
10. Chapter 10 — 83
11. Chapter 11 — 90
12. Chapter 12 — 99
13. Chapter 13 — 111
14. Chapter 14 — 122
15. Chapter 15 — 133
16. Chapter 16 — 143
17. Chapter 17 — 153
18. Chapter 18 — 163

19.	Chapter 19	171
20.	Chapter 20	183
21.	Chapter 21	195
22.	Chapter 22	202
23.	Chapter 23	215
24.	Chapter 24	228
25.	Chapter 25	237
26.	Chapter 26	248
27.	Chapter 27	259
28.	Chapter 28	269
29.	Chapter 29	275
30.	Chapter 30	285
31.	Chapter 31	291
32.	Chapter 32	300
33.	Chapter 33	310
34.	Chapter 34	317
35.	Chapter 35	329
36.	Chapter 36	340
37.	Chapter 37	349
38.	Epilogue	355
	Stuck with the Anesthesiologist	361
	Afterword	363
	About Daphne	365

Chapter 1

Bridgette

EDISON BULBS REFLECT OFF the restaurant's mahogany bar and twinkle in my best friend's lovestruck eyes.

"To the end of an era. Congratulations." I raise my glass, and our friends join the chorus toasting my last single friend's engagement.

Camille clutches her fiancé's collar, deepens their kiss, and elicits catcalls from the celebrating crowd.

She's radiant. This engagement party is the perfect way to capture Camille and Liam's happiness.

Their reflected spark warms my belly and makes me hopeful and grateful and excited for the future. They bring out the best in each other as true soulmates should.

I want what they have.

Something like envy niggles the back of my brain, but I shove it into the filing cabinet where I keep things I don't like to think about. Like bikini waxes and fatbergs.

I lock the filing cabinet and throw the key in my mental junk drawer. I can examine my loneliness when I'm on my couch with a gallon of mint chip ice cream, not at a party in the middle of a crowded bar.

Being the only single person left in our friend group isn't a hardship. I'm confident in my skin and enjoy my own company. A man will never complete me because I'm not missing anything.

Singleness just feels a little... heavier now. When I don't understand an inside joke or everyone already has plans for a Friday night, isolation creeps into the corners of my heart. I can only spend so many hours at the bookstore debating with Turner before my energy tires the septuagenarian.

I swig my champagne. Effervescent and engaging. That's me. This is their party, their happily ever after, and I will celebrate my friends like they deserve.

I snatch Camille from Liam and throw my arms around her. "I'm so happy for you!" She hugs me back, too full of joy to speak. "Let's dance."

I twine my fingers through hers and lead her to the floor. Liam and our friends join the circle. The DJ spins Taylor Swift's "Miss Americana and The Heartbreak Prince." The bass drum pounds like a heartbeat in my chest. Nica and Ethan sway while Neal spins Bailey like he's Fred Astaire. Bryce pulls Isa's back to his chest, and he whispers in her ear. A deep blush paints her cheeks.

My eyes scan the bar's active crowd for someone to dance with.

Graham leans on a table in the corner with his buddies. My on-again-off-again ex lights up my hot-guy triggers. Long and lean with shaggy brown hair that's the perfect length to run my fingers through.

We had fun a couple of months ago. The relationship had some issues—he prefers unopinionated arm candy to my firework personality—but that doesn't mean he won't be up for a dance.

Our eyes meet. Hold.

His dash away.

He hides his mouth behind his hand. His friends stare at me and break into laughter.

But it's not a fun, go-get-her-tiger laugh. There's a hard, mean edge to it that makes my eyes skitter away.

Okay, that's a no.

I toss my blonde hair off the sweat at the back of my neck. There isn't one guy in this bar I haven't dated, flirted with, or turned down except for Graham's friends, and they are a no-fly zone.

Oh well. Party of one, here I come.

I lose myself in the music. The rhythm soothes their laughter's harsh edge. Song after song plays. I dance with Camille, Isa, Nica, and Bailey until their men pull them back.

When we need a water break, Camille and I snag a quieter table in the back of the bar. I clink my glass to hers. "Here's to a lifetime of happiness."

She doesn't drink. "I feel like I'm supposed to make a big production out of this, but I've got too many things in my brain to do that, so here it goes." She clasps my hands in hers. "Will you be my maid of honor?"

"Of course!" I squeal and throw my arms around her over the table.

She sags against my chest. "Thanks!"

I release her from our hug and roll my water glass across my forehead to cool off. "Were you worried I'd say no?"

"No, but ..." She picks at her nails.

I cover her hand with mine. Camille doesn't do nervous, so whatever is causing her not to meet my eye is bad. "What?"

"I saw your expression earlier. I know this is hard for you."

I don't mean to be envious, but change is hard, especially when I'm not the one changing. Everyone else is jumping into the next seasons of their lives, and I'm stuck in neutral.

I twist my hair into a bun and pin it back. "Baby cakes, nothing in the world would make me happier than helping you plan your perfect day." It will help me get over myself and this need to be part of a duet.

Camille's nose wrinkles. "Really? It doesn't make you sad? You looked at Graham like you were sad."

I pin my eyes to her, so I don't let them drift across the bar. "Let's call it hopeful for my own fairy tale, okay?"

I don't need a guy.

But it would be nice to have someone put me first. I want my own inside jokes and booked Friday nights. I want my fairy tale.

But I'm afraid I'm not destined for one.

Camille doesn't look like she believes me, but says, "Okay."

"Enough melancholy. Have you set a date?"

She waves away my question. "I haven't done anything. Honestly, I don't even know where to start. It's all so overwhelming." She digs her index fingers into her temples. "Liam's mom keeps calling with ideas, and I don't know her well enough to tell her I'm not ready for her color swatches and seating charts."

"Forward Liam's mom to me. I'll keep her out of your hair." I pull my phone from my pocket and open my calendar. "My next day off is Wednesday. We'll spend the whole day daydreaming about what you want, then I'll get on the phone and schedule venue visits and dress appointments."

That gives me four days to grab a bunch of bridal magazines, research ceremony and reception locations, and brainstorm themes.

She squeezes my hand. "Thank you. I don't know what I'd do without you taking over."

"I'll plan you the perfect wedding." And honestly, it's the perfect distraction from my stuckness, from the fact that nothing about my life ever changes. Helping her plan gives the illusion my life has forward momentum, even when it doesn't.

She hugs me again, and we shimmy to the dance floor. Sweat coats my body, and the champagne makes my mind a little fuzzy, even as I make to do lists for their wedding.

My eyes drift back to Graham. I'll need a date for the big day, but I have no idea where I'll find one. Single men do not grow on trees around here. At least, not the ones you actually want to get serious with.

I take another water break at the bar. The cool liquid soothes my throat, sore from singing along. One of Graham's friends orders a beer, so I'm polite and say, "Hi."

He settles his forearms on the bar. "Bridgette, right?"

"Yep, and you are?" I extend my hand.

His gaze drops to my fingers, and he slowly slides his rough palm against mine. I love a man who isn't afraid of a little hard labor.

"Jason." His index finger rubs the inside of my wrist and little bubbles travel up my skin. His deep blue eyes hold mine.

Jason is promising.

I tip my head toward the dance floor. "Do you dance?"

Maybe I misinterpreted the cruel laughter earlier.

The bartender slides Jason's glass across the bar. He drops my hand like he was caught trying to snag the last snickerdoodle in the jar. "Not tonight." He takes a sip, raises the glass to me, and heads back to his table.

Awesome.

Whatever.

I take my turn in the restroom and head back toward the dance floor.

Graham's voice carries over the music. "Dude, what did I tell you? Steer clear of Bridgette."

My ears perk. Why doesn't he want Jason to talk to me? Is Graham still interested despite the little laugh-fest earlier? Did he change his mind about my fireworks?

I slide into the shadows next to their table.

"Calm down. I just said hi," Jason says.

Graham pounds the table. "It starts with hello, then she takes over. She's too much. Too loud. Too bossy. Too demanding."

I press my back against the hallway wall and bite my knuckle to keep from marching to his table and giving him a piece of my too-bossy mind.

Too much? Too loud? Who does he think he is broadcasting his cutting remarks to guys who buy scones and coffee from me every morning? I can't take their orders with a smile when I know they think I'm a demanding, self-centered princess.

Jason raises his hands to calm Graham down. "Dude, what did she do to get under your skin?"

Graham sips his beer.

The other guys give each other a look. "You're totally freaking out. Are you still into her?"

"Ha! No." He slams his empty beer glass on the table. "I introduced her to my little sister, and when she left, Willa cried in her bedroom for the rest of the night. Bridgette was so intimidating, my sister went home believing she was insignificant and ugly. I will never be attracted to someone who walks over other people's self-esteem like yesterday's confetti."

"No!" I gasp, clamping my hands to my mouth.

Willa is sweet, kind, and introverted. An unsure caterpillar.

She sat in the corner, and when I tried to talk to her, she hid behind a blanket. I never meant to hurt her feelings. She didn't want to participate in the conversation, so I filled the silence while I cooked dinner.

Hurting her was unintentional.

But that doesn't matter.

Me being me hurt her self-esteem.

I won't let that happen again. I have to figure out how to fix this.

If Graham had told me about Willa's insecurities when we were dating, I would have fixed everything. She's gone to college now, so I can't pop by their parents' house with a present to apologize.

Graham will never give me her phone number. Maybe one of Camille's athletes has it.

Graham squeezes Jason's shoulder. "I know you, dude. You want a woman who'll be your forever. Trust me. Don't waste your time with an attention-seeking narcissist like her. Bridgette will *never* be anyone's forever."

Attention-seeking narcissist!

Never forever!

Is that why everyone else is in love except me?

My best friends never made it seem like my big personality was a bad thing.

I'm not demanding. I'm decisive.

I'm not bossy. I'm a go-getter.

I'm not self-centered. I'm self-confident.

I believed them. I embraced it.

Nothing's wrong with knowing what I want and going after it. That's what strong women do.

We set goals and pursue them.

Were they wrong about me? Am I wrong? Am I too confident?

Growing up, Mom and Dad were exhausted when they had to deal with my hairbrained ideas.

When I lost the nomination for student-body president, they faked being sorry. I heard them say they were relieved I wasn't organizing the senior class activities. They didn't think they could keep up with my never-ending ideas.

Being confident and energetic are personality flaws.

My eyes dart around the bar. My friends dance and laugh in their happy coupledom. They look blissful without me acting as a weird anchor. The miniature spare tire that doesn't fit with the other pairs.

Even if they're having fun on the other side of the bar without me, doesn't mean they don't want to spend time with me. They love me.

Graham's opinions shouldn't outweigh those of the people who know me the best. Consciously I realize this, but it doesn't stop the ache from spreading across my chest and digging into my stomach like the worm in a rotten apple.

My eyes close, and I count to ten to keep the worm from migrating out of my stomach and digging through the squishy exterior of my heart.

Someone, someday will fall in love with me. I know it.

I'll find a man who loves fireworks and appreciates me the way I am.

There's someone out there like that, isn't there?

The world's a big place. I just have to pray he'll take a spontaneous trip to Emerald Bay and come into my bakery. We'll make goo-goo eyes and fall in love like what happened with Camille and Liam.

I don't care what Graham says.

But you do care. You didn't used to, but you do now.

Never forever.

I can't be here anymore. I should be able to wipe the self-incrimination from my face, block out Graham's callous remarks, and celebrate with my friends, but I can't.

I can't see them all in love and know I'll never measure up. That every time I open my mouth or show confidence in myself, I could be unwittingly destroying someone else's self-esteem.

I won't destroy Camille's party like I destroyed dinner with Willa.

"Bridgette?" Camille waves from a quiet table in the back corner and lifts a glass of champagne for me.

Never forever.

Will a champagne toast celebrate my happily ever after?

I kiss Camille's cheek. "I'm heading out. I don't feel well and have an early start tomorrow."

She scoots to the edge of the vinyl booth. "I'll take you home."

I push her back. "Too much bubbly, not enough sleep. I'll be fine. This is your party. Stay."

"Are you sure you're okay?"

Tonight is her night. I won't ruin it by dumping what Graham said on her shoulders.

I clink my glass to hers. "Here's to your lifetime of happiness."

I snatch my purse from its hiding spot next to the bar and swing my coat over my shoulders. Snow swirls in the air. Minnesota in March bites my bare legs. Thank goodness for knee-high boots.

Too bad the tears are freezing on my cheeks, and Graham's words are spiraling stronger than the storm.

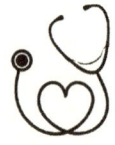

Chapter 2

Bridgette

I SHOULD GO HOME, distract myself with a Sean Connery-era James Bond movie, and soak my troubles in a bubble bath.

007 never has to apologize for being enthusiastically himself and single-mindedly pursuing what he wants. It's not his fault if men feel less manly after they see him in action.

I should take life lessons from him, but I can't get Willa out of my mind's eyes. Her downturned eyes and flat smile scrape against the inside of my eyelids and tell me I'm a horrible person for being the way that I am.

Too confident. Too proud. Too pretty.

I need a friend who'll listen. Someone who will tell me the truth instead of letting Graham's words grow like weeds in my subconscious.

Since my other friends are currently snogging their fiancés and husbands at the bar, I pound on Turner's faded yellow door and interrupt his REM cycles.

Older people wake up in the middle of the night anyway, right?

He opens the door and grunts. A red and green plaid bathrobe covers his lanky frame. Wire-rimmed glasses perch on the end of his nose. He shakes his head and walks back into his house, letting me follow in his wake.

"I'm sorry, but I didn't have anywhere else to go."

He points toward the leather sofa and continues his puttering pace into the kitchen. As I sit and snuggle under a wool throw blanket, ceramic clinks on the counter and water runs into a metal kettle.

He's making me tea.

It shouldn't bring more tears to my eyes, but the kindness is almost too much to bear after I woke him up and barged into his house.

There are those words again. *Too much.*

Why couldn't Graham's opinion have been that I was too kind or too sexy or too outgoing? That I did everything I could think of to draw his sister out of her shell.

I need clarity.

I need a tissue box to catch the emotions draining from my nose.

Turner hands me the mug. His head tilts to the side, and he fishes an honest-to-goodness cloth hanky out of his pocket. I blow my nose and mop my face.

Turner sips his tea. "To what do I owe the pleasure? I'm a little old for a booty call and you're not my type."

I lean my elbows on my knees, cradling the cup and letting the steam warm my face. "Am I too much?"

"In what sense?"

"I was at the bar—"

"Ah." He sets his cup on the table, steeples his fingers, and nods sagely. He reminds me of Dumbledore.

"Ah, what?"

"No heartwarming story ever starts with *I was at the bar*. That line is reserved for thrillers and crime dramas." As the owner of the town's bookstore, he would know.

"Drama is about right. Graham stopped his friends from talking to me and said I'm *too much*. That I will 'never be anyone's forever.'" I make air quotes. "And then he said I made his sister feel bad about herself by just being ... me." That dumb worm is gnawing through my stomach again. I hunch over to crush it, but the position intensifies my pain.

Turner lifts his bushy eyebrow. "And Graham's opinion matters?"

"Not specifically, but ... does everyone think my personality is domineering?"

That word brings to mind leather corsets and handcuffs. It's not an image I want associated with me. It's fine for other people, but I want to be a meadow with a gently bubbling creek or a perfect bite of strawberry scone with vanilla glaze.

I want to be effervescent, easy-going, and vibrant.

A boss.

Not bossy.

Turner's mouth twists to the side as he studies me.

I haven't braved a mirror, but I must look awful. Nail polish picked off. Mascara staining my cheeks. Hair sweaty and plastered to my neck, then frozen during my walk over.

He claps his hands, and I startle.

His grin turns mischievous. "I have just the thing." He rifles through a pile of magazines and novels on his end table.

"What are you doing?" Is there a personal development book hidden in one of those stacks? *Ten Ways to Get Over Yourself and Others' Criticisms, Volume I*.

He switches to a different pile. "I was going to wait, but now is as good a time as any to give you your birthday present."

I need advice, not a present. "My birthday isn't until next month."

"I know, but this is time sensitive. I was going to give it to you on Monday. Here." He hands me a manila envelope with the Amma's Tribe logo in the corner. *Twenty-six* is written across the front in my handwriting.

I finger the seal. "This is one of the prizes from Amma's Tribe's silent auction."

He nods.

Camille and Liam organized the fundraiser last spring to keep her grandmother's company, Amma's Tribe, out of bankruptcy. "You've had this for over a year. How can it be time-sensitive?"

He bats the envelope. "Open it."

I bend the metal tabs and lift the flap. It's been long enough that I don't remember what item number twenty-six was. I slide the stack of papers from the envelope.

Congratulations! You are the proud winner of one registration to the Jake Malloy Barbecue Pitmaster Intensive!

"The barbeque class? You won it?"

"We missed last year's session because of the football championship, but he does them every year." Turner bobs his shoulder. "Figured you can add to your repertoire, even if it is Texas barbecue and not Kansas City." He gives me a wry smile. We've debated the highlights of each barbecue style for years.

"How did you know I wanted this? I couldn't afford the starting bid." I scan the rest of the details as emotions I don't want to name swell in my chest.

Turner planned this gift for me over a year ago but kept it a secret. When I buy a new nail polish, I scream it to the world as I walk out of the store.

I don't deserve friendship like this. Especially not after barging into his home in the middle of the night with a mountain of insecurities in tow.

I run my finger along the dates. "April 24 through May 12 in Bubee, TX." The warm fuzzies crash into disappointment. "I can't miss three weeks of work. Where the heck is Bubee, Texas? How did this even end up in the auction?"

Turner drops his eyes to his teacup. "Jake's an old friend. He was happy to donate to the cause."

That doesn't answer the question, but it doesn't matter anyway. I have responsibilities in Emerald Bay I can't abandon: work, Camille's wedding, finding Willa's phone number to apologize, to name the most pressing few. "I can't leave."

"Leaving is exactly what you need. You need to stop worrying about other people's opinions. An adventure will do you good. Clear your head and give you the perspective you need to deal with Graham's words."

Is this Turner's roundabout way of telling me everyone here needs a break from me? That I am too much?

Stop it!

Turner has never once indicated he doesn't enjoy our banter or my tendency to crank up Bon Jovi and sing when he doesn't have customers in his store. My insecurities are making my tired brain imagine criticism where it doesn't exist.

That doesn't mean I can step out of my life for a month. "Maid of honor duties are ramping up."

"Everything can wait until you get back with recharged batteries."

"Turner ... I ..."

He scoots forward in his chair. "I never had a daughter or a granddaughter. You are an answer to those prayers." His papery hand cups my cheek and scrapes at the tear streaks. "My family ... I guess saying it's complicated is an understatement, but it is. You make the pain of missing them a dull ache instead of the stabbing pain it was. Let me spoil you like you're my kin."

"You never talk about them. I'm sure your grandson will visit one of these days."

Turner's mouth pinches, and his gaze darts away.

I want to know who his people are and where they've been all these years. I've delivered scones to his bookstore every week for the last three years in anticipation of a mysterious grandson who has never materialized. He's never spoken about anyone else. Every question I asked was met with silence or a change of subject. The hard set to his jaw tells me that's not going to change. If only he'd tell me what happened to make him estranged from his roots.

"What if Hannah won't let me take the time off?"

He taps the registration. "Do you want to go or not?"

"I ..." Growing up, I loved to travel. When was the last time I took a vacation? When was the last time I had an adventure? When was the last time everyone in a building didn't know everything about me?

I haven't been around *every* metaphorical block in this town, but I've been around enough to know what I need isn't here.

With the revelation about Willa, I'll worry about what people think of me when they order. I'll censor my actions in case I'm making someone feel uncomfortable.

That's not how I want to live my life. I need to figure out how to be myself without crushing anyone else.

This might be my only opportunity. If I don't take it, I will end up the crazy hamster lady who scares her friends' kids when she babysits.

I wrap my arms around Turner's bony shoulders and squeeze as tightly as I can. "How can I ever repay you?"

He chuckles. "Figure out how to make the best ribs in the world, and we'll call it even."

I press the paper to my chest and screech. "I can do that."

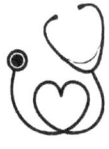

Chapter 3

Keegan

Love turns smart men into dopes.

There's no other explanation for the dumb expression on my otherwise intelligent brother's face as he stares at his new girlfriend. I bite my cheek, take another sip of my Shiner Bock, and turn my attention to the recorded A&M football game so my eyes don't roll out of their sockets at the insanity of it all.

My dad and uncle whoop and holler at the top of their lungs for a touchdown scored months ago. They slap each other on the back and tug a smile from my lips. You can take the Aggie out of the game, but you can't take the game out of the Aggie.

At least some things never change.

Too bad that can't be true for every part of my life.

"Keegan?" Grandma Daisy calls from outside.

I rise and push open the kitchen's screen door, stepping onto my grandmother's wraparound porch. The Gulf of Mexico stretches out in its most vibrant blue behind her.

The weather is perfect for Gran and Dotty Buchanan's joint birthday party. Warm sunshine and a gentle breeze drive the post-dawn chill from the backyard. "Yes, Gran?"

"Be a dear and cut this cake since your brother is canoodling with Angelina." She wiggles her fingers at them kissing their way across the lawn.

Gran's content smile broadcasts her feelings about their union loud and clear, so I school my features and try not to let my bitterness show.

It's not his fault he found his perfect partner while you were a patsy. Shut up, brain. Nobody asked you.

I scrub my hand through my hair and take the silver cake knife from Gran. I should take a cue from the sunny weather and be glad for my baby brother. He's loved Angelina for over ten years, despite how she treated him.

Or maybe because of it.

It's not his fault I'm a sour puss. I can't shake this funk I've been in for the last few months. Not surprising, considering the reason I jumped at the chance to leave my life in Dallas and escape to my hometown, even if it's just for a week.

The dual birthday party is as good an excuse as any to be in Bubee, even if it's not the real reason I'm enjoying the vacation from my orthopedic surgery practice.

After a month and a half wandering the hospital like a ghost, my boss encouraged me to disappear, clear my head before I step foot in the operating room.

Nothing clears my head like Gulf Coast breezes and Gran's lemonade.

My eyes trace the horizon. Dune strewn barrier islands. Candy-colored sailboats. Gauzy clouds. Gran's house sits on a small beach overlooking Fenner Bay. In high school, I'd sneak over here to do my homework in the pale-pink gazebo and listen to the waves hit the sand.

"So happy to finally see them together." Gran's whimsical gaze rests on Ian and Angelina. The high school nemeses turned moon-eyed, make-out experts are going at it behind the gazebo. Gran pats me on the shoulder. "When will it be your turn to find true love? Clocks a tickin'."

"Ha." I point the knife at them. "That will never be me."

I learned my lesson the hard way.

Gran doesn't know that.

No one in my family does, and I'm not going to tell them.

I've seen enough condemnation disguised as compassion to last a lifetime.

Thanks, but no thanks.

"Keegan, it's not healthy to be alone."

In my case, alone is the healthiest I can get. I slide the cake knife through the top tier of Gran's birthday cake—red velvet with cream cheese frosting—and plate slices. "I'm too busy."

It's an easy excuse. The life of an orthopedic surgeon starts at five a.m. and is jam-packed with clinic visits, hospital rounds, and hours in an operating room. When I'm on call, I'm not home until after midnight.

Medicine is a lifestyle, not a job.

The kind of women I attract ... *not going there*.

Gran picks a plate and forks a bite between her bright red lips. Her eyes flutter closed. "Yum."

I finish cutting Gran's cake and slice through Dotty Buchanan's—lemon with raspberry cream—with skilled precision.

She and Gran have been best friends since they were alphabetized by first name in kindergarten. Like twins separated at birth, they dress the same, have the same number of kids, and refused to escape our beachside enclave.

Jake Malloy climbs the stairs and picks a slice of lemon cake. "Happy birthday, Miss Daisy." His patchy salt-and-pepper beard scrapes against her skin as my ex-boss slides a kiss along her cheek.

According to Mom, he's been coming around more and more lately. Not sure what I think about that yet.

"Thank you." Gran dips her chin to hide her blush. "I saw you unloading that cooler full of ribs." Her hand rests on Jake's forearm. "You didn't have to."

He rocks forward on his toes. "Nothing but the best for the vivacious birthday girl."

Her cheeks turn as red as her lips, and she swats his arm. I bite my lip, so I don't vomit on Gran's white heels. No one wants to see their grandma flirt.

"Everything ready for this year's barbecue class?" she asks.

"Almost." His gaze swivels to me. "I need to ask a favor. When do you head back to Dallas?"

"Next Thursday." Four more days of bliss before I face rumors disguised as reality.

He scoops a bite of cake in his mouth and talks around the yellow frosting. "Any chance you can stay longer?"

"Whhhhyyyy?" I draw the word out. Jake hasn't asked me for a favor since I was his employee during my summers off from college.

"Reggie's got long COVID." He scoops another bite. This time the raspberry cream sticks to his mustache. "I need an assistant to run my class, and you're the only one with the experience I can count on."

I hand him a napkin. "You've got a restaurant full of employees, and I haven't been behind a barbecue in years."

He scoffs. "It's like riding a bike. It's not like your knife skills are rusty with all the people you carve up every day."

A smile finally graces my face. "Thanks for making me sound like a serial killer, Jake."

Only Jake would make improving my patients' quality of life sound like I'm Hannibal Lecter. No chianti and fava beans with my knee replacements.

"Well?" Jake clamps his hand on my shoulder and stares into my eyes. "Can you help an old friend out?" He doesn't flinch or blink. It feels a little like being caught in a tractor beam. Bright blue with slot-canyon laugh lines, but still a tractor beam.

"How long?"

His face scrunches like a prune. "Three weeks? Maybe four?"

I steel my expression. Part of me loves the idea. Three weeks barbecuing on the beach ... heaven. The break I crave to avoid the drama at home.

But three weeks away from the hospital might be career suicide. Rumors about my character are swirling. Will my absence feed the flames, or will they die like a fire without oxygen?

Standing on my grandma's porch, I have no idea how to fix my reputation and silence the rumors. I'm the equivalent of an ostrich with my head stuck in red velvet cake.

Instead of thinking of the three weeks as an escape, I can think of them as a strategic retreat to regroup. I'll have space to do reconnaissance, strategize, and execute a plan to undo the vitriol associated with my name.

Less hiding, more preparing.

"I've got patients scheduled, but I might be able to get someone to cover my cases. Let me make a phone call."

Jake slaps me on the back. "Saving my bacon."

"Pun intended," Jake and I say at the same time.

I shake his hand. "I'll let you know tomorrow."

He winks at Gran and ambles into her yard to chat with their other friends.

Gran squeezes my forearm. "We'd love to have you stay a bit longer."

I haven't been home for more than a long weekend since I started medical school. I wipe frosting from the cake knife and place it on the high shelf over the buffet. There are too many little kids running around to leave it out. "You want me to move into your carriage house and never leave."

"Not true. A young man needs a home of his own. Besides, you can't. I turned the carriage house into a short-term rental. Shame for it to sit empty."

My lips twist into a grimace. "Dad's okay with that?"

Her flowered skirt swishes around her calves as she turns her back to me. "Your daddy doesn't get a say."

I bend and whisper near her ear. "You haven't told him yet, have you?"

She swats me.

Crossing my ankles, I lean against the porch railing. "He's not going to like strangers parading through your home." I know I don't like the idea.

I might be afraid of my grandma, but that's because I know how dangerous she can be with a wooden spoon when you accidentally bump into a porcelain vase. "What if you get a bunch of sloppy spring breakers? I know you hate rowdy boys."

She pokes my chest. "You are the chief of rowdy boys." I smile because nothing is farther from the truth these days. "I survived being your grandma. Besides, I get to vet anyone who wants to rent from me. Handy renter-rating systems and all that. I've got a nice young lady coming for Jake's class."

"When this comes back to bite you, I'm not going to hesitate to say I told you so." Even if I will be the first one here to help her clean up the mess.

"And when it pads your inheritance, I'm going to gloat."

I mock surprise. "I have an inheritance?"

"It might just be Grandpa's cufflinks, but I'm sure there will be something left for you when I'm gone." She leans her elbows on the railing and watches our friends and family. "Not too long a wait."

I mirror her posture, bump her shoulder. "Hey! This is your birthday party. Not a wake. Stop talking like that."

She ruffles my hair. Sweet joy shines in her eyes. "For someone who deals with life and death every day, you don't have a good grasp on the concept. Everyone dies. No one makes it out of here alive."

"I do knee replacements and rotator cuff repairs. I make lives better, not necessarily longer."

Her gaze turns serious, her lips a flat line. "Are you going to take Jake up on his offer?"

"Depends on what my boss says. I've got vacation saved up, but the timing might not work."

She pats my cheek. "You'll stay."

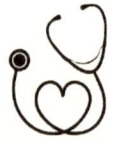

Chapter 4

Keegan

"Lay it out for me again," my boss says over the phone. I can practically hear Bud digging his thumbs into the corners of his eyes with frustration.

I kick at the wave cresting on the sand and continue pacing down the beach outside Gran's house. "I'm requesting to extend my leave of absence for another three weeks."

"If you're worried about what happened with Cynthia—"

"I don't want to talk about it." I can't dive into what happened with my ex and why the situation makes it impossible for me to return to my hospital.

The hospital is more of a home to me than my apartment, but the thought of returning churns my stomach so violently, I want to throw up.

Throwing up on patients will not endear me to them. If I step foot in an operating room at the end of the week my hands will shake, my attention will drift, and I will put my patients in danger.

I will never be that kind of doctor. My patients' health and safety are my number one priority. If someone doesn't need to go under the scalpel, I do everything in my ability to save them the risk and cost surgery requires.

"I need to figure out a plan to deal with everything that went down. I don't have any ideas yet, and a friend needs my help." I explain Jake's pitmaster class. It's not a normal excuse a Chief of Surgery should accept, but he knows my history here and at the hospital. He's my mentor and my friend. When everything went down with Cynthia, he was the first one I went to with the truth.

Bud clears his throat. "You should know, rumors hit the In-Chiefs this week. There's talk of not renewing your contract. It wasn't pretty. Nathan brought me a candidate to replace you."

I stop pacing. "What?"

Nathan's an excellent orthopedic surgeon and has a quality reputation among his patients. If Gran needed hip replacements, I'd call him.

But he's a jerk.

We don't see eye to eye on certain aspects of patient care. It also doesn't help that I beat him for the assistant director position last year.

"Your brain's been out of the game for months," Bud says. "With the rumors flying, and you not doing anything to refute them, don't be surprised if the hospital looks in another direction. It's business."

Seagulls swoop around my head searching for food. I swat them away. "Nathan just wants to fill the break room with his cronies. He hates that I'm better than he is. That my patients love me more."

He's all about through-put and adding to his five-star ratings on RateYourSurgeon.com.

"As your superior, I can't comment on Nathan's performance." I hear his scowl through the phone. "What I need to know is if I should interview this candidate. What do I tell the In-Chiefs when they ask?"

I stare at the endless ocean. Bubee is my vacation, not my life. As much as I love the beach, I can't crawl home when life gets a little tough. Stepping up and fixing my problems is the only solution. I just need to figure out what that solution will be. "I need three weeks. That gives me time for the rumors to die down and to figure out how to outmaneuver Cynthia. I promise. Don't give up on me."

"The rest of the team can't absorb your schedule. Your patients won't appreciate the last-minute change of plans."

"I know. I'll have my office manager call and smooth the ruffled feathers. It's not fair to them that I'm incapable of being in the hospital right now, but it's for their wellbeing."

"They might follow you down to Podunk."

"It's Bubee, but you know that."

He sneers. "Anywhere that doesn't have an international airport isn't worth the real estate."

"Part of me agrees with you, but you've never watched a sunset from my beach with a cold beer and hot ribs. Come visit and I'll change your mind."

"That doesn't sound like a guy who's coming back." There's a growly hesitancy to his voice.

"I promise I am. This is temporary. I'll clear my head, then I'll be your ace again. Don't let Nathan talk you into replacing me, and don't worry about the In-Chiefs. Someone will mess up next week, and they won't remember they talked about me."

Bud's quiet for a minute. He clears his throat. "Sorry, Keegan, I'll give you the time, but no promises."

Bridgette

My fingernails bite into the armrest of Turner's Toyota Camry as bare trees whip by on the edge of the highway. A grey haze hangs over Lake Superior. The smell of snow sags heavily on the air.

I glance at Turner. Hands at ten and two, wool hat pulled low over his ears, piercing eyes focused on the slick road, he's an expert driver.

"You should turn around. This weather will probably cancel my flight anyway. I don't want you driving in the snow." We're less than thirty minutes from the Duluth airport, but I can't help my nerves getting the better of me.

Why the heck am I flying to Texas when I have responsibilities here?

Turner pats my hand. "Attending the class is the right choice, my dear."

My claws relax, and I tuck my hands under my legs. "Are you sure? It was a snap decision. I'm usually more methodical. Hannah will need me." The words shoot out of my mouth without a filter.

Turner chuckles. "Spontaneous is your middle name."

"No, it's not."

He raises a shaggy eyebrow.

"Okay. Maybe it is, but that doesn't mean I should go. What if I get to Bubee and steamroll some other poor innocent soul?"

"Back to this again?"

"Graham's not wrong. I'm a lot to handle."

"There's a difference between not being wrong and missing a key piece of information."

I shift in my seat so I can see his face better. "What information is that?"

"Graham will never understand you because he can't imagine anyone else in the room being smarter, funnier, wittier—you name it—than he is. He's threatened by the possibility, and that's his loss."

"I think he has my character pretty well mapped out." I count his criticisms on my fingers. "Too loud. Too demanding. Uncompromising. Confidence-smashing. Never forever." I hold up my hand. "Look, I ran out of fingers."

"It is not your responsibility to make small-minded people feel big."

"Willa isn't small-minded. She's tender like baby greens. I wasn't careful with her fragility."

A deep scowl settles on his face. If he weren't driving, I'm pretty sure he'd be glaring at me. "If you tiptoe around everyone who might feel insecure when they compare themselves to your confidence, where does that leave you?"

I twist my mouth, pressing my lips together. "Small, insecure, and pandering to people who shouldn't get a say in how I live my life."

"Exactly." He drums his fingers on the steering wheel. "You can't fix their issues. Willa is a beautiful girl, but hiding your *joie de vivre* doesn't help her. It sets the wrong example." Turner pulls the car to the curb outside the departures concourse.

I pull him into a awkward hug over the center console. "Can I pack you in my suitcase? I'm not sure I can make it three weeks without you to help me screw my head on straight."

He pats my back. "Darling, you'll do great. Just be you. Don't hold back. Everything will work out the way it's supposed to."

"You sound like a fortune cookie."

He pops the trunk and climbs out of his seat. "This cookie says, if you continue to dawdle, you'll miss your flight. You promised me ribs, and I will collect."

I follow and hug him again. I can't seem to get enough. His wisdom, thoughtfulness, and humility are second to none. I honestly don't know what I would do if he wasn't in my life. For a girl who didn't grow up with grandparents, he slid into the honorary role like frosting on a cupcake.

I release him. "Thanks. I'll text you when I get there."

"I want pictures of everything you cook."

"Deal." I pull the handle from my wheeled bag. "I ... you ..." I hate goodbyes. I'm not good with them. My brain races with what-ifs. Turner's not young. What happens if he has a heart attack while I'm gone? Who'll check on him? Hannah agreed to bring him scones, but she's too busy to sit and chat.

He squeezes my shoulder. "I know. Love you too." He turns me and gives me a gentle shove. "Now, get out of here. I'm freezing, and a slice of pie from Betty's sounds like a good idea."

"Traitor. Don't let Hannah hear you say that."

He mimes zipping his lips and tossing the key over his shoulder. He gives me a wink and drives away.

I turn and face the sliding glass doors. "Adventure, here I come."

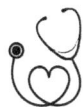

Keegan

Eighty pounds of brisket. Forty racks of ribs. Fifty-six pork butts. Sixty-four chickens. And that's just the delivery for the first week of class. I grab another slab of meat from the shipping box and carry it to Jake's walk-in refrigerator.

Jake passes me in the doorway. "Thanks for doing this."

"You owe me."

He taps the brisket in my arms. "I pay in meat."

"Nah. You're finally going to tell me what's in the secret sauce."

Jake's secret sauce is legendary and the only secret anyone in Bubee has ever been able to keep.

Other chefs try to recreate it. Employees hide in the kitchen to watch him make it, but no one has ever been able to master that perfect mixture of spicy and sweet with a little bit of tang which makes Jake's sauce legendary and draws customers to our little corner of Texas.

My teenage brain was dumbfounded when a couple from California said they devoted a week of their lives to eating their way through Jake's menu. *People plan entire vacations around the opportunity to eat at Jake's.* I couldn't wrap my head around that thought, but time and again, tourists confirmed what we already knew: Jake's barbecue is the best in the world.

I will have that recipe.

He tsks and wags his finger at me. "You're a funny guy."

I shrug the brisket off my shoulder and into my arms. "I can drop this cow right here. No skin off my nose."

His jaw flaps. "You wouldn't."

I feint losing my grip. "Whoops."

"Stop! Fine. You stay four weeks, five-star reviews from the class, and we'll talk."

I narrow my eyes. He's making this way too easy. I pulled this same stunt the week before I left for medical school, and he let the rump roast hit the dirt. Something's up.

"The class is only three weeks long. Why do you want me to stay longer?"

He crosses his arms over his chest and gives me his best, *I'm the boss* scowl. "I have my reasons."

"The hospital only gave me three weeks. Four-point-five stars, the recipe, and a box of brisket to take home, and we'll call it even," I say slowly.

His eyes pinch. "When did you become this cunning?"

"Do you know how many surgeries I'm missing to be here? How many patients are being forced to live with their arthritic knees so I can teach chefs how to properly start a fire?"

My office manager was not pleased with my unexplained vacation extension. She—like everyone else—thinks I'm hiding. Doesn't matter. I'll figure out my plan, and then everyone will know the truth. I'm not the jerk they think I am.

"You didn't have to stay," Jake says.

"You know I did. I'm not abandoning you when you need help." Jake's like my favorite great-uncle. Even though we aren't related, I learned almost as much about how to be a man from him as I did from my dad.

I owe him.

I admire him.

I wish I had turned out the be the kind of man he is instead of the man I am. Maybe these short weeks will help me see where I fall short, so I can fix it.

"Thanks, Keegan." He wraps me in a hug, smashing the brisket to my chest, and we pound each other's backs.

He's not usually affectionate, but I'm not gonna turn him down. Some don't consider hugs manly, but a quality hug is a powerful drug, and I need the calming effects.

I slap his back again. "How about a beer when we're done?"

"My staff can cover service tonight. The Boys are playing at Sobre."

"I thought we'd raid your bar and sit on the beach."

He tsks. "We'll go to Sobre. I haven't heard a live band in ages."

I glance at my sweat-drenched shirt. "I need a shower."

"Nah. We'll grab a bench on the beach. No one will care."

He's right. Flip-flops, board shorts, and a dirty shirt are as good as mosquito repellant for the kind of women who troll Sobre las Rocas on a Sunday night. Doesn't stop me from sniffing my armpits.

Meh. Repellant is one thing. Repugnant is another. "You gotta let me find deodorant."

Chapter 5

Bridgette

I STEP OUT OF the shuttle I hired to drive me to Bubee from Houston, and it's like stepping out of real life onto a movie set. Gabled rooflines, salty ocean breezes, and the sweet music of seagulls caress my senses.

Pristine robin's egg-blue shutters frame gigantic picture windows on the two-story home where I rented a room for the barbecue intensive. Pure white steps match the clapboard siding and lead to a wraparound porch, complete with rocking chairs and a porch swing.

My imagination runs wild picturing lazy afternoons, a glass of ice-cold lemonade at my elbow, and a good book on my lap. I'll push my toe against the planked floor to gently rock the swing as I gaze out over the ocean just a stone's throw away.

Could anything be more perfect than mornings learning how to barbecue and afternoons in paradise?

I think not.

I type quick texts to Turner and Camille, letting them know I've arrived, then carry my roller bag up the stairs. I inhale another breath of the sea and knock on the screen door.

"Coming," echoes from deep in the house. Shoes clip-clop against the hardwood floors louder and louder until a wisp of a woman with silver hair and a bright pink dress rounds the corner. She moves with an efficiency that belies the wrinkles around her eyes and mouth.

"You're here!" She flings the door open and wraps me in a hug like we're lifelong friends instead of email buddies who "met" two weeks ago. There aren't a lot of short-term rentals in this seaside hamlet, but I think I found a gold mine.

I squeeze her back because who doesn't love a hug from a grandma? "I hope you're Mrs. Sullivan."

She pulls back and cups my cheek. "Call me Daisy." Crystal-clear amber eyes smile back at me and sweep over my white tank top and red wrap skirt. "Aren't you a vision. Pretty as a picture."

I clasp Daisy's hand and lift our arms, spinning her to admire her dress. Pearl buttons march from her throat to her hem. The skirt flares as she spins. "You are the vision. Maybe we can organize a shopping excursion, and you'll show me the best stores in town?" I scrunch my shoulders to my ears in hope.

I want to revel in everything that Bubee has to offer, and if Daisy is any indication, it's an inviting town with no limit on spunk.

"It would be a pleasure." She takes my roller bag's handle. "Let's get you settled first. You'll be in the carriage house." She rolls my suitcase through the front door and down a hallway to the other side of the house—too fast for me to appreciate the artwork and mementos that decorate her home, but not too fast to miss inhaling the savory scent of something divine simmering in the kitchen—and out the back door, along a limestone path to a separate building with a restored barn door, red roses under the windows, and canary-yellow walls.

The door rolls effortlessly to reveal a cozy sitting room with a yellow and white pinstriped loveseat and two baby blue chairs clustered around a wood fireplace. Pictures of the beach and small seashells line the mantle. I doubt the logs are lit often, but it adds a charm that makes me a little homesick for Emerald Bay's winter.

A galley kitchen, bedroom, and bathroom with clawfoot tub complete the ten-second tour. The perfect amount of space for a single woman on a three-week holiday.

Daisy clasps her hands in the small of her back and rocks onto her toes. "Since it's your first night, will you join me for dinner?"

"I would love that." I lift my roller bag onto the bed and open the closet door. I shake out one of my sundresses. "I need to battle some wrinkles, but if you're willing, I'd like to help cook." I want to know what created that mouth-watering smell.

"Lovely." She wraps me in another hug.

Any nerves I had about this adventure drift away with her coconut scent. Turner was right. I need this. I need to get away.

I need to not be known for a minute, so I can fully embrace what it means to be me and what it means to channel my confidence for the benefit of others.

Somewhere along the way, other peoples' opinions of how I'm supposed to act sank into my subconscious. No more. That stops now.

Even if I'm too much. I will be authentically me.

I grab the hangers out of the closet and hang up my clothes. Socks, panties, bras, yoga pants, and PJs go in the bureau. I run my fingers along the cotton, silk, and satin dresses and shirts I brought. If I'm going to "be myself," I'm going all in.

I pluck a bright yellow corseted dress out of the closet and slide into the soft fabric. My hair curls around my ears as I twist it into a low messy bun. Rose gold chandelier earrings adorned with tiny crystal butterflies complete the look.

It might just be dinner with my hostess, but I feel glamourous and beautiful. I'm no longer Papa Bear's too-hot porridge. I'm just right.

My feet are tired from traveling, so I forgo my heels. Barefooted, I make my way across the lush lawn to the main house.

Sunlight reigns in Daisy's turquoise kitchen. An industrial-sized stainless-steel refrigerator reflects the sun's glow into a small seating area next to arbored windows. Parsley, mint, and oregano grow on the window ledge.

Daisy stirs a Dutch oven on the gas stove in the middle of the island. She waves steam toward her face and inhales. Her tongue runs along the outside of her teeth and lips like a snake tasting its surroundings. She sips the broth.

A contemplative look crosses her face before she executes a crisp nod and grabs a black cylinder. Fresh pepper grinds into the pot, and she repeats the snake-tasting process.

"Smells lovely." I step to the other side of the island. Carrots, onions, and celery simmer in the broth. I wave the smell toward my nose and am hit with hints of butter, oregano, and thyme.

"Italian wedding soup. My specialty."

I nip a piece of mint from the window ledge and suck on it. "What can I do?"

"Your email said you're a baker, so how about buttermilk biscuits?" She points to the door to the pantry.

"Yes, ma'am." I gather my ingredients and set to work measuring flour into the mixing bowl she placed on the counter.

"Stop this instant." Daisy wields her spoon like a sword.

I freeze with flour dribbling into my measuring cup. "What did I do?" Does she not like my technique?

She shakes the spoon at me. "I forbid you to ruin that dress." She disappears into the pantry and returns with a piece of white cloth. She holds it out to me. "Put this on."

I unfurl what turns out to be an apron. A heavily stained apron that reads, *Doctor knows best.*

I raise an eyebrow.

She lifts the strap over my head, nudges my hip, so I spin, and she ties the belt around my waist. "It's my grandson's. Makes a great key lime pie but is a bit of a slob in the kitchen." She points to a particularly large black streak. "Burnt the Christmas turkey one year because he was too busy zesting limes."

That's a lot of limes. "How many grandkids do you have?"

"Eleven." There's so much pride in her voice, it feels like a blanket.

"Must make holidays fun."

An expression halfway between whimsical and sad settles in her wrinkles. "I wish. None of them live here anymore, and it gets harder every year to get them to come home."

"I'm an only child to only children, so I can't even begin to imagine." It has always been just me, Mom, and Dad. We weren't the Three Musketeers or the Three Amigos—parenting me took a lot of effort—but we had our fun moments.

"We're a crazy lot, but we love each other. In the end, unconditional love is all that matters." She points at the apron. "Flaws and all."

Love pours from her face, and for a second, I wish I knew what it was like to be part of a big, loud, happy family. I've known Daisy less than an hour, and I want to adopt her.

I love my parents, but ... is it bad that just for a minute, I want to pretend Daisy is my grandmother? That I'm home after a long absence indulging in quality grandmother-granddaughter time?

If I'm being honest, I don't think my parents understood me. They tolerated my hurricane-force personality because they didn't know how to parent me. I was—still am—a force, and they didn't stand a chance in the path of my enthusiasm for life. They battened down the hatches and held on.

Daisy seems like the kind of person who would enjoy the thrill of riding the storm with me.

We lapse into silence as she finishes the meatballs for the soup, and I bake biscuits. Buttery, bacony aromas fill the kitchen, and I settle into my skin for the first time in a long while.

Turner was right to send me here. He couldn't have known about Daisy's welcome, but he knew I was scared to be myself at home.

I can't pinpoint when Emerald Bay stopped feeling like home. Being away puts everything in perspective. My skin felt too tight. My heart too empty.

It's like I was in a frozen lake, but I'd been there so long, I didn't recognize the signs of hypothermia.

Cooking a meal with a relative stranger has started to reverse that process. My insides are thawing.

It's a little weird and completely unexpected. Maybe the ocean air is combining with the soup and brainwashing me into contentment.

With full bowls, we make our way onto the screened section of the porch. I take my first bite, and the savory broth warms my throat. "What do I need to know about Bubee?"

Daisy tips her head, and her gaze drifts to the ocean. "Bubee isn't a town I can tell you about, sweetheart. It's a place you experience for yourself."

"Where do I start?"

"If I were your age, Sobre las Rocas is the place to be on a Sunday night. Live music. Right on the beach. The best margaritas in town. You'll have a blast."

"A bar on Sunday? I thought that was illegal in Texas."

"We call it a concert. They just happen to serve a splash of tequila in their lime juice." Daisy gives me a playful wink. She's a woman who enjoys her *lime juice*.

"I'm not sure an evening on the town is a great idea the night before class starts." I want to be fresh-faced and energetic tomorrow. A hangover would give the instructor the wrong impression. I thrive on great first impressions.

Daisy nudges my wrist. "It's the perfect idea. The bar is right next to Jake's. You'll know where you're headed in the morning. Don't stay out all night, and you'll be fine."

"A margarita does sound good." I didn't come all this way to sit in my room and watch movies. There's a big world in this small town, and I want to know every inch of it before I go home.

She mimes a chef's kiss. "They have a serrano watermelon margarita that curls your toes just right."

I shake my hair out of its bun. "Good thing I dressed up."

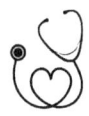

Keegan

The sun sets as Jake and I walk along the boardwalk to Sobre las Rocas. My feet scrap on the weathered wood. Jake's quiet, with his hands tucked into his pockets.

Families play on the beach, toddlers chase seagulls, and couples walk hand in hand. The smells of burgers and fried fish drift from nearby restaurants as people settle down for dinner. I never get tired of this stretch.

At the end of the walkway, the lantern-lit bar towers on raised stilts. The band sets up on a stage in the sand below. There's a decent crowd already mingling near the picnic tables and dance floor. I head upstairs and grab two beers while Jake finds a table in the back.

We settle in and wait for The Boys to start playing. Jake clears his throat. "I need to tell you something."

"That's ominous."

His cheek pinches in a half smile. "I'm looking to sell."

"The restaurant?"

"Yeah."

I sip my beer. He's been old enough to retire for a decade, but barbecue sauce runs through his arteries. I assumed we'd find him dead next to a smoker one morning. "Why now?"

"Cancer."

The word hits like a sledgehammer. "Jake—"

He holds up his hand. "It started in my liver. We fought it. Now it's back. Pancreas this time. Stage four."

That's why he's so willing to give me his sauce recipe. Shouldn't have bought him a beer if his liver's compromised. "How long?"

"Six months, maybe a year."

Jake can't die. Bubee won't be the same without him. "Anything I can do?" I'm not an oncologist, but I know some great ones who have tricks up their sleeves.

"That's what the intensive is for this year."

"I don't follow."

He picks at the beer label. "Everyone who's enrolled is a candidate to buy the restaurant. I need you to help me vet them. Who'll cherish my legacy while putting their unique spin on things?"

"That's why you wanted me?" I jab my thumb into my chest to alleviate the ache building behind my sternum, but the pain grows.

"Yeah. I figure you understand my diagnosis, and you understand barbecue. I can count on your candor."

I stare at the condensation slipping down the sides of our glass bottles. Jake's dying. He might not be here next time I come home. Goosebumps erupt along my skin. My eyes burn, but I swallow the emotion threatening to choke me.

No crying at Sobre. Jake wouldn't want me to cry in the privacy of my home.

I shift my gaze to his face. Now that I'm looking for it, I see the signs. His shaved head wasn't a style choice. He's skinnier. His skin is sallow under the patchy beard. His eyes sink into his skull when he's tired. "No one else knows, do they?"

He shakes his head. "No. The participants don't know they're being evaluated, and we're going to keep it that way."

"What if the person you pick doesn't want your secrets? Or can't afford it?"

"Every person attending, save one, has previously approached me about either buying the business or partnering with me, so I'm not worried about that." His cheek twitches. "Unless ... you willin' to give up your fancy practice in Dallas?"

I sit back and cross my arms over my chest. Am I? Even with everything that's going on at home, Dallas is still home. I miss the buzz of the OR. I can't give that up.

"I love helping my patients. The relief on their faces when I take away their pain is better than any drug. I love barbecue, but it's not my life the way it's yours. If I bought the restaurant, I wouldn't move here to run things. I'd hire someone. Would you be okay with that?"

He's silent for a minute, then meets my eyes with a sad grin. "No, I wouldn't. I want someone who loves the restaurant the way I do." He taps his beer bottle against mine. "That's why you're the perfect assistant. I never expected you to give up the life you've worked so hard to build. I'd rather not close, but if I have to, I will." He lifts his beer. "To a life well lived."

I don't lift mine. There are too many words and emotions building at the back of my throat. If I open my mouth for one of them, my sadness and regret will pour out instead of the strength I know he needs from me.

I'm sorry I'm invested in my patients. I'm sorry I won't give up my life to take care of what you love most. I'm sorry you're dying. I'm sorry I can't heal you. I'm sorry for so many things I can't bear to name.

But I keep it simple. "Jake, I'm sorry."

"Don't be. I've had a good run. My only regret is that I never took your grandma out on a date. I bet she's dynamite in the—"

I dig my fingers in my ears. "Ack. I don't need to hear that."

His laughter shakes the table. "Prude."

"Fine by me." I twist and face the band taking the stage. Milo, the lead guitarist, plays the first chords of one of their original songs. At least, I think it's original. "Name that Tune" isn't my strength.

Jake turns and rests his back against the table. He drums his fingers on his jeans in time with the music.

I can't imagine Bubee without Jake Malloy. I owe most of my success in life to him.

He gave me my first job, then rehired me every summer when I was in college. Knowing how to butcher pigs and cows gave me an advantage during medical school anatomy classes. When it came time for Residency Matching, my nearly 4.0 GPA lured the top programs.

I have to help him with his last wish even though it breaks my heart to know I'm losing him.

He drains his beer. "I'm outta here."

"I'll walk back with you." I rise to my feet.

"Nope." He pushes me back to the bench. "Enjoy your last night of freedom before the real work begins. See you tomorrow."

My beer's empty. I could follow him and make sure he gets home okay, but he's a grown man who asked me to stay, so I will. A few songs, at least.

He lumbers across the sand to the water and wades in up to his knees. He kicks spray at an approaching wave and whoops with happiness. I watch him walk toward his restaurant until the night swallows him.

I hope I'm as happy to meet death when it's my turn as he is. That I don't have any regrets and I'm content with the decisions I've made.

So far, that's not how my life's going. I have more regrets than I want to count. I'm not happy with the path my life is on.

I have three weeks to find some answers or I may never find my way.

The wind flings sand in my face. It's time for a second beer. I climb the weathered, narrow stairs and weave through the standing-room-only crowd toward the bar.

On the corner of the deck, a woman in a yellow dress dances by herself.

I can't help but watch her. Me and every other guy in the place.

Confident. Legs for days. She sways with the beat, executes a box step and spin that makes her skirt flare around her upper thighs. Her melodic singing carries over the sound of the speakers.

She holds my attention like the wild sunflowers growing in the pastures outside of town. On my drives home, I park on the side of the road and stare as they turn their petals toward the sun and dance in the breeze. Their hypnotic rhythm calms my nerves.

I enjoy their beauty but never get close enough to smell them. Never contemplated bringing a bouquet home for my mom or Gran. Spiders, biting ants, and bumblebees make their homes on those petals and leaves.

There's a reason women like her are wildflowers. They don't belong in a garden or a vase on a kitchen counter. They can't be tamed. They shouldn't be.

Stay away from sunflowers, no matter how beautiful they are.

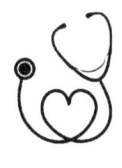

Chapter 6

Keegan

I SLIDE PAST OTHER patrons into Sobre las Rocas's upstairs bar. During the day, it's a dive restaurant serving spicy redfish tacos and sweet onion barbacoa quesadillas. When the sun goes down, chips, queso, and tequila take over the menu. They plug in Christmas lights wound through old fishing nets and pump salsa music through the speakers on the sand if a band isn't playing.

My elbows rest against the bar, and I order another beer. I silently raise a toast to Jake. Depending on how aggressive his cancer is, these could be the last three weeks I spend with my friend.

I'm glad I decided to stay and help him. I would have hated myself if he died and I hadn't taken advantage of this opportunity.

The sunflower appears at my hip and dabs sweat from her forehead with a paper napkin. Her knuckles rap the bar, grabbing the bartender's attention. "Water, please?"

The bartender nods and fills her glass.

I slide a step away.

She gives me a side eye. "I'm sorry. I didn't mean to invade your space." She exaggerates taking another step away, but the bar's too crowded for her to move more than three inches. "That better?"

I raise a hand in a placating gesture. "I spent the day moving boxes. Trust me, I'm saving you."

She steps back to her original spot, and her gaze sweeps from my flip-flops to my dark hair. "You don't look any worse for wear." She squeezes my biceps. "Manual labor suits you."

"Thanks, I think." Lifting boxes didn't build these muscles. Stress relief in the gym after hours in the operating room is the only way I can sleep sometimes. I'm so amped up from crafting anatomical masterpieces, I need to wear myself out.

I know how egotistical that sounds, even in my head, but it's true. I'm a master at what I do, and I know how hard I've worked to become a DaVinci.

I won't apologize for being proud of myself. I just keep those thoughts in my head, so people know I'm not a vainglorious chump.

Sunflower leans her back against the bar and sips her water. "Do you like the band?"

"I went to high school with them, so I have to say yes."

"Local boy?"

"Yeah." I point at her. "Tourist?"

Her entire face scrunches like a Shar Pei puppy. "Is it that obvious?"

"We don't get a lot of locals dancing on tables."

She shoves my shoulder but giggles. "I wasn't on the table."

I return her smile. "But you were headed that direction."

"Doubtful." She wrinkles her cute, upturned nose.

"My bet is it won't be the first—or the last—time either."

She tips her head at a playful angle. Her captivating golden curls bounce across her bare shoulders. "Have you ever danced on a table?"

"No."

"Then who are you to judge?"

"No one." I swallow half my beer. I want to keep talking to her, but self-preservation is stronger. I shouldn't have started flirting. I need to get out of here before I do something I'll regret.

I know how nights with women who dance on tables end, and I'm not looking for that kind of night.

Remember the stinging ants and bumblebees.

I want to wallow in Jake's news and prep myself for the next few weeks. I can't stare at him with pity in my eyes. He's kept his secret for a reason, and I can't be dumb and expose him in a moment of melancholy.

The sunflower tugs on my arm. "Come on."

I hold my seat and lift my beer. "I'm good here."

"But you'll be great on the table." Her long lashes flutter around eyes the color of the ocean on a perfect day.

Trouble.

"No, thanks."

She plops on the stool next to me. "Are you always a party pooper?"

"Pretty much." I don't want to be a jerk, but I hope my monosyllabic answers drive her away. Too much longer and I might find myself wanting to lean in and smell this sunflower.

"How about a regular dance on the floor? You up for one of those?"

"Sorry."

"Déjà vu. Here I thought I met a cool guy I could hang out with for a couple hours so I don't feel like the weird tourist in the local bar. Guess I'm wrong."

I watch her watching me. There's a vulnerability in her gaze that wasn't there before. She's worried about being alone.

I'm not a big enough jerk to leave her stranded in a crowd of strangers. "Sunflower, we can hang out. It's just going to happen at the bar or on the sand watching the band."

"Sunflower? I like that. What's your name?"

"Keegan."

"I'm Bridgette." She presses her glass to her forehead and flushed cheeks. The condensation trails across her zygomatic arches, past her mandible, and soaks into the top of her dress.

Does she have any idea what that does to me? The way I'm forgetting how to breathe? I want to trace those droplets with my fingertips.

Is her skin as soft as a sunflower's petal? I want to know. But I shouldn't.

Keep your hands to yourself, man.

Somewhere I find my rational brain and my voice. "It's cooler on the sand if you want."

"Okay." But her eyes glow with more than four simple letters.

It's just a change of scenery. Spending more time with her doesn't mean anything. I'm being a gentleman and keeping a single woman company in a strange town.

She follows me to the stairs. Several people are coming up, so she presses into me to let them by. She smells like butter and honey and something familiar, but I can't name the scent. Maybe oregano or thyme?

I shake off the instinct to fill my lungs with her.

Doesn't matter if she smells like a homecooked meal or a day on the beach. This is the only night I'll see her. I can be polite, hang out, and keep my distance at the same time.

I start down the steps. I make it two before they creak and sway with the number of people on them.

She grips my shoulder. Color drains from her face.

My hand finds her waist. "You okay?"

Her eyes dart to the sand twenty feet below and back to me. "Yeah. Um ... not a fan of heights and these stairs ..."

I take her hand. "I got you."

Her gaze dashes to my lips and up to my eyes. "Thanks."

A code alarm blares in my head. My heart has stopped beating, and I need CPR to keep me alive. This sunflower will be the death of me if I don't get away.

Too bad I'm a gentleman first and foremost. I promised to help her down the stairs and keep her company while we listen to the band, so that's what I'll do.

Without wondering if those pink lips taste as good as she smells.

I bite my lip and continue down the steps, her hand secure in mine. Her feet hit the sand, and she slips out of her shoes. They have to be three-inch heels.

"You're afraid of heights, but wear shoes like that?" The top of her head barely reaches my nose now that she's barefoot.

She quirks a smile. "Not all of us are part giant. How's the weather way up there?"

I lick my finger and raise it by my face. "Breezy and seventy degrees with a chance of rain."

Her giggle races across my skin like static electricity, sharp and stinging.

She regains her balance. I swipe my hand through my hair like it's in my eyes.

A group of rugby-types sits at the picnic table where Jake and I sat before. The rest of the tables overflow as well. So much for the hope of putting three feet of pine between us.

Bridgette skirts the sea of people and wanders to the surf-side of the stage. The breeze tumbles her long, blonde hair off her back, and she tips her chin to the sky, fluttering her eyes closed. "You were right. It's nice down here." She sways to the music with her arms in the air like a palm tree.

I swallow the lump in my throat and peel my attention to the band. "Glad I can help."

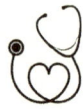

Bridgette

Daisy was right. This bar is the perfect way to start my vacation. The margarita was spicy and sweet. The sand is soft and warm. The band is loud and energetic.

I peek out of the corner of my eye at Keegan. He's the find of the night. Soft-spoken, chivalrous, with a kind face and broad shoulders that always grab my attention.

He sips his beer and keeps his focus on the band. He's not swaying to the music or tapping his toes. He doesn't seem to know the words well enough to sing along, but every once in a while, he'll tap his fingers on his thigh to the beat, so I can only assume he's enjoying himself. This close to the stage, the music's too loud to ask.

Is this his usual Sunday routine? Manual labor all day (hello, arm muscles) followed by beer on the beach watching his friends play. Must be a nice life. Simple. Low pressure.

For a local, he doesn't say hi to people. Plenty of people, mostly women, have waved, but all he does is raise his glass and keep watching the band. Is he shy? That doesn't fit with his willingness to flirt with me. I won't give myself the compliment that it's just me. That I'm the exception to his taciturn behavior.

I stretch up on my toes, so I can speak into his ear. "How much longer will they play?"

He glances at his watch. "Another hour, until ten."

"Will you keep me company until then?"

He nods, his gaze dipping to my lips again. I chew the edge reflexively. I didn't imagine the heat between us on the stairs. The tender way he held my waist to steady me. The strength in his hand as he led me to the sand.

He wants to kiss me.

And I want to let him.

Just a kiss.

Or two. Nothing more.

I don't want a vacation romance.

But a kiss under the stars isn't off the table.

The band plays another Imagine Dragons song, and I sing along. As they work through their set, the crowd drifts away. My margarita buzz is long gone, and the fatigue from traveling creeps into my legs. I yawn into the back of my hand.

Keegan cups my elbow. He tilts his head. "There's an open table. Want to sit?"

"That'd be great." The table is in the back, and I want to hear his voice before I turn into a pumpkin.

He slides into the far side of the table, and I contemplate sitting next to him, but he spreads his thighs and elbows, boxing out like he's on an airplane and needs to claim his territory.

Interesting.

I slide my leg over the bench and straddle the wood, so I can see the band and Keegan at the same time. I'll split my attention to put him at ease.

"Will you tell me about Bubee?"

His fingers drum the table. "What do you want to know?"

"Best place to get coffee?" There's a drip coffeemaker in my apartment, but sometimes a cappuccino is the only way to start the morning.

"We don't have a Starbucks if that's what you're after."

"I prefer to taste the local fare."

One of my favorite things about traveling is finding hidden gems. Restaurants, coffee shops, bars I can't get back home. What's the point of flying halfway across the country if I'm just going to eat and drink the things I would at home?

"Honey Beans is your place." He points away from the beach. "Three blocks inland, five blocks north. Tell Georgi I sent you."

I prop my chin in my hand and give him my full attention. "What do you order?"

"I don't."

"Then why are you sending me there?"

"No one makes espresso like Georgi."

"You don't drink coffee?"

He shrugs. "I make mine at home on my way to work."

"And what is work?"

He shifts his weight and leans back from the table. "Nothing special."

I've never met a guy who didn't fall over himself to parade his resume in front of me. "You're evasive." Is he embarrassed? Unemployed?

"I don't like talking about myself."

"You said you spent today moving boxes. Was that part of your job?"

He lifts his shoulder and takes the final swig from his beer. "Something like that."

"Do you have siblings? Did you go to college? Do you have a dog? Who do you think will be the next Supreme Court Justice? Tell me anything."

"Why does it matter?"

"How do I get to know you if you don't talk to me?" Every time he evades, I become more curious, not less.

Why won't he spill about his job, his life? What is he hiding?

He's like a pirate's treasure chest. The harder it is to follow the map and decipher the riddles, the more satisfaction there will be when I open it. I want to dig until I find every gold coin that makes Keegan who he is.

"I didn't mean to give you the wrong impression. I'm not great company."

I narrow my eyes. "Hmm." I swing my leg over the bench to face him. "Curious."

"What? I'm not."

"So ... a typical Sunday night is sitting on the beach, drinking a beer, listening to the band, and not talking to anyone. Do I have that right?"

He twists his mouth and doesn't answer the question.

"I don't understand you, Keegan. Are you married and hiding from your wife?"

"Ha. Never." He tugs at the collar of his shirt.

I lean across the table. "But you find me attractive?"

He jumps to his feet. "I gotta go. Nice to meet you, Sunflower. Enjoy your stay." He strides up the beach like pitchfork-wielding villagers are chasing him.

This is like Willa all over again.

Minnesota Bridgette would pout in the corner. She'd fume, watch *Goldfinger*, or find a table to dance on.

But this isn't Minnesota.

I'm on a beach in Texas being dismissed by someone who showed interest in me. Someone I would love to get to know.

Never forever.

What sent Keegan running? Did he think I was proposing or some nonsense? Was it because I sang along to the band? Swayed my hips? I *didn't* dance on the table, so it can't be that. I'm not falling down drunk or clingy.

What made him so uncomfortable he's literally running away from me?

He didn't seem uneasy around me. Quite the opposite, in fact. He seemed like he wanted to get cozier.

It doesn't make any sense, and I'm pretty well proving what Graham said about me, but if I don't ask, I'll obsess all night.

I hook the straps of my heels over my finger and run after him. "Keegan!"

He startles at my call. He glances back and runs his hand through his hair again, making it stand at adorably odd angles. Turning his back on me, he stalks closer to the water.

Graham and his crew would have a hearty laugh if they saw this. Never Forever chasing a guy she met an hour ago down the beach after asking if he was married.

Too bossy. Too overbearing. Too pushy. I am currently being all those things.

This right here is the worst version of me.

But this isn't the version Keegan flirted with and kept company. He didn't run away from crazy Bridgette.

What did I do so Keegan doesn't want to spend the last thirty minutes of the concert by my side?

I sprint until I'm in front of him and spread my arms wide. "What ... did I ... do wrong?" The words shoot out of my mouth between gasping breathes.

He steps back. "Excuse me?"

I brace my hands on my knees and suck air through my nose, holding up a finger to give me a second. Running in a corset isn't my thing, so my lungs were not prepared for my irrational sprint. "Obviously something is wrong to make you walk away from me. I need to know what it is. Was I too pushy?"

"It's not you. It's me."

I straighten and stare him down—well, up since he's so much taller than me. "At least I know you suck at lying."

He points toward the pier half a mile along the beach. "My night's over, so I'm heading home."

"Please, tell me." I grip his arm because why not add assault to my list of crimes tonight? "Back home, a guy I dated said I was *Never forever*. He said I am bossy and pushy. That I make people feel insecure about who they are—and I understand that chasing you confirms some of what he said—but before ... at the bar, what did I do? What drove you away?"

The wind whips my hair around my face, and shivers run along my arms. Is the chill from the weather or the icy reality of Graham's words?

Am I the kind of woman no one will ever love?

Keegan lays his hand over mine on his bicep. His heat radiates and soothes the goosebumps on my skin. "Sunflower, there's nothing wrong with you."

"Then why did you leave? Don't say it's because you're tired." I can't take the platitude.

He removes my fingers from his person like I'm an octopus tentacle. "I'm not looking for a relationship."

My cheeks flash hot. "That wasn't what I meant."

I shouldn't have asked if he had a wife, but I didn't want to intrude on someone else's man. Definitely shouldn't have told him the *Never forever* thing. Now he thinks I'm trolling the bar for a husband.

Good job, Bridgette. Way to alienate one of the two people you know in town.

I squeeze my hands into fists. "Keegan, I'm not asking for a relationship. If I never see you again, I'll be fine. Sort of. In all honesty, I'll probably miss your taciturn smile and the way you run your hands through your hair when you're nervous, but I'll be fine." My breath quivers, air chills my lungs. "I just need to know why people walk away from me so easily. Please. One lonely stranger to another. What did I do?"

He gently lifts my chin with his knuckle. "Sunflower, you are perfect." His eyes shift back and forth between mine like he's memorizing every detail. "But women like you don't belong with men like me."

I'm turning into a gooey puddle, but that's not like me at all. "Women like me?"

Chapter 7

Keegan

THE CONFIDENT SUNFLOWER DANCING on the deck has vanished. Bridgette shivers next to me with so much doubt in her eyes, it makes me want to dig out my spleen and hand it to her.

Why do I want to give her my spleen? I have no idea. It just feels like the noble thing to do at the moment.

The spleen cleanses blood, so maybe it's because I want to scrub away her sadness. To wash the confusion and uncertainty from her countenance and help her see she doesn't need my approval or explanations to be the strong, vibrant, passionate woman who has the courage to dance by herself in a room full of strangers.

She already possesses those wonderful characteristics.

"Keegan, I don't understand." She tucks her top lip between her teeth to keep it from wobbling.

I trace the shell of her ear and capture her wild hair in my fist. "You're beautiful, you know that?"

She slumps and steps out of my reach. "Yeah, I know." Her voice has a defeated tone.

Why isn't being beautiful a good thing?

She's one of the most beautiful women I've ever seen. It's not her body, either. Not that her curves aren't something that make my tongue fat and stupid in my mouth.

It's her posture. Her poise. Her humor and vulnerability.

She didn't have to show me this side of her personality, what others would see as a weakness, but she did, and I've never wanted to kiss a woman more than I do right now.

I snag her pinky finger with mine. It's a little touch, but it's our lifeline right now. Our small contact keeps me grounded, so I don't lose the certainty that I need to kiss her. If all I accomplish is making her smile and helping her see how desirable she is, that will be enough.

Life's too short to ignore sunflowers.

I'm selfish, and after all the little moments tonight when I wondered and wished and desired her, I have to know what she tastes like. What does it feel like to hold her in my arms?

I tug her forward. "Bridgette, I don't know where this insecurity comes from, but there's absolutely nothing wrong with you. Being beautiful isn't something people see on the outside. You're beautiful because you're honest, intelligent, and passionate. Don't think less of yourself because some idiot can't appreciate how rare you are."

"You can't know that."

"I do, though. Before you even said hello to me tonight, I knew."

"What?"

"I pinned my eyes on my beer so I wouldn't stare at your confidence."

She wrinkles her nose. "Is that a euphemism for my butt?"

A laugh bursts from my chest. "That too." I wrap my arms around her and pull her into a full-body hug, fitting her tiny, curvy frame against my chest. I inhale the mouthwatering scent of butter, honey, and salt in her hair.

Her chin tips and rests on my chest. "Thank you."

I dip my head and close what little space exists between us. Her gaze flicks to my lips.

"Please ..." I don't finish the sentence, but she nods. She knows what I don't have the courage to ask.

I mold my mouth to hers. Her lips are sweet and herbaceous, a hint of salt from the ocean air. I sink deeper into their depths and pull a sultry coo from her.

She fists my shirt and raises up on her toes. Her tongue seeks access to my mouth, and I angle her deeper.

This is everything.

Kissing this woman who is singularly incredible fogs my brain and makes me hope for every incredible dream I've ever dreamed before.

I plunge one hand into her hair, pulling it taut, so it doesn't swirl around our heads, and with the other, I grip her hip hard enough I might leave fingerprints.

If my lips weren't so busy, I'd smile at that thought. I want to belong to someone. I want someone to belong to me.

The protective, instinctive, primitive part of me growls in satisfaction. Her honesty and vulnerability are rare gifts. This is what it feels like to find the person who makes your world make sense. It's the satisfaction of a lifetime of longing.

Utter completion.

That phrase stutters in my brain. It pulls me from the sensations of Bridgette's kisses and her hands massaging my shoulders and arms like she's trying to map every inch of me.

I don't feel her touch or her need.

I try to swim back to the depths of our attraction, but it's too late. Everything's wrong.

I've had thoughts like this before. Being completed. Longing.

No! Not again.

I can't lead her on like this. She needs someone who will shine a spotlight on her brilliance and let her sparkle and glow for the whole world to see.

Being with me could destroy that. She deserves better than the kind of man I can be for her.

I grip Bridgette's upper arms and jerk away from her. Friction marks from my stubble mar her flawless chin. The hurt and confusion in her expression from before quadruple.

"I'm sorry." I wipe the back of my arm across my mouth. "I shouldn't have done that."

"I wanted you to." She reaches for me.

My foot catches on a kid's sandcastle, and I stumble backward. My arms flail, but thankfully I don't fall. "I know, but I still shouldn't have. It wasn't right."

"Why?"

I don't have a reason I can share with her. It's too shameful. Too humiliating. Every reason I'm in Bubee instead of Dallas crashes on my shoulders like a collapsing building. "This is wrong. Good night."

This time I sprint past the pier and don't stop until I reach my truck. My headlights illuminate Bridgette crouched in the sand where I left her.

I am a horrible, awful, despicable person. I shouldn't have kissed her. I led her on.

I want to kick my own butt. I hope she realizes this is about me and not her, but I doubt she will. *Never forever*, that was what she called herself.

Doctors are honor-bound to do no harm, and I've inflicted the worst harm a person can on another.

Hope is just as deadly as despair, and I gave her a lethal dose of both.

Bridgette

Keegan's hurtful words didn't keep me from dreaming of his lips on mine all night. The way his hand settled on my hip, not possessive, but stabilizing like he wanted to ground us in the moment.

I never knew a man could taste so good. That a kiss could feel so perfect.

Or that I could feel so miserable afterward.

My only hope is to never see him again. How hard will that be in a town the size of a postage stamp?

He's tall enough—hopefully, I'll see him coming so I can hide.

Because I'm a grown-up and that's how I deal with my problems. Exhibit A: Attending a Texas BBQ class instead of driving to Willa's college and apologizing.

Why am I here?

Embarrassment colors my cheeks like a sunburn. How could I be so stupid?

Asking Keegan if he's married, chasing him, practically declaring I'm hunting for a soulmate, and making out with him like he's James Bond—Sean Connery or Daniel Craig, if we're extending the fantasy.

Of course, I scared him away.

Overbearing Bridgette strikes again.

The worst part is ... I really liked him. Like, reallllly liked him.

He put me at ease and made me feel safe in a strange place. I didn't feel lonely or sad or homesick.

Why'd I open my stupid, too-big mouth?

Whatever. Time to move on.

I step from the shower and towel-dry my hair. A light pink dress with oversized poppies on the fabric calls to me. It's not practical, but I don't care. It's me.

The first day of class, I doubt we'll get our hands dirty. Most classes are theory first, practical application second.

The walk to Jake's invigorates my senses but doesn't completely mask my humiliation. Seagulls caw overhead. The sun nuzzles my shoulders. I don't let my eyes drift to Sobre las Rocas or the stretch of sand where we kissed. That would be masochistic, and I'm not that far gone.

I walk up the wooden ramp to the elevated restaurant. The views are almost as spectacular as those from the bar last night. Except no handsome stranger under the lanterns to catch my eye. Instead, four men and three women congregate in the entryway.

"Are you guys here for the pitmaster class?" I ask.

A woman with lime green glasses and bright pink hair tips her head. "Y'all are in the right place, cutie." She throws her arm over my shoulders. "I'm Amanda."

They continue around the circle introducing themselves. The introductions feel like whiplash, so I snatch one piece of information to memorize about each.

Amanda with her crazy style is easy to remember.

Juniper is a mom of six.

Brant is from Baton Rouge.

Axel is a blackjack dealer covered in impressive skull tattoos.

Tory and Tyler are twins but look like night and day in their goth versus garden pixie clothing choices.

Declan is from Dublin, Ireland with an accent that makes this woman's knees wobbly from its sheer decadence.

"Welcome!" a voice booms behind me.

I turn to the voice. A man about Turner's age with a salt and pepper beard and vibrant blue eyes pushes through the swinging door from the kitchen. "Thank you everyone for coming." He shakes hands down the line. "I'm Jake Malloy."

When he gets to me, he pauses, and the corners of his eyes pinch and his smile widens. "Bridgette, right?"

"Yes, sir." How does he know who I am? He probably does a little research his students, so he knows what to expect.

"Call me Jake. Having you is a welcome treat." He winks like we share a secret, but I have no idea why that would be. "Let's start with a tour."

He shows us around the dining room and balcony with unblemished views of the Gulf of Mexico. I stay toward the back, so my fear of heights doesn't get the better of me.

He leads us to the kitchen. The space looks similar to what Nica and Ethan built at Cuoré, their restaurant, in Emerald Bay. An expediting table gleams under heat lamps as we enter. Along the left wall is a row of ovens and a large flattop stove. On the right, refrigerators, a pantry, and empty counters fill the space.

Jake gestures for us to pull in closer. "This is where we make most of the menu and assemble the final touches, but the magic you're here for happens downstairs. That's where the smokers and barbecues are kept. It's also where we'll start today. Follow me."

We slip single file down a set of interior stairs. I'm glad there's no view like at the bar. It would make me wish Keegan were holding my hand again, and I'm not allowing myself to think about him.

At the bottom of the stairs, the only things separating us from the beach are giant screen walls. Ocean breezes and sunshine filter through without the sand or bugs. Metal tables are arranged in two rows with one bigger table at the front of the room. Barbeques and piles of wood line the wall opposite the stairs with ventilation tubes running to the exterior of the building.

Jake claps his hands. "First things first, you'll be working in pairs, so pick your partner."

Tory loops her arm around her brother's neck and rubs her knuckles against his buzz cut. "Looks like you're stuck with me again."

He wriggles out of her headlock and straightens his light green shirt. "Nah, I'm teaming up with Axel. Boys against girls."

Tory sticks her tongue out and pivots to Amanda. "Partner?"

Amanda shrugs. "No complaints here." They high-five.

Declan dips his chin, avoiding my eyes, but steps next to me. "Do ya want tuh be me partner?"

I know shy when I see it. You wouldn't expect it from this towering man, but it's evident in how he can't quite meet my gaze, his stooped shoulders.

Honestly, it soothes the raw edges of my ego that Keegan shredded like cheese on a grater.

"I'd love to." I gesture to the last empty table closest to the ocean.

"Grand." His crooning Irish lilt could knock me over with a feather. It's the kind women program into their Siris or watch Colin Farrell videos to hear. Hanging with Declan will not be a hardship for the next three weeks.

"First things first," Jake says. "Some of you brought your personal knives, some of you didn't. No big deal. I've got plenty, but I do expect them returned in the conditioned loaned. Some instructors like to start with the fire, but I figure there's no point if you can't handle your meat properly. How well do you butcher a pig? We're about to find out."

A man steps out of the refrigerator behind Jake, and I swear I know the set of those shoulders even with the pig balanced on top of them.

"What the heck?" The words slip out, and Declan's eyebrow crinkles in the middle.

"You okay, lass?"

"Like a sunflower." I prop my fists on my hips. Keegan can't see me as he carries the meat to Jake, but I'd know that backside anywhere.

What is he doing here? I thought he was a mover or a stock boy or something.

Why didn't he say he'd be here?

I think back to last night. I told him why I was in Bubee, didn't I? I don't remember. I was too busy flirting and memorizing how his eyelashes outlined his eyes.

He said he spent his Sunday lifting boxes. Were those boxes of meat?

He's going to set that pig on Jake's table and see me, and I don't know how I want him to react. Part of me wants a big grin of recognition and excitement. *Yay! Bridgette's here. Time to forgive and forget and get to more kissing.*

The other, angry part of me wants to watch him pale and freak out.

I'm holding on to my anger. He kissed me like holding me was the only thing keeping his feet on the ground, then he flung me away like I was worthless.

How do I get through three weeks of class with him right there?

My cheeks are heating again. Sheesh, is there a way to turn off the blood supply to my face or tell my nervous system to calm down and stop publicizing my feelings all over the place?

There's no room for embarrassment or regret. I don't regret kissing him. If given the opportunity, I'd do it again, but with a different outcome, so I hold on to my annoyance.

Declan gives me another side eye and concern washes through his posture, but there's also worry and anxiety. He's likely asking himself why he picked me—the woman acting all tense and freaked out—to be his partner.

Keegan arrives at Jake's table and lowers the hog to the surface. I refuse to show him I'm affected by his presence. I cross my arms over my stomach to keep them from shaking and paste a plastic smile on my mouth. I look like a Barbie doll, might as well strike a pose like one too.

Keegan's eyes sweep over the pairs on the front row, graze over Declan, then stutter to a stop on me.

His jaw clenches.

"This is Keegan." Jake claps him on the back. "He'll assist us during class. He's a master carver, so I'll let him show you how to butcher today's specimen." Jake steps back from the table.

Keegan doesn't move. He's too busy perfecting the surly frown aimed at me.

I want to shout, *I'm not a stalker*, but that's the thing mentally unstable people do. I don't need that reputation amongst my classmates.

Amanda leans over to Tory, and they snicker to themselves. Their light laughter breaks Keegan from his gloom. He picks up the knife and narrates his cuts. In less than an hour, he's completely deconstructed the hog. Ribs, shoulder, rump, and everything in between. Every part we will use is neatly laid out before him with surgical precision.

I begrudgingly have a new appreciation for watching a man's strength in action. The way his forearms bunched as he lifted hundreds of pounds of meat sent shivers across my skin. The delicate way he butterflied the pork chops turned the shiver into electrical impulses. I hold my breath to control the annoying lack of stability in my legs.

Why do I have to be attracted to a jerk who doesn't want to have anything to do with me?

"Any questions?" he asks. He doesn't give us time to raise our hands. "Grab a hog out of the cooler." He cleans his knife and turns to Jake, whispers something in his ear. They share a meaningful gaze—what that meaning is, I have no idea—but Jake nods solemnly as his gaze shifts to me. *Great. Perfect.* Now the teacher knows Keegan and I have history.

Declan returns to our table with a pig. "Would ya like to be doin' the honors?"

"Would I ever." I hone my knife and slice through the meat. If Keegan can butcher a pig in sixty minutes, I'll do it in forty-five. Perfectly. Without getting a drop of blood on my pink dress.

Chapter 8

Keegan

A CEILING FAN. An ocean breeze. I need fresh air. Anything to flush away the remnants of Bridgette's buttery, salty smell that weigh down my lungs and prevent me from drawing a full breath.

I don't have anything but the freezer. I scramble inside once Jake takes the class over.

What is Bridgette doing here? I saw her standing close to the tall Irish student whose name I can't remember, and for a second something like jealousy clawed into my chest.

But I'm not jealous.

I don't do jealousy. It's a wasteful emotion. Why expend energy wanting what someone else has?

My stomach turns. I hate how that even sounds in my head. I press my head to the frozen door.

She's not property. She's not something to be bought, sold, or traded. She's a bubbly, vivacious woman who is fully capable of making decisions for herself.

She's here for Jake's class, not the tall Irishman.

Dublin is here for the food too. Jake gave me his application to read this morning. He thinks the Irishman is the strongest contender to win the restaurant.

If only Jake had given me Bridgette's file. With a heads up, I wouldn't be standing here shivering, slack-jawed like a broken robot. This unnamed emotion wouldn't swirl behind my sternum if I'd known to expect her.

If I'd talked to her last night and told her why I'm in town, none of this would have been a catastrophic surprise. I would have said, *Hey, I'm helping my terminally ill mentor teach his barbecue masterclass.* She would have said, *I'm part of the class. I'll see you there.*

If I'd known she was a student, I wouldn't have kissed her.

Well ... maybe ... actually ...

No. Stop it.

I had to tell Jake about last night. Just the part where I was a jerk to explain the venom shooting from her eyes.

My behavior is for her safety.

My fingers dig into my scalp. I've stooped to lying to myself.

I don't want Bridgette around because she's too big a temptation.

The temptation to act like a fool to hear her laugh again.

The temptation to kiss her and appreciate her arms wrapped around my neck, holding on for dear life.

The temptation to let my guard down and tell her everything about myself.

But I can't.

Excessive honesty opened the door to all the trouble I'm in with my ex.

It might not matter to Bridgette that I'm a physician, but there's a chance once she sees the M.D. after my name, she'll only see my paycheck and reputation.

I couldn't stand it if she stopped seeing me as Keegan and started seeing me as Dr. Sullivan, husband to be captured.

She said she's looking for a ring, and I won't be that guy.

I can't give in to the temptation.

The hint of jealousy was enough. I don't need her to draw out any other emotions.

I'm stoic. Self-contained. Aloof.

I'm a jerk who has to figure out how to get through three weeks in her presence when the last hour has been torture.

I sulk in the corner while she dismembers her pig. She would make a skilled surgeon. She holds the knife like you hold a toddler's hand when you cross the street: gently but with authority.

Dublin points at something. She shifts her angle and gifts him one of her sunflower smiles.

She's a beautiful woman. I've known beautiful women before. I shake my head at my ridiculousness. We'll get used to being around each other, and the attraction will fade.

I roam to the table diagonal to Bridgette's. A guy with motorcycles tattooed on his biceps slices through the hip joint capsule. "How's it going?" I ask.

He shifts his weight left, right, left. "This is harder than I 'xpected." His heavy Creole accent places him as a Louisiana native. I wouldn't be surprised if he grew up eating alligator. This shouldn't be the first pig he's deconstructed.

I point to the muscle as it enters the joint. "Follow the muscle's grain. It will guide the knife." I show him how to track the fibers and which direction to make his cut. "Is this your first pig?"

A sheepish embarrassment pinks his cheeks. "I've got a rockstar butcher at home who does this for me."

That explains a lot. I wouldn't expect Jake to sell his business to someone who doesn't know the basics, but if this guy already has a team, he might.

The women at the next table are slicing the loin into two-inch-thick chops. I give them pointers too.

I can't ignore Bridgette and Dublin any longer. For Jake's sake, I need to know each participant's strengths and weaknesses. I refuse to make Bridgette one of mine.

What if Jake sells the restaurant to her? I'll see her every time I come home. The memory of kissing her, how she crumpled on the beach after I ran away, will always stand between us.

Bridgette's almost done with the entire pig.

I stand on the far end of the table, out of stabbing range. "Great job."

She snorts. "Why do you sound so surprised?"

"No reason."

"Sure." She disarticulates the ribcage with swift motions.

"I'm not trying—"

She plops the knife on the table. "Any pointers?"

This feels like a trick question. If I critique her work, she could take it personally. If I don't say anything, she'll think I'm a chicken.

I am.

"Dub—" I search my memory for his real name. "Declan, what do you think of Bridgette's work?"

"She's doin' grand." Hero worship shines from his expression. He's as smitten as I am by the blonde bombshell—and her knife skills.

A, s*o, there* smirk flits across her face before she places the meat in a bucket, turns her back on me, and carries it into the refrigerator.

I deserve the cold shoulder. It will make the masterclass easier if she continues to hate me.

If only my mind wasn't strategizing ways to cultivate her sunflower smile in my direction.

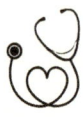

Bridgette

"You're a great partner, Declan. I hope we continue working together." I clean and pack up our knives.

He wipes the blood and fat off the table with a lemony cleaning solution that tickles my nose. "I agree."

He's almost as skilled a butcher as Keegan. Declan's initial shyness disappeared as he dislocated the hip socket, and a cheerful chatterbox took its place.

We talked about his home in Dublin. He's got two older brothers and a baby sister who are expanding their family's whiskey distillery. His grandfather taught him to cook on his farm when Declan was tiny.

The more I listened, the more I ignored Keegan's pacing the room. Listening to Declan's soft lilting vowels for three weeks might be the best part of the trip.

Once Jake was satisfied with our butchering skills, he talked us through our class schedule. Week one: Meat Prep. Week two: Fire and Smoke. Week three: Make Magic.

He's solidly in the *Barbecue Needs Sauce* camp, giving us three full days of spice and sauce instruction, so he and I will be great friends.

Declan tosses his towel in the laundry bin. "Want to grab a pint?"

A drink would be nice, but I don't want to give Declan the wrong impression. I'm here for the barbecue, not a date, contrary to my behavior last night.

"Maybe another day. I promised my landlady I'd have dinner with her." Not totally a lie. Daisy extended an open-ended invitation for every meal.

He nods and waves goodbye.

The feeling of raw meat sticks to my fingers. I wash my hands one more time and grab my purse from the cubby under the stairs.

"Bridgette?" Keegan says behind me.

I school my features and turn to face him. "Yes?"

His weight shifts to his toes, and he opens his mouth. I arch an eyebrow, but he doesn't say anything. He stuffs his hands into the pockets of his boardshorts.

I hold up my hand. "I'm not here because of you. I apologize for my behavior last night. It was inappropriate, and I didn't mean to make you uncomfortable. I thought we were flirting, and you surprised me when you left."

He scrubs his toe across the wood floor.

"Word of advice." I loop my purse strap over my head. "Next time a woman asks what you do for a living, don't lie. It will make things a lot easier for both parties. If you'd told me you were Jake's assistant, I would have asked about class and cuts of beef and the best way to make sausage."

"I never lied."

"Precision of language."

His gaze finally lifts to mine. "*The Giver* by Lois Lowry. Great book."

I bite my cheek, so I don't smile that he understood my random reference. "Have a good night. I'll see you tomorrow."

My skirt flares as I spin and walk out onto the sand. It's only four p.m. Daisy said dinner is at 6:30.

I'm taking advantage of the beach while I've got it.

I'm here to get unstuck. To figure out what makes me happy and whether I want to continue to walk the path I've tread to this point. To know how to balance being myself while honoring other people's personalities.

Might as well work that out with the ocean tickling my toes.

Bubee has miles and miles of uninterrupted sand for me to wander, stretching to a marina to the north and Sobre las Rocas to the south.

I turn north and raise my arms above my head to release the tension in my shoulders. Butchering a pig is harder than I thought it would be. I've never cut apart a 300-pound animal before. I hope Jake doesn't expect me to do the same with a cow tomorrow. I'll need a chainsaw and a crane.

Cars zoom past on Camino del Mar above the beach. Families build sandcastles and splash in the waves while an old man flies a kite shaped like a dragon. Salty air fills my lungs and caresses my cheeks. Warm water washes to the middle of my calves, and I lift my skirt to keep the hem dry.

Twenty minutes in, my tension is gone.

If only I could do this every day. Lake Superior would give me frostbite if I tried. The number of rocks along the shore make long walks illogical.

The sun creeps closer to the horizon, a chill settles in the air, and I turn toward Daisy's.

In the distance, Jake's parking lot is empty. A dip swirls in my stomach. My classmates are an interesting group. I might learn as much from them as I do from Jake, especially Declan. Too bad we didn't arrange a meet and greet last night. It's easier to get to know people over chips and queso than while butchering.

But if we had, I wouldn't have met Keegan first. I enjoyed hanging out with him on the beach. I liked listening to him talk, what little of it he did. I liked how safe he made me feel in a strange place.

But I'm not the kind of woman who chases a man if he doesn't want her. My pride's wounded. I'm irritated that he kissed and dismissed me.

But if I'm going to get unstuck, I need to focus on myself. My joy will be my doing, not anyone else's.

Chapter 9

Bridgette

Three blocks from the beach, gravel crunches behind me. A Ford F-150 pickup truck idles on the edge of the road a dozen yards back. I pick up my pace.

More gravel crunches, and I hazard another peek over my shoulder. The truck rolled forward to close the gap I created.

Just what I need today. A creeper.

The sun reflects off the windshield, blocking my view of the driver.

I spin on my heel, take a picture of the truck with the license plate legible, and send it to Camille just in case.

My fists plant on my hips, and I stare at the truck. It's not the most recent body style, but it's not old either. Maybe a 2019? Dark blue. No lift kit. No evident body damage, stickers, or other distinguishing marks. "Can I help you?"

The truck rolls toward me. I step farther into the yard behind me and angle my body, so the mailbox is between us.

I may be confrontational, but I'm not dumb. If this is an attempted kidnapping, I will put up one heck of a fight.

When the truck is level with me, the window lowers and familiar hazel eyes blink at me.

"Keegan?" I practically growl his name. "You scared the crap out of me."

He drums his fingers on the steering wheel. "I'm sorry. I was debating whether to talk to you or just drive by."

"Well, what's your decision?"

"Are you lost? Do you need a ride to your hotel?"

"I'm fine."

"Where's your rental car?"

"I don't have one."

"Why?"

"What's with the twenty questions?" He didn't care last night. Does my being in his class change his curiosity level? Am I suddenly worthy of his interest?

No ... that's not fair. Up until I chased him down the beach, Keegan and I were good.

I pushed too hard, and he couldn't handle it.

That's on me.

"I just ... Bubee's safe, but that doesn't mean you should be wandering around alone at night."

"Thanks for your concern, but I'll be fine." I shake my head and continue down the sidewalk. My emotions war with each other. Last night was magical until he left me discombobulated on the beach. He almost made it through the entire class today without talking to me.

His engine quietly grumbles as he keeps pace with me.

"I don't need an escort," I call.

"I'm headed the same direction."

"At five miles an hour?"

He silently shrugs.

"I wish I could tell if you are lying." Last night I thought I could, but this version of Keegan is calculated and calm. Not in a scary way, but in an, *I'm paying attention to every detail, so I know the best way to react* kind of way.

"I never lied to you." His words are just loud enough for me to hear. There's a hard edge to them, but there's something else lacing their tone that I can't interpret.

"You omitted the truth. In my book, that's the same thing."

He continues to follow me as I weave north and west toward Daisy's house.

My friends at home would worry if a stranger followed me home, but I'm not.

If nothing else, Keegan is a protector. He helped me down the stairs at the bar when I was afraid of the height. He noticed when I was tired and found me a place to sit.

I make the last turn onto La Playa Boulevard and Keegan speeds up so he's next to me again. "You don't live out here."

"The motel by the highway was booked, so I set up a cardboard box."

"I'm serious. Where are you staying?" I can't tell if his tone is concerned or intrigued.

This is a small town, so I assume he knows everyone anyway. I extend my finger toward Daisy's house. "She's nice."

I could say more. She's a great cook. She's witty and funny, but I don't add the descriptors. He doesn't need to know how I feel about Daisy. Keegan is a blip in my life. He doesn't trust me to walk myself home, fine. *Whatever.*

He mumbles an expletive loud enough for me to hear, speeds past, parks the truck in front of her house, and jogs to block my path. "You can't stay there."

I recoil. "Who do you think you are? You do not get to tell me what I can and can't do."

He steps close so I can count the freckles across the bridge of his nose. "I'm Daisy's grandson. Keegan Sullivan."

His name stretches. They have similar smiles and energies when I think about it.

But she wins the hospitality award, while he's Mr. Cranky Pants.

Not only does he want to keep me away from himself, but he doesn't want me near his grandmother. Peachy.

"Good to see I left such a winning impression on you. The only thing I'm going to steal is her Italian Wedding soup recipe."

"That explains a lot." His gaze dips to my mouth, and he leans forward like he's remembering our kiss and wants a second helping.

But that can't be right.

I press up onto my toes, so my eyes are level with his. "What do you mean, *that explains a lot*?"

"You tasted familiar last night, but I couldn't figure out why. She made you soup for dinner, didn't she?"

"So?"

"It's her special occasion dinner. You've been blessed. How did you find her?"

I have conversational whiplash, but the explanation tumbles out of me. "My friend found her house on the rental site. The one who gifted me the class."

His brow puckers. "You didn't sign up?"

"No, my friend won it for me in a silent auction. He knows Jake."

Keegan wags his finger in my face. "Jake doesn't know anyone in Minnesota."

I poke his chest out of my personal space. "Maybe you don't know everything there is to know about Jake."

"What's your friend's name?"

"I'm tired of answering your questions." I sidestep around him.

His arm shoots out to block my path. "Humor me."

I want to shut him up, take off my heels, and change into yoga pants. It doesn't matter if he knows the answer and Keegan's the kind that won't give up until he's got all the information he needs to make sure I won't murder his grandmother in her sleep. "Turner Donovan."

He takes three steps back. "Now I know you're lying."

"Why would I?" I'm sick and tired of Keegan's judgmental attitude. Accusing me of lying about my friend. Yeah ... nope. I step onto the grass to dodge around him. My heel sinks deep into the turf.

Stupid grass. Stupid stilettos. Infuriating man.

Bubee is officially off my list of cute coastal towns to retire to.

Keegan spreads his feet, crosses his arms over his chest, and tips his head toward me as I struggle to free my shoe. "Turner Donovan disappeared five decades ago."

"Disappeared? What are you even talking about?"

He points to Daisy's house. "He's Gran's older brother. No one has seen or heard from him since he disappeared. She won't even talk about him. The only reason I know he existed is because my great-grandmother confused me with him as dementia stole her memories. Why are you *really* here?"

I pull my phone from my purse and open my photos. Scrolling through, I find the picture of Turner and me eating scones during book club at his bookstore last month.

"Turner is one of my best friends, like my grandpa. He gave me Jake's class. I don't have an ulterior motive. I just want to learn how to barbecue." I'm not going into specifics about my little meltdown at the bar or the other reason I left Emerald Bay. Keegan has all the spilled guts I'm going to give him about that night with Graham.

Keegan cups my hand, so we're both holding the phone. His delicate touch makes me step closer even as my brain tells me to step away.

Keegan runs his thumb over the screen. His eyes widen. "No way! He looks like my great-grandfather before he died. He's been in Minnesota this whole time?" He presses his knuckles to his mouth. "Does Gran know he gave you the class?"

"I don't know. I made the arrangements. It's not like we've had a bunch of time to sit and talk." I didn't think there was a link between Turner and the woman whose carriage house he recommended. I assumed she was another acquaintance like Jake. "What about Jake? He knows Turner bought my admission from him. Why didn't he tell you about your great uncle?"

"I don't know. Everything we have is about you."

"You have a file on me? Then why were you surprised to see me?"

He lets go of my hand. "Jake never gave it to me."

I stare at Turner's picture. He always talked about a grandson coming to visit. Is this the family he kept alluding to? Did he send me here to meet them? Why hasn't he been home in fifty-odd years? Why do they think he disappeared? "We need to tell Daisy."

"That's not a great idea. Gran's fragile."

I snort. "Are we talking about the same woman? I'm not going to break her. Besides, wouldn't you want to know if someone knew where your brother was?"

"My brother wouldn't run away."

I march around Keegan. "I'm telling her he's alive." Turner is one of my favorite people in the world, and if his sister thinks he's dead, she deserves the truth.

But why didn't he tell her himself?

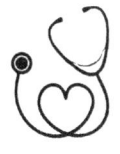

Chapter 10

Keegan

I THOUGHT MY WORLD was upside down when I saw Bridgette in class, but now I'm tumbling down a rabbit hole, and no light glows at the bottom.

Bridgette and I climb the stairs to Gran's porch. She's worrying her lip so hard, she might draw blood, but the determined set to her brow feels like someone disconnected my neurons from my muscles. I'm paralyzed to stop her from announcing her connection to Gran's brother.

I'm not sure dropping this bomb is the best idea, but Gran deserves to know her brother's alive and well. I would want to know the truth if Ian disappeared.

What is Gran going to say? Why did he disappear in the first place?

My great uncle's name is the one whispered in corners at Christmas parties when people don't think anyone is listening. Gran hasn't mentioned him in the last ten years.

But Bridgette knows him. They're good enough friends that he bought her a place in Jake's pitmaster class. That's quite a friendship.

It's not normal.

Why would an almost eighty-year-old man spend that kind of money on someone who isn't family? Why did he send Bridgette to Jake's class? Does he know Jake's selling and hoped he would give the restaurant to Bridgette?

That's a bit of a stretch, but I have to ask the questions.

I hold the door open for Bridgette. Gran sings Taylor Swift at the top of her lungs in the back of the house.

"She's got good taste in music." Bridgette shimmies to the beat. "Hopefully the vibe will make this easier."

Nothing will make our information easy. Gran's going to have a heart attack.

Where's my medical kit when I need it? Not that I can do much besides CPR. I saw bones apart then screw them back together for a living. I don't restart hearts after they learn their missing brother isn't dead.

Gran's rolling sugar cookie dough, shaking her backside like it's going out of style.

"Gran?"

She screeches and brandishes the rolling pin like a sword. Bridgette jumps behind me. Her hands grip my shoulders, using me as a shield.

"Glad to know you're willing to sacrifice me," I say over my shoulder.

"Keegan!" Gran wraps her arms around me, trapping Bridgette against my back in her excitement. I'm like their Oreo frosting, and I don't want to admit how nice the honest affection feels. "I thought you went back to Dallas."

"Dallas?" Bridgette's grip tightens, but I don't respond to the condemning squeeze. "Local boy, my biscuits," she whispers so quietly Gran can't hear.

Gran releases me and wipes the flour from my T-shirt. "I wish I'd known you were coming, but this is such a nice surprise." Her gaze jumps from me to Bridgette. "This means you're helping with Jake's class. Is that why you're coming home together? Did he walk you?"

"Stalked is more like it. Followed me in his truck because he didn't trust I belong here."

Gran presses a sailboat-shaped cookie into Bridgette's hand but levels her glare at me. "Women don't appreciate being followed, no matter your good intentions."

"That's not ... I ..."

Gran narrows her eyes and looks down her nose at me. "I watched you drive away. You said work couldn't wait and you needed to get home."

"Jake needs me. Who else will be your cookie tester?" I snag a cookie from the cooling rack.

Gran tries to bop my hand, but I'm quicker. She's not really trying anyway. It's the game we play where she pretends she doesn't want to give me a cookie, but she genuinely loves that I'm stealing them.

It's also a good way to steer the conversation away from what's waiting for me in Dallas.

Bridgette sits on a barstool. "Seems he likes to keep secrets from everyone."

I need to control this conversation before Gran spins it in a direction I don't want it to drift. "Gran, did Bridgette tell you how she learned about Jake's class?"

Gran washes her hands. "Jake's a great teacher. I assumed she read about it in a magazine or something." She picks up the rolling pin.

"Your brother gifted her the admission."

Bridgette shoots me a look, but I don't know her well enough to interpret it. Annoyance? Frustration? Yeah, my declaration lacked tact, but just rip off the bandage, right?

I shove another cookie in my mouth and step out of arm's reach.

Gran cuts another sailboat. "How do you know Warner?"

"Turner, Gran. She knows Turner."

Gran's eyes drift to Bridgette's. "Turner?"

Bridgette shows Gran the picture she showed me. "Turner Donovan. He lives in Emerald Bay, Minnesota. He runs a bookstore and makes horrible latte art. He's the surrogate grandpa I always wanted." Bridgette's expression holds so much love and respect it makes me squirm that I didn't believe her.

Gran wipes her hands on her apron and takes the phone. Her finger hovers over the screen. "Time hasn't been kind to him, but I recognize the eyes." She looks at me. "They're the same hazel as yours."

"When was the last time you saw him?" Bridgette asks.

"When he deployed to Vietnam. He never came home, but we never received word from the Army saying he was captured or killed in action. He just disappeared."

"Call him," I say.

Gran shakes her head and returns the phone to Bridgette. "No. I don't wish to speak with the boy who abandoned our family." Her arms drift over the cookie dough like she's not sure what to do now. She shakes her head and steps back. "Bridgette, be a dear and finish these. I'm going to lie down."

Bridgette clasps Gran's hands to steady them. "Sure, Daisy. Anything special you want me to do?"

"I ... whatever you'd like, dear." She unties her apron and loops it over Bridgette's dress.

Gran's fingers skim over the counter, refrigerator, and cabinets as she makes her way out of the room, almost like she needs to touch everything to know it's solid.

When Gran's door clicks shut, Bridgette swats my chest. "That was awful. Why'd you tell her like that?"

"Beating around the bush would have been worse. Now she knows." Turner's secret is revealed and mine is safe.

My strategy was selfish, but what was Bridgette going to do? Drag out the revelation over an hour-long conversation? It's better this way. Gran can process alone in her room, then she'll come back and ask Bridgette questions. We'll figure out what Gran wants to do and be done.

Bridgette slides a full cookie sheet into the oven and sets the timer. "What do you think happened?"

"War changes people. It's possible he couldn't face what he'd done." I don't know anything but the Forrest Gump version of the Vietnam War, so I can only guess.

Bridgette balls the cookie dough and kneads the stray pieces together. "Turner isn't a traumatized soldier. He's sarcastic, opinionated, and extroverted."

"Maybe it's repressed." During my intern year, I met a lot of soldiers with PTSD. Some were extremely skilled at hiding it. "It's been five decades. He could have he gotten help but still doesn't have the courage to face the people he left behind."

"That's not it. Every Thursday, I delivered fresh scones to the bookstore. He said they were for his grandson, but no one ever came. He always seemed lonely."

I take a seat across from her, grab a piping bag, and outline the sailboats in white. We settle into the silence, lost in thought. Jake needs to explain how he knew about Turner and why never told my grandma. I need to figure out how to get back to Dallas to clear my name.

Bridgette slams the dough onto the counter and rolls it flat. "I want to bring him here," she says in almost a whisper. Like if she admits her desire too loudly, the universe will stop her from making it come true.

But that is my job. "Gran doesn't want to see him."

"Maybe if I figure out why he never came home, I can heal their relationship. I'm sure he has a good reason."

"Or he's a coward."

Her pointer finger dashes into my face. "You don't know him."

I ignore the finger and tone and continue decorating the cookies. "What kind of man ignores his family for half a century?"

Bridgette's ears turn bright red, and her nostrils flare. "What kind of man is embarrassed to be a line cook in a barbecue restaurant?"

"I'm not embarrassed."

"Oh, right. What about living in Dallas? You said you're a local." It's amazing how her voice and posture can be so tense and frustrated while her hands continue to gently cut and place the cookie dough on the cookie sheet.

I roll my shoulder. "I grew up here. That makes me a local."

"If it takes you hours to get to the *local* coffee shop, you are no longer a local."

"Why does it matter?

"I don't appreciate being lied to."

"I never lied." I omitted. I redirected. But I never lied.

Technically.

She flattens her palms on the floured counter and leans forward. "Keegan, hear me loud and clear. You don't want me to get to know you? Fine. Whatever. I'll leave you alone. You can't stop me from reuniting my friend with his sister. I don't need your permission."

I rise to my feet. "I won't let you upset Gran."

"Don't you think she wants to know why he left? Deep down."

I point toward her room. "You saw her reaction."

"That was shock because you've got the bedside manner of a mortician."

"A mortician? That's the best you've got?"

"Sour lemon. Moldy cucumber. Pick your metaphor. You suck."

The temptation to open my mouth and let the truth spill out makes me dig my teeth into my tongue.

I have excellent bedside manners. I once told an NFL-bound quarterback he would never play again, and he thanked me. Tears in his eyes, relief skated through his body. His mom sends me Christmas cards. He's an engineer for NASA with a wife and three daughters.

Bridgette mistakes my silence for acquiescence. "I owe this to Turner. He's the sweetest, loneliest man I've ever met. He's always been there for me when I needed a friend. I'm going to help him reconcile with his sister."

I can't stop Bridgette. She's persistent and a little pig-headed. She'd move the beach a grain at a time just to prove she could.

"You're not doing it without me." Bridgette doesn't get to dig through our family history without a chaperone.

She pops to her toes and glares at me. "Worried I'll spread some dirty Donovan family secret all over town?"

"People usually have good reasons to keep their secrets."

I know I do.

Chapter 11

Bridgette

Keegan scoops the sailboat cookies off the tray and slides them onto the cooling racks. After our standoff, he used the rest of the frosting to decorate the prebaked cookies then disappeared to an upstairs bedroom, returning in a mint green T-shirt that hugs his chest and biceps and jeans that leave little to my overactive imagination. Apparently, he keeps a second wardrobe here, and he's mouthwatering in fitted clothes.

I try to keep my attention on the cookies, but he's distracting. Hauling meat has perfected his physique. Who needs dumbbells and a treadmill when you move cows?

Stop staring! Make the cookies. Daisy will expect them to be done when she wakes up.

Since he used the end of the frosting on the last batch, I mix powdered sugar, milk, corn syrup, and vanilla with a hand mixer, adding drops of blue food coloring until it's the color of the ocean outside the window.

My mind swirls like the ingredients in the mixer. I don't want to believe Turner is the man his sister paints him to be.

He's kind and helpful. He wouldn't abandon the people he loves the most in the world unless he had a good reason.

I need to help him reconcile with his sister, but I have no idea where to start. The easy answer is to call him and ask.

But if I do that, he'll know I'm digging into his past. He left for a reason and if that reason is as shameful as Keegan insinuated, I can't afford to alienate Turner.

He knew I needed to be here. I owe him for my current sanity. If I were home, I'd flinch every time the bakery bell rang, wondering if it was one of Graham's friends coming to laugh at me. I'd worry being myself was making someone else lose their self-confidence. I'd watch my friends waltz around with heart eyes bonking out of their heads and wonder why no one wants more than a night or two with me.

Turner deserves to know his sister as she is now. She deserves to know him.

Soft feet pad down the hallway. Daisy smooths her hands down the front of her soft cotton tunic as she enters the kitchen. She claps her hands together. "Time for dinner. Grilled chicken with asparagus sound good? Keegan, be a dear and fire up the barbecue." Even though the menu sounded like a question, her rapid-fire directions brook no argument.

Keegan raises his hand and strides toward the door. "Mom and Dad are expecting me."

Daisy waves away his words. "You're not fifteen with a curfew. You're here. You'll eat with us."

He scrubs his hands around the back of his head. "I'll call them." He steps onto the porch.

"Start the barbecue while you're out there," she calls. "Bridgette, the asparagus is in the crisper. Second drawer on the left." She points to the massive refrigerator.

I open the door. It's surprisingly well-stocked for a woman who lives alone. Spinach, apples, milk, eggs, cream cheese, Sriracha, and a dozen other hot sauces. "Do you have people drop in for meals a lot?"

"More than you'd think. I love to cook, and there's never a shortage of people who appreciate a home-cooked meal. The couple three houses down the way just had triplets. She's too tired to cook, and he's at the BioTech factory all day. I like to help where I can."

My mind drifts to the bookstore in Emerald Bay. "Turner's the same."

Daisy stiffens.

"I'm sorry. I didn't mean to ..." I don't finish my sentence because I did mean to bring him up. I want to know who he was before I met him in Minnesota.

She shrugs. "I'm not used to hearing his name spoken so openly."

I grab the asparagus. "Will you tell me what he was like as a kid?" I snap the bottoms off the spears.

A crease pulls at her silver eyebrows. "Covered in mud. Sneaking frogs into his bedroom."

"I can see that. He constantly sneaks my friend's dog slivers of venison jerky when she brings the puppy to the bookstore."

"A dog in a bookstore? That's odd."

I lift my shoulder and let my gaze blur until I picture Turner's craggy face in my mind's eye. "That's Turner. He makes everyone feel welcome. That's why we're great friends. He always has a warm greeting and a listening ear, no matter how off the wall my rant of the day seems to everyone else."

Daisy hones her boning knife. "He's always been charismatic. He could talk the wings off of a butterfly." She crunches through the chicken's ribs, spatchcocking it for the grill as easily as if she were buttering toast. She's where Keegan gets his culinary prowess.

The warm, homey feeling I had during dinner with Daisy last night creeps to the door of my heart and knocks to remind me how wonderful this town and this family are, despite events with Keegan.

These are people Turner used to belong to. He's more entitled to—and deserving of—experiencing this atmosphere and feeling their love than I am.

Daisy needs to give me the key bits of information that will help me decide how to reconcile them.

"What else can you tell me about him?"

"He loved playing baseball and sailing." She lifts a cookie and traces it with her finger. "I still have his boat. Mama saved his trophies and personal effects in the attic. I didn't have the guts to throw them away when Mama and Daddy died."

"This is the house you grew up in?"

"Of course. We southerners love our heritage."

"Barbecue's hot." Keegan spins tongs on his long index finger. "How do you want the chicken seasoned?"

"Chef's choice," Daisy says.

"Lemon pepper it is." Keegan rifles through Daisy's cupboards, completely at ease in this little cooking cocoon they've created.

There are so many things I want to discover about this family. These two love each other unconditionally, and I get the feeling the rest of the family is the same way.

Except for their feelings about Turner, but hopefully, I can change that.

"Daisy, can I see Turner's things?"

"If you'd like." She wrinkles her nose. "They're probably covered in spider webs."

Through the open sliding glass door, Keegan smirks.

A few bugs will not deter me.

"Keegan can squish them." I stick out my tongue in his direction.

It's Daisy's turn to smirk. "You'd think a big, strong man like him would take on that task, but you would be wrong. He screams like a little girl when he finds them in his bathroom."

Red shoots up his neck. "Gran!"

"What? You've never liked bugs, and Ian loved putting them in your bed."

"Ian?"

"His little brother. He's in medical school in Houston."

That explains the doctor apron. "Fine. I'll protect you *and* squish the spiders if you brave the attic with me." Two sets of hands are better than one.

"Let's eat first. I have a romance novel that needs my attention." Daisy waggles her eyebrows, and I don't want to interpret their meaning. I love a good bodice-ripper as much as the next woman. That doesn't mean I need to talk about it with my hostess and her super-sexy grandson.

Keegan cooks the chicken and asparagus while Daisy makes a mixed green salad and I finish frosting the sailboat cookies. We work in harmony like this is a normal Monday night. Like I've known these people forever, not just two days. It's weird to feel so at home in a place where I should feel like a stranger.

I don't feel this comfortable in Hannah's kitchen. Maybe that's because of the boss/employee dynamic. At the end of the day, she holds my career in her hands and can fire me if I don't do a stellar job.

There's no pressure in this home. If Daisy laughs about burning a Christmas turkey, a wobbly frosting line won't garner criticism.

I sneak glances at Keegan at the grill. I don't understand him. He bops along to music playing in his head. His hips swivel hypnotically. It's like he's a different person here than he was last night at the bar or today during class.

This is relaxed Keegan. Fun Keegan. Jokester Keegan. I thought I wanted to get to know Shy Keegan from the bar, but Homebody Keegan is almost irresistible.

Almost.

I can't let myself forget what happened on the beach. After the kiss. Because I should probably forget the kiss if I'm going to act like a sane person, not an attention-starved groupie.

He doesn't like me.

He doesn't want me.

It doesn't matter if I want him.

He's here for Daisy and to protect his family's reputation, not to get to know me.

"Why is a baker learning how to barbecue?" Daisy asks as she places chicken breast slices on my plate.

I inhale the delicious chicken aroma. "There's nothing better than a perfectly executed pulled-pork sandwich on a brioche bun. I've got the buns part handled. But after hours and hours with the meat, I can't seem to get it right. Once I learn how to smoke the pork perfectly, I'll be able to expand the menu at our café back home."

Keegan squeezes his fork tighter. "You own a restaurant?" His tone is slightly accusatory.

"No," I clarify. "But my boss gives me carte blanche to modify our menu. There's no reason to open my own restaurant. Emerald Bay can't support more than what we have." Definitely not a second bakery or a third diner/café. "Besides, Hannah's Bakery is the only place I've ever wanted to work. Since my best friend, Camille, and I started working there in high school, it's been a second home. It's comfortable. I know the routines."

Daisy taps Keegan's hand with the end of her fork. "Keegan's dad arranged for him to work at Jake's in high school to keep him out of trouble."

"I didn't steal the car." He tears thigh meat from the bone. "It was Milo's idea."

"You were caught behind the wheel. Thank goodness your daddy was good friends with the sheriff and Mrs. Shaw didn't press charges. That would have ruined your life. All those scholarships you earned would never have materialized in the first place."

"Mrs. Shaw didn't press charges because she knew free labor when she saw it." He turns to me. "Milo and I spent the summer relandscaping her entire property."

"That couldn't have been too bad."

"105 degrees. One-hundred-percent humidity. Three acres of rose bushes. I have scars all over my hands." He spreads his fingers wide and shows me the back of his hand.

I trace the centimeter-long marks. "Poor baby," I deadpan. "Don't do the crime if you can't do the time."

Keegan leans on his elbow, drawing his face closer to mine. "Let me guess, squeaky clean record without a hint of villainy in your system?"

"No, I have never been arrested. I don't even speed."

"What fun are you?"

"My own kind." I nibble the inside of my cheek. I'm not the kind of fun I want to talk about in front of Daisy, but I don't miss the way Keegan's eyes fixate on my mouth. His Adam's apple bobs in understanding.

The charred barbecue scent radiating from his skin is better than any cologne you can buy in a store. I fill my lungs and watch him watching me. The centers of his irises are a subtle forest green with gold and brown radiating to the darkened edges to make them appear hazel from a distance. They catch the kitchen lights and sparkle like the stars have taken up residence in them. I didn't recognize that in the bar's low light.

That's the thing about Keegan. You have to pay attention and convince him to let you lean in close to get to know him.

His five o'clock shadow is patchy, so he wouldn't be able to grow a full beard to run my fingers through. There's a slight left turn in his nose. Did he break it doing something else illegal? How do I get him to open up and tell me about himself?

"I'll bet." He licks oil from his lips, and I swear my heart's beating in my neck.

"As much fun as your staring contest has been ..." Daisy reaches across the table and lifts the cookie plate.

My cheeks burn and I shovel three quick bites of chicken into my mouth to keep from doing something else dumb like tracing my tongue across his mouth.

Daisy rises. "I'm taking these cookies to the porch to read my book. Keegan, you know how to get the ladder down for the attic, right?"

"Yes, ma'am." Cool and collected, he leaves the table and rinses his dish at the sink.

"Great. After you finish the dishes, show Bridgette how to get upstairs. Turner's things are probably in the far back corner."

Keegan shivers. "I hate the attic."

"I'll do it myself." I need distance right now, not claustrophobic spaces with a sizzling chef. "Just show me where."

"That place is a death trap. I'm not letting you go by yourself." His gaze skates over my dress. "You're going to want to change."

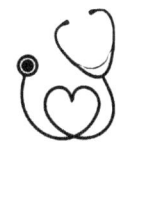

Chapter 12

Keegan

I SCRUB THE LAST of the chicken from Gran's serving plate and dry it with a teal tea towel. Dinner was surprising. Gran loves Bridgette. She would call them kindred spirits, talking about food as if it were an old friend not just nutrition.

"Ready." Bridgette stands in the doorway to the yard. The night sky silhouettes her like she's in a spotlight. Hands on her hips, one knee slightly bent in front of the other, she reminds me of a pin-up calendar Jake used to have in the restaurant. A bright yellow bandana holds her hair off the back of her long neck. Her vintage camp shirt and short running shorts highlight her curvy frame.

I almost swallow my tongue. The serving plate slips from my hand. If I thought her pink dress in class today was distracting, the way she looks right now is flabbergasting. I catch the plate before it falls to the counter.

A big grin splits her face. "You okay over there?"

"Just used too much soap."

She nods, but her smile tells me she doesn't believe my lie. I'm not convinced either. She's a knockout, and she knows it.

That's part of the problem.

"Where's this attic?"

I hang the towel on a hook and store the platter in the cabinet over the stove. "This way."

I lead her through the sitting room and up the stairs to the second floor. I grab a pole with a hook on the end from the linen closet and pull the attic ladder out of the ceiling. "Ladies first."

"Not too dangerous?"

"I'll let you catch the spiders for me."

"Such a knight in shining armor. I'll protect you. Don't worry." She grabs the rail and ascends the ladder.

I should be a gentleman and drop my gaze to the carpet, but it's hard not to stare at her backside as she climbs. The thoughts that run through my head are PG-13 bordering on R-rated, so I keep them to myself. "There should be a pull string for the light bulb up there."

She pulls her phone from her back pocket and shines it around the space as her head disappears through the dark hole. "Got it." The bulb clicks, and light shines down into the hallway.

I follow her into the dank, crowded space, ducking under the rafters. My great-grandparents and my grandparents were pack rats. *Never give away something that might be repurposed or have a use in the future.* Lamps, rocking chairs, trunks, cardboard boxes, doll houses, and a thousand other remnants of their lives are scattered around us. I'm not sure how they got some of the things up here, they're so big.

Bridgette blows a loose curl out of her eyes and scrubs her fingernails down her thighs. "Where do we even start?"

By not staring at her legs, that's where I start. "What do you hope to find?"

"Honestly, I have no idea. Knowing who he was back then will give me a better idea why he left."

"It's not like there's going to be a box labeled *Turner's Secret*."

She shoves my shoulder. "You are such Mr. Sunshine. I'm so glad you're here to help."

I poke her side because apparently, we're flirting like handsy teenagers. "I'm here to make sure you don't step through the ceiling of my bedroom."

"So, you have bedrooms here and at your parents' house?"

"Yes."

"And your place in Dallas."

"So?"

"That's a little weird."

"It's nice to be loved."

"Do you have any other bedrooms?"

Thinking about bedrooms makes me think about beds. And beds make me think about what it would be like to share one with Bridgette. And holy ... my brain needs to stay away from those thoughts. But is she having the same ones?

"Why are you curious about my bedrooms?"

She eyeballs me, her gaze traveling from my tennis shoes to the top of my head and back down. She twists her mouth and nibbles the corner. "Just trying to figure you out."

She's an arm's length away. I could snag her waistband and bring her to me. Bury my hands in her hair and continue the torture we started on the beach. It's not a smart idea, but I want more of every part of her. I shift my weight to my toes. "I'm a simple guy." Simple wants. Simple needs. Complicated life.

"Ha. You are anything but simple." Her sharp tone breaks the lusty spell. She climbs over a cardboard box on the far side of the attic and opens the flap.

Distance is better anyway. I'm letting the irrational idiot part of my brain make decisions. I stopped kissing Bridgette for a reason on the beach. I need to remember that relationships with a woman like her are a bad idea for guys like me. She deserves more than I can give her, and I need to protect myself from repeating past mistakes.

I sweep my finger through a thick layer of dust on one of the old trunks my great-grandfather used when he traveled by train for work. "We should have brought hazmat suits. Who knows what's living up here?"

She picks another box and peels the tape from the lid. "Suck it up, buttercup. A little hard work and elbow grease never hurt anybody. If you're too delicate, I promise to be safe. You can go downstairs and eat cookies with your grandma."

I settle on the floor. "You're snarky."

"You say that like it's a bad thing."

"It's irritating." In the same way a good hot sauce burns my tongue, not like sand on my cornea, but clarifying would be counterproductive.

She stands and pops her hands on her hips. It's adorable because she's still taller than the rafters and has to hunch over. Any threat is lost. "We've already established that you don't like me. I don't care if I irritate you. I am who I am, and you can either tolerate my presence or not. It's up to you."

The muscles in the back of my jaw clench. How can she say that after the way we stared at each other over dinner? If she'd been in my head all day, she'd have the full-color version of how much I don't hate her and want to get to know her intimately.

I loved listening to her talk to Gran. Their heated debate over condiments at dinner was entertaining. Why does she have such strong opinions about barbecue sauce? I want to know more about her and how she became a baker.

But I don't ask any of the questions burning the back of my tongue. I don't share any of the visions in my head.

I vowed to keep my distance and that's what I'll do.

As soon as I start asking questions about her, she'll start asking questions about me, and we've already determined I'm not telling her anything. "I'll start in this corner."

I crawl over a faded pink dollhouse and unlatch another trunk. Skimming my fingers through the layers of fabric, I dig to the bottom. It's just old clothes, nothing that will help Bridgette. I move from box to trunk to box and filter through the lives of my ancestors.

It's interesting what they thought was important enough to store for future generations. I highly doubt anyone will wear the moth-eaten wedding dress hidden behind a mauve, ruffled tuxedo hanging in the corner.

I don't see anything with Turner's name after the first hour. Bridgette moves along the other side of the attic with as much energy and determination as she did first thing this morning deconstructing the pig.

How does she have so much energy after the day we've had? I check my watch. It's almost midnight. No wonder my eyelids feel like sandpaper. I've had my contacts in for almost nineteen hours.

"We should start again after class tomorrow."

She stands and braces her hands on the small of her back, pinching her shoulder blades together to stretch. "I'm good," she says with a yawn.

"You're going to be dead on your feet tomorrow. That's dangerous, with the knives we use."

"Fine." She lifts her leg and hops over a crumbling cardboard box. Her toe catches, and she stumbles. Her arms pinwheel. She pitches forward.

I dart to the middle of the room, wrap my arms around her waist, and pull her back to my chest. Our toes graze the edge of the truss. A gap wide enough for her to have fallen through to the bedroom below stretches in front of us.

Her heart beats so rapidly, I feel it in my chest. She presses on my forearms to get me to let go.

"Not yet." I pull her tighter. "Give me a second, please?"

"Okay." She grips my forearms and rests her head on my shoulder.

We stand in the musty attic, me hunched over her in the tight space, steadying my breath. If I hadn't caught her ... if she'd fallen through the ceiling ... I don't want to think about that.

She strokes her fingernails along my arm. "I thought I was going to fall."

"I won't ever let that happen." My cheek presses into the side of her hair to stabilize myself as much as her.

I shouldn't love holding her as much as I do. I shouldn't squeeze her tighter, hoping the comfort of my arms stabilizes the rapid breaths pulsing from both our lungs.

Maybe I'm being an idiot, and I should give her a chance. Lay out all the facts about who I am, why I'm in Bubee, and why I'm scared to trust new people.

We could see where this attraction takes us.

Am I willing to risk *everything* again for a pretty—gorgeous, magnetic, sweet, snarky—bombshell of a woman?

When I put it like that, the answer is easy.

No.

I've worked too hard to let myself get roped into a miserable relationship where the woman I've fallen for only wants me for my title and reputation. I learned that lesson with my ex. She only saw me as her ticket to the luxurious lifestyle she craved.

Bridgette wants a husband who'll worship her, and I can't be that. I'm too guarded. Too jaded.

But loneliness doesn't sound like the right answer either. I want to marry my best friend and fill a house with laughter and happiness. Those images danced behind my eyes when I kissed Bridgette. Holding her feels right.

I rest my mouth next to her ear. "Is this your way of getting back into my arms?"

She stiffens.

I squeeze my eyes shut and curse myself. "That came out wrong." I step back and give her space. "I'm sorry. I didn't—"

"You think I'm shallow enough to risk permanent injury to steal a hug from you. I get it. I shouldn't have told you about Graham and what he said."

"That's not ... the world needs people like you who aren't afraid to be authentic. I just want you to be more careful."

"If only that were true." She climbs down the ladder and races down the hallway before I can ask her what she means. Does she think the world doesn't need her genuine openness or that I'm not worried about her safety?

Because both options make my stomach lurch like I'm going to throw up. I'm a jerk and an idiot. I hurt her when I left her on the beach, but I didn't think she cared so much about my opinions that she would blame herself.

I was so busy protecting myself that I never thought about how Bridgette would interpret my callous, grumpy wall.

I hustle down the stairs and slide the ladder into the attic. The lights are out in the rest of the house.

I run out the side door toward Bridgette's carriage house. The windows are dark. Did she go inside and straight to bed? I wasn't that far behind her.

She deserves an apology. I don't mind saving her. I don't mind her body pressed against mine. My soul craves the way she looked at me in those adrenaline-filled, tender moments when we realized everything was fine.

Why do I want to protect her so much? She's not mine to protect. I've made it clear I don't want a relationship. If she's with me, I can't be what she needs.

But when I hold her, my brain wants to beat its chest and stake a claim like I have any right.

I pound on the door, but she doesn't answer. I scan the yard and the rest of the beach. Clouds cover the moon, so I can't see much. She's not in the gazebo.

I hope she didn't go for a walk. It's treacherous when you can't see where you're going. Kids dig castle moats that break ankles.

"Bridgette?" I pound on the door again. I need to unbreak us.

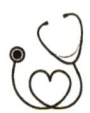

Bridgette

The sun's barely up, but I couldn't sleep last night. The bags under my eyes and messy ponytail attest to that fact. Caffeine is the only solution to my brewing headache, but I'm not in the mood for the bitterness of coffee today. I've got enough of my own after Keegan's commentary on my life choices last night.

I thought we were making progress toward friendship. I was embarrassingly wrong.

Sunlight pours through Honey Beans' floor-to-ceiling windows and illuminates the bookcases lining the coffee shop's back wall. Each shelf is themed by color; starting with white on the top right shelf, the rainbow effect cascades diagonally through the novels until you reach the black-spined books on the bottom left. A vinyl bench with half a dozen tables sits full of customers opposite the barista's counter.

It is freakin' adorable. It's the kind of place you want to meet your best friend after work, chill on a solo Tuesday morning, or pop in to check out your next book boyfriend from their lending library.

A barista about my age leans her ripped-jean-clad hip against the counter. "Welcome in. What can I get y'all?"

In an asymmetrical paisley top that leaves one shoulder bare and the other covered in ruffles, her presence reminds me of Julia Roberts, but her auburn hair is pure Bryce Dallas Howard. Either way, her infectious smile lightens the heaviness in my chest.

"Chai latte, please."

The barista tosses her braid over her shoulder. "Vanilla or spiced?"

"Hmm? Which do you recommend?"

Her chin tips, and she leans over the counter to analyze my silver espadrilles, lavender peasant dress, and chunky, heart-shaped pendant. "How sweet do you like your drinks?"

I hold my fingers four inches apart. "Sugar." Then scrunch them down to one inch. "Everything else."

"You'll like vanilla better. Name?"

"Bridgette."

"Welcome to Bubee, Bridgette. I'm Georgi." She grabs a box of chai concentrate from the refrigerator below the counter. "How are you likin' Jake's barbecue class so far? Are the Bubbles being kind to ya? Making you feel at home?"

"The Bubbles?"

"That's what we call ourselves." She gestures to the patrons sipping coffee while reading on their eReaders and tablets. "Bubee Bubbles. Some people think it's juvenile, but I appreciate that we don't take ourselves too seriously. We have permission to be playful and whimsical when we want to be." She the words pour from her like the milk she's pouring into the metal frothing cup. This woman has never met a stranger.

"How do you know I'm in Jake's class?"

"Small town. Everyone knows everything."

"That's pretty universal, isn't it? You can't order a chocolate croissant at my bakery back home without everybody knowing you broke your diet before lunch."

A twinge of homesickness hits me. I need to text Camille about wedding stuff today. I haven't heard from her since I arrived. Normally, we don't go a day without a text or call. She must be busy planning wedding stuff and Amma's Tribe's summer sports camps.

Over Georgi's shoulder, she gives me a mischievous wink. "It also makes news when Keegan Sullivan spends an entire evening with a mysterious blonde at Rocas."

I'm not sure what to think of this new piece of information. I knew he was shy at the bar, but I didn't think talking to me would be that big of a novelty. "How do you know it was me?"

She gives me a look, but I already know the answer. "Small town," we say at the same time.

Ten minutes and I already love this woman's spirit. She reminds me of Camille with a little less filter.

"Every woman with a pulse has been trying to land one of the Sullivan boys since they turned fourteen. My sister, Angelina finally succeeded with the younger brother, but Keegan's elusive. Doesn't help that he disappeared up to Dallas after graduation and rarely comes home."

"I got the impression he was here all the time."

She reaches for a ceramic mug with a honeybee on the side. "Are you staying?"

"I wish I could, but I have to get to class."

Georgi plucks a paper cup from the stack. "Nah. Keegan was here for our grandmas' birthday—seventy-five is a big hurrah around here—and Jake roped him into stayin'."

"Our? You're related? But your sister ..." They do things differently in the South—Ashley and Melanie Wilkes were cousins in *Gone with the Wind*—but I thought kissing cousins fell out of fashion centuries ago. Because eww.

"Oh, no." She flaps her hands. "No incest here. His grandma is best friends with my grandma."

"I'm staying with Daisy."

A blissful expression ignites her face. She grips my hand. "Ask her to make you Bayou Goo pie. Chocolate pudding, toffee, whipped cream, chocolate swirls. It's heaven. Between you, me, and the wall, everyone thinks Keegan's here to take over Jake's place. I hope he adds her recipes to the mix."

My mouth falls open. He's not just a line chef. He's the heir apparent. My disappointment turns into a stewing cauldron. Why doesn't he want to tell me about his life? "Learn something new about that man every day. He likes his secrets."

Georgi pops the lid on my drink and slides it across the counter. "Enjoy your chai."

"Thanks, Georgi. I'll see you tomorrow." I left Daisy's house early specifically to avoid him but now I have more questions.

Before I pause to consider why I care so much, I shoot through the coffee shop's door and pound down Tiburon Avenue to Jake's. Keegan said he's only in town to help Jake, but if he's negotiating to take over, he lied to me again.

I don't care about this specific lie—who cares if he's taking over Jake's, they can do what they want—but frustration boils when I consider how many times he's lied.

I need to know why.

Chapter 13

Keegan

"Keegan Sullivan!" Bridgette growls my name as she stomps down the stairs to the classroom.

Today she's wearing a purple dress that hugs her waist and stops just below her knees. Her heels are at least three inches again, and they sparkle.

She looks ready for the runway or dinner at a Michelin star restaurant, not to be one of the chefs preparing the meal. I can't tear my eyes away, and if she asked, I'd probably dig them out of my head and give them to her.

First, I want to give her my spleen and now my eyeballs. Something is seriously messing with my head, and her name is Bridgette Christianson.

Jake chuckles and claps me on the back. "You're in for it now." He tips his hat to her. "Good morning, dear."

"Hey, Jake." She offers him a warm smile and returns her glare to me.

I slide my knife into its case. The silver skins on these baby back ribs can wait. Based on her feral snarl, I don't want to put a weapon in Bridgette's line of sight. She's likely to stab me and I haven't done anything to her. Today.

But I'm glad she's here. When she disappeared before I could ask her to join me for breakfast, the unwieldy feeling in my chest doubled. We need to talk.

She marches up to me and sticks her finger in my face. "What is wrong with you?"

I gently push her hand down, so she doesn't accidentally stab me with her manicured fingernail. "I tried to talk to you last night." Pounded on her door for thirty minutes and left my self-respect on the doormat, in fact.

"That's not what I'm talking about. You're taking over Jake's? I felt like a fool when Georgi told me. I don't understand why you keep lying to me. You aren't his temporary assistant. You're his heir. What is it about me that makes you not want to tell me the truth?"

"First …" I hold up one finger. "Georgi has a big mouth. Gossiping is not limited to Daisy and her friends in Bubee. Second …" I hold up a second finger. Bridgette's eyes narrow and her scowl deepens. "I never lied. I just didn't tell you every detail of my life. Why should I? We're not friends."

I want to be, but after my behavior last night, we aren't.

She staggers as if I struck her.

That wasn't the reaction I expected. I thought she'd double down, get in my face, and demand I account for my friendly behavior at dinner and in the attic.

This morning I wanted to make her breakfast, apologize, and get us on the road to friendship, but I've mucked it up again. I didn't expect to reach this degree of self-loathing first thing in the morning, but here I am. I need to learn to keep my mouth shut—or only say what I actually mean.

I take a deep breath and reach for her hand. "Bridgette—"

She raises her hand to stop me. "We're not friends." Her hand drifts to the table next to her. She plants her palms and leans over for support. "I'm sorry. I forgot. Dinner with your grandmother confused me, made me think we could hang out in the same room and not kill each other. I guess I should have focused on the part in the attic where you called me deceitful. My mistake."

She spins, the skirt of today's sundress flaring like flower petals. No matter what she wears, she reminds me of flowers and the beautiful, intricate, dynamic world we live in.

I just ran over her wild field with a tank.

Her back vibrates like she's trying to control her emotions. I'm not sure if the emotion is rage or sadness though.

I don't know how to read her. I've barely known her for two days, even though dinner last night felt like she was an old friend. It felt like it wasn't the first time we'd climbed into my grandmother's attic.

I stuff my hands in my pockets and step back three paces until my thighs hit the prep table. I suck at apologizing. I suck at relationships. This is why Bridgette and I can never be anything.

I don't want Bridgette to hate me, but my default over the last several months has been not to trust new people with my true self.

It's easier to push her away than admit the reason I'm being a jerk is because I don't want to risk learning her motives are disingenuous and let her hurt me. My reasons are selfish. I know, but that reality doesn't stop them from being what's best for me.

She hasn't given me an explicit reason not to put my faith in her, but my ex didn't show her true motives until the end of our relationship. I can't risk starting something with Bridgette if it could end the way things ended with Cynthia.

"Look, I'm sorry about last night, but I'm not taking over Jake's." I scuff my foot on the ground. "Why does it matter?"

"It's not about you," she whispers.

"But you're mad at me."

"I'm mad at myself."

"Because I didn't tell you my life plan?"

She stretches her fingers and arms at her side, shaking her entire body like she's molting. "You know what? You're right. It doesn't matter where you live or what you do for work. It doesn't matter if you tell me anything about yourself. I understand the whole tourist/local dynamic. I'm here to learn about barbeque, not get to know you. Thank you for the reminder. Where's Jake?"

She stomps up the stairs but disappears into the women's bathroom until class starts. She won't meet my eyes as I instruct everyone how to clean and trim baby back ribs.

When class is over, I corner her in the entryway. "I'll walk you home."

"I'm not going to Daisy's."

"Where are you going?"

"Why do you want to know?"

It's on the tip of my tongue to confess I can't get her off my mind, but Bridgette deserves so much better from me.

"Have a nice night." I check my pockets for my keys and phone. Right where they should be. I slide my sunglasses over my eyes and step into the bright sunshine. It's better for her to stay away.

But what if it isn't?

Maybe what happened with Cynthia wasn't so much your fault as a perfect storm of her insecurities and your misplaced enthusiasm.

I ruminate on the dissenting voice gnawing at the back of my head as I drive to Gran's house.

Daisy rocks on her front porch swing, a pitcher of sweet tea at her elbow. "Two days in a row. I'm a lucky grandma."

I climb the stairs and kiss her cheek. "Are there any cookies left?"

She levels her *grandma-eye* at me. "Bridgette's not here."

"I know. She was walking toward the pier when I left Jake's."

She pats the seat beside her. "Why does that woman have you so twisted up?"

"I don't know, Gran." I collapse and drag my fingers through my hair.

She pours me a glass of tea. "You'd best figure it out."

"I'm trying." Part of me wants to slump into the chair and spill my secrets. Tell my grandma a woman broke my heart, and I'm finding it hard to trust anyone. Especially someone as breathtaking as Bridgette.

When she unloaded her fears on the beach that first night, she said she was afraid she would never be someone's forever. I'm taking one moment of vulnerability and stereotyping her, but the last thing I need is to get mixed up with another woman who just wants to get married and doesn't care who her husband is.

I may be an orthopedic surgeon, but in my heart I'm a country boy who prefers spending my days in the backyard grilling bratwurst, playing catch with my friends, and curling up at night with the love of my life.

I thought my last girlfriend was like Bridgette: honest, brave, outgoing. Now I can't go home because rumors and lies have turned everyone against me. They think they know what happened between

Cynthia and I, but they don't. I can't look them in the eyes and tell them how easily I was fooled.

The worst part is I didn't love my ex. We weren't a good fit from the start, but I was too excited about the possibility she represented to recognize the signs until it was too late.

I broke up with her, but the way it happened, what she did after ... took a chunk of my heart with it. My heart beats asymmetrically beneath my ribs. This brokenness is something I never want to feel again.

If I hadn't opened my heart so willingly, Cynthia never would have gone to the lengths she did to ruin my reputation. I can't forget the part I played.

If Bridgette is half as sweet as I want to imagine she is, she deserves better than a broken man wallowing on his grandmother's porch.

Man, I've got it bad already. This will end in disaster if I don't lock down whatever this is. I shouldn't be here. The urge to talk to Gran or to stare at the street and wait for Bridgette to appear is too strong.

I need to move.

I kiss the top of Gran's head. "I'll be in the attic if you need me."

Finishing the search for Bridgette is the least I can do to apologize. I'll prove there's nothing here to find. Gran won't have to see her brother. Bridgette can go back to Minnesota satisfied with her time in Texas and never look back.

My heart will be safe.

I bring cleaning rags and bug spray into the attic and pick up where we left off.

In the far back corner, under an old record player, I find a box with Turner's name scrawled across the side in faded marker. I haul it to the space in the center of the attic. It's got to weigh fifty pounds. I open the flaps.

Three medals rest on top of a pile of papers. I don't know anything about service medals, so I tuck them in my pocket to ask Gran. I inspect each piece of paper. Some are letters from Turner to his parents during the war. Others are report cards from school— he wasn't the best student. Several are paperwork from the Army.

Someone jammed a crumpled envelope into the corner. I straighten it against the edge of the box and remove the sheets inside.

Dishonorable Discharge from Service to the Army of the United States of America, September 5, 1967.

Well, that is a good reason to hide from your family. I doubt Turner would return home with the shame of a dishonorable discharge hanging over his head.

Does Gran know about this? It would explain why she doesn't want to see her brother. She wouldn't want to associate with someone who'd lost the town's respect.

I leaf through the rest of the box but don't find any other records related to his discharge or military service.

I close the box and climb down the ladder to the second floor. Bridgette and Gran's voices drift up the staircase from the kitchen. I take a steadying breath, make sure no cobwebs are in my hair, and head toward their voices.

Bridgette's smile drops to a scowl when she sees me over Gran's shoulder.

"What on ..." Gran turns to me. "Oh, how was the attic, Keegan?"

Surprise washes through Bridgette's body language.

I hold up the envelope and scatter the medals on the kitchen counter. "What can you tell me about these?"

Gran picks up a yellow and red striped medal with a gold disc dangling from the bottom. "This was Turner's Vietnam medal."

"What about the other ones?"

"These were my grandfather's from World War I. I'm not sure what he did to earn them."

I take the discharge papers out of the envelope and spread them flat. "What about this?"

Gran's eyes flit over the page. "I've never seen this before." Her face hides her emotions. I may as well have handed her a recipe for chocolate chip cookies.

Bridgette lifts the papers from the counter. "This can't be right. Turner never would have done anything to be dishonorably discharged."

"He did, and I would bet good money that's the reason he never came home." I'm not sure I want to know a man guilty of something bad enough to get him kicked out of the military.

"There has to be a good reason." Bridgette shakes the envelope like I forgot to take the rest out.

"My dad always said Turner was a perfect soldier. He would have told me if something had happened to prove otherwise." Gran stands from the barstool. She kisses the top of my head. "Thank you for finding these. I appreciate the modicum of closure. Now, if you'll excuse me. Dotty and I are hosting Bunco, and I need to spike the punch."

She grabs her keys from the hook by the door and leaves Bridgette glaring at me.

When the door thwaps closed, I glare back. "Do you ever hide your thoughts? Or do you prefer to have them splashed across your face for everyone to see?"

Her glare hardens. If her eyes were rocks, they would've just transformed from granite into diamonds. "Why did you show her the discharge? Now she'll never want to see him."

"She might have known something."

She shoves the paperwork back into its envelope. "This was supposed to be a surprise reunion."

"Our search isn't going to end with a fairytale happily ever after. There won't be any running across an open meadow to happily embrace. Turner's not the person you think he is. Or he wasn't. You have to accept that."

"No." She slams her finger into the counter. "He's a good man. There has to be a reason for his discharge."

I pull my phone out of my pocket. "Call him and ask."

Bridgette's ponytail whips back and forth before I finish my sentence. "No. He can't know I'm doing this. He would be too embarrassed. If there's any hope of getting him to come home to Texas, we have to know the whole story before we talk him."

Embarrassed is a good word. Ashamed or mortified might be better.

What kind of man gets dishonorably discharged? Yes, I'm judgmental, but I can't believe the version of this man Bridgette is trying to sell me.

"Are discharge records sealed?" she asks.

"How would I know?"

"You are a know-it-all, so I guessed." She takes my phone and swipes up. Then frowns. Only my face will unlock the screen. She taps it again, flashes it in front of me—long enough to unlock, but not long enough for me to snatch it back—and opens the screen.

Her eyes roll to the top of her head. "Of course, your background is a car."

"It's not just any car." I tap the screen and enlarge the image. "It's an Aston Martin DB5."

Contrary to everything I said earlier about being a simple county boy, I am a car guy. The day I retire, I'm buying myself something that goes 0 to 160 at lightspeed.

She hugs the phone to her chest and snorts. "I know James Bond's car."

"You do?"

"Sean Connery is the best actor of all time. Misogyny aside, James Bond knows how to satisfy a woman and drives a cool car. The silver one in *Thunderball* is my favorite."

I choke on my tongue. It's fat and heavy and cutting off oxygen to my lungs. That has to be the explanation because I do not believe the direction this conversation is taking.

Bridgette knows Bond well enough to know his car.

True, it's the car he's famous for, but still. Most women I know are like, *Oh, wheels!* when they see the picture.

She shifts the phone. "Dishonorable discharges more than fifty years old are public record." She types and talks to herself. "Fill out the form. Pay the fee ... with your saved credit card." Her attention shifts to me. "It's not safe to keep your credit card information saved to your phone, you know. That makes it easier to steal." She types again. "In forty-eight hours, we will know the charges against Turner."

Her self-satisfied smile makes her look like a cat that ate the entire pet store of canaries.

"Glad I could finance this lunacy." Glad I didn't put my credentials on my credit cards.

"I'm hungry." She spins—she can't seem to move without adding a twirl—and digs into Gran's pantry. "Oh, pancakes. Yes!"

"Glad you're making yourself at home."

"You're glad a lot today." She runs her finger along the shelves. "Even though we aren't friends and you hate being around me, I'm going to be a bigger person. Would you like pancakes? We can tolerate each other for an hour ... probably ... if you cook the bacon in the fridge."

I lean against the counter. "What kind of pancakes are you making?"

Her head pops out of the pantry. "Do you have a request?"

"You have strong opinions about barbeque sauce. I have strong opinions about pancakes."

"The size of your face. Light and fluffy with crispy edges."

"I have a big face."

She makes right angles with her thumb and forefinger and frames my face. "You have a big head. There's a difference."

Why is she so sexy when she's mocking me? Why do I want nothing more than to enjoy a quiet night drizzling maple syrup with her?

Lock it down, man. Stop staring at her lips.

I drum my fingers on the counter. "I'll see you in class tomorrow."

"What about the bacon?" She looks truly distraught that I'm not joining her for dinner.

Maybe, just this once, I can ...

No. Stop while you're ahead. "I'm becoming a vegetarian." I pat my stomach. "Better for longevity."

Her nose scrunch is back. "I'd rather have a short, happy life than one without bacon."

I'd rather continue this conversation licking whipped cream from her neck, but sanity must prevail.

Chapter 14

Bridgette

To paraphrase Ms. Swift: It's me. I'm the problem. One hundred percent, totally me.

I can't trim the tenderloin correctly, and Declan's sweet smile has morphed into frustrated annoyance.

"Try ... no ... why don' ya ..." He shoves his gloved fist in his mouth.

I hand him the knife. "I surrender. You take over." My mind isn't in the slice-and-dice anyway. Turner's records should arrive in my inbox today. I stashed my phone in my locker at lunch, so I stopped obsessively checking it after Georgi blew it up.

Unknown number: Girls night

Bridgette: Who is this?

Georgi: Georgi

Bridgette: How did you get my number?

Georgi: I called Dotty who called Daisy who agreed to give it to me in exchange for delivery of a flat white

Georgi: Sorry no punctuation running

Bridgette: What does girls' night look like?

Georgi: Sangria under the pier with my sisters and our friends

Georgi: We call it SUP club to make it sound classy

Bridgette: I'm in!!! When?

Georgi: Saturday night

Bridgette: What can I bring?

Georgi: Barbecue of course

Georgi: And the lowdown on how things are going with doctor love

Bridgette: Doctor Love?

Bridgette: There is no Doctor Love

Georgi: Fine be that way

Georgi: Still bring food

After the last few days, I could totally use some girl time. Amanda, Juniper, and Tory only ever want to talk about meat or kids, and I've run out of things to contribute.

Hanging out with Daisy is fun, but it's not the same as hanging out with women my age. It will be nice to have a conversation that doesn't get turned around to Keegan or Turner. Just women being women with some wine-spiked fruit.

Declan expertly trims the rest of the pork. Tension ebbs from his shoulders as he accomplishes the task I failed to complete for the last thirty minutes.

Jake wanders to our table and rests his chin in the palm of his hand. "Clean work. Now what do you do with it?"

"Aren't you supposed to teach us that?" I ask.

"You're allowed to have ideas too."

Declan mirrors Jake's posture. "Salt. Black Pepper. Cayenne pepper. Maybe some cumin."

"What do you use as a slather?"

I answer this one. "Mustard."

"What kind of mustard?"

"Plain ol' yellow. Anything else will overpower the flavor of the spices."

"Or they could compliment the flavor palette."

"I want the wood smoke's flavor to sing, so I'm not adding anything extra to this one."

"We haven't covered the smoke part yet."

I bounce on my toes. "Can we start early?"

It's the end of the first week, and Jake and Keegan lit every barbecue and smoker so far. I expected we would have at least built our own fires by now, but Jake's set on perfecting the butchering and seasoning before he gives us matches.

"Maybe." Jake winks his vibrant blue eye.

"I'm not falling for that. You promised me smoke. I want smoke."

"Tomorrow?"

"Deal."

Out of the corner of my eye, I catch Keegan watching our exchange. His expression is contemplative. He catches my eye and lifts a lazy shoulder. I stick my tongue out because I'm classy like that.

He frowns and turns to help Amanda slather her brisket with hot sauce.

I like Amanda. She's forthright and creative. Her family's hosting a picnic Sunday afternoon for the class, and I'm curious to meet the rest of her clan.

When class is finally over, I snatch my phone from its cubby and leave before Keegan can read over my shoulder. He shouldn't have dropped the dishonorable discharge on Daisy without consulting me first. I won't give him another opportunity to tell her information without all the details. We need to figure out the reasons behind

Turner's actions before we broadcast them to the rest of his family and further tarnish his reputation.

Besides, he said we're not friends. He turned down my pancake olive branch. I'll continue this search by myself. Wouldn't want to burden him into spending time with me when he doesn't want to, right?

Tapping the screen, I open my inbox and scroll through the emails. *National Archive's National Personnel Records Center* jumps out third from the bottom under the ad from Pottery Barn.

A happy screech bursts from my mouth. One step closer. I loop my purse over my shoulder, walk to the beach, and find a secluded spot next to a dune. Seagrass dances in the breeze. The softly crashing waves soothe my anxiety.

This is a big moment.

A dishonorable discharge is no small matter, especially for a guy who made loyalty a keystone of our friendship. Not just anyone would drive the four-hour round trip to drop me at the airport.

I open the file. I've never read military records before, so I'm not sure what I'm looking at. I understand words like *dereliction of duty*, *absent without official leave but without intent to desert, forfeiture of all pay and allowances, confinement of not less than one year*. "Oh, Turner. Where did you go? Why did you leave?"

I read the words out loud to help myself understand them, give them gravity, and convince my confused brain they're real. "Private Turner Donovan failed to report for duty 13 April 1967, 0800, Fort Bragg, North Carolina." I scroll down. "Private Donovan returned to base 21 April 1967. Court martial. Fifth Amendment ... refused to name the location of his disappearance. During questioning, Private Donovan assaulted JAG officer Lieutenant Commander Fuller."

I shut down the screen on my phone. I can't read anymore. The ache building in my heart is overwhelming. The Turner I know braved a blizzard to rescue a kitten. I've never seen him lift a hand in violence or anger or frustration.

Assault? It's printed there in black and white, but I don't believe it.

This isn't the whole story. Where did he go? Why did he leave the post? Why did he go back?

A breeze whips my hair into a frenzy. I loop it around my fist and turn to face the wind.

"There's more to this story. I will figure out what happened, and I will reunite Turner with his family. He's given me a new start, so I'm going to give him one," I shout into the wind. "Do you hear me? This is just the next stone along the path. I'll figure out what happened that week in 1967. I will find out where Turner went. I'm salvaging his reputation."

He saved me from mine. Proving he's not a deserter who abandoned his family is the least I can do to pay him back.

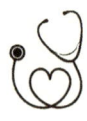

Bridgette

My fingers fly over the phone's keyboard searching for headlines from April 1967. Nothing in the national news catches my attention. NASA landed an unmanned ship on the moon. A comedic James Bond movie was released. North Korea shot missiles over the border into South Korea, but none of that would have made Turner desert his post in North Carolina and then return to the Army a week later.

His reasons have to be personal. I could ask Daisy, but she's extremely hesitant to speak about her brother. She said she'd never seen the dishonorable discharge paperwork before, so she wouldn't know where he went during that week of desertion. Plus, the news that he went AWOL is not going to endear him to her after their five-decade separation.

What would make me leave my post?

If my parents were hurt. Wouldn't the Army give him leave for that? What if a friend needed help?

My gaze skims over the bustling ocean-front stores. Speckled white and tan, their walls are made of limestone and seashells. Something about the composition helps the buildings weather storms better. I can imagine teenage Turner strolling to the ice cream parlor on a date with a special girl or grabbing a boogie board and catching a wave.

Maybe his desertion had something to do with this town. Did something happen here that made him come home? If that was the case, Daisy would have mentioned seeing him. Wouldn't she? Or did he sneak in and out?

I have no idea where to start, so I might as well search old newspapers and town records. Does Bubee have a newspaper? Another round of searching informs me their paper closed its doors in 1983. Town Hall, however, is still open.

I brush sand from my backside and follow the map on my phone toward Town Hall. Three blocks from my destination, Honey Beans sits like a friend inviting me in to relax. I could use a stress reliever and some caffeine. Georgi's auburn hair glows through the windows, solidifying my decision.

I push the door open and wave. "Hey, Georgi."

"Hey there, girl."

"Can I get a mocha?"

"Dark or white chocolate?"

"Dark chocolate." I run my fingers over their pastry case. "Can I have a peach scone as well, please?"

She grinds coffee beans. "How's class going?"

That's a multi-pronged question. Learning how to butcher and season the meat is going well, but my mind isn't fully engaged in class. It darts to Keegan and Turner and then up to Emerald Bay, wondering what my friends are doing.

In all my frustration, I didn't text Camille after my last trip to Honey Beans. I'll send her a text while I walk to Town Hall.

Georgi hands me my scone, and I give her the only answer I can. "Class is fair."

"There's more to that story." She drizzles chocolate around the inside of my cup.

"I'm distracted."

"By the handsome assistant?"

"No ..." Why does she always assume the only thing on my mind is Keegan? How much do I want to tell Georgi about the family mystery I'm trying to solve?

She could be a great friend, but Keegan called her a gossipmonger. She already hinted at me spilling details about my relationship with Keegan ... even though we don't have a relationship, just a mutual antagonism.

People talking about me behind my back sent me running from Emerald Bay. I won't replicate that situation here.

Plus, I respect Daisy and Turner too much to hint at Turner's discharge before I know the details. When Turner comes home, he'll have enough to deal with overcoming his disappearance. I don't want people to have preconceived notions about who he is because of his military record as well. "Just some stuff from home."

"Don't let that keep you from sangria." She hands me my cup with a wink.

"I wouldn't miss it for the world." Meeting Georgi and her friends will help me get a better read on whether I can trust Georgi with my search.

"Great! Meet me here, and we can walk over together."

I wave as I leave. It's nice to have something to look forward to that doesn't have any expectations for me except to show up and have fun.

I shoot Camille a text as promised. *Hi, Miss you.* I could say more, but I'm not sure what to add, so I hit send and tuck my phone away.

Town Hall is built out of the same limestone-seashell mixture as the buildings along the ocean. I run my hand along the rough surface. One story with slits in the rock for windows, it's like a little fort without cannons.

Someone obsessively loves their bright pink flowers. Petunias and zinnias overflow the boxes under the windows and in pots along the front steps.

The inside is decidedly dated, but not in a historical fashion. I'm greeted by peeling linoleum and glaring fluorescent bulbs. A sea of empty desks spreads out in the main room filling every available inch of space.

"Can I help you?" A girl who can't be more than sixteen, maybe seventeen years old sits with her feet on top of the desk to my left.

"I'm looking for town records from 1967."

She blows a large bubble and lets it pop. "Why?"

"Research?" Why did I make that sound like a question?

"About this junkie old town?" She blows another bubble. It pops and laminates her cheek. Her jagged fingernail digs under it, and she sucks the pink string back into her mouth.

I might throw up. "Who are you?"

"Tipsy."

"Tipsy?" No way. She's got to be lying. No one in their right mind names their kid Tipsy.

She holds her palms out to me and scrunches her face. "I fell over a lot as a kid. Nickname stuck."

I guess that makes sense. "Why not ask people to call you by your name?"

Her left eyebrow slowly rises, and she tilts her chin to glare at me. "Because everyone knows me as Tipsy." Another bubble pops between her teeth.

I'm not sure if I want to feel sorry for this girl or snatch the gum out of her mouth and enroll her in an etiquette class.

While I may have an overwhelming personality, at least I have manners. *Please*, *thank you*, *you're welcome*, and a sweet smile will gain you access to a lot of places and smooth a lot of harsh edges when need be. This girl needs to learn that lesson before her reputation runs amok.

I use one of my sweet smiles. "Do they store town records here or not?"

"Depends what you're looking for. I mean, besides a life."

"You're just adorable," I deadpan.

She blows another bubble, this one popping back into her mouth. "Back at ya, Barbie."

"I wish I could say you're the first one to lob that insult my direction. No sting left. Nice try."

"Henrietta, leave this nice lady alone." Stepping out of an office to the right, a woman in a trim gray pantsuit with the same eyes as the snarky girl extends her hand. "Forgive my niece. I'm Mayor Buchanan. How can I help you Ms. ...?" She raises an eyebrow like I need to finish the sentence for her.

"Bridgette."

"Nice to meet you, Bridgette." She folds her hands demurely in front of her.

"I'm looking for events that occurred in town in April 1967."

"Hmmm." Her eyes narrow, and she taps her finger to her lips. "That's a long time ago. Any specific direction I can guide your search? Real estate, marriage licenses, birth certificates? Criminal records are archived at the courthouse."

I haven't considered the courthouse. That will have to wait until Monday if there aren't any answers here. "I'm not sure what I'm looking for. I'll know it when I see it though."

I hope.

"Henrietta, show our guest to the records room." She spins on her nude high heels. "Best of luck." Her walk can only be described as a sashay as she returns to her office and shuts the door.

I turn my smirk on Tipsy. "Henrietta, huh?"

"Now you know why I prefer people call me Tipsy. At least it has a personality that doesn't need a walker."

"I think it's sweet."

"Whatever. Follow me." Her sneakers thud to the floor, and I follow her down a wood-paneled hallway to a room marked *Records*. "Here." She opens the door and gives it a light shove. Her hand flails on the inner wall, flipping a switch and illuminating the cramped room.

Filing cabinets line every wall from floor to ceiling. Six rows, a foot and a half apart.

"I'm not cleaning up after you." Tipsy pops her gum again and leaves me to my task.

"What a delightful rebel." I rub my hands together. "Here goes nothing."

After four hours of searching, I'm not any closer to finding an answer. This was a waste of time. I lean against the cabinets and rest my chin on my knuckles. I can't do this by myself.

Keegan's face pops into my mind's eye. He found the paperwork in the attic and insisted on helping, aka chaperoning to control the dissemination of information.

When I read the AWOL statements, I knew Keegan would run to Daisy and tell her what a horrible human Turner was accused of being. He would confirm all her prejudices.

I couldn't let him do that. I thought searching alone was the right choice, but now I'm not so sure.

I need someone to help me figure this out, and he's the only one I trust to care about this search as much as I do. Even if his reasons aren't juxtaposed to mine.

My cheeks heat at the implication of asking for his help. I don't want a reason to hang out with him. Despite his harsh behavior, his hazel eyes do unwanted things to my lower belly. I won't even talk about the daydreams that involve his lips.

Yes, he has moments where he's a jerk, but he also has moments of sweet kindness. Why is he inconsistent? Figuring that out might be harder than clearing Turner's name.

Chapter 15

Keegan

PEACHES, SUGAR, FLOUR, BUTTER, salt, vanilla. Gran lines them up to make my favorite peach cobbler. I snatch a sugared peach from the bowl fast enough that she can't slap my hand.

"You keep doing that and there won't be any left for your dessert." Gran greases the bottom of her pan and transfers the fruit out of my reach.

"You always cut extra."

The corner of her cheek twitches because we both know I'm right. "Still. Maybe we should save some for Bridgette?" Gran pauses her movements. "How's she doing in class?"

"Honestly, she's one of the best." Contrary to what Jake thinks—he's still team Declan—she would do a wonderful job taking the reins of his restaurant. She would maintain his legacy but add her distinctive flair and flavor. Both of which this town desperately needs. But I'll never add those details to my description for Gran. I will definitely never tell Bridgette. She's unlikely to believe me.

"Have you figured out why she gets you all twisted?"

"No." Not specifically. Jealousy tastes like burnt tires watching her easy camaraderie with Declan. Again, not something I want to share with my grandmother.

It's my fault she and I aren't friends. Bridgette asked for honesty about my life, and I refused to give it to her. Shallow and self-serving as my laconic behavior might seem to others, they have no idea what I've been through. Until they walk a mile in my shoes and deal with the repercussions of Cynthia's deceit, they won't understand.

I'm just going to steal more peaches instead of opening myself up to getting hurt again.

Gran leans over the counter and looks out the window. "Wonder where she got to." The lights in the carriage house are still dark. The sun set an hour ago. Bridgette snuck away from class before I had an opportunity to talk to her today.

I shrug. "She'll be fine." She was distracted. I assume she learned something new about Turner and didn't want to share.

I hoped to catch her here to see what she'd learned. Instead, I got Gran, baked salmon with broccolini, and peach cobbler. I'm not complaining, but I'm disappointed. I keep screwing up with Bridgette. I don't know how to be casual acquaintances. That's the only choice for our relationship. I need to get her to see that.

Gran assembles the cobbler while I steer the conversation away from Bridgette and tell her about the other students. "The group gelled quickly. Today, Axel and Tyler hovered over Jake, telling him different ways to build his fire for premium heat distribution. Juniper snaped her fingers, and they scurried to their table. Jake nodded appreciatively and stacked the logs the way he taught me ten years ago.

Brant's knife skills have improved too." He's making a solid bid for the restaurant.

I don't tell Gran the last part. She doesn't know Jake's retiring. I doubt she knows he has cancer. She's got enough to deal with concerning Bridgette's mission to reunite her with Turner.

I don't get why their reunion is so important to Bridgette. It goes beyond wanting to help a friend. If that's all it is, why not call him? That's the simplest, most logical solution to her problem.

The door bangs open. "Do you live here now?"

I hop off the stool.

Bridgette's in the doorway with her fists on her hips. She favors that particular pose. Like she can't decide if she wants to be Wonder Woman or Harley Quinn. Part warrior hero, part crazy seductress. Not that I'm comparing her to my all-time favorite comic book characters. Her legs would look spectacular in Wonder Woman cosplay though.

"I live in Dallas, remember? You yelled at me about it." Why do I always jump to the defensive around her?

"As previously discussed, you could also be taking over Jake's, so moving in with your grandmother isn't outside the realm of possibility. Why aren't you at your parents' house? Are you hoping to drive me away so you can live in the carriage house?"

Gran gasps. "You're taking over Jake's?"

"I'm not. I'm just helping." I pin a glare at Bridgette. "We also previously discussed *that* fact." I retake my seat and point to the casserole dish on the counter. "And as for why I'm here ... not that I need to explain myself. Gran's peach cobbler is better than my mom's." *And because I was waiting to see your smile one more time before I slink off to bed, but now I know how stupid that idea was.*

Casual acquaintances. That needs to be our thing.

I lift my fork to keep the focus on the cobbler. "Try some. It's a religious experience."

Bridgette drops her bag on the counter and takes the fork. "No offense, Daisy, but I doubt it. I make the best peach cobbler in the world." She eats a bite. Her shoulders bob in a way that says, *It's good, but no big deal.*

Gran and I share a look. "Is that so? You're going to have to prove it." I grab my apron from the pantry and loop it over Bridgette's neck. "You know the way around this kitchen. Dazzle us."

She unties the strings. "I don't want to make cobbler. You may not have my secret ingredients."

I step closer, remove the strings from her hands, and tie them around her waist. My hands linger at her hips. I don't miss the way her cheeks flush and her breathing increases when I'm this close.

Even though my brain wants to chant the casual acquaintance song, the rest of me knows that's a pipedream. I'm too attracted to Bridgette not to want more when she's this close.

If only we didn't have this animosity between us—but it's my fault. I need to be the one to fix it if I ever want ... whatever I can have with Bridgette.

That means getting over my issues, admitting I'm a doctor, and strategizing a plan to clear my name in Dallas, so there's space in my heart to share with Bridgette.

I should have worked through my strategic plan this week instead of following Bridgette around like a lost kitten.

That's a problem for another night because she just insulted my grandma. "You can't diss Gran's cobbler and not step up."

Bridgette stares up at me. Her lashes flutter, and her muscles contract under my fingertips like she's enjoying my hands where they are.

She huffs out a breath. "Fine, but I will not share my secrets, so you need to leave the kitchen."

Gran taps her finger to her lips.

I bob my shoulder. "Gazebo?" Gran nods and I grab a bottle of Moscato wine and two glasses. "We'll be in the gazebo."

Forty-five minutes later, and three trips back and forth to the carriage house, Bridgette carries a tray with four bowls to us. "Blind taste test. I warmed yours up, Daisy, so temperature won't give away whose is whose."

I lift the first dish and look at it from every angle. Bright orange peaches. Streusel crumble falling down the sides. It looks like Gran's. I lift another bowl. They look exactly the same.

"How do we know you aren't serving us four plates of Gran's cobbler?"

Bridgette shifts her weight, pops her hip, and scowls. "You'll know."

I take a tentative bite. Sweet, slightly creamy with the perfect amount of crunch in the topping. I move to the second bowl and repeat my process.

The flavor on this one is richer, deeper, the crunch just a little bit crunchier. There's something to the sweetness that's different. It's the difference you get when you let a peach ripen three more days on the tree. It's fuller. The juice more likely to run down your chin as you indulge in bite after bite, not caring that you're making a mess, just wanting to eat every drop before someone steals it from you.

Bridgette crosses her ankles. "So, which is better?"

Gran pats my shoulder. "Which do you like best?" She bats her eyelashes innocently, but I know how heavy the question is. I thought it would be easy to tell them Gran's is superior, but I can't.

Perjury isn't a good color on me.

Gran prides herself on unparalleled, uncontested kitchen domination, and I'm about to ruin it. "Um ... it's ... I ..." I will lose my Favorite Grandson status because I know the second one has to be Bridgette's—and it is better.

And not just a little better.

This peach cobbler deserves statues erected in its honor.

Bridgette bites her lip and hides it behind her fist. Her grin says she knows I don't want to tell Gran the truth.

I slide my fork onto the tray. "I'm sorry, Gran. They're both fantastic, but Bridgette's is better."

Gran takes bites from both bowls. Her eyes flutter closed. "Wow. Bridgette, you win. Is that extra nutmeg? Or ... it's not allspice or cinnamon. Hmm?"

"Gran, I will not let her win this." Maybe I'm only trying to soothe Gran's pride, but I scoop my grandma's cobbler in my mouth and make happy sounds.

Bridgette scoffs and steals my bowl with her cobbler. "Whatever. More for me."

Gran pats my thigh. "Credit is due where credit is earned." She digs into her serving of Bridgette's cobbler with gusto. "And by gosh, she has earned it. You have to share your secret."

Bridgette mimes zipping her lips, locking them, and throwing the key over her shoulder.

I want to snatch that key, place it to her lips, and make her tell us because, oh, my gosh, this is delicious. I will never be able to eat another peach cobbler without fantasizing about this one ... and the woman who made it.

What *can't* she do? Why have I been trying so hard to keep her at arm's length? She's kind, talented, knows her strengths, and isn't afraid of her weaknesses.

Why did I ever assume she was like my ex?

They are nothing alike.

Bridgette's last boyfriend obviously didn't appreciate what a spectacular woman she is if he said she would never have forever with someone.

Every day I'm with her, I'm willing to step up and volunteer as tribute. It's such a cliché, but I'll stand on the bench and wave my arm, shouting, *pick me, pick me* if I can earn her forgiveness and bring the sunflower smiles back to her eyes.

"You can thank me by not making me do the dishes." Bridgette splays her hands. "I hate dishes. They're bad for my cuticles. If I never have to do another dish for the rest of my life, I'll be a happy woman."

I abandon the dregs of Gran's cobbler. "You make more cobbler, and I'll be your personal dishwasher until the apocalypse."

Her cheeks redden, and she ducks her head. "Don't need to go that far."

"You deserve it." I gather the bowls and silverware and retreat into the house before any other stupid declarations jump out of my mouth.

Our relationship is already rocky. We need baby steps to bring us back to friends.

I clean every dish, pot, pan, serving spoon, and measuring spoon Gran owns. These women do not know how to cook economically.

Halfway through the process, Gran kisses me on the temple and wishes me goodnight. "I left Bridgette in the gazebo with the wine." She winks. "She needs company."

"That's not a good idea." Especially with the swirling thoughts a simple dish of peach cobbler induced. One sweet concoction and I'm ready to forget every cautionary tale I learned dating my last girlfriend.

Because Bridgette isn't like Cynthia. She never has been. Don't let fear rule you.

It's like Gran can read my mind. "Keegan, you have to let someone in." She nods toward the back door. "She gets my vote."

I dry my hands and rest my hip against the edge of the sink. Through the window, I watch Bridgette. She's leaning against the railing with a glass of wine in her hand, staring up at the stars, completely and utterly at peace.

The way I see it, I have three options.

1. Slip out the front door and call it a night.

2. Go to the gazebo. Thank Bridgette for the cobbler and say goodbye.

3. Share a bottle of wine under the stars with a woman who is stealing pieces of my rumpled heart.

My last relationship burned me like bacon left in the oven for twice as long as it should have been. My heart is way past crispy, almost too charred to be recognizable.

I don't want to be this man anymore. Figuring out how to fix my inability to trust should be my top priority.

Bridgette is a stranger.

I've known her less than a week.

But it's been one heck of a week. Watching her dance at Sobre las Rocas, her vulnerability on the beach when we kissed, how she unapologetically takes charge in the kitchen, and her dedication to reuniting my family—all of these things make Bridgette someone I want to trust.

I flake the char from a corner of my heart and reveal the tender flesh underneath. It's not much, but wine and starlight are a place to start.

I tap my knuckles on the gazebo's wooden support, so I don't scare her as I approach. "May I join you?"

"Are you going to be nice?" Her tone is as cold as a November breeze.

"Yes."

She narrows her gaze, then steps to the side to make room for me on her railing. "We'll see."

"Thank you."

"For what exactly?"

I sit on the railing, so I'm facing her. "For the smile you put on Gran's face. She loves having someone to cook with again. Daddy doesn't cook. Since we grandkids moved away, she hasn't had anyone to share her creations with."

"She told me about a family down the street."

"She cooks *for* them, not *with* them. It's different."

"I get that. I used to cook all the time with my best friend Camille ..." Her shoulders hunch, and she exhales a labored breath. "She's getting married and took over her grandma's company, so I never see her anymore."

"It's funny how you can miss people even when they're not gone, huh?" Or that never were, but that's not a story for tonight.

"Yeah, that's a good way to put it." She sips her wine, rolling the liquid around her mouth like a true connoisseur. "I need your help."

"With what?"

She hands me her phone. "I got Turner's discharge records, and I don't know what to do with them."

"I told you we would figure this out together." I scan the page. Dishonorable discharge. AWOL. *Assault*. "Holy cow."

"Yeah, I know." She tucks her thumbnail between her teeth and chews. "You can't show this to Daisy."

I'm not sure I want to meet this man. The paperwork doesn't read like the same guy Bridgette described. Can people change that much?

She points to the dates Turner was missing. "Do you know anything about April 1967?"

"No." History was my worst subject.

"I can't find any major events in the war, Texas, or Bubee that might explain why he would have left Fort Bragg for almost a week and then gone back to his unit. He had to know he'd get in trouble."

"It's not called Fort Bragg anymore."

She swats my arm. "Not the point."

"What do you want from me?"

Her shoulder lifts, but there's no force to it. "Perspective. You found the letter in the box."

"You would have too, eventually."

She rests her hand on my forearm. "You know your family's history. You'll know if something is important or not. I spent all day at Town Hall, but I don't know who people are or if they're connected to Turner. You have to help me decide what's important."

I cover her hand with mine. "Only if you make me more cobbler."

She looks at my hand like it's a poisonous snake. "You're okay with me continuing to dig into this? You won't run to Daisy with every detail until we know what they all mean?"

I want to spend time with her outside the kitchen. I want to learn what makes her tick, and if this is how I do it, then so be it. "It's my family's history you're unraveling. I want to know what you find."

"So I don't spread rumors?"

"Rumors destroy lives." I know that better than anyone. It's time I put my life back together.

Chapter 16

Keegan

Jake's is nearly empty at this early hour. A skeleton crew maintains the fires in the mornings. The meat they'll serve happily smokes away, the tantalizing aroma filling my lungs, but it doesn't clear the heaviness from my chest.

If I ever hope to get my life back, I need to deal with the rumors back home. I need a game plan.

Cynthia destroyed my reputation. Everyone thinks I'm a callous, heartless swine. They think I broke up with her when she was at her most vulnerable.

They don't know her vulnerability was the lie. She took my overeager dreams and twisted them for her own ends, so it's her word against mine.

If I shout the truth from the rooftops, everyone will think I'm an angry bully with a vendetta—and with one tear-streaked statement from her, I can kiss my career goodbye.

I pull a rack of ribs from the refrigerator and remove the silver skin. The knife's balance reminds me of a scalpel. I miss my OR and my patients. The precision required to filet steaks doesn't carry the same weight as the intricacy of a rotator cuff repair or meniscus debridement. If I miscalculate my angles here, no one is maimed for life.

I miss the pressure. I need a new perspective.

I drizzle the ribs with mustard and a basic sprinkling of salt and pepper. A simple meal for a simple guy.

Simple.

I'm not sure I can call myself that anymore. Not with how complicated my life has become.

Why didn't I see through Cynthia's lies before it was too late? Why did I let her pull me in so deep that I couldn't see the surface anymore?

I thought I was a good judge of character, but she makes me question every friendship, every interaction, every request people make on me and my time.

A friend asking me to go to a Cowboys game used to be a simple invitation for fun. Now, I worry they're trying to buy my vote at the next staff meeting.

While the seasoning works its way into the ribs. I add wood to a small barbecue and stoke the fire.

I activate my Bluetooth and dial my boss.

Bud answers after the first ring. "So?"

"So, what?"

"Are you coming back?" His voice is gruff and distant. He's multi-tasking me too. I'll make our conversation quick and to the point.

"Of course, I'm coming back."

"When?"

"Two weeks."

"Are you getting your head back in the game?"

"I need your help."

"Mine?" His voice is clearer. I have his attention.

"What did Cynthia say this week?"

"You know I don't listen to gossip," he grumbles.

"I know, but you still hear it." Try as he might, the doctor's lounge and PACU are infested with gossip. "If I don't know her newest lies, I don't have a way to combat them."

He sighs. He's probably running his hand through his goatee. "The nurses were talking. They think you're interviewing in Bangor, Maine because you can't face what you did to Cynthia."

Except I didn't do anything to her. "Did Cynthia start that rumor?"

"I don't know."

"Is she still talking about her fake pregnancy?"

"Yes." The word drops like a hammer striking an anvil.

If she's still claiming she miscarried, garnering sympathy, my uphill battle is steep and treacherous. "Do you have any suggestions to counter her claims?"

"As the mother, she holds all the rights. It's too late for a paternity test."

The one I refused to get initially because hope is dangerous.

Cynthia knew building a large, loving family is my most sacred dream. It's why she chose to pretend to be pregnant in the first place.

If I hadn't told her my dreams so early in our relationship, she wouldn't have assumed I wanted those things with her.

That was my fatal mistake.

I gave her too much, too soon, and led her to believe we had a deeper relationship than I was capable of having with her.

She wanted to build a castle on the sand, but I didn't see it was quicksand until I'd shared too much of my heart.

"I'll be back in the OR on the fifteenth. My PA will load my schedule to make up for the lost time. I'll figure out what to do by then."

He huffs into the phone. "Thank the surgery gods. Nathan has been breathing down my neck to replace you. The guy he suggested is Chicken Little. The sky is falling every day. Nothing good happens to him. His problems are always somebody else's fault. That's not the kind of guy I want on our team."

"Sounds exactly like Nathan."

"Nah. Nathan knows when he's wrong, and he owns it. His problem is that he's rarely wrong, and it's gone to his head."

Time for me to own my mistakes.

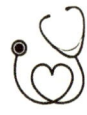

Bridgette

Me and my picnic basket of barbecue chicken, coleslaw, and mashed potatoes push through Honey Beans' doors for Sangria Under the Pier Club. I was reluctant to leave the shore this afternoon to cook dinner, but I couldn't arrive at my first SUP club without my offering.

Georgi waves from behind the register as I set the basket on the counter with a thud. I never got a head count, so I packed enough to feed a small army.

She flares her hands toward the espresso machine like I'm going to win it on a game show. "Do you want something?"

"I'll save myself for this famous sangria I keep hearing about."

She winks. "You bet your bottom dollar it's famous. My shift's done in ten."

My ringtone roars from the bottom of my purse. I dig it out. Camille finally texted me back.

Camille: I miss you too. How's Texas?

I'm not sure how to answer her question. Jake's class makes it educationally delicious.

Georgi and Sangria Under the Pier make it excitingly fun.

Keegan makes it heart-flutteringly complicated.

Turner's mystery adds brain-scrambling confusion.

That's too many words to type with any clarity. Especially since I don't have a whole lot of clarity myself.

Bridgette: I love the ocean.

I send her a picture of the waves and dunes I snapped when I walked to Sobre las Rocas the first day I was here.

Camille: That's gorgeous.

Camille: Can I bother you with some wedding stuff?

Bridgette: You are never a bother.

I'm honestly surprised she hasn't blown up my phone with ideas, suggestions, and questions all week.

Camille: Are you okay with green bridesmaids' dresses?

Bridgette: It's your wedding.

Camille: You have to wear it, and I want you to be happy.

My heart contracts a little harder. I press the phone to my chest to hold in the swell of homesickness. Ethan and Nica eloped. This is the first wedding I've helped plan, and I will not miss a minute of it.

Bridgette: It means so much that you want my opinion. As long as it's not lime or neon green, I'm good with whatever.

Camille: Great! Will you set up appointments at these bridal shops the Monday after you get back?

The websites for the bridal shop in Emerald Bay and two in Duluth pop up on the text message feed.

Camille: Oh, and we moved the date to June 10, so they'll need to rush the order once we pick what you like.

Bridgette: Like in 6 weeks?!

The three dots appear, disappear, appear again. It feels like ten minutes before she texts back.

Camille: We just want to be married.

I pinch the bridge of my nose. How do I plan a wedding in six weeks when I'm not even there? I just do. I'll figure it out. That's who I am.

Bridgette: I'll make your magical day happen whenever you want it. Don't stress.

Stressing will be my job. She asked me to be her maid of honor. I knew what I was getting into. Her happiness is all that matters. She deserves this. I can make phone calls and send emails from Texas. This isn't the Stone Age, requiring carrier pigeons.

Bridgette: Who else will be bridesmaids? How many appointments do we need?

Camille: You, Nica, Bailey, Isa, and Keira. But Keira can't get to Emerald Bay until the ceremony, so she'll text us her measurements once we pick stuff out.

Bridgette: Will you do me a favor and see if you can get Willa's phone number from one of your players?

Camille: What's up?

Bridgette: I need to talk to her about something Graham said.

Camille: Graham? You're talking to Graham again? Bridg, I thought you were finally over him?!

Bridgette: Totally done with him. He said some things during your party that I need to clear up.

Camille: That's why you left early.

Camille: What did he say?

Bridgette: Nothing. Don't worry.

Camille: Uh huh. Spill. What'd he say?

Bridgette: It's not a text conversation and I need to go.

Camille: Is this why you went to Texas?

Bridgette: I'm here for barbecue.

The three dots appear and disappear several times.

Camille: Fine. We'll talk when you get back.

I'm glad she dropped it. I should have told her everything Graham said before I left, but I was so heartsick, I didn't know how to explain without breaking down like I did in front of Turner.

Camille would have helped me, but she might have also sent her football players to "misplace" Graham's car inside his office. I don't need to add pranks to the drama.

I send her a thumbs-up emoji and click on the first store's website. I fill out the appointment requests, create a group chat for the bridesmaids to confirm their availability, and create a checklist of everything I need to do to make this wedding perfect in six weeks.

My news feed knows I was researching the year 1967, and several articles flow across the reel. My three millionth internet search for events in April 1967 is as unfruitful as the others.

It's weird how the world spins and a million things happen in people's lives, but none of them seem important. No world event stands out that would have been big enough to make Turner leave his post. Whatever drove him to go AWOL was personal. A sinking feeling settles in my stomach. I'm going to have to ask him what happened if I want to solve this mystery.

I'm not ready for that yet. How do you ask someone you love about the shameful secret they've hidden for more than fifty years?

Hey Turner, why'd you go AWOL? lacks tact. Those harsh words could destroy his trust in me.

"You wish," Georgi snarls.

My head whips up. Back pressed into the counter behind the register, Georgi's arms cross over her chest, and she shoots a glare at the guy ordering that would kill if she were a superhero ... er, villain.

Three women in dresses that look more like birthday party napkins than fabric—his friends, I assume—giggle at the confrontation. There's a man hanging with them too, but he looks just as confused and freaked out as I feel.

I rise, ready to defend my friend.

She extends her hand toward me in an, *I got this* motion. "Dr. Sanchez, just because your daddy's factory is responsible for fifty percent of my town's revenue doesn't mean you have anything to offer me."

He leans an elbow on the counter. "I've asked you to call me Theo." His rich accent purrs in a way that makes my pulse sizzle. It's like the caramel drizzle on a flan, creamy and decadent.

But based on Georgi's sneer, he's a dessert you avoid at all costs.

Georgi pulls a paper cup from the stack next to her hip. "*Dr. Sanchez*, do you want to order something or not?"

"I'll take a small drip coffee, black, and the ladies will take ..." He steps back and extends his hand to the women. "Ladies, what can the lovely Georgi get you?"

The first woman steps forward. "What do you have that's decaf, sugar-free, fat-free, and lactose-free?"

"Air." Georgi delivers the line with a straight face I couldn't hold if my life depended on it.

The woman scowls. "That will get you a one-star rating, Lovie."

"What makes you think I care about stars?"

Napkin girl taps her stiletto. "I'm an influencer. My ratings and reviews will keep this place open."

Georgi puckers her lips, a, *You poor thing* expression crinkling her forehead. "You believe that don't you? What's it like having an ego the size of the Gulf of Mexico and no real use?"

Ouch!

The woman turns and grasps Dr. Sanchez's lapel, tugging him toward the door. "I'm not thirsty. Let's go."

He brushes her off and chuckles. "She's right, Lexie. You have ten followers."

Lexie's face matches the setting sun over her shoulder: purple and fiery. "You're going let her talk to me like that?"

Theo's adoring gaze settles on Georgi. "Honey Beans thrives because of Georgi's skill, and you will never stop her."

Something's going on here that I don't understand, and after the hard time Georgi gave me about Keegan, you can bet I'll pry the details out of my friend as soon as this disaster leaves the coffee shop.

Georgi scowls and points at Dr. Sanchez. "A newer version of you will be with him next weekend. Don't feel special."

The woman huffs and storms out, the rest of the group follow as quickly as their four-inch heels can carry them. The guy gives a broken wave and follows while Dr. Sanchez ambles back to the counter.

I shove my fist in my mouth to keep from laughing uncontrollably.

"Can I still get that coffee, please?" Doctor Sanchez says.

"Whatever." Georgi spins and fills a small cup with black liquid.

He pulls out a wad of cash and drops it on the counter. I see a couple of hundred-dollar bills. Georgi picks it up and flings it back at him. "It's on the house if you promise never to come back."

He tucks the cash in the tip jar instead. "Not on your life, Georgi. I love our little meetings. I'm sorry about Lexie. I'll talk to her about being nicer."

He takes a slow slip of his coffee, his gaze never leaving her eyes. I want to pluck at the collar of my shirt and fan my chest, there's so much tension between them.

He licks his lips. "Delicious. See you next weekend." He strolls from the coffee shop like he's on a runway.

Georgi collapses across the counter and screeches. "I hate that man."

I rub her back. "Who was that, and what just happened?"

"Dr. Theodore Esteban Alejandro Frederick Sanchez IV. His dad owns a company that builds anesthesia machines, heart rate monitors, biomedical whatsits." She sits up. "He thinks he's God's gift. Every Saturday right before closing, he parades a new group of people into town. They're always beautiful, sometimes they're nice, but usually they're as vapid as Miss Sugar-Free. Can you believe he has the audacity to flirt with me in front of them?"

"That's gross." Gross isn't the right word, but I can't think of what I should say.

Georgi is a thousand times prettier than the three women who were just in here, based on her personality alone. There's more to Georgi and Theo than Georgi wants to admit. She's too sorrowful for this to be just an annoying man with his cringeworthy friends.

She drops her apron on the counter. "I need sangria."

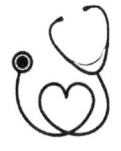

Chapter 17

Bridgette

From the coolers in the back of the coffee shop, Georgi and I retrieve three pitchers filled to the brim with burgundy liquid and five different varieties of fruit. Instead of turning right and heading toward the beach, we zig-zag left until we stop in front of Town Hall.

At my confused expression, Georgi laughs. "I'm not kidnapping you. We're getting my cousin." She glances at her watch. "Three, two, one. Blast off."

The door bangs open, and Tipsy stomps out. She stops short when she sees us. "I don't need a babysitter."

Georgi hands her the fruit containers. "But you do need positive role models and quality time away from …" She points toward Town Hall with her chin. "This is Bridgette."

Tipsy tucks the plastic cube under her arm and scowls. "The history buff. Yeah, I know her." She shoulders past me and stomps toward the beach.

"Delightful," I mumble.

Georgi hears and steps beside me, nudging my elbow. "She's a good kid. My aunt and uncle are a special brand of horrible. My sisters and I are trying to prove that life doesn't have to be chain-smoking in a double wide while she waits for her next welfare check."

"That's awful. If I'd known …" I did to Tipsy what I hate everyone doing to me.

I'm worse than Graham. His harsh criticism was based on an entire relationship. I jumped to conclusions about Tipsy after one interaction. I didn't consider anything except the snark and bubble gum popping before judging her.

I need to be better and give people the benefit of the doubt.

Georgi loops her arm in mine. "You're a new Bubble. It takes time to learn our ways."

Warm goosebumps sweep across my skin. "I get to be a Bubble? I'm only here for a few weeks."

"Honorary for now, then we'll decide if we gift you permanent status."

"Don't you mean if I earn permanent status?"

"Nope." Her ponytail swishes. "Our friendship isn't earned. That would make it transactional. Friendship should be rooted in love and acceptance. Bubbliness is gifted because we want you to be part of us."

Permanent. As in make Bubee my home. I expect the idea to make me homesick, but it doesn't.

I'd be lying if I said it wasn't attractive. Ocean-kissed skin, humidity-fluffed hair, barbecue and sangria every Saturday night.

Maybe my adventure is finding a new home, not just a vacation.

Georgi catches up to Tipsy. The teenager's shoulders relax, and a smile flits across her face as they talk.

Georgi has that way with people. She makes them comfortable with their place in the world. At least she's done that for me and Tipsy.

I follow them down the brick sidewalk to the beach and reexamine my interactions with Tipsy. I have so many questions, but I don't want to be nosy.

Gossiping for gossip's sake is always a bad idea.

Tipsy seems like a lost puppy who needs love and encouragement. Like Willa. I don't want to crush her by coming on too strong.

Georgi waves at a group of women sitting underneath the pier. "Let me introduce my sisters ... well, the ones who are here."

Camp chairs and a few tables sit in a semicircle facing the water. Tipsy drops her containers and wanders into the water. The waves swallow her ankles, and she stares at the horizon.

Georgi adds the sangria to the table and fills plastic mason jars someone else brought.

"Nora." She hands a cup to a woman in faded, light blue scrubs the color of the chair in the front of Turner's bookstore. "Nora's a cardiology resident at Third Coast Regional. She loves to sleep in late on Saturdays, hike fourteeners in Colorado, and rebuild antique guns," Georgi explains.

She hands over the next drink. "Julietta." This sister's hair is in a messy, brunette bun on the side of her head like she got halfway through a Princess Leia hairstyle and gave up. "She's on spring break from her second year of medical school at Tulane. She says she loves their dedication to underserved communities, but we're pretty sure it's because she wants to do an Emergency Department rotation during Mardi Gras."

Georgi hands me my cup. "Sisters, this is Bridgette. Baker, barbecuer, and coffee connoisseur."

We clink our glasses together. "Cheers." The sweet, tart liquid is the perfect mixture of wine and juice. I roll it around my tongue. "You are so right. This is divine." I nod to Julietta and Nora. "Two doctors in the family? Wow."

"Three. Angelina's going to be a dermatologist." Georgi raises her glass. "I'm the disappointing underachiever of the group."

Her sisters boo. "You hold us together, big sister."

The women share the details of their weeks: troublesome surgeries, brain-rotting tests, escapist time travel novels. I settle into my chair and listen, not adding much to the conversation.

I sip the sangria and will the gentle wash of the waves against the sand to lull me into blissful paradise. Instead, my brain catalogs my week: meeting Keegan, the shock of the first day of class, Jake's crooked smile, planning Camille's wedding. Then I jump to Turner and all the questions I have about his past and why he's hiding.

Why did he send me to his hometown in the first place? He ran away and never looked back, so why did he think this was what I needed?

Tipsy joins us. Georgi pours her a cup from the other pitcher. "Non-alcoholic," she assures me.

An olive-skinned woman with gold ribbons woven through her braids hugs Nora from behind.

She jumps to her feet. "Rach! You came. It's so good to see you."

"It's not a proper Saturday night without SUP club." Rachel sags in the chair between Nora and Julietta. "When was the last time I had a Saturday night off?"

"Too long." Georgi hands her a cup. She points her thumb in Rachel's direction, but says to me, "Emergency Department nurse."

Rachel waggles her finger. "Not just any nurse. You are looking at the new nurse-in-charge."

"What's that?" I ask.

"It means she's the bo-oss," Julietta singsongs. "Congrats, killer. It's about time."

We raise a toast.

"The only downside is it means more time with Dr. Crumb Bum. But sacrifices must be made to achieve our goals. Am I right?"

"Undoubtably," Julietta says, draining her cup.

I lean into Georgi. "Dr. Crumb Bum?"

Rachel rolls her eyes. "Don't ask. Let's just say cookies were destroyed for no good reason. When you get between me and my mama's oatmeal raisin, I hold a grudge."

The Bubbles have enough stories to keep me busy for months' worth of SUP clubs. "Oh-kay then." I pull the picnic basket into my lap. "Speaking of cookies, is this everyone? Should we eat?"

Nora throws her head back and laughs. Everyone else joins with chuckles and giggles.

"What'd I say?"

"We are always ready to eat, and there are ..." Georgi counts on her fingers. "Fifteen women in SUP club?"

Fifteen? Where are all the other members?

Julietta lifts the lid of my basket and nods. "With Bridgette, yeah, fifteen. I'm not sure Lane counts anymore. She skipped out last time she was in town to go make out with George." She grimaces like she ate a stale black licorice.

"George?" I ask.

"Our cousin," Georgi and Julietta say at the same time Tipsy says, "My brother. She dated him for a minute before he dumped her. He's a simp."

"I'm still hung up on the names. You're Georgi, and he's George? And you're cousins. Who's Lane?" Can I get a family tree or a phonebook to catalog these people?

"I'm older." Georgi raises her cup. "My aunt, Tipsy's mom, isn't the most creative woman. She named her kids after British royalty: Harry, George, Philip, and Henrietta. She didn't care that I was already Georgi."

My head spins with the new names and facts. "And Lane?"

"Lane is Keegan's little sister," Nora clarifies. "We assumed Daisy talked your ear off about her superstar granddaughter. Didn't she just sell a screenplay or something?"

That's the thing about small towns. It's hard being an outsider. When everyone knows everyone, and everyone knows everyone's business, you're expected to keep up. Camille and I talk about the people in Emerald Bay the same way.

"I need flashcards to keep everyone straight."

"Nah." Tipsy points at the women in the circle. "These are the ones you need to know. They matter."

Georgi, Julietta, Nora, Rachel, and Tipsy. I can keep them straight. Name tags with identifying characteristics for anyone else, though.

We pass around plates and dig into the dinner I packed. Eyes roll back in their heads as they take their first bites.

"So good."

"Shazam, that's amazing."

"Permanent dinner provider."

"Yeah, no more of Georgi's stale leftover sandwiches."

If all fifteen women had shown up, we wouldn't have had nearly enough food with the amount these ladies consume. It will be nice to meet them eventually, in small groups so I can keep them straight.

We settle in, and my gaze drifts to the lit porch on the back of Jake's BBQ. The restaurant is hopping. We're too far away to hear the music playing over their speakers, but people mill around in the sand.

Is Keegan working? I haven't seen him since last night, and I hate that I always scan Daisy's kitchen for him when I step out my front door.

Julietta tells Rachel and Nora a story about something in anatomy lab, and Georgi nudges my elbow. "You okay?"

"A little overwhelmed."

"Keegan?" Her tone has a slightly disdainful quality.

"Why do you think it's him? You always ask about him."

"Men tend to be problems. He was your problem last time you got the weird look on your face."

"He doesn't get to take up residence in my head."

Okay. He's got real estate, but I don't want to explain the tense relationship we've established.

The Peach Cobbler Incident twisted me into knots, so we buzzed around each other but never talked while Jake taught us how to build our fires in class yesterday.

"Good." Georgi pats my knee. "He's a hottie, but he and Theo are cut from the same cloth."

I swivel in my chair and face her. "Hmm. Interesting. I thought he was strictly Dr. Sanchez?"

Her eyes roll skyward, and she fans herself. "Oh, let me tell you ... the first time I talked to him, he was Theo. Handsome, charming, witty. I thought I'd died and gone to hottie heaven. Just saying his name ... Theo ... sent shivers down my spine." She plants her hands on her knees and digs her nails into the skin. "The second time, he paraded a group of model-esque women into the coffee shop, and I knew I'd been scammed. The rest is sad, sad history."

"Why are the cute ones always jerks?"

She clacks her cup against mine. "There's the ultimate question."

"My ultimate question is what happened between April thirteenth and twenty-first in 1967."

Georgi raises a sculpted eyebrow. "Our grandparents got married."

"Really? How do you know that?" I have no idea when either of my grandparents' anniversaries were. Neither marriage lasted and they died when I was young, so maybe that shouldn't be a surprise.

Her arms stretch wide to encompass the whole town. "Grammie Dotty and Peepa Auggie threw a massive party every year until my grandpa died three years ago. They wanted everyone to remember and celebrate their fairytale story."

I tuck my feet underneath me and lean toward her. "Tell me."

My skin tingles in anticipation. I love a good romance. I don't know if this is the break I need to solve Turner's mystery, but I need to hear a happily ever after. I need to believe in true love.

Georgi scoots down in her chair, rests her head on the headrest, and digs her feet under the sand. Her gaze takes on that faraway look people get when they reminisce. "He was a bomber pilot home on leave. She was the girl he'd loved from afar. She blew a tire, and he stopped to help her change it. Three weeks later they were married."

"How romantic."

"Peepa brought Grammie flowers every Tuesday. He held her hand in church. She fed him after his first stroke. See? Fairytale."

"Your grandma is Daisy's best friend, right?"

"Yeah. Daisy was their maid of honor too."

"Interesting." Would Turner have cared if Dotty and Auggie got married? Was he friends with either of them? Would he have skipped out on the Army to see his friends tie the knot?

I hug Georgi. "Thanks for this. I need to go."

A serious look spreads across her face, and she nods sagely. "Worried about vampires?"

"No." Her awkward comment breaks the strain building in my shoulders. "You're the best, you know that? I'll see you later." I need to ask Daisy whether Turner was at Dotty's wedding.

I skid in the sand and spin to Georgi. I have a better idea. Daisy said she hadn't seen Turner since he left for Vietnam, and the dishonorable discharge was the closure she needed. That means she didn't see him at the wedding, but maybe Dotty or Auggie did.

"Will you introduce me to your grandma?" I ask.

"Why?"

"I want to hear all the romantic details about her wedding." Like whether Turner was there. Was August his best friend?

Maybe he went AWOL to celebrate his friend's marriage because the Army refused to grant him leave. If their love was as fairy tale as it sounds, there may not have been time.

It's not a great reason, but people have done stranger things for the people who are important to them.

"I'm having brunch with her tomorrow," Georgi says.

"Shoot. Amanda's having her picnic."

Georgi frowns. "She rescheduled for next weekend. Her son's soccer team made the playoffs."

"How do you know that?"

She taps her watch. "Town text group."

"You have a text group for the entire town?"

"It's supposed to be for emergencies like tornados and hurricanes, but ..." She shrugs. "Delayed picnics are kind of an emergency. Also trust me, if she asks you to help, say no. You'll end up knee-deep in crawfish heads with no hope of escape."

"I would not have guessed that." Amanda doesn't seem the crawfish type. "Can I join you for brunch, then?"

"I guess. Just be prepared to have your every life choice analyzed and torn to shreds."

I plop back into my camp chair. "Can't wait."

She refills our cups. "You are strange. I'm so glad we met."

"Me too." I wrap my arm around her shoulders and settle in while Nora tells Rachel something about heart valves and violin strings.

Chapter 18

Bridgette

Georgi stares at her phone as I walk up the sidewalk to her grandmother's house. In a fit-and-flare cantaloupe-orange dress with white pumps, she's almost unrecognizable from the hipster-barista I see at Honey Beans. "Who are you, and what have you done with my friend?"

She spins, and her skirt glimmers. "Dotty has a dress code."

I glance down at my seersucker pinafore. "Is this okay?" I don't bother with other people's opinions of my wardrobe most of the time, but a good first impression does matter. Dotty could be the key to my search, and I want her to like me enough to open up about her courtship.

Georgi picks something from my shoulder. "You always pass. I've never seen you in something that doesn't scream Southern debutante."

That's not the look I'm going for, but if that's Georgi's interpretation, I trust her. We stride to the bottom of the stairs. Tulips and irises line the paving stones to the two-story Victorian. It looks like a birthday cake balanced on toothpicks: scrolling gables, pink shutters, and white trim lifted fifteen feet off the ground.

"You ready for this?" Georgi cringes.

"She can't be that bad if she's your grandmother and Daisy's BFF."

"Uh-huh. Just remember I warned you." She climbs the steps and opens the screen door. "Grammie, we're here."

"In the kitchen." Her melodic voice floats down the central hallway.

I follow Georgi past rows and rows of family photos going back generations. I pause and stare at an old tintype of two scowling miners.

Georgi taps the wall next to the frame. "Those were Peepa's great uncles. They tried to strike it rich in the California gold rush. Made it as far as San Francisco before they got sidetracked by whiskey and women, or so the tale goes." She wiggles her eyebrows with dramatic exaggeration. "Slunk home penniless. Quite the cautionary tale."

"I'll bet." What is Dotty going to think of me and my spur-of-the-moment trip to Texas? I guess we'll find out.

Oak cabinets line every wall in the small kitchen. Dotty whisks eggs in a glass bowl in the corner next to the sink.

Where Daisy is silver and athletic, Dotty looks like a porcelain baby doll. Bouncing burnt sienna curls frame rosy, cherub cheeks. Her nude heels are as high as Georgi's. They're a coordinating set in their pale orange dresses.

Georgi kisses her grandma's cheek. "Thanks for letting me bring Bridgette. She was dying to meet you and hear about Grandpa." She exaggerates the word *dying* like brunch will literally save my life. It might save Turner's if I can reunite his family.

Dotty's gaze assesses me, from my updo to my flats. "Nice to meet you as well. Let's cook first, chat second. Grab an apron and beat these eggs." Dotty hands the bowl and whisk to me. "Georgiana, brioche is in the pantry." She pulls out a cutting board and slices strawberries and mangoes into a bowl.

I mouth, *Georgiana*? Georgi ignored that little tidbit on the beach last night.

Georgi wrinkles her nose. "Mom wasn't much different from Aunt Sally in her naming strategies. She hated her boring name, so she named us after Regency romance novel heroines. Georgiana, Angelina, Leonora, Julietta. Lysander got made fun of so badly, he started going by Lee in kindergarten."

"I can imagine." That must have been an interesting home to grow up in.

Dotty flaps her knife. "Lisa is a fine name. No one ever stumbles over it like they do with your epithet."

"She also never got her happily ever after, and she's convinced it's because her name wasn't romantic enough to keep Dad around," Georgi whispers in my ear.

The reasoning is silly, but how can Georgi be so indifferent to her parents' failed relationship? Camille was devastated when her parents divorced. It's taken her years to speak to her father again. I want to ask about Georgi's parents, but Dotty levels a pointed glare at me and the unwhisked eggs.

We set to work making French toast and conversations over naming conventions die. After Dotty finishes the fruit, she lights the gas stove and sets a griddle over the burners. "Oranges." She points to the fruit bowl.

Georgi grabs a hand juicer from the drawer, and we squeeze fresh orange juice. I love this simple domestic routine grandma and granddaughter have established. It makes me thankful for Turner and our afternoons with his espresso machine and horrible latte art. He is the only one who doted on me and created traditions with me just because he could, not because he felt obligated.

We take the platter of French toast onto the deck. A small community garden and playground stretch before us. Neighborhood kids run and giggle down the slide while their parents cultivate early tomatoes and artichokes.

Dotty already set the table with fine china, cloth napkins, and silver cutlery. A bowl of pink and blue hydrangeas sits next to two tealights, adding romance to the already elegant spread.

Dotty prays over our food, and we pass the serving dishes around the table. "Georgi said—"

Dotty stabs a strawberry with a sharp clank. "Georgiana. Let's use proper names, shall we?"

"Yes, ma'am. Georgiana told me last night about your whirlwind romance with her grandfather."

Dotty places a minuscule bite of mango between her teeth and scrapes the tines across them. "And?"

I let the grating sound die in the small space. "It sounds romantic, and I hoped you'd tell me the whole story."

"Why?" Dotty asks.

Romance isn't enough of a reason? Based on the sense of propriety and decorum I've already witnessed, I don't think she'd appreciate the real reason. I'm running out of resources to scour for April 1967.

If I don't find something, I'm going to have to ask Turner, and I still don't know how to have that conversation. If he reacts badly, I will have ruined our relationship for no reason except for being a busybody. "Curiosity?" I try instead.

Dotty cuts another bite. "I'm sure Georgiana told you the whole of it. She loves a good yarn."

"She wasn't there. She doesn't know every detail."

"I'm not one for reminiscing."

I scrunch my napkin in my lap. Could this woman be more confusing? "Then why do you throw a party every year?"

She dabs the corner of her napkin to her mouth. "That was August's doing. Any reason to host a party."

I'm not sure what else to ask if she doesn't want to reminisce. Should I move the conversation to Turner, decorum be damned?

"It must have been hard to plan a wedding in just a few weeks. Did distant guests have to scramble to get here?"

She refills our orange juice. "In Texas, people have had shotgun weddings since shotguns were invented. We know how to get the important things done."

"I didn't realize it was a shotgun wedding. You were pregnant with Lisa?"

Georgi chokes on her juice and sputters into her napkin.

"That is an impertinent question, young lady."

"Yes, it is," I say.

Dotty raises an eyebrow, but I don't break eye contact. In this moment, I don't care if I'm being too much: too bossy, too forthright, too impolite. Dotty's being too impassive, and I need answers. I will use the resources at my disposal to get those answers.

"Mom's not the oldest. Uncle Hoyt is," Georgi says around her napkin.

Dotty's scowl shifts to her.

Georgi shrinks into her chair. "What? He is."

Silence stretches between us. I rest my chin in my palm and stare at Dotty.

She huffs. "Hoyt was born four years after we were married when August was discharged from the Air Force."

"What made you finally notice him?" I ask.

Dotty dabs toast in her syrup and slowly chews the bite. "He was handy with a lug wrench."

"That's it?" He had the tool she needed when she needed it, so she married him. So much for one of the greatest love stories of our time.

That's not how happily ever after is supposed to start. Where were the racing hearts and the can't-live-without-him vibes? Jane Austen must be rolling over in her grave.

"Not everything is sunshine, lollipops, and rainbows. Sometimes marriage starts as friendship and grows into love." Dotty squints at me. "Don't tell me you believe you have to be in love for a marriage to be successful?"

"It can't hurt." It sounds like a better place to start than lug wrenches.

Dotty folds her napkin next to her plate. "Trust me. *Love* ..." She says the word like it's a highly contagious disease, "... doesn't sustain a marriage. Love sets impossible expectations on fallible people. Love might be patient, kind, and not remember wrongs, but people do. When times are tough, it's not the love that sees you through, its commitment, friendship, and loyalty."

"Your marriage wasn't a fairytale?"

She gives a clipped nod. "It was what August and I needed it to be."

Dotty's pragmatic approach to relationships both reinforces and contradicts what I witnessed as my friends fell in love. Commitment, friendship, loyalty, and *love* are equal cornerstones in their relationships. They support and reinforce one another.

But their relationships are new. Will the elements rebalance as they get older? Will love fade and commitment take its place? I hope not.

"You don't regret marrying August?"

She spreads the fingers on her left hand and admires the simple gold band. "August was loyal and provided a comfortable life for me and our children. Why should I expect anything more? Why should I put pressure on him to fulfill some silly fantasy? That's not his job."

I collapse against the back of my chair. Her version of marriage leaves an ache in my chest. I want to feel like I can't live without my partner. That's how Camille feels about Liam and how Ethan feels about Nica.

If all I wanted was a buddy, I could have settled down years ago with a guy who was nice to me. I want my heart to race, my pulse to gallop. I want the silly fantasy.

Does that make me unrealistic?

Is it too much to hope for?

If my friends found it, why can't I?

I swirl my orange juice around the bottom of my glass. Maybe things were just different in Dotty's era. It wasn't long ago that marriages centered around farm contracts and dowries. Maybe Dotty is a relic from another time. "That was a fateful flat tire."

Georgi snorts. "Daisy wrapped the wrench and stuck it with the wedding gifts as a joke."

Might as well dive in. "Did her brother come to your wedding?"

Dotty pauses before putting her next bite into her mouth. "Her brother?"

"Turner Donovan."

Dotty's countenance doesn't change, but something in the air shifts, like the charge before an electrical storm. Her movements become more measured as she cuts and chews her next few bites. "How do you know that name?"

"He's a friend."

"That's impossible. Turner died before you were born."

"He's very much alive. He owns a bookstore in my hometown."

Dotty's knuckles whiten on her utensils. "The Turner I knew hated to read. He organized the town's first and last book burning."

"That doesn't sound like the same person." Turner proudly stocks banned books in his front window. No way would he ever burn books.

"He was spoiled, self-centered, and conceited. He only ever cared about himself." Dotty jabs her fork into a strawberry and points it at me like an accusing finger. "I suggest, if you desire to eat at my table, you never speak of that ... that man again. Am I understood?"

"I—"

"Am I understood?"

"Yes, ma'am."

There is so much more to Turner's mystery than I imagined. What did he do to make Dotty hate him so violently? Daisy never mentioned anything.

If Dotty wanted to stop my search, she should have pretended she didn't care. Now I'm a greyhound in the starting stall. I smell my prize, and I won't stop until I catch it.

Chapter 19

Bridgette

My mind swirls and trips over itself like a drunken sailor as I drag myself back to Daisy's house.

Dotty hates Turner.

Vehemently.

None of what she described matches the kind man I know.

Daisy kneels on a green pad next to her flower garden. She squints at me, blocking the sun with her hand. Her expression scrunches, and she grasps my hand. "Y'all all right, sweetheart?"

I sink to the ground next to her. "I'm ..." Confused. Heartbroken. Dismayed. Angry. "I had brunch with Georgi and Dotty, and it didn't go as planned."

"Did she burn the quiche again?" Daisy squeezes my hand and releases it. She scoops dirt out of the ground into a small pile. "I keep telling her she needs to turn down the heat on her oven, but she doesn't believe me. Burns the bottom of the crust before the eggs set."

I smile. It would be nice if something so simple caused my bewildered mood. "I wish eggs were the problem."

"Grab a spade and dig in. We've got snapdragons to plant."

I take the offered shovel. "It's not too early?"

"Not in south Texas. It'll be 106 degrees before you can blink. Now, tell me, what did Dotty say?"

I pull a baby snapdragon from its biodegradable container and gently set it in the hole she created. "She said Turner burned books."

"Still stuck on my brother?" She backfills the hole and pats the dirt level.

"I don't understand how the man I know can be the man she described."

She hands me the next flower. "What did she say?"

As I repeat the conversation on Dotty's porch, Daisy nods along. "He was all of those things."

"He couldn't have been. He's never condescending or pushy or egotistical. He goes out of his way to help people."

She sits back on her heels. Her sweet, grandmotherly countenance washes over my face. "Do you believe people change?"

"Yes, but the amount of change we're talking about is like a personality transplant."

"Sweetheart, he was good at only showing the side of himself he wanted people to see. His appearance was impeccable. He could talk a bee out of its honey, but he could be a bully when it suited his purposes."

I shoot to my feet. "You're wrong. Turner is kind. You're mad he ran away, and you want to destroy his memory."

"Hey!" Keegan growls behind me.

The little hairs on the back of my neck bristle, and I spin to face him.

He jogs the distance between us and sets a protective hand on Daisy's shoulder. "You will not speak to my grandmother like that."

I fling my arm toward her. "She's lying."

His chest puffs with indignation, and anger turns the tips of his ears red. "Gran isn't a liar. You're too stubborn to hear the truth."

"You don't know anything about me, and you don't know Turner." Why do I even bother with these people? They don't deserve to know Turner.

Keegan leans his weight onto his toes. "I know you're too opinionated to let people speak their minds."

I suck in a breath. *Too stubborn. Too opinionated. Too much of the wrong kind of woman.*

That's me. I'm too *everything* to be acceptable.

I don't want to care about Keegan's accusations, but they burn in my gut like he stabbed me with a fire poker. Daisy's eyes blink with pity. Pain condenses behind my eyes and burns down the back of my throat.

The shame of my outburst drops me to my knees. I shouldn't have yelled at Daisy. I shouldn't have had breakfast with Dotty. None of these people know Turner like I do. He's not the man they accuse him of being.

I need to figure out why he left so I can prove he's become a genuinely loving man. Not for them, but for him. To repay the debt I owe him. "I'm going to go take a shower."

I tuck my metaphorical tail between my legs and disappear into the carriage house. The room's stillness calms my racing heart. I'm missing the key piece of my puzzle, and the deeper I dig, the angrier people become.

Does that mean I'm getting closer to a truth they don't want me to find?

Or is it like Keegan said, and I'm too opinionated and stubborn to see the truth?

Are they right? Turner's not the man I believe him to be, and he's lied to me our entire friendship.

I'll never believe that. I'm not wrong. They are.

He deserves to be known as the amazing man he's become. I'll find a way to prove it.

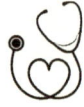

Keegan

Daisy loves her flowers. I'm not sure if my great-grandmother was prophetic in naming Gran, or if the love of flowers is because of her name. Either way, my soft physician hands are covered in mud. The callouses I work hard to prevent have formed thanks to chores around Gran's house and chunking firewood for Jake.

I wash my hands in the sink, grab glasses of sweet tea for both of us, and join Gran on the porch swing. "We were wrong about Bridgette."

I can't believe the way she yelled at Gran. What right does she have to accuse her of lying about a man whose record confirms everything Gran said? The more I learn about my great-uncle, the lower my opinion sinks.

Desertion. Assault. Dishonorable Discharge.

Bridgette's dedication to him makes me question her as well. The buzzy feeling in my stomach when I rounded the corner and saw her—before she started yelling at Gran—felt a lot like the desire burning inside me before I kissed her at the beach and again when she made the peach cobbler.

I thought Bridgette was different.

This is another instance of me not being able to read people. I hadn't given her enough time to show her true self.

The buzz is still there, but I don't trust it.

If I can't trust my gut, what can I trust?

Gran pauses her cup halfway to her mouth. "How were we wrong?"

I lift an eyebrow. "She went crazy."

Gran tsks. "That wasn't crazy. That was defensive. She was more cornered dog than riled up tiger."

"She shouldn't have yelled at you." I don't need to hear Bridgette's side of the argument to know Gran doesn't lie.

"Bridgette is an emotionally driven woman. Strange how much she reminds me of my brother."

"What do you mean?"

"Turner had these outbursts—"

I open my mouth, but Gran holds up her hand to stop me.

"My parents never taught him how to process or control overwhelming emotions, so when they got out of hand, he sailed to the shack or took them out on random walls. He became an expert at repairing drywall holes."

"The shack? The one on Willard's Island, where we hunted hermit crabs?" We spent weeks on the island every summer when I was younger.

We call it a shack, but it's more than that. A small kitchen, living room, and bunkroom raised twenty feet off the sand. When I was in middle school, my dad wired a portable generator so we could cook on a hot plate. The only thing it doesn't have is indoor plumbing, but no one's been there in years.

Gran nods. "Turner built it when we were in high school. He'd disappear out there for days at a time."

"I never knew that." What other nuggets of our family history don't I know?

"It's a relief to talk about him. It made Mama too sad to hear his name after he ... well, anyway."

Why haven't I ever asked her about how we came to own the shack? She's lived a full life, and I only know bits and pieces of it. I need to do better by the people I love.

Gran finishes the last drops of her drink. "Those roses won't trim themselves."

I steady the swing as she stands. "We're making sausage in class Monday. I'll bring you dinner. Do you want potato salad and bread pudding too?"

She bumps my chin. "Apologize to Bridgette while you're at it."

"She doesn't need an apology."

Gran cradles my face in her warm palms. "No matter how truthful your words, they were delivered in anger. You need to apologize for your tone, if not the meaning behind it."

"Gran—"

She taps the center of my forehead. "This is not optional. We raised you to be a gentleman, and gentlemen apologize when they've injured someone's feelings."

"Fine," I say around my clenched jaw.

"In fact ..." Gran points over my shoulder. "Now's as good a time as any."

Bridgette walks around the side of the house. Shoulders back. Spine straight. Her blonde hair flows in the breeze. She changed out of her overall thing and is wearing calf-length black pants and a flowing green top. The late afternoon light casts her in an ethereal glow.

My heart zigs sideways in my chest. I was cruel to her. I shouldn't have said what I did. She's not too opinionated or stubborn. Her dedication is admirable.

I just didn't like her yelling at Gran. I thought I finally understood Bridgette, but watching her yell, I realized how little I know her.

I knew hoping for joyful evenings in the kitchen taste-testing peach cobbler was just another way to pummel my heart.

I don't trust myself when I'm around her. I'm too easily deceived by what I want to see in Bridgette instead of looking below the surface to who she really is.

Is she a woman who takes her frustrations out on little old ladies when she doesn't get her way?

Is she someone who resorts to yelling when she's frustrated and can't find another outlet for her rage?

I don't know.

Even if I get to know Bridgette well enough to feel safe falling for her, it's too soon.

Cynthia's unresolved lies are an unscalable wall.

Regardless of the future, I owe Bridgette an apology.

I kiss the top of Gran's head and jog down the steps. "Bridgette, wait for me."

Her shoulders tense, so I know she hears me.

"Come on. Wait up."

"I'd rather not, thanks." She doesn't turn around or slow her pace striding down the street toward the center of town.

"Where are you going?"

"Nowhere."

"Then you've got time to wait."

"Go away, Keegan." Her voice is rough like she's been crying.

"I'm sorry for my tone. I'd rather not apologize to the back of your head."

She waves her hand over her head. "I don't care if you're sorry."

"Really?"

She spins. Her eyes are bloodshot, and dark circles ring the delicate skin underneath. She spreads her arms wide and lets them collapse. "Why would I? We were attracted to each other, but you've proven over and over that we aren't compatible. You don't trust me. You believe everything Graham said about me to be true. I need to get over my crush. Walking away and finding a boat are the best ways to do that." She pivots and jogs down the sidewalk.

"A boat?" I chase her. I should deal with the whole *incompatible, get over my crush* part of that comment, but ... "Why do you need a boat?"

"What makes you think I'm going to tell you? I'm too stubborn and too opinionated for you to talk me out of this."

"I don't even know what *this* is. Would you just wait?"

Two blocks in, she turns north—the opposite direction of Jake's—toward Tiburon Avenue. Maybe a boat isn't a floating watercraft, maybe it's something from Honey Beans, but Bridgette breezes by the coffee shop like she doesn't even see it.

"Stop following me."

"I'm not letting you wander around by yourself when you're upset."

"Why do you insist on treating me like a little kid? I got all the way to Texas by myself."

My snarky mouth opens. "You got on an airplane. The pilot did the rest." And I immediately stick my foot in it.

She slams to a stop, turns, and jams her fists on her hips. "Why did I ever let you kiss me? What was it about your stupid hazel eyes that made me think you were the kind of man I want to spend more than five seconds with?"

"You chased me."

"And now you're chasing me. Funny how the tables have turned."

"Just tell me why you need a boat."

Her eyes pinch. "And you'll leave me alone?"

"Maybe."

"Ugh. You are so annoying. You're like the bad stray I can't get rid of."

She crosses Camino del Mar and jogs into the Bubee Yacht Club. So, she's looking for a real boat. I follow her to the reception desk outside the restaurant and bar area.

She leans across the desk and bats her eyelashes. "Do you rent boats?"

The concierge straightens the lapels on his navy blazer with one quick jolt. "No, ma'am. This is a members-only facility."

She smiles her sunflower smile as if she didn't hear the disdain dripping from his voice. "Do you know if anyone here might be willing to take me somewhere?"

"This isn't a fast-food restaurant, ma'am." He rises, steps around the desk, and ushers her toward the front door with a pushy hand on her shoulder. "If you don't know any members, I'm going to have to ask you kindly to leave."

I give him a condescending look of my own and step between them. "Bridgette, what are you doing?"

"I thought that was obvious." She cranes her neck to look in the bar. She points. "Oh, I know him. Bye." She strides into the bar and sits next to Theo Sanchez. "You're Dr. Sanchez, right?"

He swigs the clear liquid in his glass. His eyes trail across her face, and I can't decide if I want to punch him for the enthusiastic way she's looking at him or clap him on the back in congratulations for not letting his eyes wander down her body.

Neither thought is rational, and I shove my hands in my pockets to keep from doing something I'll regret. Theo's a good guy. I haven't had much opportunity to get to know him, but he and his family do great things for Bubee.

Theo extends his hand. "And you are?"

She shakes his. "Bridgette Christianson. I'm a friend of Georgi's."

"And she sent you here?" Hopefulness fills his tone.

Bridgette grimaces and rasps a strained laugh. "Oh, no. She would kill me if she knew I was talking to you."

His shoulders cave in. "Then why do I have the pleasure?"

"I need a ride to Willard Island. Can you help me with that?"

My ears perk. Willard Island? I cut between them. "Why do you need to go to Willard Island?"

She shoves me out of the way and trains her attention back on Theo. "Ignore him. So, can you? Take me, I mean."

"The sailboat can get you close, but the draft is too deep to navigate close to the island. We'll have to use the zodiac to get on shore."

She claps her hands. "Perfect." She weaves her arm through his and tugs him out of his seat. "Let's go."

I plant my palm on his chest to push him back down. "You are not getting on his boat."

She tosses her hair over her shoulder and yanks on him again. "You don't have a say in the matter."

Poor Theo's stuck like the rope in a game of tug-of-war. His eyes dart back and forth between me and Bridgette as we stare each other down.

"Why do you want to go to Willard Island?" I repeat.

Her eyes narrow. "You know why."

"The shack?"

She crosses her arms and bobs her shoulders. "So?"

"You were eavesdropping?"

"It's not like you were going to tell me anything I need to know. You've made up your mind about ..." Her eyes dart around the bar. "Him."

It's not crowded, but every ear is tuned to our argument. I appreciate her not spewing family secrets all over the place.

"That island is miles long. You have no idea where you're going."

"I'll figure it out."

Theo raises a finger, but I talk over him. He doesn't need to get mixed up in our spat. "Ours isn't the only place." There are a dozen houses sprinkled along the dunes. At this time of year, most of them will be boarded up.

"It's called a shack. I think I can figure it out." She plops in the chair next to Theo.

"Adding breaking and entering to your CV?"

Her chin juts forward, and her forehead wrinkles. "What's a CV?"

"It's like a resume but for doctors," Theo chimes in.

I scowl at him, but it's my fault for not using terminology that would be familiar to her. I'm so jealous of her getting on Theo's boat, I didn't watch what I said.

She swivels her chair, bumps her knee into my hip. "According to the handy search on my phone, the only way to get to that island is by boat. If you're going to be a baby and not tell me which shack is yours, you have to take me."

I take two steps back. "No."

"Either you take me, or he does. Either way, I'm going today."

I pull my hair until my scalp stings. "Bridgette you are ..."

She unfurls from her chair and drums her fingers along her pelvis. "I know what I am. I done apologizing for it. The way I am makes me formidable." She raises an eyebrow challenging me to contradict her.

But she's right. She is formidable. That's one of the qualities that makes her so appealing. She never gives up. She attacks problems with a vigor I applaud and envy.

"Are you going to cave and find me a boat or walk out the door and leave Theo and I alone?" She stares at me. Her lips press into a flat line waiting for me to make my inevitable decision.

I won't let her go with Theo. Not because of him. I run my hand around the back of my neck and pinch my eyes closed, tight.

I can't stomach the idea of her on a starlit cruise with anyone but me. I'm so in over my head. The hold she has over me eclipses my better judgment.

I want to say I'm drowning, and she's my life preserver, but I fear she's the ocean pulling me under.

"I'm not sure Gran's boat is even seaworthy, but we can check."

Chapter 20

Bridgette

Of all my reckless ideas, this might be the dumbest. Daisy's boat is a bath toy compared to the Sanchez's super yacht. Theo's boat would have had me at Willard Island in five minutes. Keegan's will make me a cast member on *Gilligan's Island*, but it will take twelve hours to sink instead of three.

I back away up the dock. "I'm sure Theo will still take me."

Keegan lifts his head from the compartment next to the big steering wheel. "Get on the boat."

"You're bossy." I'm not sure if I like it or not.

He spins the wrench in his hand. The muscles bunch and stretch in ways that make my mind wander and heat race to my cheeks.

"You either put up with my bossiness, or we don't go to the island."

What the heck is wrong with me? We just had a blowout fight and now I'm drooling. My stupid heart can't decide where it wants to fall concerning the sexy sous chef. "What do I need to do?"

"Inventory food and water. If we don't have enough for dinner, they should have everything up at the club. Tell them to put it on *Gypsy*'s tab."

"*Gypsy*?"

He knocks the wrench against the bench seat. "The boat is named *Gypsy*. Every boat has a tab."

"Is this your boat?"

He shakes his head. "No, in an ironic twist of fate, it was Turner's, but Gran took it over. She lets me borrow it from time to time."

"You do know how to drive this thing, right?"

"The term is sail. I can sail her to Australia if that's where you want to go."

"Touchy." I climb into the galley. I think that's the right word.

The boat is cozier than I expected, in a good way. Light pours in. Paperback novels line the headboard of the full-size bed in the boat's nose. A small table next to the kitchen is painted with a Scrabble board design, but the points are listed in M&M colors instead of numbers.

It would be a relaxing place to recharge after a grueling day in the bakery. In the secret part of my heart that I'm not even going to admit to myself—because I'm not a masochist—I imagine Keegan stretched out on the bed with his head cradled on his bicep. A single, long finger beacons me to join him. The mischievous smile on his face would make me run and jump into his arms.

But like I said, I'm not a masochist, so I ignore the burn low in my belly that thinks a night with Keegan would be a good idea. I don't dare to dream about a lifetime with him. We're too different. Too untrusting. Too confrontational.

A search of the cabinets amounts to three eight-ounce water bottles and stale saltines. That's not going to work.

There's a small convenience store next to the yacht club's restaurant. While Keegan and I fought over Theo, I watched a woman picked up a picnic basket out of the corner of my eye.

I snatch a menu. Yep, to-go ordering to the rescue. The waiter takes my sandwich order for our picnic dinner. While I wait, I grab several bottles of water, Cokes, pretzels, chocolate chip cookies, gummy worms, bananas, fruit salad, Oreos, and saltines. I snag a bottle of wine too because why the heck not.

I've never been on a boat before, so I also add Dramamine and ginger ale. I don't need to lower Keegan's opinion of me any further by puking off the edge of his boat ... his grandmother's boat ... Turner's boat.

The cashier charges me an extra two dollars for reusable bags with the Texas flag on them, and the stuffy front desk man carries them down to the dock.

Keegan's eyes bug out of his head. "Did you buy the whole store?"

I smile but don't let it reach my eyes. "Almost. Was there something you specifically wanted? I can go back."

"No." He climbs off the boat and wipes his grease-stained hands on a rag. "The boat is in good condition, but I checked the weather report. A storm's brewing. We can't go tonight. We have to wait until after class later in the week. Next Saturday would be best."

"Ha. No way. We made a deal." I jump the gap from the dock and the boat sways under my foot.

"Springs storms are unpredictable. It's not smart."

I look pointedly at my watch. "How long will it take us to get there?"

"An hour to an hour and a half."

"When is it supposed to storm?"

"Tonight."

God, keep my eyes from rolling out of my head. "Thank you, Mr. Specific. It's 2:15. Three hours round trip, plus an hour there. We'll be back in plenty of time."

He braces his foot on the boat railing and leans forward in what might be an intimidating posture but reminds me of the satiric Old Spice commercials with the guy pretending to be a pirate. Keegan looks just as foolish and non-piratey. "What do you hope to find?"

"Answers. Turner built the shack, so it has sentimental value. Maybe he left something."

"He hasn't been there in decades. None of his stuff is left."

"I have to try."

"Not tonight."

"Fine." I hop off the boat and scoop up the picnic basket. "Theo's boat is a better option anyway." I watch longingly as Theo cannonballs into his pool on the middle deck of his mega yacht.

Too bad Georgi thinks he's such a jerk, and he parades women through Honey Beans like show ponies. He seemed nice. Maybe not *nice*, but willing to help me annoy Keegan, which is a win in my book.

Keegan swats his rag against the side of his leg. "Big boats? That's what you care about? The bigger the better. Fancy trips, diamond rings. You're one of those."

"Those?" The word tastes vile on my tongue.

"The less refined term is gold digger."

"You keep thinking that, Keegan."

Why are the cute ones always so misguided? The only thing I like better about Theo's boat is that it will get us to the island faster. It will be more stable in a storm.

If Keegan didn't have such a low opinion of me, I would correct his illogical train of thought. I've never had money, and I've never been envious of lifestyles like Dr. Sanchez's.

Nothing sounds more isolating than a fancy trip without someone you care about. If nothing else, Theo looks as lonely as I was back home.

This could have been a fun evening. I'd love for Keegan to teach me to sail.

But the only thing sailing out of here is my hope that Keegan could get over himself.

His loss.

Hopefully, Theo will accept my picnic dinner as payment for the trip.

Keegan lets me get halfway across the dock before his fingers wrap around my elbow. "Please don't get on his boat." He says the please with the same tone of voice he used when he asked me to kiss him.

It's a pleading, hopeful, heartbreaking sound.

My eyes flutter to his lips, and the yearning in my chest rears its stupid head like a lion offered a T-bone.

"Please. If we leave now, we'll get back before the storm," he says.

I nod because I don't know what to say to the vulnerability poorly cloaked in his eyes. He's been so closed off and guarded since our first night on the beach. This peek into his soul calls to me, makes me curious and hopeful that he'll finally let me in the way I've wanted him to since we met.

He takes the picnic basket, his hand presses into the small of my back, and his thumb rubs small circles as we walk.

I carry the bags into the galley and store the food in the refrigerator and pantry space while he finishes futzing with the engine.

I want to read meaning into his touch. But as nice as it would be to stick my head in the sand and be blindly optimistic, I need to be pragmatic.

He called me a gold digger. He doesn't know me. He doesn't want to get to know me. He just doesn't want me near Theo. I need to resign myself to that sad fact and ignore how Keegan's thumb felt against my skin.

I straighten my spine and push away my longing. My fingers grip the banister, and I put my foot on the lowest step to climb above deck.

The boat lurches left, and I stumble. "What the heck?" I tighten my grip and pop my head out of the cabin. "What just happened?"

"We left dock."

"Warn a lady next time."

I climb the rest of the way on deck and sit on the bright blue cushion next to the steering wheel. Keegan stands with his feet braced against the bases of the benches. His arm relaxes over the top of the steering wheel. The afternoon sun kisses his pale cheeks, and the foolish pirate image is replaced by one that could be on the cover of a yachting magazine. "When did you learn to sail?"

"I was on this boat before I could walk."

"Must be nice." Even though I grew up on Lake Superior, we never went sailing. Mom and Dad aren't water people. Mom doesn't even like the bathtub.

Keegan and I pass a set of buoys into open water. He pulls some cords, and the sail unfurls, revealing a pink flamingo on a turquoise background. "Nice."

He shrugs. "My little sister picked it out."

Georgi told me about her. "Lane, right? Georgi said she's going to be a pediatrician."

"That's her plan."

"That's a lot of doctors for such a small town."

"Third Coast Regional Medical Center is here. We're the biggest hospital until you get to Houston."

"You have two doctors in the family? Georgi's sisters give yours a run for their money with their three."

"It's not a competition."

"My parents would disagree. They used to say they wanted a baseball team of kids. I was born, and they couldn't imagine taking care of more than one of me, I was such a handful." I hate the pensiveness in my voice. I shouldn't have said anything.

My gaze shifts out to sea as I swallow the guilt and discomfort weighing down my shoulders. It's no wonder my parents and I aren't close. They wanted a different life than they lived but didn't pursue it because my big personality overwhelmed them.

Keegan taps the wheel, drawing my attention back to him. "Do you want to steer?"

"Me?"

"No, the redhead sitting behind you."

I stick my tongue out but stand and grasp the steering wheel with both hands.

I expect him to take my spot on the bench, but he wraps his arms around me, so his chest presses against my back. His hands rest on top of mine, and he peels my fingers from their death grip. "Hold her the way you want to be held."

His breath tickles the side of my neck, and I squirm to brush off the sensation.

"What are you doing?"

"A little left." He applies pressure to my hand and guides me to steer the boat into a wave. My arms move with his prompting. "Great," he says. "We'll stay on this course for a bit."

His thumb is back in action, rubbing slow circles across my wrist as he applies gentle pressure to help me steer. I can't bring myself to destroy the peaceful moment. We aren't fighting. He trusts me with the boat. He told me a little about his sister.

It's progress.

This is what I want, what I've wanted since I met him at the bar. Being held in Keegan's protective arms with no other cares in the world besides enjoying his company as we get to know each other.

I settle into his embrace as clouds sweep overhead. The sail pulls us forward.

He whispers directions in my ear. "A little left. Watch the sail. Just like that. That's my girl." With every mile, I gain more and more confidence controlling the ship and contentedness wrapped in Keegan's arms.

I feel like I finally belong. Keegan and I might be able to share more adventures if he figures out how to trust me.

I've decided I don't care what other people think of me.

Turner was right. I can't pander to other people's expectations. It's not my fault Willa was uncomfortable and chose not to speak up. Making myself small doesn't help her find her strength. It encourages her to stay silent.

Keegan's cheek nuzzles the side of my head, and my hair sticks to his unshaven whiskers.

A pelican swoops across the boat, startling me, and my happiness splashes apart.

Keegan and I can't be like this.

His sexy hands don't get to make my brain sizzle like a grease fire. He can't whisper insinuations in my ear. It doesn't matter how good it feels to be cradled in his arms or how right this feels. Less than an hour ago, he called me a gold digger and I vowed not to be an ostrich with my head in the sand.

Romantic boat rides won't brainwash me from the unpredictable swings in his behavior.

I press my stomach to the steering wheel so I can't feel the heat from his chest radiating against my spine. "Please stop."

He squeezes my shoulders but doesn't comment on our snuggling. "Nice and easy. The wind's steady, so just keep her on this course for a bit." He climbs down the cabin stairs.

"Where are you going?" I hate the anxiety piercing my voice.

"I thought I'd take a nap."

"Don't you dare. Get back up here." If I wasn't so scared to take my hands off the steering wheel, I'd point to the spot right next to me. That way if anything goes wrong, I can jump out of the way, and he can save the day.

There's a look in his eyes that twists my stomach. I want to interpret it as a longing to do exactly what I asked. To stand close to me. To help me.

If that's what you want, then why did you step out of his arms? You don't believe he thinks you're a gold digger, right?

But a mischievous wink shatters that notion. "I'll be back."

"You are not the Terminator," I call after him.

His only response is a thumbs up over the edge of the hatch as he waves goodbye.

My knuckles whiten. He left me in charge of this behemoth. I called it a bath toy before, but I was wrong. I'm steering the Titanic, and even in the Gulf of Mexico, I'll find an iceberg.

My heart beats louder and louder, trying to burst from my chest.

I can't do this.

I can't control my temper, what makes me think I can control this boat?

We dip and weave. I try to tighten my grip, but there's no more strength. I'm at one hundred percent and don't have a hundred and ten.

I fix my gaze on the horizon.

Steady my breathing.

I have to do this.

I *can* do this.

I'm too much, so I'll be too stubborn to let a little thing like not knowing how to sail make me crumble. Keegan's words filter through my mind. "Hold her the way you want to be held. Follow the waves. Not too tight. That's my girl."

The salty ocean air tingles my nose and clears my mind. I relax my grip and cradle the steering wheel. I let it shift against my palms and give the ocean permission to glide the boat forward instead of muscling it against the current.

The call of seagulls replaces my heart banging in my ears, and I lift my face to the sun.

I am strong.

I am capable of great things.

I can do hard things because that's the kind of woman I am.

Keegan chuckles.

I don't open my eyes. I'm not ruining my blissful moment with his condescending smirk.

"You're a natural," he says.

"I'm ignoring you."

"I wish I could ignore you."

My eyes fly open. "What?"

He twists his gaze away from mine to the horizon. "Nothing."

"You can't unsay something like that. Why can't you ignore me?"

The sexual tension between us is a tightrope, so that part I get, but what about the rest? Yelling at me. Calling me dumb and deceitful. Gold digger. Are those his defense mechanisms because he's developing real, deep, scary feelings for me?

Or is the tension what he wishes he could ignore because he thinks I'm a gold digger?

"You know why." The wind whips his whisper away.

"You're mercurial, so I don't. One minute you're yelling at me and the next you're wrapping your arms around me. I need you to explain."

Kissing me, running away, staring at me across the classroom, yelling at me, chasing me to the marina. I wish I knew where his head was at. I wish he'd make up his mind.

"Want a Coke?" He holds the red can out to me.

I reach for it, just so he has to get closer. I want to see his eyes as he answers my question. "Tell me."

Unfortunately, he drops his gaze to his shoes. "You are an unstoppable force."

"A hurricane." Destructive, chaotic, unstoppable.

He shakes his head. He threads his fingers through my hair and traces his thumb across my jaw. "Gravity."

I can't hear the seagulls anymore.

Keegan thinks I'm *gravity*.

My fingers wrap around his forearm and will him to close the distance between us. He's called me so many things, but ... gravity ... anticipation and elation bubble in my stomach like the froth crashing against the nose of the boat.

He shakes his head and drops his hand from my face. "The closer I get, the closer I want to be. But if I get too close, you'll crush me."

Like I crushed Willa. "That's not a compliment. Why are you afraid of me?"

"I'm afraid of myself around you." He sips his drink and walks to the nose of the boat.

If this thing had cruise control, I'd follow him and ask him to explain himself. Before, I blamed myself for him walking away. I pushed too hard. I came on too strong. I didn't let him control our timing.

But ... he's afraid of himself? What happened to destroy his self-confidence?

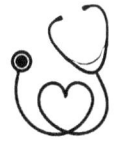

Chapter 21

Keegan

The wind pushed us past the barrier islands faster than I expected it to. The sun's still high as Bridgette and I approach Willard Island.

I drop the anchor offshore and lower the dinghy. Bridgette gathers the oars, food, and water from the cabin.

She hasn't pushed for me to open up after my slip earlier. Maybe she doesn't want my explanation. I'm not ready to give one. I shouldn't have held her while she sailed the boat. I should have stepped away and kept the buffer between us, but I didn't make myself.

Watching her with Theo cracked something in me. Something I need to name but am scared to.

Our family's shack sits at the southwestern edge of the island, amid dunes and seagrass. Wild horses roamed this stretch of beach a hundred years ago, and it's not too hard to get lost in the peaceful beauty of the place.

Somehow our little shack withstood everything nature has thrown at it over the last sixty years. Like all the other buildings along the coast, it's raised off the sand to prevent hurricane-level storm surge from washing it away.

Bridgette pauses at the bottom of the stairs and shakes the railing.

"I'll go first to make sure it's stable."

She juts her chin. "I'm fine." Her foot slides onto the first step. She sucks in a breath and marches up the stairs. The weathered boards need another coat of paint, but they don't creak as we make our way to the top.

I try not to stare at her butt, but my willpower hasn't improved since she climbed the stairs to the attic. Her curves are perfect. People pay my plastic surgeon colleagues thousands of dollars for what she has naturally. I appreciate her as the work of art she is.

Rust laces the edge of the combination lock, but with a little muscle, the dial spins and the hinge slides. I push the door open and step back to let Bridgette enter first.

What little we see through the door looks solid. The design is modest with clean, efficient lines. The front room doubles as the living room and kitchen, with bunkbeds in the room off the back. The wall facing the Gulf holds two picture windows perfect for framing the sunrise if we remove the storm shutters. Shelves and the dining table sit opposite. A place for everything you need, and no room for the things you don't.

The roof didn't leak. No plumbing and we didn't bring the generator, so the hot plate and lights won't work. We won't be here long enough to need them anyway.

We drop our bags, and I flick on a flashlight. There should be a battery-powered lantern around here somewhere. My light glints off the plastic on the kitchen counter, and I push the buttons to turn on the lantern.

No luck.

I search for batteries in the drawers and replace them. The room illuminates to reveal spiderwebs and at least four years' worth of dust.

Bridgette opens the first cabinet to her right and piles the contents on the floor.

"What are you doing?"

She gives me a look that can only be described as, *are you dumb?* "Looking for clues."

This is why we're here, but I'm still amazed by her tenacity. She's not even taking five minutes to enjoy the space. "Just make sure everything gets back where it belongs. We need to set sail in forty-five minutes." I leave her to her task and turn to wipe dust from the countertops and cobwebs from the furniture.

Bridgette sifts through playing cards, blankets, and flashlights. Pots, pans, and cereal bowls. When she puts things back in the sixth cabinet, she slams the door.

I could help, but she needs this. She needs to sort through everything, so she can't blame me for missing something. She'll see for herself that this was a waste of time.

She needs to ask Turner where he went if she wants to solve her mystery. Reuniting the family is never going to happen. There's too much anger and sadness between him and my grandmother.

That's what you get when you disappear from someone's life.

Bridgette moves on to the bunkroom. All she's going to find in there are rolled up sleeping bags, but it means she's almost done.

I kick my flip-flops off at the top of the stairs and walk to the water. I miss the warmth that tickles my toes the most when I'm home in Dallas.

Ocean breezes. Sand escaping from under my feet as the tide washes it away. The disconnected calm.

I could stay here forever.

Lightning strikes the water in the distance.

Thunderheads build over the ocean faster than they should.

I jog back to the shack and vault up the steps two at a time. "We need to leave."

"No!" She's surrounded by blankets, hangers, and a laundry basket.

"Sunflower, there was never anything here to find."

"Don't call me that."

"Sorry. It slipped out."

I haven't earned the right to use endearments with her. That would require me to name the emotions that swirl inside me when I'm with her, when I think about her late at night, when I imagine my future and Bridgette's part of it.

I'm terrified I know what those emotions are.

I don't trust myself to have them, to believe they're true and not an overeager manifestation of what I want to be true.

But naming my heart has to wait until she's safe again. We can't ride out the storm in the shack. It's too unpredictable. "We need to go."

"Keegan … I … why? Ugh. Never mind. There has to be something here. There's nowhere else to look."

The urge to yank her into my arms and hold her, take away the strain etched into her face, almost gets the better of me. Instead, I drag her onto the deck and point to the horizon. "If we leave right now, we can probably beat the storm to the Yacht Club."

"Probably?"

I grab our bags and lock the door. "The wind is moving faster than I'd like, so it will be close." I tug her down the stairs. "We'll come back another day."

She twists out of my grip. "I may not have another opportunity. Class days are getting longer, not shorter. I promised Amanda I'd go to her party next weekend." She grasps the front of my shirt. "Turner isn't who you think he is. I have to prove it."

"Why does this matter so much? Gran's been fine without him her entire life. She doesn't need him now."

"But he needs her. He's lonely."

"Then you need to call and talk to him. That has been the solution all along."

"He won't come."

"Why are you beating yourself up for people who don't care about each other?"

"It's not about them," she screams.

"Then what's it about?"

She collapses on the top step and buries her face in her hands. Her body heaves. I kneel on the step below her and tuck her wind-whipped hair behind her ears. "Sunflower, talk to me."

"It's too embarrassing. You'll think I'm ridiculous."

"Usually, your ridiculous is pretty cute."

That draws a smile from her, and she lightly shoves my shoulder. I wipe the single tear that escaped across her cheek.

"Turner treated me like a beloved granddaughter from day one. He accepted me, no questions asked. I need to return the favor. I need him to know he's loved as much as he loved me, even when I didn't deserve it."

"Everyone loves you."

"No, they don't. They tolerate me. They indulge me. I'm too much for most people, so they batten down the hatches until I move on. *Never forever*, that's me. Except with Turner."

"That's not how I see you."

"Too overbearing. Too inflexible. Other people have called me domineering and pushy. I don't care what you think of me, what anyone thinks of me—but ... but ... I need to fix Turner's reputation." Her shoulders sag. "I owe him." She barely whispers the last words.

I sit next to her, gently nudge her head onto my shoulders, and wrap my arms around her. "I'm sorry."

Bridgette *is* pushy, but it's not in an egotistical or self-centered way. She pushes people to be better versions of themselves. She pushes them to see beyond what's right in front of them to what could be. She pushed me to trust her even when it scared me.

"You are strong and forthright. I'm sorry I made you feel insecure because I didn't want to hear the truth." I brush my lips across her hair. "You're right. Gran should meet Turner. If he's half the man you make him out to be, we'd be crazy not to welcome him home. He deserves a chance."

Guilt washes from my chest to my stomach. I choke back bile. She's baring her soul, and I can't bring myself to tell her something as simple as my profession. There's no reason to keep it from her anymore.

I know who she is. I know her heart, and she would never use me the way Cynthia did. "Bridgette, we—"

"I know."

My heart jumps into my throat. "You know?"

Here I thought I'd done a good job avoiding conversations and distracting her from the fact that I'm a physician.

She strokes little circles on my thigh above the hem of my shorts. "I'm sorry."

"How did you find out?"

She lifts her head from my shoulder. "Find out? I'm watching the clouds."

The clouds. The storm. "Why are you sorry?"

"We can't get back in time, can we?"

The horizon morphed into premature dusk over the last ten minutes. If we hurry we might beat the storm. I'm not sure which is safer, racing the storm or weathering it here.

Maybe the better question is what happens if Bridgette and I stay in the shack overnight? Will being cut off from the rest of the world help me find the words to tell her all my secrets?

I want to find out.

"It's not safe to ride out the storm on *Gypsy*. Were there any supplies we can use inside?"

"There's another lantern and a bunch of candles."

"How'd the sleeping bags look?"

"I didn't unroll them."

"See what we can use to get us through the night. Will you be okay while I get *Gypsy* ready for the storm?"

She wraps her fingers around my arm. "Be careful."

I kiss her forehead. "Don't worry."

I row out to the boat, seal the hatches, check the anchor, and gather the supplies we'll need to ride out the storm in the shack. I radio the harbor master and let him know where we are, just in case. I was annoyed Bridgette bought so much food before, but now I'm thankful. Gummy worms and Oreos will make a great dinner as the rain beats down on the old tin roof and I find the words to tell her about Cynthia and my life in Dallas.

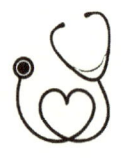

Chapter 22

Keegan

BRIDGETTE'S BUTT STICKS OUT of the storage space on the side of the shack when I get back from getting *Gypsy* ready for the storm. I'd love to stand here all day and watch her, but we don't have time. The storm's imminent, and we need to be ready. "Find what you're looking for?"

She rests on her heels. "No."

"What's in there?"

"Rusty shovels, a hammer, and an ancient surfboard."

I hold up the gummy worms. "Snack?"

"Might as well. I think a spider is laying eggs in my hair." She bends over and ruffles her hair.

How is she so calm if she thinks there's a spider in her hair? Most women—and men—would run around screaming, *get it out get it out* but never pausing long enough to find the critter.

Bridgette is definitely one in a million.

Nothing falls out of her hair. It has a mesmerizing windblown look now. Tendrils drape across her forehead. I shove my hand in the gummy worm bag so I don't clear the strands from her face.

She stretches her arms over her head. Her back pops as she twists side to side, giving me a brief glimpse of the soft, pale skin around her belly button.

For all her insecurity, Bridgette is completely comfortable in her skin. She's the kind of woman who doesn't care if the extra slice of Thanksgiving pie sticks to her hips. She cares more about the pleasure of the apples and cinnamon on her tongue.

She snatches the bag of gummy worms. "Should we call Daisy and let her know where we are?"

"No cell service. I radioed the harbor master and told him. What else do you need to search?"

"I don't know. I've looked through everything I can find inside. Are there any more storage lockers like this one outside?"

"No." I lift the rest of our bags.

It's time to tell her about my job. First, I should apologize for my behavior. I can't believe I called her a gold digger. I know better. In truth, she deserves better, but I'm hoping against hope I haven't ruined everything already.

Friendship and forgiveness first. Build trust, then see where the relationship takes us.

She crosses her ankles. "Where's the bathroom?"

"The ocean."

"You've got to be kidding me." She stuffs gummy worms in her mouth.

"There used to be an outhouse about a half a mile down the beach, but it washed away in the last hurricane. No one ever rebuilt. Most people don't come out here anymore. They prefer the more civilized beaches close to town."

"What am I supposed to do? I didn't bring a bathing suit."

"Skinny dipping is always an option."

If the storm weren't imminent, and I hadn't told myself we were going to take this relationship nice and slow, I might recommend a moonlit swim.

She circles her finger in my face. "I see those wheels turning. Not on your life, buster."

"You can use the rusty shovel to dig a hole like a Boy Scout."

She grabs the shovel. "This is humiliating."

I climb the stairs and give her privacy.

She disappears for ten minutes. When she comes back, I don't ask. Raindrops speckle the front of her top, molding it to her chest.

I swallow the lump in my throat and busy myself unpacking our food. Thunder rumbles, and dust floats from the rafters.

She squints at the roofline. "Was there a loft?" She points to the beams crisscrossing the peaked ceiling.

"Not as long as I've been alive, but someone may have modified it before then."

She climbs onto the dining table and stretches her arms to reach the beam. The legs totter, and she scratches at the wood for balance.

I drop our water bottles and race to her. "Hey, get down." I grip her waist to steady her and the table. If she falls and hurts herself, I can't get her to a hospital quickly.

I didn't bring my first aid kit. All we have are the minuscule supplies that were already on the boat: bandages, alcohol wipes, and antibiotic cream. Those won't do anything for a broken leg, concussion, or internal bleeding.

"It's fine. Calm down." She slides her hands over the wood, flexes her fingers, and swings her leg over the ledge, pulling herself to sit on top of the beam.

She flashes her sunflower smile down at me. "See."

She inspects the ceiling and beam she's sitting on, digging her fingers where the two meet as if she's trying to loosen something.

"Don't put a hole in the roof."

She holds her hands out. "If I can destroy it with my little hands, it's not structurally sound anyway, and we should take our chances with the storm." She gestures around the room. "It doesn't look like there's water damage in here, so it'll be fine."

"What are you doing?"

"Looking for hiding spots."

Her search is moving past ridiculous, but I'm going to keep my mouth shut and savor the peace we've established.

"Aha." She scoots to another beam and rotates onto her back with her head next to the eaves. She's digs at something, but I can't tell what from down here. When she sits up, she clutches a stack of envelopes to her chest. "I knew it looked weird up here. The beams aren't aligned. There's a gap here full of letters."

She lowers herself to the ground. A self-satisfied smirk dances in her eyes. "My turn for I told you so."

"You haven't opened them yet. You don't know what they are."

She sticks her tongue out and sits on top of the table.

I tug her foot. "Come here. I want to see too."

Her eyebrow arches. "Oh, now you care?"

I level my gaze at her. "We've come this far together. No reason to stop now."

"Fine." She hands me the stack and climbs down. She rubs her arms.

"Cold?"

She gestures to my board shorts and T-shirt. "Aren't you?"

"This way." I unroll a sleeping bag on the lower bunk bed and unzip another to use as a blanket. "Climb under."

The wind batters the shack. Rain pounds against the roof and storm shutters relentlessly. *Gypsy* is likely being tossed like a cork in a blender outside.

Here, side by side, we're protected and insulated from everything. The drama of Cynthia's lies, Bridgette's ex, Jake's cancer.

Nothing can hurt us.

She gently opens the top letter. "It's from Turner to someone he called Gypsy." She presses her fingertips to her lips. "It's a love letter!"

She reads it out loud. "16 July 1966

My darling Gypsy,

Deployment orders arrived this morning. We depart in three weeks. I'm forbidden to share where we're going. It's for the best anyway. I don't want you to worry if you hear reports of fighting near my platoon. I promise to keep myself safe.

I'm glad it's finally our turn to leave base. Watching other platoons rotate in and out makes me feel worthless. Why am I here if not to fight?

I know you don't like my melancholy, or that I'm here, so I'll leave my sentiments to those. It's supper time. I'll drop this in the mail as soon as I can. Give my love to my sister.

Always yours,

Turner

Bridgette turns wide eyes on me. "He was in love with someone. Daisy knew who." She shakes the letter at me.

I leaf through the rest of the letters. There have to be over fifty in the stack. Some from Turner, some from this the mysterious Gypsy. "These are private. We shouldn't read them."

"Why not? It's not like Turner's coming back for them. This is the break I've been looking for. Maybe something happened with Gypsy that made him leave base?"

"A lot can happen in a year. Maybe they'd already broken up."

"Reading these is the only way to find out."

"Bridgette, we can't invade their privacy."

I would hate if someone pried into my love life without my consent.

We do and say stupid things when we're deceived by love.

We don't think rationally. I didn't.

If I'd written letters to Cynthia, none of what I would have written at the beginning of our relationship is true anymore. We can't rely on Turner's sentiments for Gypsy to be anything more than lovesick ramblings. How do I get Bridgette to understand that?

She clutches the letter to her chest. "I thought you wanted to help me find the truth?"

"Not like this."

She tears open the next letter. "You thought Turner's reason to disappear for a week was going to be something innocuous like a broken-down car, didn't you?"

"Well, no." I never thought we'd find the truth.

"You don't have to read along." She unfolds the next one and my eyes track with hers as we read the next letter.

22 October 1966

My darling Gypsy,

Our weekend pass was a kick. I spent an entire day following Kurt from ladies' shop to ladies' shop looking for the perfect birthday gift for his wife. He settled on a light pink dress you would love. Little blue flowers line the hem of the skirt. They remind me of the ones you painted on the tea set two summers ago.

My stomach twisted watching Kurt smile so big when the saleswoman handed him the bag with his purchase. I wish I could buy you such an extravagant gift. I'm still saving to buy you a wedding ring, my darling, one with a stone the size of Texas.

Besides, we both know your father would never let me send you such a personal gift. He won't even let me post this letter to you. I hate that we have to hide. Someday, I will be the lucky man who showers you with everything you desire for all the world to see.

Until that day, know you have my entire heart.

Always yours,

Turner

"See." She points to the final paragraph. "Scandal is the only reason he would leave the Army. Scandals don't get any more salacious than secret love affairs."

Thunder shakes the tin roof, and wind howls across the beach. She's right about the letters being the clue she needed. But who was Gypsy?

Bridgette and I read letter after letter, the romantic picture crumbling with each new missive.

12 November 1966

Turner, my love,

I don't need expensive gifts or a ring the size of Texas. I just need you home. Daisy read me the letter you sent your mother. They cried all the way through it. You'll be proud of me for maintaining my composure, but we miss you.

We hate to hear how dangerous the fighting is and how many men are dying unnecessarily. I still don't understand why you didn't take the college deferment like your friends. Jake is home every other weekend. There are plenty of other boys willing to fight.

Thanksgiving is coming. We'll be dining with your family again. I'll save you a slice of pie.

Please be safe.

Forever,

Gypsy

I point to Jake's name. "We never talked to Jake about Turner. Do you think he knows why my great uncle disappeared? Does he know who Gypsy was?"

"Why did she use a nickname, but Turner didn't?" Bridgette opens the next envelope.

25 December 1966

My darling Gypsy,

Merry Christmas, my love. As I sit here in our mosquito-infested camp, I realize this is the first Christmas I've spent without you since we were children. If tradition stands, you and my sister exchanged gifts last evening, and today you'll join the rest of the choir to carol around town.

I would give anything to hear your sweet voice sing to me.

There are so many words I wish to write, but I can't bring my pen to the paper to describe what I'm experiencing here. I won't put those images on your soul as they are burned into mine.

This isn't a very Christmasy letter. I'm low on paper, so I can't crumble it and start over. You deserve a Merry Christmas, not this dreary missive. I apologize and beg you to remember the cheerful times we had last Christmas.

Know that I love you. I long to hold you. There are rumors my platoon will rotate home next summer. I hold out hope.

Always yours,

Turner

Bridgette presses the page to her chest. "He's so sad."

I slip the pile from her hands. "The rest of them don't have postmarks."

She reads the next one out loud.

11 February 1967

My darling Gypsy,

I feel a little silly writing a letter I'll never send. At this point, I write more for myself than for you. I need to keep my connection to the man you love, the man I used to be, the man I hope to be again.

Things are different than I expected them to be here. It's little things. It's so hard to keep my feet dry. I miss the minty toothpaste I use at home. I miss the rhythmic waves crashing against the hull of my boat when we sail.

I don't tell you about the fighting because I know you don't want to hear it, and I can't bring myself to write the words.

I miss you. I miss your laughter. I miss your sassy little jabs when I do something stupid. I miss your lips. I know it's probably hard for you to not hear from me again, but my silence is for both of us.

Silence is better than having you learn I'm not the man I want to be for you. I'm not strong enough. Everything will be okay when I get home. We will rebuild our relationship and start our happily ever after on a solid foundation.

Always yours,

Turner

Bridgette brushes her finger under her eyelid. "He kept writing, but he never sent the letters."

Thunder rattles more dust from the rafters. Bridgette flinches and draws closer to my side.

I wrap my arm around her, comforting her as she reads Turner's history, and it breaks her heart.

"War does things to people. It changes them in unexpected ways," I say.

"You sound like you have firsthand experience. Were you in the military?"

"No, but I ..." Now would be a good moment to tell her about my career, but I don't. The weariness in her eyes over Turner's doomed relationship is enough of a burden for her right now. I'll wait for a more opportune moment when she's not already heartsick and can hear me with an open mind.

"I've worked with a lot of veterans." I pick the letter from the bottom of the stack. "Read this one next."

"You don't want to know what happened in between?"

"I'm pretty sure this one tells us everything we need to know." I point to the date. "He wrote it while he was missing."

15 April 1967
Mrs. August Buchanan,
Bridgette's eyes bulge. "That's Dotty! She was his Gypsy."

This is the last letter I will write. In all honesty, it was hard to address it to your married name, but you aren't my darling anymore. You aren't my Gypsy. You haven't been for some time, it appears.

And I know that's my fault.

I should have sent the letters I wrote. I should have continued to tell you that I love you and begged you to wait for me. I won't explain why I didn't. You don't want to hear my excuses.

I'm sorry I upset you. I know today was supposed to be full of happiness, but I needed to try and explain. I hoped maybe it would be enough, but ...

I'm taking Daisy's advice and leaving Texas for good. I won't burden you with seeing my good-for-nothing face every day once this war is over.

I don't know where I will end up. First, I have to face the consequences of my actions. I'm sure there's a court martial in my future, but at the moment I can't bring myself to care.

I didn't know a broken heart would hurt this badly. As I sit at the shack I built for us, the life I thought we would have crumbles like a sandcastle. The children we would raise, the dreams we would create, your laughter when we're eighty. They wash away with the tide. A silent tomb for our love.

I'm not sure what else to say besides I'm sorry, and I wish you the best of luck with August. He's a good man. I understand why you chose him and would not run away with me. He will never abandon you like I did. You made the right decision.

~~Alw~~ Best wishes,

Turner

Tears gather on Bridgette's eyelashes. "Do you think he ever gave this to her?"

"Probably not if it's here with the rest of his unsent letters."

She rubs her sternum. "My heart is breaking for him. He thought he was protecting her, and instead, he drove her away."

"You can't ignore somebody for months on end and expect them not to react." I leaf through his other letters. He wrote almost every week. Sometimes two or three times, but he never let her know he was safe. Never told her he loved her despite their separation.

Bridgette shakes her head. "But to marry one man when you're in love with someone else? That's big."

"What makes you think she didn't love August?"

Dotty and August were a fixture in our home growing up. They doted on each other. I would have never guessed they weren't happily married.

She looks down her nose. "Turner broke her heart, so she picked someone safe. She knew she couldn't love August completely. It gave her the freedom to protect herself but still live part of the life she wanted."

"That's callous." August and Dotty loved each other. At least from an outsider's perspective, it looked like they did.

But we can never know what's happening in someone else's relationship, can we? I know from personal experience. Everyone thought Cynthia and I were perfect. They didn't know she was manipulative and demanding, or that I was distant and distracted.

"You should have heard her talking about August at brunch. He was a comfortable partner, not the love of her life." She tucks the letters into their envelopes. "Do you know what it feels like to be in love?"

I flinch. I don't want to answer her question. I wanted to be in love. I'd hoped Cynthia would be my *one* when we started dating, that was why I told her so many secrets so quickly, but we soured even faster.

Bridgette tips her head, waiting for my answer, so I give her a half-truth. "I haven't found the person I want to spend the rest of my life with."

As I say the words, staring into her eyes, I wonder if I'm wrong.

If I can get over my fears completely and love Bridgette the way I've always wanted to love a woman, all of the heartache of the last few months might have been worth it.

Side by side, her hip pressed into mine, my eyes trace the slope of her nose, the bow of her mouth, the angle of her jaw. She's breathtaking.

When I add in her loyalty, humor, charisma, and unstoppable work ethic, I know she's unlike anyone else I've ever met. She's earned my trust one impulsive, driven, confident moment at a time.

Only someone with a will as strong as gravity could have pulled me from my guilt-ridden, untrusting shell.

She did.

Being completely authentic proved she's the woman I need.

My hand drifts to her knee. She tilts her shoulders, and her hair falls across my chest. I tuck the strands behind her ear and tip her chin. "Please, can I kiss you again?"

"I thought you were afraid."

"Not anymore."

She leans forward and captures my mouth. Her arms thread around my neck, and I lose myself in the beat of her heart against my chest.

Her kiss is stabilizing. It takes the swirling unknown of the last several months and drops everything unimportant to the ground like the wind stilling after a tornado. There's still wreckage, but there's the promise of a better tomorrow as well.

Promise and passion and sincerity.

Dreams I stopped dreaming because I couldn't trust people. Couldn't trust myself.

I trust Bridgette.

The storm rages outside, but everything in my heart is finally clear.

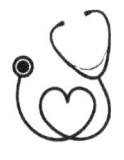

Chapter 23

Bridgette

KEEGAN KISSES ME LIKE it's an Olympic sport and he's devoted his life to winning the gold medal. I will give him thousands of medals if he keeps kissing me like this.

His enthusiasm matches mine. His strong hands thread through my hair. His hungry lips caress my skin. His fervent devotion captures my heart.

No one has ever made me feel this wanted and desired.

His mouth angles over mine, caressing my lips to deepen our kiss to a steady rhythm. I practically purr in response.

I love that kissing Keegan is about us being together. I'm safe, comfortable in my skin as the biggest, loudest, most enthusiastic version of myself.

I love who I am, and Keegan has become secure enough to stand beside me and let me be me without feeling eclipsed or diminished.

Lightning sizzles and thunder crashes outside, the wind chucks sand against the windows and bangs on the roof. I flinch into his chest.

Keegan pulls my attention from the shack's structural integrity to his desire-glazed eyes. "I should probably feed you." He trails kisses along my jaw.

"I won't turn down food, but it's not a priority."

He kisses the tip of my nose. "We have time."

Do we?

Time tonight? Time before I go back to Emerald Bay, and he goes back to Dallas?

Or time in the grand scheme of a relationship that doesn't have to have an expiration date because it's that amazing?

Is that where we are?

Is that where I want us to go?

Two make out sessions, and I'm ready to start thinking in terms of decades instead of days?

Do I want that last thought to be a question or a statement?

Two make out sessions and I'm ready to think of my relationship with Keegan in terms of decades instead of days. Period. End of thought.

If my best friend told me something so silly, I'd check her for a fever or a lobotomy.

But it's not just the kissing. It's all the moments in between. It's how safe I feel when I'm with him. It's his loyalty to his grandmother. It's him looking at me like he sees decades too.

He could be my forever. He could be the greatest adventure of my life—and I could be his. And that doesn't terrify me like it probably should given his inconsistent behavior.

But I don't care. I want to bask in the glow of what falling in love with Keegan feels like.

Is this love? No.

It's falling. It's the journey toward a love that lasts decades.

We piece together our meal and eat quietly at the table. The melody of the storm plays like a scratchy vinyl record in the background.

I lick sauce off my thumb. Keegan's eyes heat watching my every movement. I rise to my tiptoes, lean across the table, and kiss him again. "I like you a lot, against my better judgment."

"Your better judgment, huh? Why is that?"

I nip his lip. "Can you blame me? Our relationship hasn't exactly been smooth."

He hooks his foot around the leg of my chair and drags me to his side of the table. "I promise to do better. I'm sorry I didn't tell you about myself before. You deserve better, but I hope you'll give me a chance to make amends."

I trace my finger along his forearms. Pressure builds in my stomach dreaming about what amends might look like. "I just need you to talk to me."

He grips my hips and plops me across his lap. "It's hard to talk when you look at me like that." His lips press against my throat and work their way across my collarbone to my shoulder. "You taste like the ocean."

"That's a good thing?"

"It's fantastic." His breathy voice flutters against my skin, eliciting tingly goosebumps. "The ocean is my second favorite thing in the world."

"What's your first?"

He nips at my neck. "This, here, with you. We should stay a while."

"I can be persuaded." My hands roam his back and massage the tight muscles at the base of his skull.

He laces my fingers with his and brings them to his chest. "Texas doesn't have the best beaches, but they're my favorite because they're home. Sharing this with you makes it even more special."

I tip his chin and draw his forehead to mine. "You surprise me."

"Why?"

"You have a romantic heart, but you hide it. I don't understand why."

"Not exactly manly."

He leans in to capture my mouth again, but I lean back. "No, that's not the reason. If you were worried about being manly, you wouldn't spend your free time with your grandmother."

"I just want the free peach cobbler. I have a new source now, don't I? Gran will be disappointed she won't see me as often."

I scrub my fingers along his scalp. "You're such a dork."

He groans. "But you like this dork. What does that say about you?"

"I must be a dork too." A dork who's falling hard and fast for this man.

His hands slide up my thighs. "You're too beautiful to be a dork."

"Why can't pretty people be dorks?"

"You can be whatever you want, I just don't think you're a dork. Dorks lack the social charm that radiates from you like electrons from the sun."

His words bring heat to my cheeks. "Even your compliments are dorky. I love it."

His body stiffens at my words.

The L-word. He's afraid of it. *Noted*.

He scrubs his hands up and down my arms. "I think the rain stopped. Are you cold? Still hungry? We should check on the boat." His shoulders hold new tension.

I'll have to watch how I say things from now on if one little L-word scares him so easily.

He lifts me, and I climb off his lap and open the front door. The storm has passed, and brilliant stars dance across the night sky. "I love being away from all the light pollution."

He leans against the door frame next to me. "Me too."

I step to the edge of the porch and settle my forearms on the railing. The darkness pushes my fear away. This high, I can't see the ground, so I can't be afraid of plummeting to my death.

The ocean is peaceful. A quarter moon provides enough illumination to tell the boat is where we left it.

I turn to face Keegan and lift myself onto the railing. "What made you pick Dallas?"

The beams creak under me. Something shifts. Pops sound like firecrackers below us.

"Bridgette!" Keegan screams.

The only thing I see is the fear in his eyes as they disappear above me.

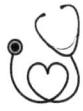

Keegan

Sand and wood particles coat Bridgette's unmoving body in the dim moonlight. "Bridgette!" I scream her name over and over, my heart like a foghorn in my ears, but she doesn't show any signs of life.

I can't tell if she's breathing under the debris. She's stomach-deep in sand and broken two-by-fours from the deck. Her arms, head, and torso haven't moved since the dust settled.

Miraculously, the stairs are intact. I gingerly press my weight onto the top step. It creaks but holds. The last thing we need is for me and the rest of the shack to collapse on top of her.

One step at a time, I crawl down the stairs, spreading my weight so they don't detach from the pylons.

My feet hit the sand, and I scramble closer to her on my hands and knees. Is there a sink hole?

How did it even collapse? It was fine before.

Did the wind weaken the structure? Did the rain push enough sand against the supports that they shifted? If I get too close, will the pile shift and suck her deeper?

It doesn't matter. I have to get to her. I have to know. Can I save her? Or is it too late?

Puffs of air swirl dust around her nostrils.

She's alive. *Thank heavens.*

Relief hits me, but I don't relax. Too much adrenaline. Too much fear. Too much shame at my failure to protect her.

I have to get her out of here before I can feel real relief.

A new wave of adrenaline hits me, and I triage the situation.

She's breathing. I stretch across the wood separating us and press my fingers to her carotid artery. Her heart rate is strong and stable. No apparent head wound or upper extremity fractures.

I run my fingers over her scalp. "Bridgette, sunflower. I need you to wake up and talk to me."

She moans, turns her head. "I hate heights."

I grin. "They don't like you much either." I squeeze her hand. "Sunflower, squeeze my fingers."

She does.

"Does anything hurt?"

"Does everything count?"

"I'm glad you didn't break your sense of humor." That's a good sign. If she'd broken a bone or was bleeding internally, she wouldn't be cracking jokes.

Unless the damage is so catastrophic, she's in shock and bleeding out ... but we're going to assume door number one until proven otherwise.

She lifts her head and flops onto her back. "I want to file a complaint with management. Your deck sucks."

"We need to get you out of here. Can you move?"

"I think so." She blinks to clear the last shreds of unconsciousness from her brain and braces her hands against the boards at her hips and shoves. She doesn't move. "My foot is pinned." The boards next to her sink deeper into the hole.

"Don't move."

I slide around the pile and examine the pieces. It's the highest stakes game of Jenga I'll ever play. One wrong move and instead of the pile clattering to the table, Bridgette will be maimed, sucked underground like quicksand, and I won't be able to put the pieces back together to start over.

"I'm going to pull boards out. Tell me immediately if anything moves or pinches or ... just anything."

Fear settles in her eyes.

I cup her cheek. "I'll take care of you. You trust me, right?"

She nods.

I press a swift kiss to her lips. I grab the first boards and throw them as far as I can from us. Thank you, stress-relief-gym sessions.

Never thought I'd have to use my strength for anything more strenuous than hauling Jake's meat from the truck to the fridge, but here I am.

Our progress is slow. Bridgette lifts herself and slowly shifts so her hips are visible, then half her right thigh.

"My foot's stuck. I can't get out." She whimpers. Fear and fatigue make her shiver.

I lay my upper body across the boards at the edge of the hole. "I'm going to reach in and see if I can free you. When I move the board, pull yourself up next to me."

My fingers glide down her thigh, past her knee, to her calf. I stretch and twist. I feel the end of the jagged board wedging her foot. My hands don't have the strength to move the board on their own. I need to move deeper into the hole. My feet brace against the boards on the sand, and I reach deeper, trying to get enough leverage so my biceps can move the board.

The pile shifts. Lancing pain shoots down my arm to my fingers. Reflexes take over, and I rip my arm back to my chest. "Ack."

"Keegan!" Bridgette's face pales. Her mouth gapes. "You're bleeding."

"We have to get you out." I try to extend my left arm, but the pain intensifies down to my fingertips and up into my eardrums. A jagged tear bisects my antecubital fossa and anterior arm. Blood flows freely from my elbow into the sand. "I need to free you."

"It's fine. I'll do it. Your arm can't—"

"I'm saving you." I clench my left fist and hug my arm to my chest.

I'll do this one-handed. With my non-dominant hand. In the middle of the night, with only moonlight and the faint cast of the lantern glow out the shack's front door.

Why didn't I grab the lantern? It doesn't matter.

Do no harm.

Bridgette trusts me to keep her safe.

I can't let her down.

I settle myself over the pile. "On three, I'll pull the beam and you crawl out. Okay?"

"But your arm."

"I'll be fine. It's just a little cut. It looks worse than it is," I lie.

Her eyes pinch, but she doesn't fight me. Every moment we bicker is more blood dripping from my body, mixing into a slurry in the sand.

I reach deeper into the pile, wary of invisible nails and jagged boards but determined to see this through. "One. Two. Three." I lift the board, and she tugs her leg. Not much moves, but it's something.

"Again. One. Two. Three." I tug, and she lifts. Her knee slides past my arm, and she scrambles out of the debris, pulling me behind her.

We collapse onto the sand. My uninjured arm wraps around her, and my lips find her forehead, and I don't stop myself from kissing her.

She's clammy, but she isn't stuck in that awful pit anymore.

She's safe.

Well, safer.

She presses up onto her elbow and cups my face. "Are you okay?"

"Fine."

"But your arm ..." Her eyes dart across my face, down my torso, to my arm. "Keegan!"

The world's a little hazy, so I'm not sure why she's screaming so loud.

She shoves my shoulder. "Keegan. Wake up. I need your help. It's a lot of blood."

I glance down at my arm. "I've seen worse. I had a patient once lacerate his femoral artery. That was a lot of blood."

She blinks like she didn't hear me correctly. "You had a what?"

I sit up and pull my shirt over my head. It's dirty and gross, but whatever. I wrap it around my arm, and now she can't see the wound, so she'll stop freaking out. I run my hands over her arm, down her ribs, to her hip. Her pants are torn, and angry red scratches mar her beautiful thigh.

"Can you move your ankle?"

She grabs my hands, so I stop feeling her up. She has nice legs. I'm glad we saved them.

She twists my face to look at my arm. "Keegan. I appreciate you taking care of me, but you need to let me take care of you right now. You're bleeding. Badly."

"It's just my median cubital vein. Probably. If it was the brachial artery, I'd be dead already."

I didn't think her face could get any paler, but it does. "We need to get you inside and clean this up. Stop the bleeding."

"It's not safe."

She levels a flat glare at me. "Where's the first aid kit?"

I slump. *Ugh*. One of us has to go inside. I have to climb the rickety stairs and grab our stuff and get her to the boat. No more romantic stargazing for us.

"Yeah, upstairs." She loops my good arm over her shoulder, and we struggle to stand. "Come on, big boy."

"I'll go." I lift my arm from her shoulders, but the world wobbles, and she grips me tighter.

"You can't stand by yourself, and I can't fix your arm without more light."

Her arm around my waist feels nice.

Why's my brain so fuzzy?

Have I lost that much blood already? *Nah*.

Maybe this is what it feels like to come down after your body dumps so much epinephrine into your arteries you could outswim Jaws if you wanted to.

And then maybe wrestle a grizzly bear. I could totally do that right now.

"One foot after the other, buster." She leads me to the stairs.

Fear flashes in her eyes as she looks from the bottom step to the top. She grabs the railing and shakes. It doesn't move.

Warm rivulets slide down my elbow and plink on the step.

"Up you go."

We slowly make our way up the stairs and into the shack. She deposits me on the dining chair and scrambles around the kitchen grabbing water, the first aid kit, and the gummy worms.

"Eat these." She shoves a worm into my mouth.

I chew dutifully. The sour sugar clears my brain a little. I rest my arm on the table and cautiously unwrap my T-shirt.

The cut isn't that bad. It's long, but not deep. I flex and extend my fingers. Flex and extend, pronate and supinate my wrist. The pain brings tears to my eyes. I don't want to break the clots already forming, so I stop examining myself.

Her hands flutter over the supplies like she's not sure where to start.

"Grab a bowl." Gran will be upset if I get blood all over the floor.

More blood.

Bridgette goes straight to the cabinet. That's the nice thing about her search earlier—she already knows where everything is.

I lay my arm over the bowl and pour water over the wound. I won't be able to get all the sand out of it without better disinfecting and debridement equipment, but it's something.

"Grab the antibiotic cream. We don't have any sterile swabs, so just squirt it over the top."

She does as I say. Her lip trembles.

I lift her chin so I can get a better look at her face in the light. "What's wrong?" Did I miss a bruise? Does she have a head injury I couldn't see under her mass of blonde hair?

"How do you know how to do this?"

"I ..."

She blinks at me. The color has returned to her cheeks, but now there's a wariness in her gaze. She nibbles her lip. "How do you know about median cubital veins and brachial arteries? What did you mean when you said you had a patient ... I don't even remember what you said happened ... how do you know all of this?"

"Would you believe I was a Boy Scout?"

She shakes her head and snatches the gauze from the table. "Right. Because every Boy Scout knows those things." There's so much bitterness in her voice, it hurts to take my next breath.

"I'm an orthopedic surgeon."

"Of course, you are. How stupid of me not to realize that sooner." She wraps the gauze around my arm, pulling tighter than necessary. "Are you the grandson who burnt the turkey?"

"Yeah."

"Awesome."

"Bridgette ... I ..." How do I even begin to explain why I didn't tell her the full truth? Even without the pain and blood loss making it hard to think clearly, I wouldn't have the words.

"No. I get it." She pastes on a fake smile. "Gold-digging, husband-hunting, untrustworthy stranger. I chased you up the beach when you didn't want to have anything to do with me and then showed up in class unannounced. Top it all off with me living in your grandma's carriage house. Hunting to reunite a brother and sister who don't want anything to do with each other. I wouldn't trust me either. Smart move." Her tone is dead.

I've killed us.

My reasons for keeping my career a secret seemed so valid before.

"I wanted to tell you—"

"Do *not* lie to me." She tucks the tail of the gauze into the top. "That should hold. Time to get you to the hospital." She stalks to the kitchen and shoves the rest of our food into a bag. "Eat this." She tosses me a package of salami and a bottle of water.

She adds Turner's letters to the top of our bag.

I grab the blankets. "Can we talk, please?"

Her jaw flexes, and she stops scurrying around the shack long enough to give me a withering look. "I don't have it in me to listen to you right now. It's taking everything in my power not to scream. I can't get us back without your help. You will tell me how to sail *Gypsy* to the marina. I will get you to the hospital. When you're taken care of, I never want to speak to you again."

I didn't think I could see someone's heart break in their eyes, but I'm watching it in Bridgette's. They're little windows to her soul, and she's fracturing like a femur crushed by an oak tree.

I can't put the pieces back together.

It doesn't matter how many rods, plates, pins, or screws I use. It will never be what it was before.

One little omission shouldn't matter this much, but it was the perfect storm of my fear crashing into hers.

I didn't trust her, and that was the only thing she needed from me.

She shoulders the bags and walks away.

She doesn't realize my heart is as shattered as hers.

But after what I've done, she probably thinks I deserve it.

Chapter 24

Bridgette

IN THE MOONLIGHT, THE rowboat sits upside down on the beach with sand piled against the hull. Keegan paws at the grains.

I pull him away. "Save your strength to tell me how to drive the boat. I'll do this."

"I'm fine."

"You're swaying on your feet." I gently nudge him to the ground.

I scoop handful after handful away from the bottom. The exertion helps temper my dark mood and the sucker punch that steals my breath every time I think about Keegan being a doctor.

Not just any doctor. An orthopedic surgeon.

I can't believe he lied to me. I can't believe he didn't tell me something so simple about himself. Why didn't he trust me with the barest fact about who he is?

He devoted years to training. His life is about healing people. Why didn't he want me to know?

Because I was honest with him, that's why.

If I'd lied and kept my insecurities to myself that first night, he might have told me.

But I opened my stupid mouth and told him about Graham.

Never forever.

It's my self-fulfilling prophecy.

Find a good man who's kind, loyal, intelligent, achingly handsome. Show him my flaws and the crevices in my armor, and he uses them against me.

Every.

Single.

Time.

I'm a fool for thinking something was growing between us. If he couldn't—wouldn't—tell me what he does for a living, there's no hope for a relationship.

But we never had a relationship, did we?

We had tension and attraction.

We had kisses on a secluded beach.

I let my desire get the better of me. I was lulled into a stupor when he called me gravity. Turner's broken romance made me susceptible to Keegan's whispered words and the storm's hypnotic romance.

I ignored Keegan's hurtful comments and lack of trust.

I believed him when he apologized, but the apology was incomplete. He didn't actually trust me. He was just sorry for being mean.

Aches and pains set in from my fall. How did I fall twenty feet, and he's the one with the life-threatening injury? Karma, perhaps.

I dig the boat free and slide my fingers under the edge. Keegan appears at my side. "It will take both of us to flip this thing."

"You can't. You'll hurt yourself."

"Stop arguing with me. I'm helping."

"Your arm will start bleeding again." I may be mad, but I don't want him to die.

"If you try to turn the boat and drop it, we have no way to safely get to *Gypsy*. Then where am I?"

I suck my lips between my teeth and count to twenty. He's right. I need what little strength he can offer.

Not only am I too much, but I'm not enough.

How do I manage that?

"Fine. Whatever." I puff strands of hair out of my face. "Only use your good arm."

He squats beside me and wedges his fingers into the space I created. "On three. One ... Two ... Three."

My grip tightens, and I straighten my knees, lifting the edge of the boat out of the sand. Keegan braces the edge on his chest. "Go around to the other side, and I'll lower it down to you."

I do as he says. I hate that I can't tell him to sit down. Take a break. Let me do this. He won't listen. Stubborn. That's what he is.

I guess you have to be to keep your life's work a secret.

How did he get the whole town to keep his secret? Why didn't Georgi tell me?

But she did, didn't she? She called him Dr. Love. I missed the signs.

We glide the boat onto its bottom. Keegan slides his hands over the hull. "Looks good."

I push it to the shore break and load our bags inside. I hold the end while Keegan climbs in.

"Bridgette ..." he says softly, but he doesn't continue.

I hate the way my name curls out of his mouth like a caress. It's like watching a campfire dance and curl and sway around the logs. A crackling rhythm of seduction.

I force myself to remember it doesn't turn out so well for the logs.

Keegan

Bridgette's arms strain against the oars as she pulls stroke after stroke. I can't say I mind the view, even as it makes me feel like an incompetent perve. I shouldn't stare at the way the moon sparkles in her eyes. I shouldn't want to trace my fingers down the slope of her neck and mop the sweat from the hollow between her collarbones.

She wouldn't appreciate my touch anyway, so I turn my head and stare out to sea. She has every right to be mad. Furious even.

I withheld important information to protect myself. I had my reasons. At the time, before I knew her the way I do now, they were valid, but I should have tried harder to tell her about my career once I knew she was authentic.

Even if it wasn't my intention, I hate that I hurt her. She doesn't deserve to suffer the consequences of my ex's actions. I sacrificed her self-confidence to my fear.

That's never okay.

With Cynthia, I told her everything. No filter.

How many kids I want, where I want to raise them, what I hoped my marriage would be like. I assumed if I shared enough, we could decide if our relationship provided the foundation for the happy marriage I envisioned.

But she assumed since I talked about my version of the white picket fence, I wanted those things with her. I said too much, too fast before

I knew she was only out to marry a doctor and she didn't care who that doctor was.

With Bridgette, I swung the pendulum too far in the other direction. I withheld too much.

Even though I want to tell myself my lack of information was for her protection as much as mine—so she didn't get tangled up with an emotionally unavailable sucker reeling from his ex's lies—I know it's a lie.

Bridgette never misrepresented who she is or what she wants.

Now we both pay the price for my stupidity.

Bridgette rows to *Gypsy*. New meaning coats the boat's name. It's easier to think about the mystery we're attempting to solve than figure out how to fix my mess of a life.

Turner built the boat for Dotty—when she was Dotty Rios—before she was a Buchanan, married into the founding family, with all its implications and privileges.

Being a Rios was just as powerful in Bubee when my grandmother was a child. They built the railroad and made sure Bubee was a prime stop.

My family didn't arrive until Daisy's grandparents opened the grocery store in 1910. We have status but will never have the prestige of the Buchanans or Rioses.

Is that why Dotty's parents didn't approve?

Why would they love Daisy but not Turner? There are pieces to this puzzle that don't make sense.

Bridgette bumps into *Gypsy*'s hull next to the ladder. Thankfully the old girl rode the storm well. The strain in my shoulders relaxes a little knowing we should be able to get back to the marina without calling the Coast Guard.

As long as the motor works. I know Bridgette can't sail us back. Not in the dark. Not when she's had one sailing lesson.

The adrenaline from watching the deck collapse under her has settled. The deep, crushing pain of my injuries digs in.

I grit my teeth to distract myself, but it's pointless. I'll be useless as a wayfarer unless I get a dose of painkillers. We don't have anything besides breath mints in the galley.

I wiggle my fingers, prick their ends as Bridgette climbs onto the boat. My motor control and neurological signs are still normal. No nerve damage, no major musculoskeletal injuries. Just blood loss. A few stitches, and I'll be fine.

Bridgette stores our supplies while I collapse on the bench next to the steering wheel.

When she comes above deck, she tosses a shirt at my face. It's Ian's, so it will be too small, but something is better than nothing right now.

"You'll have to drive." I rub my hand over my face and around the back of my neck to wake myself up.

She steps to the steering wheel and slides her fingers over the varnished wood. "You should sleep."

I slide my injured arm through one sleeve, pull the collar over my head, and then pull the other arm through, wincing with every breath.

Crud. My arm throbs when I don't press it to my chest. "No, I'll stay up."

I'm worn out, but I can't sleep. Not until I help Bridgette get us home safely. There's still the possibility that she has an injury I can't see. I won't leave her vulnerable.

"Don't trust that I can get you back alive?" Her snarky tone pulls my attention to her expression. Even in the moonlight, I can tell she's using anger and sarcasm as defense mechanisms.

"There are sandbars as we motor around the island. You don't know how to read the buoys."

"Keegan, you need to rest. Just tell me what to look for." Her voice is confusingly soft. Where's the snark and bitterness from five seconds ago?

"Push the throttle forward halfway."

She does as I say, a firm line set on her lips.

I point to a lighthouse in the distance. "Keep her nose pointed that way until we get around the island."

"And then what?"

"And then I'll tell you what's next," I snap.

"You don't need to treat me like this."

"Like what?"

"Like I'm ... I don't know ... an inconvenience."

My gaze drifts to the dark horizon. I clench my jaw.

"You're not even going to acknowledge me?"

My head drops back on the edge of the bench. "I'm too tired to fight right now."

That's what she wants. She needs a place to dump the anger brewing inside of her, but neither of us is thinking clearly. The words that come out of our mouths won't be the right ones. They'll be defensive and mean, spoken from a place of hurt, not from a place of reconciliation.

She deserves better than I can give her right now, but I don't have the energy to form those words and make her understand that waiting to have this conversation is the wiser choice.

She flexes her fingers around the steering wheel. "I'm not asking for a fight. I'm asking for an explanation."

"You won't like what I have to say."

"Try me."

Fine. I'll give her an explanation. I squeeze my injured arm against my chest, plant my feet on the floor, and glare at her. "Why did we have to go to the shack *tonight*? Why couldn't we have waited until after the storm?"

"We found our answers."

"You found another puzzle piece."

"An important one."

"Those letters have been there for over five decades. They would have waited a day and a half for the storm to pass and me to properly supply the boat." My rising frustration spikes my blood pressure. My pulse pounds in my arm, amplifying my pain. What I wouldn't give for acetaminophen.

"Neither of which would have prevented the deck from collapsing. The shack may not have survived that storm. The letters would have been lost."

"Reuniting my grandmother with her brother is not worth *your life*. You've been running around so worried about what Gran has to say, did you even consider Turner's point of view? Does he want to see her? Does he want to be reunited with Mrs. August Buchanan?"

"I don't know," she screams at me. "I don't know."

I step next to her and lean across the steering wheel. My breath whispers stray hairs from the nap of her neck. My eyes hold hers. "If those boards had fallen a different direction ... if the entire deck had collapsed ... you could have been crushed. You could have ... I ..." My gaze dips to her mouth, and I lick my lips. "Bridgette, if you ..." I can't bring myself to finish my sentence out loud.

Bridgette is too important for me to finish the thought.

Even if she hates me for the rest of her life, I need her to be alive and well. I can't imagine walking this Earth knowing her brilliance isn't shining on someone deserving of her.

She shoves my chest. "Don't make this about your concern for me."

I lock down my hurt before she can read it in my eyes. "Fine." I walk to the nose of the boat and sit with my back to her.

I told her she didn't want to hear what I had to say.

It's easier to blame me than take responsibility for her part in this disaster of a day.

Chapter 25

Keegan

Third Coast Regional Medical Center sounds a lot grander than it actually is. Three stories of glass and concrete house the 106-bed hospital. Bridgette parks the harbor master's truck in the Emergency Department lot. "See you in class."

I balk at her. "You're not going anywhere."

She leans against the driver's side door. Her eyes narrow and short, sharp breaths shoot from her nostrils. "Excuse me?"

"You fell off the deck. At the very least, you're getting a CT to make sure you didn't sustain a subdural hematoma."

Her neurological status seems stable, but brain bleeds can be slow, silent killers. I can't let her leave. I would never forgive myself if I let her walk away without someone checking on her.

She pulls the keys from the ignition and drops them in my hand. "I'm fine. Daisy's house isn't far."

A scowl burrows into my forehead. "You would sacrifice your health to get away from me?"

"Read my lips. *I am fine*. I don't need a medical bill to tell me that."

"I'm sorry I lied to you. I have my reasons." I should have said that on the boat, but late is better than never, right?

She scoffs and jumps from the truck.

I climb out my side and slam the door. "Only one of us gets to be a stubborn idiot today. I already claimed that right." I don't have the strength to haul her over my shoulder and carry her inside. The only peace offering I have is to tell her the truth. I step between her and the sidewalk. "Ask me anything, and I promise to be completely honest if you let a doctor examine you." I take her hand in mine and gently squeeze it. "Please. Don't hurt yourself because you're mad at me."

"Anything?"

"Anything."

It's enough to get a slow nod out of her.

At the check-in desk, a woman with gold ribbons in her braids gives us a soft smile. "Bridgette, what happened?" She sweeps around the counter and wraps Bridgette in a hug.

"Hey, Rachel." Bridgette points to my arm. "Keegan hurt himself."

That's a simplified version of the facts. I point to the dressing Bridgette applied. "Twelve-centimeter laceration to the antecubital fossa and anterior arm resulting in significant blood loss a little over two hours ago. Innervation and motor control remain baseline distal to the injury. No systemic symptoms."

Her eyebrow hitches.

Yeah, I speak the language.

She casts a glance at Bridgette, who just shrugs. Rachel grabs a clipboard from behind the counter. "License and insurance, please. We'll bring you back when a room is available."

"Bridgette needs a CT too."

Rachel turns her hitched eyebrow on Bridgette. "What did you do?"

"Fell, but I'm fine. He's just being bossy."

"Either way, fill these out." Rachel hands Bridgette another set of forms.

No one else is in the ED waiting room at this early hour, so we have our pick of grey plastic chairs. Bridgette grabs one next to the window and slumps into it. The first rays of dawn peek over the horizon.

She's exhausted. Dark circles under her eyes, messy hair, torn pants. She needs a hot meal and twelve hours in her bed.

I grab my wallet from my back pocket and stare at the paperwork.

Bad news: I'm left-handed, and I don't know how to write ambidextrously. The pen slips in my right hand.

I write a *K*, but it looks more like a wonky *X* with a funny tail. The *E* isn't any better.

My head drops back, and I stare at the tiled ceiling. "Bridgette?"

She purses her lips.

I show her my illegible penmanship. "Will you help me fill out the forms?"

She shifts to brace her elbows on her knees and drums her fingers on her chin. "That was hard to admit, wasn't it?"

"Please." The single word seems to be her weakness.

She slips the pen from my fingers without touching me. "Social security number?"

I give her the important information the hospital needs to bill me hundreds of dollars for something I could do myself if I had the supplies ... if I'd injured my right arm instead of my left, that is.

She turns our paperwork in at the front desk and brings back two bottles of water and a bag of pretzels. She tears the top open and hands it to me. "You should eat."

The salt revives my senses. "Thanks. You can have the rest."

"Dr. Sullivan?" a nurse calls from the security door.

I push to my feet and hold my hand out to her. "Come on."

Bridgette stares at my hand. "Scared I'll run away?"

"Because it's my fault this happened, and I need to make sure you're uninjured." I wanted to blame her, but ultimately it was my call to take the boat to Willard Island. We might have made it back to the harbor before the storm, even after she cried on the steps.

Part of me wanted to escape reality and hide in the shack. I wanted to know if, when the rest of the world didn't matter, the attraction we felt was real or circumstantial.

I got my answer but destroyed her faith in me. If she'll let me, rebuilding that faith will take time. Taking care of her is the first step.

Her mouth twists, but she finally takes my hand and follows me through the security doors.

The nurse deposits us in one of the rooms and shuts the door with a quiet click. I climb onto the bed, and she sits in the abutting chair, drumming her nails on her thighs.

I press my hand over hers and lace our fingers together. "Nervous?"

She shakes her head. "No. You?"

"No."

I'm not scared of needles. I know the process to repair my wound—undress, inspect, debride, sanitize, suture, redress. Immunizations for tetanus and antibiotics. CBC, type and cross, transfuse if necessary—but Bridgette's presence adds a layer of calm I wouldn't have otherwise.

Even though she's mad at me, having her hold my hand loosens the knot in the back of my throat. Bridgette is in the room because she cares, not because she's required to be. "I appreciate you staying."

She opens her mouth with a snarky smirk but snaps her mouth shut. "You're welcome."

I nudge her knee. "What were you going to say?"

"Nothing. It's not important."

"Tell me." I almost pull out the please.

She tucks her foot under her bottom and shrugs. "I know your personal information now. I'm one credit card application away from an all-expenses-paid European vacation, so you kind of have to keep me close. Gold digger, right?"

"I shouldn't have said that. You've never given me a reason to assume that about you. That was my insecurities talking."

She snorts.

"My behavior over the last few weeks doesn't reflect my feelings. I'm sorry."

"Why didn't you tell me you were a doctor?"

"Most people see my title and jump to conclusions. They want something from me. I'm tired of being used."

Hurt flashes in her eyes. "I'm not that kind of person."

"I know that now."

"I never should have—"

A well-built Black man in faded blue scrubs steps into the room. "Dr. Sullivan?"

"Call me Keegan. This is Bridgette Christianson. She's on your list too."

He extends his hand to Bridgette, then to me. "Then I'm Jeremiah. I'm the attending tonight. Want to tell me what happened?"

Jeremiah nods along as I give the history of the wound and my general health. Jeremiah unwinds the bandage. The scab has woven through the gauze. When he tugs, dried blood and interstitial fluid give a smacking pop, and the end dislodges from the wound.

He inspects the cut. "Nice work, ma'am. You likely saved his life."

Bridgette chews the end of her thumb. She's obviously uncomfortable. Was it selfish of me to ask her to come in the room? Yes. Should I let her leave? I don't want to, but that's what's best for her. I've been selfish and need to put her first instead.

"She needs a CT. Maybe she can do that while you stitch me up?"

She shakes her head. "No. I'll stay."

"Are you sure?"

"I'm fine." Bridgette scoots back in her chair and sucks a large breath through her nose. She's not green, but she's not calm. She's sticking by me even though I'm a stubborn jerk who owes her the biggest apology in the history of apologies.

I'd wrap my arm around her shoulder and pull her tight if I could get closer to her.

The wound isn't as bad as I thought. The bleeding stopped. The margins will approximate nicely, so I won't have much of a scar. Maybe twenty stitches to facilitate healing and decrease the risk of infection.

Jeremiah pulls a vial from the medication cart. "I'll administer a dose of lidocaine, and when it's effective, I'll sew you up. Any questions?"

"When will he be able to use his arm like normal?" Bridgette asks.

"No lifting anything over five pounds for the next two weeks or so. Work up the weight a little at a time." Jeremiah draws up the numbing agent and injects it around my wound. The skin bubbles slightly with the increased pressure.

He swivels his chair to Bridgette. "Your turn." He gives her a thorough neurological evaluation, inspects the scrapes on her thighs, and checks her vital signs. "I agree with Keegan. You may not remember hitting your head, but that was quite a tumble. A CT will make us all rest easier."

She chews her lips. "Do I have to?"

Jeremiah chuckles. "Doctors' orders. Both of ours." He leaves us to collect the suture supplies and order Bridgette's tests.

"How are you going to help Jake? Does this mean you're going home?"

I run my thumb along the back of her hand. "You worried?"

"No, just ..."

"It's okay if you're worried. And no, I'm not going anywhere. Jake still needs me."

He's still dying, and I still need to help pick his successor. Does Bridgette want to move to Texas? Since Turner bought her the admission, I doubt relocating is even on her radar. She thinks this is just a class, not an interview.

Another important piece of information I'm keeping from her, but this omission isn't mine to share. I have to keep Jake's confidence.

If she were here, would I come home more often?

I'm not sure I can answer that question until I know if she'll forgive me. I don't like the idea of never seeing her again when class is over, but that might be the extent of our relationship.

She leans over my arm, swallowing hard. "I've never seen a cut that bad. Not a lot of opportunity in a bakery. We specialize in burns."

"Got any good stories?"

She rolls up her shirt sleeve and points to a two-centimeter line along her biceps. "Leaned too far into the oven."

I roll up the side of my shorts and show off a three-centimeter, crescent-moon-shaped scar on my lateral thigh. "During my psych rotation in medical school, a patient stabbed me with a pencil."

"Let me guess, you told her something she didn't want to hear?"

"I was trying to give her a bag of Skittles."

"She was an M&M girl?"

"I never found out. The nurses restrained her and took her to the safe room. If I'd ever doubted psychiatry wasn't my calling, I knew then."

"Is your lack of bedside manner why you're a surgeon?"

I flex my right arm. "I like using power tools."

Her eyes roll. "You could have been a carpenter."

"Not in my family. Advanced degree or bust."

She settles deeper into her chair and yawns. "Glad I'm not part of your family. My parents were relieved I finished high school with a job."

My gut clenches with her admission. She'd fit in quite nicely in my family. Gran already loves her. "My mom's an artist, so it doesn't fully ring true. They just expected a lot from us growing up."

"Why settle for a B when you could get an A?"

"One hundred percent effort, one hundred percent of the time. No shortcuts."

"Isn't that exhausting?"

"Sometimes."

Jeremiah pushes the door open with his hip. "Did the lidocaine kick in?"

I palpate the perimeter of my wound. "Numb."

"The nurse will be by in a minute to take you to imaging." Jeremiah lays the suture kit on the counter next to the sink and slides the tray table in front of me. "Place your arm on the tray, please."

I do as he says. He washes his hands and dons sterile gloves. He cleans the wound, swabbing it and the surrounding skin with antiseptic. "Ready?"

He pulls out the curved needle, suture, and forceps, and the color drains from Bridgette's face. She shoves the side of her fist between her teeth.

"Will you get me a bottle of water?" I shake my empty one at her.

She balks. "Now?"

Jeremiah glances between us. Understanding dawns on his face. "He's severely dehydrated. I'd prefer not to give him an IV bolus, so he'll need several more bottles. Nurse Abadi will help you."

She rises on shaky legs. "Um, okay. Anything else you need?"

"Maybe some apple juice and crackers," I say.

Her fingers rest on the edge of the bed next to my hand. "You'll be okay without me?"

"No." I wink. "But I'm thirsty."

She nods and escapes into the hallway.

Jeremiah closes the door behind her. "Shouldn't have her walking around. She looked ready to pass out."

"She's exhausted and is putting on a tough face. I think blood makes her squeamish."

"You had quite the adventure."

"You have no idea."

Jeremiah and I trade medical school and residency stories as he sews me up. He ties the final knot and applies the bandage. "You know what to watch out for. Keep the wound clean and dry. Drink more water. Eat well. Rest. Nothing strenuous for the next few weeks, and you'll be fine."

I clap him on the back. "Thanks, man."

"Now I know who to call when I give in and get my knee fixed."

"What's wrong with it?"

"Torn meniscus."

"That's quick. Can't the ortho here help you out?"

"We don't have one anymore. She quit about six months ago, accepted a better position in Corpus. We've had locums guys covering. You looking?"

"No. I love Dallas." *Most of the time. This injury will make driving home a chore, but I need to deal with Cynthia. Especially now that I've realized how much I like Bridgette and am learning to trust again.*

Jeremiah tosses his gloves in the garbage can and puts the sharps in their container. "No knee manipulations for a few weeks. Let the rest of the surgical staff get the patients on the OR tables."

"All things I know."

"But I have to say them."

"CYA. I get it."

"Not covering anything. In my experience, medical professionals are the worst patients. They don't follow instructions, think they know better, and end up back in my ED with compounding injuries. I'd rather grab a beer than more sutures."

"Deal."

When we leave the treatment room, Bridgette is sitting in a wheelchair at the nurses' station talking to Rachel. "They buzzed my head. Just need someone to tell me I'm fine."

Jeremiah swings around the end of the desk. Rachel's sitting in front of the computer. He stares down at her, glances at the computer, then back to her.

She bats her eyes in return. "Anything I can assist you with, Dr. Crumb Bum?"

Bridgette points between the two of them. "Rachel, is this …?"

"Yep." Rachel lets the *P* pop with a heavy dose of disdain.

"If you'll kindly move, Nurse Stabby, I'll read the CT and let them be on their way."

Bridgette hides a laugh behind her hand.

I've missed something.

Dr. Thompson is embroidered on Jeremiah's coat, and her tag reads *Rachel Abadi*, but the way Jeremiah avoids eye contact with Rachel keeps my lips sealed shut. Not my business.

She rolls her chair backward, giving him a tight, annoyed smile.

Jeremiah clicks a few keystrokes. "CT's clear. You two are discharged."

Bridgette hugs Rachel. "See you under the pier?"

"Wouldn't miss it." She points at me but looks at Bridgette. "I need the rest of this story."

"And I need the rest of yours." Bridgette pointedly looks at Jeremiah.

When we get in the car—Bridgette driving and me downing my first dose of extra-strength Tylenol—I swivel. "What story?"

"Us at the shack."

"Did you tell her about the letters? About Turner, Dotty, and my grandmother?"

She shrugs like what we discovered is no big deal. "No."

"Don't." My words snap like a whip.

"Why?"

"We don't know the whole story yet. The last thing we need is for people to know my great-uncle tried to destroy one of the pillar relationships in our community. Rumors ruin lives."

She's quiet for a minute. Staring at me. "What rumor ruined your life?"

Chapter 26

Bridgette

Keegan is quiet the entire drive to his parents' house. Not like it's far, maybe five minutes, but still, he doesn't answer my question. Something is definitely wrong in Keegan's life.

I'm disappointed in myself for expecting anything but silence. He promised he'd tell me everything if I saw the doctor, but again, he lied.

Why did I expect more?

I park the truck at the curb and grab his bags. He can return it to his friend when he feels better.

He doesn't try to take the bags from me and follows me up the sidewalk. He's exhausted and the pain medication is working its magic.

His parent's house looks a lot like Daisy's: white siding, light green shutters, wraparound porch, and a gabled roof. It's not as big, though. The yard has more weeds and fewer flowers.

I knock on the front door. "I'll tell Jake about your accident."

He reaches around me, turns the handle, and walks into the entry way. I guess that makes sense. This is the house he grew up in. He doesn't need to knock.

"Keegan?" An eager voice calls down the hall.

"It's me, Mama," he calls back. His voice has a slow southern drawl to it now that he's tired and dopey. Under other circumstances, I might call it sexy.

But Keegan can't be sexy anymore.

I set down the bags and slip out the front door. I'm not ready to meet his parents. Not after the night we had. Not with the disappointments layered on my heart.

I thought we had something. I thought we could be something. I can't meet the woman who belongs to that sweet voice and not wonder *what if*?

Keegan palms the side of the door, sliding it open. "Where are you going?"

"You expect me to hang out on your parents' couch all day?"

His shoulders sag. "I ... umm."

I peel his fingers from the door. "Sitting by your hospital bed doesn't mean I forgave you. Keegan, I'm done with your games. I deserve better. I can't trust you to trust me. Let your mama take care of you, get some rest, and leave me alone." I shut the door in his face.

I'm too exhausted to fight a battle that's already lost. I can't do anything about my relationship with Keegan, but I can help Turner. Daisy said she hadn't seen him since he deployed, but she told Turner to leave on Dotty's wedding day. She owes me an explanation for her lies.

Keegan won't appreciate me digging deeper into why his grandmother kept her secrets, but I need to know every detail before I call Turner.

Keegan's parents' house is on the opposite end of the peninsula from Daisy's. Exhausted as I am, the walk gives me plenty of time to figure out how to approach her.

Or at least you'd think it would. By the time my tired feet walk down the limestone path to the carriage house, I'm no closer to a plan of attack than I was when I left the Sullivan's place. I'm freezing and hungry.

A quick shower helps me feel human again.

The bed beckons me.

Come lie down.

Rest your weary head, sad girl.

But, through my window, I see Daisy bustling in her kitchen. I throw my hair into a messy bun, slide on pale pink capris, a white cotton T-shirt knotted at my waist, and my navy cardigan.

I flick through Turner's letters to Dotty and grab the last few. I need to ask Daisy about them before I lose my nerve. With a fortifying breath, I climb the well-trodden stairs and open her kitchen door.

"Where have you been?" Her voice holds a playful lilt. There's nothing condemning in her tone or her body language.

She reminds me a little bit of Isa in her playfulness and spunk. My heart squeezes.

I miss my best friends. I miss our easy conversation and trust. I miss knowing they love me unconditionally, and I'm never too much for them. But I left them behind to have an adventure of my own, and I'm not done trying to bring Turner home.

I set the stack of letters next to the butcher block on the center island. "I found something important, and I need you to tell me the truth."

She tips her head to the side and blinks at me like I'm speaking a foreign language. "The truth?"

I open Turner's final letter, smoothing its rough corners. "Your brother was in love with your best friend. He tried to stop her wedding. You told him to leave Bubee and never come back."

I watch for signs of remorse, but her face doesn't pale, her cheeks don't redden, and her shoulders stay erect.

"You told me Turner and Dotty didn't have a relationship."

She casually sips her coffee. "My brother's shenanigans are not my story to tell."

I don't believe my ears. "He was in love with her. Based on the letters, she was in love with him too. What happened?" There's a desperate whine in my voice that makes her eyebrow arch.

"Nothing *happened*. Nothing ever was going to *happen*."

"Why not?"

She sets her mug on the counter and folds her hands over her stomach. "I refuse to talk about this."

"This is why Turner hasn't come home. You told me it broke your parents' hearts, and you had the answers all along. You could have fixed everything."

"It is not my story to tell."

"That's a cop-out. You told him to leave, and you lied to keep him away. Why?"

Why didn't she want to see her brother again? Was it only about Dotty, or is there more to the story that I don't know? If there is, who's going to answer my questions if not Daisy?

"I will not be interrogated in my own home." Her voice still holds a pleasant tone, but her eyes have turned into ice picks.

"Turner deserves—"

"He does not deserve anything." She spins on her heel and clomps down the hallway, slamming her bedroom door so hard, the pictures rattle.

I fold the letter into its envelope and carry the stack back to the carriage house. I don't want to be here anymore. This isn't the home away from home it seemed to be.

The love and care aren't real. They're only handed out when convenient. When they benefit the giver.

There has to be another place for me to stay until my class is finished.

The closet doors squeak as I jam them open. I don't bother folding my clothes, squishing them into my suitcase.

So much for a nap. Class starts in two hours. That should be plenty of time to find a hotel if I ignore the reality of my finances. I grab my purse and flick open my wallet. Forty-seven dollars cash. One emergency credit card.

Does my reaction to Daisy's lies count as an emergency? My savings account is laughable, so I can't use that. The emergency room bill coming in the mail won't help either.

I hang my head.

I'm being stupid and dramatic. There's no reason to leave.

I just need to avoid Daisy and Keegan for the next few days, then I'll go home and none of this will matter.

Bridgette

"Welcome to the halfway point." Jake ambles to the front of the class with his thumbs tucked in his belt loops. "I have an announcement before we get started today. I did a little bit of a bait-and-switch with y'all. This is the last pitmaster class I will ever teach." Gasps echo around the room. He holds his hands up and continues. "Because I'm selling Jake's BBQ."

Mumbles grow, and people talk over each other as the news settles in.

I wish I had a better understanding of what this means to them. Restaurants are bought and sold all the time. Jake's is an institution in this town, but selling isn't the same as closing.

People will still get their brisket and roasted chicken with a side of bread pudding if they want it.

Keegan's still recovering, so I can't see what this announcement means to him. Does he already know, or will he be surprised when he finds out? Does he want to buy it? Would he give up medicine to take over Jake's legacy?

"Now for the surprise." Jake rubs his hands together.

"That wasn't enough?" Amanda says, slapping her towel on the table.

"'Fraid not." Jake chuckles. "I've chosen to sell to one of you."

"Who?" Tory asks.

"I don't know right yet. That's the surprise. Whoever shows me they are the best fit to take over Jake's will win the opportunity."

I could win Jake's?

My life would change if I did. I wouldn't go home.

That idea doesn't scare me like I expect it to.

Even though the last few days have been horrible, this town has grown on me.

Maybe the bigger truth is nothing has changed in Emerald Bay. I love it. It's home, and it will always be one of my favorite places in the world, but it's not where I want to be right now.

When I get back, Graham and his friends will still see me as the selfish princess who destroyed Willa's confidence.

Staying here is akin to running and hiding from a situation I don't want to deal with, but it's also stepping out of a toxic environment where I will never truly be accepted as I am.

I came to Texas to live for myself, to stop worrying about other people's opinions, and decide who I want to be and how to be comfortable in my skin. Keegan distracted me. Not anymore.

Getting on a plane in two weeks is scarier than putting down roots here.

If I win Jake's, I'll buy a little house with a view of the ocean and be in charge of my future instead of answering to someone else.

The boss.

"What if we can't afford your asking price?" I ask.

"We'll negotiate. I care more about this ol' place ending up in the right hands than making a pile of money from it."

I could add buttermilk biscuits to the menu and revamp the desserts. The bread pudding is fair, but I have just the recipe to make it a main attraction. Add my peach cobbler and more than the barbecue sauce will make headlines.

Desire for something all my own grows and grows until it's the fuel in a furnace moving my arms and legs to scurry around the kitchen.

Determination flickers in my chest. Not a full-blown fire, just a spark.

But it's more than I had when I left Daisy's house this morning.

I tie an apron around my waist and slot three chickens on a baking sheet.

Declan holds up two spice blends. "Lemon pepper or ancho chili?"

My knife slices through the bird's ribcage, and I smash it flat. I love spatchcocking chickens. The skin is crispier, the meat is juicier, and it cooks in half the time. I have yet to see the downside. "One of each."

"Number three?"

"Furikake."

His nose wrinkles and his mouth smashes to the side. "Not sure that'll roast. Too much sugar and the seaweed may burn."

I lift my shoulders. "Never hurts to try. What's that quote? Failure is just a steppingstone on the way to success."

Declan pops the top on the olive oil. "Who said that?"

"I heard it from Oprah, but I'm not sure if she said it first." We lather the birds and cover them with the spice mixes.

"Let's get these birds cooking."

We slide them into the oven, and he steps back and looks at me like he's seeing me for the first time. "Your energy is different today. You want this restaurant?"

I take in our surroundings: the line of barbecues and smokers, the screened walls, and ocean in the distance. I love this room. I could spend every day here for the rest of my life and be happy. "I want to try. Don't you?"

"Nah. At one point in time, I approached Jake about a partnership, but Texas is too hot. I miss me drizzle and grey clouds. I'll help ya if that's what ya want."

I nudge his elbow with mine. "I'd appreciate it."

"How about dinner after class? We can strategize." There's something extra in his gaze that wobbles in my stomach.

"Are you asking me on a date? Or as a colleague?" I spritz the birds with a little vinegar to hide my nervousness.

"Which gets ya to spend the evening with me?"

Keegan ambles down the stairs, and he's like the north pole, pulling my compass needle back to him.

I catch his eye. He holds my gaze long enough I think he might have something to say, but his eyes fall to his shoes, and he retreats upstairs.

That tells me everything I need to know. Our two kisses were the end links in chain reactions following romantic moments. We were lulled by the crash of the waves, the twinkle of the stars, and the hope of something more.

But they weren't the beginning of anything more than memories.

"It can't be a date, but Sobre las Rocas has excellent margaritas," I offer.

A grimace crunches Declan's cheeks. "I'm a peated whiskey guy, but I'll try one."

When the timer on my watch dings, I open the barbeque. Our three birds glisten golden brown. Smokey ancho chili, tangy lemon pepper, and umami seaweed scents waft from the grill in a decadent mixture. My mouth waters and eyes tear at the beauty of it all.

It doesn't even distract me that Keegan's downstairs now, helping Tyler temper his fire.

Declan holds the cutting board, and I lift the birds from the grate. After resting for fifteen minutes, I carve the furikake chicken. Steam billows from the breast. Juice runs down my knife and channels into the cutting board grooves.

I slice a piece and hand it to Declan before grabbing my own. He sniffs it, examines the color and texture from every angle.

Jake joins us. "What are you playing with?"

"Japanese furikake."

"One of my favorite ways to fry, but never tried it on the barbecue."

I cut him a bite and raise mine like I'm offering a toast. "To legacies, delicious food, and the opportunity to learn from a master."

Red races from the collar of Jake's shirt across his cheeks to the tips of his ears. "Are you sucking up, Miss Bridgette?"

"I pride myself on honesty." I don't let my eyes drift to Keegan, but I see his shoulders hunch in my peripheral vision.

Jake touches his chicken to mine and then Declan's. "Bon appétit and bottoms up." His head tilts back and drops the meat in his mouth.

He gags and spits the chicken into the garbage can. "Ugh."

"What?" I take my bite. Burnt salt coats my tongue. I spit it into the garbage can right along with Jake's. "That's awful."

"Over seasoned," Jake says.

"Ya think?" I scrub my tongue with a towel.

Jake drains an entire bottle of water. "Now we know what not to do."

"Stick with deep fryin'," Declan says.

"I was heavy-handed. Next time, I'll make my own umami blend instead of relying on something I picked from a store aisle."

"At least there's a bright side." Jake dumps the chicken in the garbage can.

Declan's eyes widen, and his nostrils flare. "Do we even want to try the other two?"

"They're here. Might as well." I slice through the ancho chicken's breast meat and hand Jake and Declan bites. They hold it like it's toxic.

"Big babies." I sink my teeth into the meat. This one is perfect. Spicy with a little tangy zing on the back end. Juices coat my tongue and run down my chin. "Mmm. So much better."

They share a look, a shrug, and eat their bites.

"You can cook, my dear." Jake snags another bite.

I shake my head. "This one's all Declan. All I did was smash it."

Jake bows to Declan. "You, sir, are a master." He winks as he stands.

My heart sinks at the lost opportunity to dazzle Jake. Declan must be the front-runner to win the restaurant.

But he doesn't want it. Jake didn't say what he'll do if the person he picks doesn't want the restaurant. Will he pick a second favorite?

Watching Declan shine, it doesn't matter if I failed.

Declan is a fantastic chef. I will not deny him praise for a job well done.

I just need to do better. I'll learn from this mistake and move on.

"Can I try?" Keegan holds out a fork to me.

I gesture to the cutting board. "Sure."

Soon, the rest of the class gathers around our table sampling our chickens. Amanda bumps Declan's shoulder. "Dang, dude. If I knew you were this good, you'd be catering parties with me. How about you swing by early for the graduation party?"

He blushes. "I appreciate the compliment, but I'm no caterer."

Amanda slides up to me, so we're pressed together like slices of sandwich bread. "What about you, honey? You're half of this genius. Will you help me with the graduation party?"

I appreciate her confidence in my ability and the compliments, but I didn't earn them.

"Graduation party? Shouldn't that be at the end of class?" I ask.

Amanda gives a clipped nod. "Week from Friday."

"I thought it was this Sunday?"

She wiggles her phone. "You need to get on the text stream, my love. Lawrence made the championships, so the party moved to the Friday after class is over."

"Sure, I guess." It will be as good a chance as any to say goodbye to everyone before I head back to Minnesota.

Or it will be the perfect way to celebrate the next phase in my life. Whatever the heck that looks like.

Chapter 27

Keegan

WATCHING BRIDGETTE WALK THROUGH the sand with Declan, tilting her head, and smiling her sunflower smile at him, laughing at whatever he's saying, stabs my gut.

Waves of jealousy and envy crash over me.

I'd stupidly assumed her presence in the Emergency Department meant we'd reached a truce. I was wrong.

I've spent every minute since she left running the events on the island through my head over and over. As my imagination toyed with them, they morphed into worst case scenarios: Bridgette impaled through the abdomen. Bridgette with a crushed skull. The lift draining out of her eyes as her blood pumped past my fingertips.

In every situation, I was helpless, powerless, impotent to stop her from dying.

That's why I couldn't look at her when I first stepped into the classroom today. I'm just as helpless watching her walk away ... unless I do something. Take a different tact.

My pride can't get the better of me. I run after them. "Bridgette! Bridgette, stop."

She spins, waves washing over her ankles. "Yes, doctor?"

"Can I talk to you for a second?"

"Declan and I have dinner waiting for us, so no."

"I promised you an explanation."

She sighs like shackles hang on her limbs. "I'm tired of explanations. Three times I asked you for the truth, and three times you lied, whether by omission or outright fibs. I'm tired. I'm thirsty. You apologized. That's enough." She weaves her arm around Declan's and drags him down the beach. "Let's go."

Declan casts me an apologetic grimace. "You can talk with him if you'd like," he offers.

"Nope. I need a margarita, a business plan, and menu ideas. I do not need a medical diagnosis, injection, or Band-Aid, so there's no reason for me to speak with a doctor."

Her words burn into my chest.

I was just trying to keep myself safe.

But this isn't safe. This is broken for no reason except for my own cowardice.

Bridgette

Declan is freakin' adorable. I wish I'd latched on to him sooner. His thick brogue washes over me and tingles my eardrums, but it doesn't stir anything deeper.

I sip a blueberry coconut margarita with sugar on the rim. Declan is classic lime with salt. He does a cute little nose scrunch every time he takes a sip.

He doesn't like his drink, but he's humoring me, and I appreciate the gesture.

I set my drink on the table. "What are you going to do with your barbecue pitmaster knowledge?"

"I told you me siblings have a distillery. They're leasin' me space ta open a restaurant."

"No nepotism?"

"They're successful. My part isn' guaranteed. The Irish love their whiskey, but barbeque isn' popular."

"What did you do before?"

Our conversation ebbs and flows around topics we've touched on before but never did a deep dive. I knew he had brothers and a sister and that they were distillers, but learning about Declan's hopes and dreams, his plans for the future, paints him in a new light.

He's sweet and kind. He's driven, but his version of success doesn't revolve around numbers on a balance sheet. He wants his food to serve the community, draw it together, and deepen its roots.

That's what I want too.

Meals should be about the people around the table, not ingredients in a pot. That's what made my job in Emerald Bay so wonderful. Hannah, my boss, cares about the people eating her food. She knows what they want to order before they do. She feeds their souls with conversation and community as much as she feeds their bellies.

Georgi does that at Honey Beans.

If I win Jake's, I want to continue that tradition. To do that, I need a better understanding of what makes Bubee tick. I need to spend time with Georgi and the Sangria Under the Pier women so I can see where I fit.

Because even if I don't fit with Keegan, I love this town and my new friends enough to leave Minnesota.

I'd miss my best friends, but they're all entering new seasons in their lives anyway. Moving doesn't mean we won't be friends.

Texts, phone calls, email, video chat, and airplanes are modern conveniences that allow friendships to thrive over long distances. We just need the motivation to use them.

Loving my friends is enough to make them a priority, even as their lives get busier and mine takes on a dimension I never expected.

"And yourself?" Declan asks.

I blink at him. I was so deep in my head, worrying about myself, I didn't pay attention to what he was saying.

I press my fingertips to my lips. "I'm sorry. What did you say?"

A soft smile tugs his lips. "It's fine. I'm not interesting."

The self-deprecation stings. "You are interesting. I'm just ..."

"Distracted."

"Yeah. Leaving Minnesota is a big step. I'm not sure I'm ready to make it."

"What would convince ya?"

"A Magic 8-Ball with all the answers."

He pulls his phone from his pocket. "I can help." He swipes up, and the screen illuminates his face in the dark booth. He turns it to face me. An app with the Magic 8-Ball fills the screen. "Ask your questions."

I gingerly take it from him. I don't believe an app will tell me the future, it's fun to pretend, right?

"Will I take over Jake's restaurant?" I shake the phone and the white square "floats" into view on the screen. It reads, *Better not tell you now*. I show Declan. "That's unhelpful."

"Ask a different way."

"Should I move to Bubee?" I shake it again. "*As I see it, yes.*" I shake again. "Will I work at Jake's?"

Declan reads the 8-Ball's answer, "*Don't count on it.*"

I hand his phone back. "Well, there you have it. I move to Texas, but I don't have a job. How do you think I'll pay my bills?"

"Amanda mentioned hiring you."

"I don't know if I want to work for someone else. I love the independence I've had to set my own hours the last few weeks and to create whatever strikes my fancy."

He cringes at another sip of his margarita. "Bein' your own boss is addictive, but it also means ya never get a day for yourself."

"I guess I never thought about the other side of being the boss. I just don't want to answer to anyone else. I'm tired of trying to be the perfect employee."

"You wanna be the perfect boss?"

"I want to be the perfect version of me."

He leans his chin on his palm. "And who is Bridgette?

I mirror his posture. "That's the question, isn't it? I thought I knew. I was the fun, spunky, outgoing baker. I am those things, but I want to be more. I don't want to censor myself because I'm worried I'll make other people uncomfortable. I don't want to hide in the shadows when I have a bad day."

He shakes his head like what I'm saying is preposterous. "Who says you canna have a bad day? Everybody has 'em."

"When everyone expects their breakfast pastry and cup of coffee to come with a flirty wink or hilarious joke, I worry what they'll say if I don't give them the anticipated version of me." I shake my head. "I'm sorry I'm dumping all this on you."

"I think you needed a safe listener."

"I did. You're good at this." Too bad the only attraction I feel for Declan is the wish that he was my psychologist. He has all the hallmarks of a perfect boyfriend.

But I don't wish he would reach for my hand or caress my cheek or try to make any kind of move.

My imagination pictures Keegan and the future we could have had as I describe my fears and longings. I wanted him to be a part of the life I'm rebuilding.

He's not an option anymore.

"It's too bad you're going back to Ireland. You and I would make a great team."

"Aye. But I don't think it's the same for me. I wish I'd gotten to know you before the doctor broke your heart."

"How did you …"

"Ya did just yell at him at the beach. It's hard not noticin' the tension between the two of ya. The way ya avoid each other, it's pretty obvious somethin's happened."

My face flames hot. "How did you know he was a doctor? Am I the only one who didn't figure that out?"

"Don't beat yourself up. Sometimes you only see what you wanna to see."

"Why wouldn't I want to see his career?"

"That's a question only you can answer."

Knowing Keegan's a doctor doesn't change my opinion of him. His lies did that.

It's harder for a doctor to pick up and leave his career than it is for a chef. Hanging my hope on Keegan as a chef who could move back to Bubee is entirely different than loving Keegan the doctor with a fully established life in Dallas that he'll never leave.

I want to win Jake's, but if I fell in love with Keegan, I would have to pick between the two.

I guess one good thing came from Keegan's deception: I don't have to decide to follow my heart or my passion.

My phone buzzes on the table, and Camille's face fills the screen. She's called several times over the last few days, but I haven't had it in me to be perky and happy for her as I wallow in my sadness. My wallowing needs to be over.

"Do you mind?" I ask Declan.

"Take it."

I step from the table and walk onto the deck. Shania Twain pumps from the speakers tonight, but it's quieter out here so I can hear my bestie. I slide my finger across the screen, and the video connects. "Camille?"

"Bridge! Why haven't you answered my phone calls?" She sounds distressed and worried.

I could open my heart and let her see how broken it is, but I've already cracked open my insecurities with Declan tonight. I'm not ready to dissect them anymore.

Talking about Keegan will inevitably lead to talking about Jake's and me considering a move to Texas. Until I know what I'm doing, I don't want to lay that worry on her. "Things have been ... busy. How's everything up there?"

She flashes the camera around. All our friends stand in front of Emerald Bay's City Hall dressed in suits and gowns. Ethan and Nica hold Delia's hands. Bryce's arm is draped over Isa's shoulder. Bailey and Neal hold hands. Turner, Hannah and her husband, Liam's family, Camille's dad and grandma wave. Handsome barks out of view.

Camille's in her wedding dress. Liam's wearing a black suit. The camera pans back to her face. "I've been trying to get ahold of you to get you home. We're getting married today."

"Right now?"

"Liam's parents, brother, and sister flew in two days ago. Dad leaves tomorrow. We're tired of waiting. Liam doesn't have another trip for two weeks, and the Tribe is on break. We can fit in a honeymoon and not have to rearrange our schedules. The only thing missing is you. Why weren't you answering? Is everything okay?"

No.

Nothing is *okay*.

But I'm not telling her that on her wedding day.

I refuse to tell her not being home to celebrate her marriage is breaking my heart.

I'm not mad at them for wanting to start their life.

I'm mad at myself for being self-centered. She asked me to be a pivotal part of her wedding, and I abandoned her to learn how to smoke meat.

I don't regret coming, but I hate missing out.

If I move here, it will only get worse. I'll miss anniversaries, birthdays, and babies.

The emotion clogging my throat makes it hard to swallow, but I manage.

"Congratulations! I'm so happy for you guys." I tilt the phone away from my face, so she can't see me blinking away tears.

Camille sighs. "Bridge?"

"Yeah?"

"I'm sorry, babe." She circles her finger around the screen. "I know that face. You're upset."

I could never hide anything from her. "I am. I shouldn't be here. I should be there."

"No, you shouldn't. You're where you need to be. I'm sorry we aren't waiting, but I am so proud of you for sticking it out down there. You're a rockstar, and you deserved this trip. Can you manage long-distance maid of honor duties?"

She knew exactly what I needed to hear. Her confidence in my choices helps lessen the sting a little.

Words are impossible, so I nod.

She hands the phone to Hannah, and they walk inside. My best friend promises to love, honor, and cherish until death do they part as my stomach cramps and tears stream down my face.

After Camille kisses Liam, she takes the phone from Hannah. She presses her fingertips to her lips and then to the screen. "Thank you for being here for me. I love you. We'll have the reception when you get back. Liam's mom can plan the whole thing, and all we'll have to worry about are dresses and champagne. How's that sound?"

"I do love an excuse to dress up."

"Perfect. See you soon."

"Love you too." I end the call and stare at the horizon for far too long. I need to get back to Declan, but I want my stomach to settle first.

All of my best friends are officially married.

And I'm in limbo.

I plop into the booth and give Declan as much of a smile as I can muster. He slides his margarita toward me. "This thing is gross. You wanna finish it?"

"You don't have to ask me twice." Because tonight tequila is the solution to my life's problems.

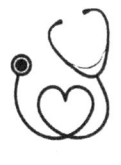

Chapter 28

Keegan

I RUB MY FINGERS over the rough, worn seat of Gran's gazebo bench. Gran hasn't painted in a while. It's more pale pink than the bubblegum color it used to be.

Makes sense. Most seventy-six-year-olds don't frequently grab a paintbrush and slather latex paint over a piece of furniture they rarely use.

This is my haven, not hers. I haven't been here to paint it for her.

I tilt my head and stare at the cloudless night. Millions of stars shimmer, providing a glimpse into the past. They remind me how small I am.

What I do with my life doesn't matter in the grand scheme of things. Where I live, the work I do, who I love, are all infinitesimally small compared to the grandeur of the universe.

But they matter to me.

I don't want to be this cynical, cranky, skeptical, SOB I've become. The only way to become the man I want to be is to go back to Dallas and face Cynthia. Closure will give me the peace I need to get on with my life.

It's just like planning a complicated surgery, I need the perfect set-up. I need to know the exact entry point, what the tissues look like inside the joint, and prepare for possible complications along the way.

Every tool at my disposal needs to be prepared. I also need to assemble my team. It's not safe for me to sit in a room with Cynthia by myself. I'll chicken out—or she'll find a way to exploit the situation, so I look even worse than I already do.

Who can I rely on to help me when my boss is the only one who knows she lied about her pregnancy? Even though Bud would help, I can't drag him into this. It's professionally inappropriate to involve him in my private life.

No, this has to be an objective observer.

Someone I don't get along with but whose integrity is pristine. I pull my phone from my pocket and stare at the screen.

I can't believe I'm doing this. I open the contacts and swipe to Nathan's name. We've run into each other multiple times at the gym, so I know he's a night owl.

The phone rings three times before he picks up. "Sullivan?"

"I need a favor."

A low laugh crackles across the line. "You want me to take over your practice? Sure, no problem."

I run my hand around the back of my neck. This may be worse than dating Cynthia in the first place, but my gut says Nathan's the man I need at my side. I want to trust myself, so I'll trust him. "That's not what this is about."

"You've had it out for me since day one. Now you want a favor? What gives?"

"I need a wingman."

"Complicated surgery?" His voice takes on a serious tone. It's his professional, no-BS tone, and I appreciate that he can switch modes so effectively.

"Can you meet me in my office Monday morning at six a.m.?"

"Not until you tell me what this is about."

I dig my fingernails into my forehead. I have to tell Nathan the truth to fix my reputation and stop the buzzing rumors. The reasons don't make it any easier to tell my rival my deepest, darkest secret.

Thankfully, he listens patiently and doesn't interrupt as I spill my guts. When I finish, he's silent. I appreciate that he's processing everything I said and doesn't just laugh at me for being a dumb doormat.

"Will you help me?"

He blows out a long breath. "Yeah, I got your back. We can't have her painting targets on surgeons' backs. I'm at a conference in San Diego beginning of next week. Can you survive if we push until Thursday?"

My head falls to my hand in relief. "No problem. Thanks, man."

Most people don't understand the pressure on surgeons to live up to everyone's expectations. We aren't rockstars or famous athletes, but people still hang on to our coattails. Associating with us is a status symbol. Somedays, I wonder if I would have pursued this career if I'd understood the pressure to fit the image.

We hang up, and I take a cleansing breath.

It's almost over.

Lights from a sedan illuminate my hidey-hole and activate Gran's exterior security lights. Declan's long frame climbs out of a car so small, he shouldn't fit inside. He walks to the passenger side, opens the door, and lifts Bridgette into his arms.

I'm seeing red and stomping across the grass before I realize what I'm doing. "What happened?"

"Her friends got married."

Her head rolls against his chest until she's glaring at me out of half an open eye. "Hello, Liar McLiarpants." The words come out more like *yello wire migwirepans*, so I know she's trashed.

He shifts her in his arms, readjusting his grip, so she's higher against his chest.

"Let me help." I reach for her.

He shifts his weight back. "I don't think she would appreciate that."

Her arm flails in my direction. "Nobe, I vud nah appeciate tha ad all."

"Bridgette, I'm sorry. Let me make it up to you."

She rubs her nose against Declan's chest. "You smell like rainbows and leprechauns."

"What does a leprechaun smell like?" he asks.

She snores in response, snuggling deeper into his arms.

Watching him cradle her against his chest brings dumb Neanderthal, possessive, over-protective tendencies to the surface. She shouldn't be snuggling into him and enjoying the way he smells.

Three days ago, *she* was in *my* arms. *My* lips were on *her* body.

She and I were on the precipice of something universe-defining.

But I let my secrets drive her away.

My jealousy makes my skin crawl.

Irrational jealousy was the first clue that something was wrong in my relationship with my ex. The idea of being like her makes me wary of myself and my actions.

I scrub my hands over my face. What is wrong with me? My motivations for wanting to take care of Bridgette should be selfless and pure. I want to help her because it's what she needs, not because I don't want Declan to earn her favor.

Declan gives me a sad, knowing smile. "I'm not getting in a pissin' contest with ya, chum. Just bringin' her home safe. I care about taking care of my friend, and you are persona non grata at the moment."

"I know. Follow me."

Gran gave me a key to the carriage house a long time ago. I pull it out and unlock Bridgette's door, sliding it wide enough for Declan to carry her inside. "The door on the left." I follow him in and watch helplessly as he lays her on her bed.

"I got it from here." I slip her sandal from her foot.

He eyeballs me. "You broke her heart. Not sure she'll wanna see ya when she wakes up."

"I'm glad she has a friend like you. I know you don't like me, and you don't trust me, but I promise I will not hurt her again."

He holds his hand out for me to shake. "I trust you'll be a man of your word."

I grip his hand firmly, without any animosity. Declan is a good guy, and we're both lucky to have him in her corner. I understand why Jake thinks he would be the best option to take over the restaurant. Declan is loyal, dedicated, and genuine. He would never do what I've done to someone he loves.

He scribbles a note and his phone number on a piece of paper and puts it on her bedside table. "'Til class tomorrow."

I wait for the door to click shut before removing her other sandal and covering her with a blanket. I add a glass of water to the note. I retrieve ibuprofen and the electrolyte mix I keep in Gran's kitchen and add them to the water.

Bridgette has wiggled her way under the sheet. Her hair fans on the pillow, and she tucks her hands beneath her chin like a little kid without a care in the world. It's nice to not see the crease of frustration that has lived between her eyebrows since Willard Island.

I cram myself on the tiny sofa in the living room and wait for her to wake up. I'm going to finally tell her the truth, even if it makes her hate me more.

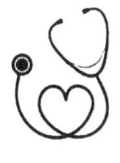

Chapter 29

Bridgette

A LOCOMOTIVE POUNDING THROUGH my brain.

A hurricane churning in my gut.

A jackhammer eroding my skull.

I'm not sure which analogy is best for how crappy I feel this morning.

Daisy was right.

Those margaritas are stronger than they seem. I should have left Declan's alone, but I hate seeing good food and drink go to waste.

I jam my fingers into my eyes, but it doesn't relieve the pressure. My temples throb. Massaging them helps a little.

I blink my eyes open and find water, beige pills, and a packet of electrolyte mix next to a note from Declan. That was sweet of him. I'm relieved he's understanding and kind.

I would be horrified for Keegan to see me in this state. I can see the judgment in his eyes already. I slowly push myself to a seated position and wait for the room to stop spinning.

It takes about ten minutes, but whatever. It's the price I pay for drowning my heartache in sugar-coated tequila. The pills slide down easily, and the water eliminates my cottonmouth.

After a stop in the bathroom to scrub the slime from my tongue, I gingerly make my way to the kitchen. I shove my head in the refrigerator, hopeful for something to ease my stomach.

A snore stops me cold. I turn slowly and find Keegan passed out on the sofa. He's too tall to fit on the loveseat. One leg dangles over the back while the other hangs off the edge of the armrest. His bandaged arm's thrown over his face, and his shirt has curled up to reveal the six-pack my fingers traced the other night.

As much as I appreciate the view ...

What the heck?

What is he doing here?

He's the last person I want to see. I smack his foot.

He jerks awake, flailing to his feet. "Code blue OR five," he sputters before he realizes where he is.

"What are you doing in my apartment?" I want to tap my toe, but the movement reminds my stomach it wants to be nauseous, so I stop.

He digs his thumb and forefinger into the corners of his eyes. "Making sure you don't die of alcohol poisoning. You're welcome."

"It was four shots of tequila. I'm a lightweight, not an idiot. You can leave now."

"We need to talk."

"My brain is not ready to comprehend anything you have to say, so let's put a pin in that until the Tuesday after never."

"You don't need to be this pigheaded. I'm here to apologize and to tell you what happened so you know why I didn't tell you the truth."

I rake my hands through my snarled hair. This is the conversation he promised me. The opportunity to finally understand why Keegan is jaded and cagey appeals to my caretaker side like chocolate appeals to a five-year-old. It would be ridiculous not to listen and cling to my frustration.

If I'm going to be mad at him, it can't be because he didn't try. "Let me make coffee first. Maybe a batch of blueberry scones. Do you like blueberries?"

His cheek twitches. "I love them."

I turn on the coffee pot and grab ingredients out of my cupboards. I'm only here three weeks, but I fully stocked my pantry. Baking whims are real and must be delt with swiftly. Like blueberry scones for a hangover.

Besides, scones take thirty-five minutes. That gives the ibuprofen enough time to do its thing.

Keegan stretches and rubs his hands over his arms and chest as if he's trying to revive himself. "Can I help?"

"Nope."

He flips a dining chair around and straddles it. "I love watching you work in the kitchen. It's your element."

"No sweet talking, please."

"Sorry. I'm working on honesty and full disclosure."

"Work on it silently. My head is killing me."

When the coffee is brewed, the scones are golden brown, and my headache is a four-point-oh on the Richter scale, I grab a tray and load it up.

Between my hangover and his hangdog expression, this tiny living room is stifling.

I need ocean breezes to listen to whatever he has to say. "Gazebo?"

He takes the tray and follows me outside. I pick the bench facing the water, curl my knees to my chin, and wrap my fingers around my coffee cup like it can provide a semblance of comfort and protection. "I'm listening."

He takes the seat adjacent to me. "I noticed Cynthia a little over a year and a half ago at a directors' meeting. She's one of my hospital's senior VPs. My boss was away at a conference and asked me to fill in at the last minute. When I walked into the conference room, she was regaling the head of neurosurgery with a story about her most recent humanitarian trip to Haiti. It took me six months to get up the courage to ask her out for coffee." He taps his fingernails against his mug with a wry expression on his face. "She seemed brave and compassionate, and I couldn't avoid her magnetism."

"You fell in love with her?" The bitter bite to my tone makes his eyes widen.

"No. I was infatuated ... bewitched." He stares into his coffee. "Duped." He takes a small sip. "Her friend had a dinner party four months after we started dating. Cynthia spent the night bragging about how great it was to be a doctor's significant other. She said once I popped the question, she would use my money to buy herself a mansion, spend her days shopping, and never worry about anything ever again. She called me her golden ticket and paraded me around like a show pony."

My throat tightens. Every relationship has its issues but come on! I didn't do anything to make Keegan think I care about the number of zeros in his bank account.

"Because she was materialistic and shallow, you assumed I would be too?" I throw a scone at his head. "Thanks for that."

He catches the pastry midair and shoves a bite in his mouth. His eyes flutter closed. "Man, is there anything you can't bake? This is extraordinary."

"Oh, my goodness. Seriously? You just accused me of being superficial and greedy, and now you're poetic about a scone?" I push to my feet and jog down the gazebo steps. "I don't have time for this. I need to … call Camille about bridesmaids' dresses." I don't—my best friend got married without me—but it's the first thing that pops into my head.

He dashes around me and holds his hands up. "She didn't care about me. She cared about my title. Not who I was as a person."

"But I did. I fell for you when I thought you were just a chef. Yes, I told you I want to get married, but I never said I want to marry you. I'm a small-town baker who's only aspiration in life is to feed people well."

He hangs his head. "I know."

"Do you? Because it doesn't seem like you know me at all." All those days we spent cooking and searching for the truth about Turner's story, and he couldn't tell I wasn't anything like that woman. I was more delusional than I thought.

He rubs the side of my arm with the back of his hand. "Let me finish, okay?"

My hangover beats against my eardrums. I need a glass of water ASAP. "What more could there be?"

"More than you can imagine." He drops his forehead against the side of the gazebo, his voice barely above a whisper. "She was parroting the dreams I'd shared with her like it was the checklist to win herself a husband. I want three kids, so she told her friends the names she'd picked. I want to spend summers here at the beach, so she emailed me real estate listings all over the Gulf coast. I was dumb enough to give her the information that convinced her she could manipulate me into giving her the cushy life she wanted. I broke up with her as soon as we got in the car. I could never marry someone who only wanted to use me as a piggy bank."

"That makes sense. No one wants to be used, but that doesn't explain why you lied to me. What did I do to give you the impression I would ever treat you like that?"

"I'm not done yet." He sinks onto the step. He swallows three times before he continues. "Two days after I broke up with her, she called me and confessed she was pregnant."

I gasp and bite my knuckle. Pregnant! "Why are you here? How far along is she?"

What is he even doing here talking to me? Why did he kiss me? The urge to scrub the feeling of him off my body overwhelms me. I'm a cheater. A homewrecker.

"She said she had this whole big reveal planned, but I'd ruined it. Because I broke up with her, she said she'd contemplated not telling me, but she knew she couldn't hide it and I would want to know. She hoped I'd be excited, even if the circumstances weren't ideal."

The pain in his eyes knifes into my chest. To father a child with a woman who only saw him as a means to an end would be horrible. To know you'd helped her snare you into a relationship you never wanted would make me jaded too.

Jaded enough to lie? I'm not sure.

"I thought doctors knew better. Always use more than one form of protection. Better yet, don't have sex with sociopaths."

He gives me a side-eye. "The timing was suspicious. She was volatile as it was. Any accusations on my part would make things worse. I want to be a dad. Have a family. Just not with her. We made an appointment with an obstetrician, but she rescheduled it for a time when I was in surgery. I never heard the heartbeat."

The tightness in my throat threatens to choke me. "Wait, why is that sentence past tense?"

He holds up a finger.

Patience? Yeah, that's not going to be easy. I take up the pacing he was doing a minute ago and give him an, *Out with it, keep talking* hand-flap. I need to hear the end of this story before I have a heart attack.

"She told everyone at work how excited we were, how she'd move into my apartment, and eventually we'd set a date for a wedding. People stopped me in the halls to pat me on the back and shake my hand. Inside, I hated her more and more every day, but I couldn't let anyone see it. She was carrying my child. I felt so ashamed of myself for doubting her. For not wanting *her* baby. For being trapped."

"Is it a boy or a girl? Have you picked a name?"

His chin falls to his chest, and he struggles to take a deep breath. "When she would've been sixteen weeks, she left a panicked message in my voicemail saying she was in the Emergency Department at a hospital on the other side of town. She'd lost the baby. I missed her call by ten minutes. She didn't pick up when I tried calling her back. I ran every red light to get to them. Redialed over and over. I pulled into the parking lot, but she still didn't answer. I burst through the doors as a text came in saying she was already home and didn't want to see me."

"Keegan, I don't know what to say." The shame and the relief must have eaten a hole in his soul.

The baby he didn't want was gone, but so was a precious life that would never be born.

That little boy or girl would never learn how to ride a bike, graduate from high school, or fall in love.

He fists his hands in his hair. "Over the next few weeks, she clung tighter. But only at work. She showed up in the OR waiting area and begged me to take her back in front of my patients and their families. She didn't answer my phone calls, but she popped into the physician lounge sobbing. She ranted to her coworkers that I wouldn't let her move into my place, but when I tried to talk t0 her in private, she was always running to meetings and couldn't be bothered."

He keeps rambling. "It got to the point I was nervous to go to work. My hands shook during surgery. She wanted our friends to see her heartbroken, to see me as the asshole for not comforting my grieving girlfriend. I couldn't do it anymore. Her story didn't add up. If she'd had a miscarriage, they would have admitted her for observation at the very least.

"One of my old interns works at the hospital she went to. I asked him to look up the attending who oversaw her care. She didn't even have a patient chart. I talked to the obstetrician." His chin wobbles. "Cynthia was never even pregnant. She lied so I wouldn't break up with her, and then when she would have started showing, she faked the miscarriage. Everyone believes she's the suffering mother who lost her baby. I was so angry and heartbroken and bitter. I couldn't do my job because she'd gotten so deep in my head, I doubted everything I did or said. I needed to get away from the hospital and from her. Jake's masterclass—it saved me."

Poor Keegan. My reaction should be so much deeper—angrier, more hurt, more resentful—but those are the only words I can think. "Did you ever tell anyone?"

"My boss knows, and one of the other surgeons, but no one else."

"Why didn't you defend yourself and tell everyone she lied?"

He blinks at me like it's the stupidest suggestion. "Who was going to believe me? Her reputation at the hospital is impeccable. I didn't have a way to prove her lies without providing documentation I can't get without breaking multiple laws. HIPAA denies me any rights as a father to know about the well-being of my child. The only thing I could have done was a paternity test, but because of the supposed miscarriage, there wasn't any fetal DNA to sample."

I shove a scone in my mouth as I digest everything he's told me. His brutal, enthusiastic honesty drove a manipulative gold digger to fake a pregnancy *and* a miscarriage. It breaks my heart for him, but it doesn't entirely explain his behavior.

"I'm … I'm sorry she did that to you. I'm sorry you're so jaded you couldn't see the possibility someone could love you for you." The next question claws at my throat. It demands to be asked even though it's heartless and cruel. "I'm sorry to make this about me, but how could you think I could be like that? What did I do to make you think I was selfish, self-serving, and manipulative like her?"

He stands and steps toward me like I'm a skittish kitten, hands extended, steps slow, gaze never fully meeting mine. "This isn't about you. This is all on me. I was in love with the idea of partnership and building a family with someone. My gut didn't tell me to steer clear of her, so I didn't mete out my trust appropriately. I leapt before I looked. I haven't told my parents or Gran. I'm too ashamed I fell for her lies and let it interfere with my work. I screwed up, and I should've trusted you with the simple facts of who I am, but I didn't know how. How could I trust anyone else when I didn't know how to trust myself?"

"And now?" I bite my cheek for the hope in my tone.

"I'm sorry, and I know a simple apology isn't going to earn your forgiveness, but I hope that you will. I hope that we can … start over is the wrong word."

Everything about my relationship with Keegan has been quick starts and slammed brakes. If we are going to have the kind of future I imagined while we were at the shack, I need to process what he's said.

Not just what his ex did to him, but how he reacted and what he's learned from the experience. What have I learned about him?

"I need to think about this."

"I'll answer any questions you have."

I can't think with his soul-bared eyes clinging to me like I'm his last hope. "I'd like you to leave. Please."

He grips the railing and chews the inside of his cheek. For a fraction of a second, I think he's going to ignore my request. Conflicting urges to wrap my arms around him and punch him in the face make me grip the step tighter and keep my butt in a seat.

Finally, he nods and leaves. He doesn't even pause long enough to say hello to Daisy on her porch stairs. Her gaze shifts back and forth between my face and his back, but she and I aren't going to have a heart-to-heart about my relationship with her grandson. She continues to refuse to speak to me about Turner, so maybe a taste of her own medicine will loosen her lips and help bring everyone the closure we need.

Chapter 30

Bridgette

AFTER KEEGAN LEFT THIS morning, I made myself a plate of scrambled eggs and another blueberry scone, then went back to sleep because ... yeah ... no ... I just couldn't deal with all *that* and the hangover.

Half the class met this morning with Keegan to practice building and maintaining their fires. Now it's time for Declan, Tyler, Axel, and me to put our skills to the test.

Keegan's truck pulls out of the parking lot as I round the corner onto Camino del Mar. Thank the biscuits I was divided into Jake's group.

Keegan and I need our space. But Jake probably knew that.

I don't know what to say to Keegan. I wish his revelation brought clarity, but it just made me more confused.

What could I have done differently to show Keegan I wasn't like Cynthia? Will he ever trust me fully or will the ghost of a baby that never was always linger in his mind?

I want to trust him.

I thought I wanted to fall in love with him.

I can't do that now. Not without more answers.

Like do I even want to stay in Texas.

Winning Jake's place will go a long way toward helping me decide because there's no point in dreaming about my future if I don't know where I'll be living. I'm not the type of woman to move across the country for the possibility of a guy. Especially one dealing with the heavy emotions Keegan revealed.

Jake assigns our smokers. He slaps a log against the palm of his hand. "We've got some good Texas post oak for our fires. What other woods do you want to try today?"

Axel raises his hand. "Pecan or apple?"

"Sounds like we're making pies," Tyler quips.

"Good thing we've Bridgette, then." Declan winks at me. "She'll teach us a thing or two."

I take the log from Jake. "You boys get to make your own pies. I want brisket." I build my tower in our smoker's firebox according to Jake's instructions. The sweet, earthy aroma of burning logs fills the space.

Declan prepares our brisket with cayenne, salt, and garlic while I tend the fire. Once the brisket is on the grill, Declan, Tyler, and Axel disappear upstairs to raid the kitchen.

Meaningless banter feels futile today, so I stay and shift the logs to help increase airflow to the fire.

Jake's squats next to me. "You're a natural at this."

I don't try to hide my smile. His praise makes me feel like a million bucks. The first ray of sunshine after a tornado. "Thanks, Jake. You're a good teacher. I'm glad I made the last class."

"I knew Turner wouldn't send me a bad chef."

Jake should have been the first one I asked since Turner bought the class from him. "How long have you two been talking?"

"Never stopped. He told me all about his whip-smart, sassy friend, and her tendency to argue over barbecue sauce recipes."

"What is in your sauce?"

"Not tellin', but nice try."

"Do you know why he left?"

"He never told me anything besides wanting a change of scenery."

"You believed him?"

"I knew better than to ask questions that would hurt my friend."

"Daisy never asked where he went? She never tried to track him down?"

He hands me a small log to add to the fire. "He asked me not to tell her. She never wanted to know. Warner was out on his own by then, so she pretty well became an only child when Turner vanished and that seemed to be okay by her."

"How do you think she would respond if I asked Turner to come home?" It's a silly question, considering the confrontation she and I had when I got back from the shack, but Jake's known her longer than I have. Maybe her reaction was more about the shock of my accusation than about her never wanting to see her brother again.

He rubs his hands together. "I'll bring the popcorn to those fireworks."

"That's what I'm afraid of." The rift in this family feels insurmountable. I don't understand why they hold grudges and cling to broken memories so fervently.

"She's a little stubborn, but you know it runs in the family."

I stretch my neck. "You're talking about Keegan."

"I am. Does that bother you?"

"Bother? No, he doesn't bother me. He confuses me."

"Can I help with any of that confusion? I've known that boy a long time."

How do I ask Jake to explain Keegan's character and behavior without betraying his trust? Jake doesn't know about Cynthia, so he can't tell me why Keegan acted the way he did.

He pats my shoulder. "I know it's on the tip of your tongue. Child, let me help."

Cynthia broke Keegan's spirit, and he hid to protect himself. It wasn't about me, but I was the unfortunate recipient of the consequences. I understand that.

What I don't get is why, after all the time we spent getting to know each other, he decided not to trust me with who he is.

Will the next bump in the road send him skittering to hide again? Or, if I give him my heart, will he protect it and keep it safe?

All the confusion and indecision comes down to one question. "Is he trustworthy?"

"Absolutely. I trust him with my life."

"Then why did he lie to me?"

"Now that's a little bit stickier. What did he lie about?"

"Why he is in town. His profession. Everything he spent his entire life building."

Being a doctor is an integral part of who Keegan is. Why wouldn't he want me to know that about him?

You don't accidentally go to medical school. It's not like Keegan couldn't decide what to do with himself, so he spent years and years in school and residency until he figured something else out. Or maybe he did. I don't know.

I don't know why he made the decisions he's made. Until I fully understand who he is, my heart needs to stay firmly in my chest, not on my sleeve for him to smash.

Jake rocks back on his heels and scrubs his hand over his bald head. "As to why he's in town, that's all on me. I begged him to stay and not tell anybody about me quittin' the masterclass."

"Why are you quitting? Or is that another secret?"

"When I'm ready, I will tell you, but until then, some things need to stay hidden."

These men and their mysteries. *Ugh*. "You sound exactly like Keegan."

"Pretty sure I taught him that one. His mama prides herself on never keeping secrets. Can't tell you how many times I've heard her say, *There are no secrets under my roof*. And you'd better believe there are none. Poor Lane. Whole town found out when she got her first menstrual cycle."

I slap my hand over my mouth. "Why would you share that?"

He shakes his head. "No secrets."

"That's not a secret, that's ..."

"It's a secret, but one that everyone is happy to keep."

"That still doesn't explain Keegan's behavior."

"Then let me tell you this." He settles his weight against one of the tables and crosses his arms over his chest. "That man has given up the last month of his life to be of service to me with no expectation of reciprocity. He's honorable, hardworking, kind. You'd be lucky to count him as a friend."

Heat tingles in my cheeks. "What if he's not asking for friendship?"

"More than friends?"

I nod and chew the corner of my lip.

"Don't let pigheaded stubbornness keep you from something that could be the best *something* in your life."

"If you had a daughter and you got to pick who she fell in love with ..."

"I would pick Keegan first every time." He squeezes my shoulder. "Watch those coals in the back. They're getting a little clumpy, with today's humidity, you need to let that air circulate."

I use the shovel to level my coal bed. "Thanks, Jake."

"Out of curiosity, do you want my restaurant? Or do you plan to follow Keegan to Dallas?"

"I want both." Jake's perspective is what I needed to forgive Keegan.

He went through hell. He's loyal to a fault, and his loyalty was used against him in the most grievous of ways.

I'd be more worried if he wasn't guarded in future relationships.

And I am the first. There was no way he wasn't going to keep secrets from me.

Jake winks. "We both have some hard decisions to make, don't we?"

Keegan's not moving to Bubee. Not when he has a thriving practice he loves in Dallas. Do I want to live here without him?

"Which do you think I should choose?"

"Always choose the one you can't live without, but ..." He taps the side of his nose. "That doesn't mean I'm promising you my restaurant. We're still operating in hypotheticals here."

"Noted."

"One last piece of advice." He hands me another log for the fire. "I've learned, with brisket, if you focus on the fire, everything else has a way of workin' itself out, given enough time. Kinda works for most of the rest of life as well." He holds up his index finger. "Find that one thing that matters most to you, tend it with all your heart, and things work out."

"You sound like Turner."

He pops his collar and swaggers to the stairs. "Age and beauty. Who woulda thought?"

Chapter 31

Bridgette

Honey Beans is nearly empty at this late hour. Georgi whirls something pink in a blender for the little old lady at the register. The woman is scantily clad in a neon yellow bikini under a woven dress that leaves nothing to the imagination. I hope I have the courage to wear an outfit like that when I'm her age.

Georgi tosses me a wink and chitchats with her customer before ushering her out the door, locking it, and flipping the closed sign.

"Fifteen minutes early is close enough. Want something to drink?" She pulls a black sweatshirt over her head that reads: Eat fish. Drink water. Enjoy the sun. Be a seal.

"If my body didn't already hate me, I'd say sangria. I'm not going to do that to myself."

"Had a little too much fun the other night. Who's the lucky guy?"

Too much fun. I don't know what that is anymore. So much has happened in the last few days. Jake's announcement. Camille's wedding. Keegan's revelations.

"There's no lucky guy." Even though I've forgiven Keegan, that doesn't mean he's my *lucky guy*.

"I have it on good authority that one fine Irishman took you out for drinks, but another swoony country boy left your apartment early the next morning."

I bury my face in my hands. "I'm not even a local, and people are talking about me?"

"Don't fuss. Amanda told Dotty about your barbecue partner, and Daisy told her about Keegan this morning. She told me when I dropped Tipsy off before my shift. I didn't think you were that kind of girl."

"I'm not." Even though I dated most of the eligible bachelors in Emerald Bay at least once, I'm not promiscuous. Monogamy and commitment all the way over here. I don't do one-night stands.

"The only person in my bed was me. I drank too much at Sobre and remember getting in Declan's car. I have absolutely no idea how Keegan ended up on my sofa. Nothing happened."

Besides his big confession which he doesn't want Georgi to know. Rumors ruin lives, right? That's his mantra. Now I know what rumor ruined his life.

I can't even imagine what it would feel like to walk into work and have everyone think I'd ditched my girlfriend when she miscarried our baby.

That's heavy in a way I can't begin to fathom.

The number of conflicting emotions running through his body must have twisted him more than spaghetti in a blender.

"Well, do you wish one of them *had* been in your bed?"

Until he and I talk, I have to give her a safe answer. "I need to figure me out first. That's what brings me here."

She boosts herself onto the counter. "What are we figuring out?"

"If a girl ... a woman we're contemplating moving to a certain small Texas town, where would she start looking for a job and a place to live?"

Because there isn't a guarantee I'll win Jake's restaurant, even though he asked me if I wanted it. I need to cover all my bases.

Georgi raises her hands over her head. "Am I supposed to be squealing and jumping up and down, excited you might be staying or worried you're having a midlife crisis? I don't know which reaction to give you."

"I don't know which reaction I want. This is scary. My friends back home are going to flip out. I think I need someone to tell me this isn't a crazy idea."

"People relocate all the time. It's how the Indigenous Peoples lost the United States to my conniving ancestors."

"That's a random reference."

"At one point in time, I had my heart set on opening a museum dedicated to the tribes who populated this area, but nobody wants to learn about European colonization and genocide while they're at the beach, so my head is full of random knowledge without an outlet. I gift you my silliness. You're welcome." She scrubs her eyebrow with her fingernails. "Are you thinking of staying because of Keegan?"

"He's going back to Dallas." Once he deals with the fallout from his ex and Jake's class is over, he'll be gone. But Bubee is closer to Dallas than Emerald Bay, so it gives us a place to start.

"If it's just our pretty little town that makes you want to stay, you might want to hold off on that decision until you experience Bubee in August. It is Satan's armpit, and I don't recommend it, even with our wonderful coastal breezes. Oh, and wait till we get a hurricane. Those are super fun. You never know if your house will be here when you get back after an evacuation. And we *always* have to evacuate. Even if it's projected to hit New Orleans five hundred miles away."

"That's not the sales pitch I expected." I expected a list of festivals and town quirks that make it idyllic, but I appreciate her brutal honesty.

"It's not meant to be. I have fallen in love with you." She presses her hands to her heart. "But I want you to understand what you're getting into if you decide to stay."

"Do you want to be my roommate? Move out of your uncle's trailer and live like a grown-up?"

"That's a tempting offer. Tipsy is almost done with high school and is doing a better job of standing up to her dad and brother, so I might be able to."

That's better than nothing. I appreciate her warning me about the awful weather. It's best to have all the facts before I decide. Can't say I'll miss scraping ice off my windshield at two a.m. after a blizzard dumps three feet of snow.

I slide onto the counter next to her. "I have something else I need to talk to you about, and I'm not sure the best way to do it."

"Sorry, honey, I said I love you, but men are my jam, even if you're hot enough to make me consider otherwise."

"That never crossed my mind, so we're safe." I wrinkle my nose. "I figured out why Turner left Bubee and never came back."

She props her chin on her fist. "Am I gonna be the first to know?"

"It kind of concerns you, your family." This may not be the best idea, but I need to talk to someone. Georgi knows her grandma and can help me decide what to do next. "Turner tried to convince your grandma to run away with him on her wedding day, but she said no."

She pats my knee. "Contrary to her contrariness, she was super in love with Peepa Auggie, so that makes sense."

"Did you know she was dating Turner? According to the letters I found, they were going to get married after the war, but he stopped writing to her." I chew on my lip. "I think she married your grandfather to spite Turner."

"That's a lot of assumptions I'm not sure I want to agree with, but it would make for a good movie."

"Yeah, I don't know what to do about this. I want to reunite Turner with Daisy, but what about Dotty? Does she want to see him? Will she explode if she sees him walking down the sidewalk? Your grandmother didn't want to talk to me before. She won't talk to me now if I confront her with any of this."

"Grammie strongly believes you have to suffer the consequences of your actions."

"I have to call Turner, don't I?"

"It's about time."

I hop off the counter. "This is not going to be fun."

She holds her arm out toward me. "Do you want me to hold your hand?"

"I need to be alone. I'll take one of those pink drinks though."

She spins, slides across the counter, and lands on her feet. "Dragon fruit, strawberry, mango smoothie coming up." She twirls the blender cup on her palm. "Do you want a shot of protein powder or immune booster?"

"Whatever will help my body feel like it belongs to a human again would be great."

After one final wave to my quirky friend, I sip my smoothie and walk the few blocks to the beach. Finding a spot next to the pier, I stare at my phone until the last rays of the sun warm my cheeks. I suck in a breath and dial Turner's phone number.

Will he have a good explanation for this wild goose chase he unwittingly sent me on?

Bridgette

"Bridgette?" Turner sounds sleepy answering the phone.

"How's Minnesota?"

Something clicks in the background. Maybe he's turning on a lamp. "Frozen and sconeless. How's class?"

I'm not going to beat around the bush. If I don't just ask him my questions immediately, I'll lose my nerve—or he'll hang up before I get the opportunity. "Why didn't you tell me this was your hometown?"

He hesitates. "Didn't think it mattered."

"I'm staying in your sister's carriage house. She was surprised to learn you're *alive* and own a bookstore in Minnesota."

He coughs and something tinks in the background. "I'm not a great correspondent."

That's a cruddy excuse if I've ever heard one. I dig my feet into the sand. "Why didn't you come home?"

"That's not why you called."

"You should visit." That sounds so lame.

But it's better than, *Hey, you haven't seen your sister or the girl you asked to run away with you on her wedding day in five decades, so why not pop down for the weekend and reunite? I mean, what could go wrong?*

Yeah, nope.

He clears his throat, so his words are strong and clear. "I have no place in Texas."

"Don't you want to see your sister? Meet your nieces and nephews and their kids? You have an entire football team of people whose lives you've missed."

I may be coming across too strong, but that's what I do best. If nothing else, this trip taught me to use my voice, speak my mind, and embrace my dogged confidence.

"It's too hard for me to travel these days," he says.

"That's garbage. You run 5ks every month. You sent me here to pave the way for you to come home."

"There's too much ... she doesn't ..."

"By she, do you mean your sister or Dotty Rios Buchanan?"

Yep, I went there, definitely pushing too hard. Too late now.

"What do you know about Dotty?" His voice isn't quite a growl, but it's on the way there.

"You showed up on her wedding day and asked her to run away with you, but she refused."

"I was a young fool." His voice is muffled like he's dropped his head into his hands but didn't move the phone.

"Turner, you told me I needed to have an adventure to find myself. I'm giving you the same advice. You need to come down here to find yourself. You can't pretend this part of your life doesn't exist. You need to talk to your sister. Meet the family members you don't know. You putter around that bookstore every day like you're looking for a lost volume. It's down here. It's the people you've ignored for half a century."

"It's too late," he whispers.

"Are you dead? Because the only way it's too late is if you're dead." Life is one and done. We don't get do overs or extra chances. We need to do the best we can with the time we have. The best Turner can do is embrace who he is now and let the people who used to love him, love him again.

"Why does this matter to you?"

I clutch the phone to my ear. "Because I love you, and I want to see you happy. I want you to be satisfied with every aspect of your life. I know you. I know you won't be satisfied knowing your family thinks you abandoned them."

"Daisy knows I didn't abandon her."

"You aren't the boy she remembers, and you need to prove that to her, or I'll ... never make you another scone."

"That's a low-down, dirty trick."

"I may never come back to Emerald Bay, so if you want more scones, you have to come to Texas."

"Jake got his hooks in you?"

"I'm trying to win his restaurant—did you know he's retiring? I could use a partner who knows how to run a small business. If you're interested."

His laugh's full-throated and belly-deep. "Ultimatums and a job offer. You're full of surprises today, dear, but what do I do with the bookstore?"

"The Bubbles need a good bookstore down here. Franchise."

"What about our friends in Emerald Bay? Have you even talked to Camille or Ethan about this plan? Hannah?"

"I won't worry them until it's necessary. I have to win Jake's contest first." They deserve for me to talk to them about my plans. They've stood by me since we met in elementary school and never judged me for the way I am. I love them, but it's not the same now that they're all married.

I get their behavior now that there's the possibility of a life with Keegan. When Jake announced the contest, I didn't want to rush to call Camille or any of my friends in Minnesota. Even though I was pissed off, I wanted to tell Keegan my plans and see his reaction. I guess that tells me more about where my heart is than anything else.

He's become my person, even on our worst days.

He and I have so much to talk about, but I need to fix Turner's relationship first. I owe him. "I'm buying your plane ticket."

"So I don't have a choice?"

"You don't have to use it, but I hope you do. I want to give you the same gift you've given me. Please, Turner, come to Texas."

"I like your scones too darn much to say no to you."

We hang up, and I stare at my phone. I need to prepare Daisy, and hope this isn't the family reunion equivalent of Mount Vesuvius.

But that's not what keeps my finger hovering over the text message icon. It's time to clear the air.

Bridgette: We need to talk.

Keegan: When and where?

Bridgette: Gypsy. 7 am. Bring coffee.

Chapter 32

Keegan

"How does Bridgette take her coffee?

Georgi eyeballs me over her espresso machine. "She doesn't have a usual, but wouldn't a good boyfriend know something like that?"

"I'm working on it, okay?" That Bridgette has even given me the opportunity to speak to her again is a big step in the right direction. I won't let myself be overly optimistic and assume this is a reconciliation, but I'd be lying if I said I'm not hopeful.

Georgi leans across the counter and taps her finger on the wood. "Work harder."

"What'd she tell you?"

"I'm not sure I want to answer that question."

"The town gossip wants to keep a secret?" I press my hand to my chest. "I might die of surprise right here."

Georgi isn't as bad a gossip as her grandma. She only shares strategic tidbits that help people. Right now I need her strategic tidbits.

She grinds coffee beans. "Your sarcasm is noted but not appreciated."

"Help a guy out." Showing up to the boat with a drink she hates will send the wrong message. This could be one of the most important conversations of my life, and starting with bad coffee will sink us before we leave harbor.

"Why should I help you?" she asks.

"Because ... I owe her."

"Wrong answer. Try again." She fills a cup with drip coffee.

Spilling my guts to Georgi might be the only way I get that perfect cup. Bridgette only asked for one thing, and I can't screw it up. "Because she's the best thing that's ever happened to me."

"Closer, but still not right." She tosses a look over her shoulder that says I'm holding out on her.

I hold my hands out, palms up. "I'm not telling you I love her."

"You don't?"

"How can I fall in love with her if she still hates me?"

Georgi sets the cup in front of me and leans on her elbows. "If you only love her *if* she loves you back, it's not love and you don't deserve her."

"If she hates me ..." I can't explain to Georgi how devastated I'll be if Bridgette doesn't forgive me. To have my heart torn to shreds twice. I'm not sure I can recover from that.

But Bridgette is worth the risk. A life with her is everything.

Georgia's face softens. "Does she set your soul on fire?"

"Is that a barbecue question?"

She flicks my forehead. "No, dummy, it's an emotional one."

"Brighter than a Bunsen burner."

"Not a raging wildfire?"

"Have you known me to do anything resembling a wildfire?"

"Besides steal a car?"

"That wasn't me." It wasn't *just* me.

"I know, but it's fun to make the vein pop out on the side of your head."

"Can I get the coffees, please? I'm late."

"Keegan." She lays her hand on top of mine. "I may not have gone to medical school like all you other geniuses, but I did take a few anatomy and physiology pre-recs. Trust me when I say what I'm about to say. Nod if you understand."

I nod.

Her grip tightens around the back of my hand. "Bridgette is one of the best people I've ever met. She's sweet, nurturing, open-minded, and open-hearted. She deserves infinitely better than the way you've treated her since she got here."

"I know." Oh boy, do I know.

"For some reason she loves you like I love Sangria Under the Pier. I can't live without it."

"You think she loves me?" Maybe a wildfire is a better analogy for how important Bridgette is to me. Fire heats me from the inside, and I want to let the full force of what Georgi's implying consume me.

Her nails dig into my palm. "Shush, please, I'm not done yet. Back to the point I was making before you so rudely interrupted. I think she does—however, I'm not sure about you. You have that fancy, fast life in Dallas, and that's not where Bridgette belongs. She's a Bubble through and through. If you screw up my chance at another best friend, I will remove your twig and berries like they taught me in Anatomy 301." She twists my wrist, and pain shoots up my good arm to my elbow. "Do you hear me?"

Tears pop to the corners of my eyes. She might break my ulna, tear a ligament, but the absurdity of the situation makes me laugh. "Twig and berries? Come on, Georgi. How can I take you seriously when you say things like that?"

She releases my hand. "Because you know me, and you know the extents I go for the people I love." She slides two drinks across the counter and taps the one on the right. "This one's Bridgette's. White chocolate lavender mocha. You get plain light roast."

"Thanks, Georgi."

"Go convince our friend to be a Bubble."

"Yes, ma'am."

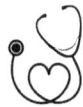

Keegan

Bridgette sits on *Gypsy's* bow with her arms wrapped around her shins. The sun's early rays add a golden glow to her skin.

I stand on the edge of the dock. "Permission to come aboard."

She scrambles to her feet with her hand clutched to her chest. "You scared me."

The words, *I'm sorry* will come out of my mouth about a million times during this conversation, so I'm not going to lead with them. "Coffee? Georgi sent you a white chocolate lavender mocha."

Her mouth twists. "We make those at home."

"You can have my black if you'd prefer."

She grips the boom and steps toward me. "No. It just makes me homesick."

"Ah." Does that mean she doesn't want to stay?

She's not in love with me like Georgi assumed. She doesn't want Jake's, and this is the beginning of a painful goodbye.

I sip my coffee to drown the nervous energy building in my limbs and chest.

She hasn't said anything yet. Don't jump to conclusions. That's what got you in this mess in the first place.

I step onto the boat. "Do you want to take her out?"

"No. I knew this would be a place where we would have privacy."

"What do you want to talk about?"

"I thought you were the smart one?" But her eyes sparkle with impertinence.

"I've been pretty dumb these last few weeks."

She nibbles the corner of her lip. "You have."

"Do you want me to apologize again?"

"I've heard plenty of apologies." She presses her hand to her chest. "It's time for me to apologize."

"For what?" I rack my brain but can't think of anything Bridgette has done that would require her to apologize.

"I put a lot of pressure on you. I made demands that I shouldn't have because I was insecure."

"That's nothing to apologize for. We're good."

An adorable crinkle forms between her eyebrows. "How come you get to be the only one to apologize?"

"Because I'm the only one who screwed up."

"I shouldn't have demanded you tell me every detail about your life when we were just getting to know each other. Yes, normal first dates include things like careers and hometowns, but they aren't required. It took years before my best friend told me the details of her parents' divorce and what that did to her. Why would I expect a stranger to be an open book?"

"I still don't think you need to apologize, but apology accepted." I climb into the cockpit and lean against the helm. "Is that all you wanted to talk about?"

"Maybe. Why? What else do you want to talk about?"

If I don't sit down and put space between us, I'm going to try to touch her, so I grab a seat and cross my shin over my knee. "I kind of dropped a big bomb on you about my ex, and you haven't said anything about that, so I'm kind of wondering what you think." The words come out in a rush. She has to know how nervous I am.

She picks at the lid on her cup. "She is a horrible human being."

"Agreed."

"There's no way you could have known what she was going to do."

"Also agreed, but it doesn't excuse the way I acted."

She sits across from me. "Never forever. That's what Graham said about me. I told you immediately how insecure I was about never finding someone who'll love me. I could have been exactly like Cynthia. You thought the only thing stopping me from seducing you into marrying me was your fear of falling for lies like hers again. I get it. It's okay to be afraid and not let everyone know everything." She sighs. "I wish you'd told me about your career sooner, but it doesn't matter anymore. There are a million things we don't know about each other. Intimacy takes time."

"I should have been as vulnerable as you were." Even though I was scared, once I learned her intentions, she deserved for me to open up. Relationships aren't only built on physical attraction—which we have in spades—we have to share every aspect of our lives to really get to know each other.

She shakes her head, causing a few whisps of hair to soar in the morning breeze. "You can't think in absolutes. Life is a spectrum. Our actions and decisions slide us back and forth on the vulnerability scale daily. She was cold-hearted and manipulative. Anyone with a modicum of protective instincts would have done what you did."

I lower my foot to the hull. "So I'm off the hook?"

She tilts her shoulder and takes a slow sip from her mocha. "Until the next time you screw up."

I slide to the edge of my seat. "There gets to be a next time?"

She scoots forward so our knees are six inches apart. "Do you want there to be a next time?"

"Georgi said something, and it got me wondering."

Her giggle catches on the breeze. "What did our gossip-prone friend say now?"

"She thinks you fell in love with me."

Her eyes widen. "That's presumptuous of her."

"Is it true?"

She slides back against the backrest and crosses her knees. "Did you fall in love with me?"

"I asked you first."

"I asked you second."

"Bridgette, I don't want to spend another day without you."

"That's not the same as loving me." She lifts her cup. "I don't want to spend another day without coffee, but I'm not going to marry it."

My heart thuds in my chest like it's trying to escape. "Marriage? We're jumping there?"

Her cheeks flush. "Figuratively speaking, I mean. We haven't known each other a month. I would never presume. I might hate the way you fold towels."

I raise my hands. "If laundry is a deal breaker, I need to walk away now. My clean clothes live in the basket until I wear them again."

"It's nice to know you're capable of operating a washing machine."

We're too far apart. My fingers don't want to wrap around a paper cup, they want to caress her cheek. I stand and join her on her bench. "All this banter is delightful, but you still haven't answered my question."

"I don't want you to think I'm saying it because you asked me."

"Well, in that case." I thread my fingers into her hair, trailing my thumbs across her cheekbones to tilt her head toward me. "I do love you. If you don't feel the same, I don't expect you to say the words. I respect you for not saying them and being honest with me. But know that I'm all in."

"All in? What does that look like?" Her lips are so close, air moves across mine when she talks, but they're still far enough away to let cooler heads decide whether we take this where I hope it leads.

"You want my life plan? As of a few weeks ago, I was going to help Jake and then go back to Dallas and deal with my mess of a reputation alone. But I met this sexy blonde, and she pretty well threw that plan in the woodchipper. I have no idea where to go from here without her input."

Her gaze darts to my lips, and she leans half a millimeter closer. "She likes Bubee, and she'd like to stay, but she's also willing to break every rule she ever set for herself and follow you to Dallas if that's where you're going to be. They're bakeries up there, right?"

"Small-town girl wants to move to the big city?"

"I just want to be with you. I love you too."

Her lips press to mine, and I know in my soul this is where we belong. No one but Bridgette could have brought me back from the deep misery I lived with after Cynthia.

My sunflower's effervescent, uncompromising authenticity led me back to the light.

I hold her tighter and luxuriate over the feel of her body pressed to mine, her mouth learning me, and my heart loving her.

This was fast, but we couldn't have fallen any other way.

She kisses the angle of my jaw. "By the way, Turner will be here on Tuesday."

"Excuse me?" I lean away so I can look into her eyes. "When did this happen?"

As annoying and ill-timed as her revelation is, I'm glad she's still taking care of those she loves.

"I convinced him last night."

"He does want to come home?" I never thought the reunion would happen and now it's days away.

She scrunches her nose and tucks her head like a turtle. An adorable turtle, but still a turtle. "I may have threatened to never bake him another scone for the rest of his life if he didn't come talk to Daisy."

"Good to know you fight dirty."

She snuggles under my arm. "I always get what I want. Like you."

I scoot away. "Honestly? Those words make me nervous."

She smacks my arm. "Oh, my goodness. I meant the hot guy with the big biceps who's good at moving boxes and is kind enough to keep a tourist company on her first night in town without pressuring her to take him home."

I swing her legs across my lap. "That's what I thought you meant. I just needed clarification."

"That is not what you thought." She grabs my face and smashes my cheeks. "I'm smitten with the orthopedic surgeon, but I'm in love with Keegan Sullivan. I realize it will take time to rebuild your trust in people but know that you can trust me."

"I do. Now what do we do about Daisy and Turner?"

She scrunches her face. "They both like barbecue."

I guess that's a start. To a couple of things, actually.

Chapter 33

Keegan

Turner is taller than I expected him to be. He's not a hunched-over old librarian-type with half-moon spectacles and a moth-eaten sweater.

He's elegant in a trim pinstripe blazer, khaki pants, and a bright yellow bow tie with ducks on it. With my grandmother's hazel eyes and my great-grandfather's long limbs, he carries himself with an air of gentility.

Turner wraps his arms around Jake, and they pat each other on the back twenty times before letting go. Jake squeezes Turner's shoulder. "About time you got back."

"My scone maker threatened to revolt if I didn't." He tosses a warm smile at Bridgette. She nods her head in a, *you bet your bottom dollar* expression.

Turner's attention shifts to me. "You helped Bridgette get us together?"

I hold out my hand. "Keegan Sullivan, sir."

He takes my hand and shakes it firmly. "It's nice to meet you, Keegan. You better be nice to her because I'm the one you answer to if you're not."

Bridgette swats his arm. "Turner."

"What? I see the way he looks at you, and I am no old fool. If you don't see it, you'd better start watching him with the same intensity he's watching you."

Her hands wrap around my biceps, and she squeezes into my side. "I'm watching."

"Do we need to talk about the birds and the bees?" he jokes.

She buries her face behind my shoulder. "Oh, my word, kill me now."

Jake gives Turner a tour of the restaurant and kitchen. Turner keeps casting Bridgette glances I don't understand.

They have a connection, a silent bond I envy. They've obviously spent hours and hours getting to know each other and perfecting this silent form of communication.

At the end of the tour, Jake pats a stack of to-go boxes. "Dinner is all set. Tell your sister, *hey* for me."

Turner flicks his thumb over his shoulder. "Do you want to come with us? She might be less inclined to yell if you're there."

"Not on your life buddy. I am not getting anywhere near your sister's wrath if things go sideways. I need her to like me when this is all over."

Turner grins. "Always looking out for number one."

Jake spreads his arms to encompass the restaurant. "I have a thriving business to bequeath. I can't lose my limbs before that's accomplished."

"Any chance Bridgette is the front runner?" Turner asks.

"Sorry, not givin' any hints."

She grabs the to-go boxes. "Let's go before anyone says anything else embarrassing."

We climb into my truck and drive to Daisy's house. Bridgette and I lean against the side while Turner climbs the steps and knocks on her front door. He gives us a thumbs up. We return it and cross the fingers of our other hands.

Daisy doesn't know Turner's in Bubee. We didn't know what she'd do if we prepped her. A wild hair might send her to Zimbabwe.

"It's open," she calls. Her voice is followed by a series of feminine giggles.

Turner looks to Bridgette with a raised eyebrow. I share a glance with her, but she's as confused as we are. He grips the door handle, pushes it open, and steps inside.

"Who else is here?" I ask Bridgette.

She nibbles the corner of her lip. "I don't know."

"What did you tell Gran?"

"Just that we had a surprise and would bring dinner."

"Sheesh. She probably thinks I proposed and invited the whole town." I take Bridgette's arm and yank her toward the house.

She digs her heels in. "Proposed? Why would they think that?"

I cradle her face in my hands. "Because ... even though it's too soon and I still have to fix everything in Dallas, someday I will ask you to be my wife. Grandmas know these things. She's jumping the gun a bit."

Bridgette's gaze darts back and forth between my eyes, her breaths turn short and shallow, and her hands fidget at our sides. "Keegan, I ... but ..."

"Sunflower, I know." I kiss her forehead, and her breathing calms to a smidgen below hyperventilating. "I'm not proposing. I love you. Let's see where that leads us before we pick matching Aston Martins."

Something shatters in the kitchen. Someone screams. Bridgette's eyes widen, and she dashes up the front stairs.

Forever will have to wait.

Bridgette

Keegan and I race the final steps to the kitchen and smack into each other when we round the corner. Turner quickly doffs his hat. At the stove, marinara drips down Daisy's hand. Shattered porcelain covers Dotty's feet. She presses her hands to her mouth.

Georgi lifts her glass. "Cheers to family reunions and engagements."

"Hello, ladies. Long time, no see." Turner worries the brim of his hat.

"What are you doing here?" Daisy's question is aimed at Turner, but her eyes are fixed on me and Keegan.

I straighten my spine. "Surprise."

Dotty unties her apron and slaps it against the back of the chair next to Georgi. "Daisy, I'll see you at Bunco. Georgi, let's go."

Turner raises his hand and steps toward her. "I'm not here to cause trouble. You don't have to leave. We have enough food for everyone."

Her lips pucker as she assesses him. "I will leave you to reminisce with your sister. Good day." She smooths her skirt and walks out the back door without a backward glance. Her heels clip down the wooden stairs faster than I would expect for someone of her age and breeding.

Georgi twists her mouth. "I guess we're leaving." She grabs the top takeout box from Keegan's pile. "Thanks for dinner." She hugs me. "I'll see if I can calm her down." She lifts my empty left hand. "Oh, well. Maybe next time."

I pull my hand away and nudge Turner with my elbow. "Don't you want to talk to Dotty?"

"She doesn't need to speak with me if she doesn't wish to."

I can't stand here and watch the hurt in his eyes. "You guys are ridiculous." I march after Dotty calling her name. She stops on the sidewalk. "Will you please come back inside?" I ask.

She jams her finger toward the house. "I have nothing to say to that man."

"It's been fifty-six years. Why do you still hold a grudge?"

"A grudge? This has nothing to do with a grudge."

"I read the letters he wrote. You were in love. What happened?"

She runs her hands down the front of her skirt. "I will not be the laughingstock of this town ever again."

"I don't understand. I thought your romance was a secret."

"He forgot about me." Her chin quivers.

"It wasn't like that. I have the letters in my room. I'll get them for you to read." I step toward the edge of the house.

"I have no interest in whatever you think you found."

"Grammie." Georgi laces their fingers together. "It wouldn't hurt to—"

Dotty shakes her off. "I can't. I refuse."

"He didn't know how to tell you about the horrible things he'd witnessed. He wanted to spare you the horror. He was trying to protect you."

"Protect me? Ha. We were supposed to support each other through thick and thin. He unilaterally decided I wasn't strong enough to be his partner. He promised me the world, and at the first sign of trouble, he fled. Tell me, what would you have done if he'd shown up on your wedding day? Would you have run away with a man who didn't believe in you?"

"When you look at it that way ..." Turner's attempt to protect her was a strong commentary on what he believed about her.

War is awful. There's no way a soldier can avoid the emotional and mental trauma. By hiding behind his protective tendencies, he didn't have to relive the worst days of his life. He could bury everything in a box in the back of his heart and never think about it again.

He probably didn't consider Dotty would interpret his silence as a commentary on her ability to be his partner. She wanted to share his burden, but he denied her the privilege.

"I'm sorry you felt devalued and judged by him. I don't understand how that makes you a laughingstock."

"I buzzed around town like a silly, lovesick schoolgirl. Everyone knew. We weren't hiding our relationship from anybody. Then he disappeared, and every time I stepped into a room, conversations stopped. I knew they were talking about me. About how the Rios girl couldn't even keep the attention of the grocer's son."

"None of that matters anymore. He's here." This can't be the end. Keegan and I didn't spend all this energy searching for Dotty to run away and refuse to talk to him.

"Why does that change anything?" Dotty asks.

"What if he still loves you?"

Her laughter is so condescending, I feel foolish for even mentioning their former relationship. "That's his problem, not mine. August became the love of my life when he stopped to help me change my tire.

He complemented me, put his confidence in me, and treated me as an equal."

"Let Turner apologize. He deserves the right—"

She jabs her finger into my chest. "What right do you have to preach to me about right and wrong? It was never your right to invade our privacy, dredge up events we no longer wish to remember, or invite him into Daisy's home. You have stepped out of line, young lady. Stop meddling in places you do not belong. I hope he takes you with him when he goes back to whatever hole he crawled out of." She stomps past a slack-jawed Georgi.

"He won't," I call. "This is my home now, and I'm hoping it will be his as well, so you just have to get used to us."

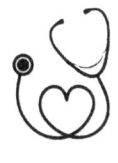

Chapter 34

Bridgette

I guess I'm never going to learn to keep my big mouth shut. I haven't decided to move to Bubee and Keegan hasn't hinted that he wants to stay, so I have no reason to believe that this sweet, coastal town will be my home.

Score one for impassioned outbursts. If I don't stay, that will tarnish Turner's reputation even further.

Oh, wait.

I don't care about Dotty's opinions.

I feel sad for her. She lives her life so worried about being hurt again she refuses to take half the happiness she's offered.

I'm not asking her to fall in love with Turner again.

That's silly.

Fifty-six years is a long time.

People change.

She had the white-picket-fence happily-ever-after. I understand wanting to honor August's memory, but why can't she and Turner be friends? All it takes is a meal, a conversation, and an open mind.

When I get back to the kitchen, Keegan is the only one who's moved. He leans against the island, shoving sugar cookies into his mouth. Daisy stirs marinara on the stove, and Turner stands in the middle of the hallway staring at his shoes.

"You people. Get over yourselves. Turner, take off your jacket and sit down. Daisy, why are you making spaghetti sauce? We told you we would bring dinner."

Her eyebrow creeps up her forehead, and she points the spoon toward the wall. "It's for the neighbor. He's having his hip replaced in two weeks, so I'm stocking his freezer."

"Oh, sorry. Stir away." She rolls her eyes. My permission is not required. "Keegan, will you help me unload the barbeque?"

"I'd love to." He kisses my cheek and takes the bags to the table.

I hand out porcelain plates. "Who's covering the bookstore?"

"Isa convinced Bryce to hold down the fort for me."

"What? Aren't you afraid he'll scare off your customers?" At Keegan's confused expression, I say, "They're some of my best friends from home. Bryce is a dog trainer with a more flexible schedule than his wife's, but he can be extremely grouchy, even on a good day." I hand Turner his silverware.

"He has very strong opinions about Dan Brown and James Patterson. If he growls at too many customers, Isa will let me know."

"How long are you in town?" Daisy asks.

"Until Sunday. I didn't want to overstay my welcome."

"Hmm." She turns her back, adds basil to the sauce, and hums a song I don't know. It's like the rest of us aren't here.

How do I break the ice between these two? I meet Keegan's eyes and widen mine, hoping he understands my silent request for him to help engage them in conversation. He just shrugs and loads sausage and baked beans onto his plate.

What's that saying? Control what you can and give the rest to God? I grab a plate and load it with ribs. Maybe uncomfortable silence will do what I can't.

I tear into Jake's ribs, and my eyes flutter closed. I don't know how he manages the perfect balance between sweet, tangy, and spicy, but his sauce is the best I've ever tasted. The ribs fall off the bones. I would lick the plate if I could get away with it.

Does winning the restaurant come with the sauce recipe? It had better, or I'll revolt ... if I win.

Keegan shovels his last bite of sausage into his mouth and rubs his stomach like a content pregnant woman. Turner nibbles at his food but doesn't dig in like us.

Daisy turns off the burner and ladles sauce into a container. "You didn't come back for Daddy's funeral."

Turner twists in his chair and braces his elbows on his knees. "I know."

She bangs the ladle to remove the remaining sauce. "Why not?"

"A blizzard grounded my plane. By the time the flight was rescheduled, it would have been too late, and I knew that would have been worse."

"You didn't call either."

"What would I have said? Warner was here."

"It's not the same. Mama wanted you. She cried more because you weren't here than because Daddy died. She'd expected his passing. She didn't expect you not to care."

Daisy's anger at her brother takes on a new dimension. Not only was she mad about him ditching her best friend—and trying to ruin the wedding—but he wasn't there for her when their dad died. He broke his mom's heart. She needed her big brother, but he never materialized.

He rakes his hand through his wispy hair. "I did what you told me to. I stayed away."

She leans her hip against the counter and stares at him. "Sometimes I think maybe you shouldn't have. I shouldn't have let my anger get the better of me at Dotty's wedding."

"I'm sorry for the heartache I caused."

They share an unspoken connection. The truce and healing have begun. Keegan squeezes my hand under the table. *We did it.*

Daisy dries her hands and sits in the chair next to him. "A bookstore?"

He loads her plate with ribs, beans, and potato salad. "Books were my only diversion during the war. I wanted to help other people find that sense of escapism."

"You always had an entrepreneurial spirit."

"Tell me about your kids."

Daisy's smile widens, and she spends the next hour regaling Turner with her children's and grandchildren's accomplishments. There's no shortage of gushing over Keegan's position as the associate director of orthopedic surgery at his hospital in Dallas.

I roll my eyes at the freedom with which she tells Turner the information I had to pull teeth to get.

"You just asked the wrong question," Keegan whispers in my ear. "She would have just handed you the soup recipe and told you stories about me that first night if you'd asked."

I elbow him in the ribs.

Turner's smile doubles. "I see you found your happy place."

My mouth twists, and I lean away from Keegan, scrutinizing him. "Something like that."

"Was this adventure all you hoped it would be?"

"It's better."

Turner reaches across the table and covers my hand. He squeezes lightly. "I haven't seen you smile this bright ... ever."

"Thank you for sending me."

He tips his head toward the front door. "Thanks for sticking up for me. It's nice to be home." He clears his and Daisy's plates from the table. "Sis, how about we go for a walk, reacquaint me with town, and let these guys clean up?"

"Wonderful idea. Let me change my shoes."

Daisy disappears to her bedroom, and Turner envelopes Keegan and me in a hug.

"I found that grandson you kept expecting to visit. Why did you lie about that?" I ask.

"Sometimes sad, lonely old men tell lies to encourage kind friends to bring them scones on chilly winter mornings."

I break the hug. "I knew it. I almost got frostbite that one time."

"But you didn't, and we had such a nice chat about Clive Cussler."

I squeeze him tighter. "Thank you for being the grandpa I never had."

"Thank you for being the granddaughter I always wanted."

Keegan wriggles out of our embrace. "You guys are so sweet, I'm getting a cavity."

Turner and I laugh at Keegan's discomfort. I love my cobbled-together family.

"Turner?" Keegan asks. "Will you keep Bridgette company for a couple days?"

"Where are you going?" I ask.

"Cynthia."

I wrap my arms around his waist. "I should go with you."

"I wish you could, but she'll freak out if she sees you."

"Maybe you need her to freak out to demonstrate how crazy she is."

"Don't worry. I've got a plan." He kisses my temple.

"That doesn't make me any less worried." That woman was willing to fake a pregnancy and a miscarriage to manipulate Keegan into marrying her. What else will she stoop to?

Turner pats my shoulder. "I'll keep her busy making scones, so she doesn't have time to worry."

"I do not like being ganged up on here, guys."

Keegan holds his hand out for Turner to shake. "Then you probably shouldn't have introduced us."

I'd rather be ganged up on than not have them both in my life, so I guess I'll deal with it.

And find a way to use it to my advantage.

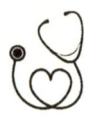

Keegan

"Thanks for doing this, man." I signal our waitress, and Nathan and I order iced teas.

She shares a shy smile with him. Black hair, shaved on the sides, long on top. Muscled like me. He stands out in a crowd.

He sits across from me in a booth in the back of my favorite hamburger place across the street from the hospital.

I figured the crowded restaurant would keep the fallout from Cynthia's theatrics to a minimum. We couldn't meet at the hospital. My personal life should not interfere with my professional life, even when the line between the two is hazy.

He drums his knuckles on the table. "No problem. You'd do the same if roles were reversed."

"I'm pretty sure you never would have found yourself in this situation."

"There's that, but nobody's perfect. Except me."

"I see nothing changed while I was gone." Somehow his cockiness calms my nerves. The people who support me are the same. They don't care about the rumors Cynthia instigated. They know who I am, what I stand for, and will continue to stand by me in my worst moments.

Even people who are part rival, part friend.

Nathan nudges my shoulder. "She's here."

Cynthia speaks with the hostess, a gentle smile on her face. I didn't have any expectations about how I would feel seeing her again.

Part of me guessed rage, contempt, irritation.

But all I feel is pity.

What does it feel like to be so insecure you think lying is the only way to get people to stay with you?

Where would our relationship have gone if she'd wanted me, not just my last name?

It doesn't matter now.

Bridgette is a million times the woman Cynthia could have ever pretended to be.

Bridgette is real, compassionate, and vulnerable in a way that makes her the strongest woman I know. She's not afraid to let life knock her around a little because she always gets up again.

Nathan switches sides of the booth so Cynthia can't sit next to me. The hostess points toward Nathan and me, and Cynthia's smile falters. She tightens her arm around the purse at her side and weaves through the tables to join us. "Keegan. Dr. Nguyen, good evening." She's pristine in a grey skirt and jacket with pearls around her neck. Her brown hair is coiled into a bun at the nape of her neck.

"Please, have a seat." I gesture to the empty side of the booth.

She looks at Nathan. "May I ask why I'm here?"

He gestures to me and remains silent.

"We need to clear the air." I point to the booth. "Please sit."

She pops her hip and scowls at me. "I have nothing to say."

"I guess it's a good thing I have plenty."

"I don't have to listen."

I retrieve an envelope from my pocket and set it in the middle of the table. "True, but by tomorrow the entire hospital will know you faked both your pregnancy and the miscarriage. If you would like Dr. Nguyen to hear your side of the story, now is your opportunity."

"Why is he here? He's not your boss or mine. He's not part of HR." She wiggles her fingers at Nathan. "I didn't think you guys were even friends."

"Friends might be too strong of a term, but we are colleagues who respect each other, and he has a vested interest in this situation. It can't be open season on physicians. Fake a pregnancy, snag a husband is not a game that can continue."

She sneers. "What does he get out of it? Are you paying him to lie?"

"He has no reason to lie, unlike you. Please sit down."

She glares at the seat, but the people around us are starting to stare at her with quizzical expressions, so she slides into the booth and sets her purse on the table between us.

The waitress delivers our iced teas. "What can I get you to drink?" she asks Cynthia.

"Ice water. Three lemons."

"Would you like some time with the menu?"

I fold the menus and hand them back. "We're not eating but thank you."

Disappointment flickers across her face. "I'll get that ice water." Our meeting is costing her tips. We'd better make it quick.

When the waitress is out of earshot, I fold my hands on the table. "Cynthia, before we start, I need to apologize to you."

"It's about time. You've wrecked me."

I hold up my hand. "I'm sorry my honesty led you on. It was never my intention for you to believe my feelings were stronger than they were. I didn't love you. But you didn't love me either."

"Yes, I did." Her chin quivers, but I've learned it's one of her tells when she's lying.

"Why did you pretend to be pregnant?"

She digs her nails into the sides of her purse. "I *was* pregnant. How could you even …"

"I checked with the obstetrician. You never tested positive for hCG. No hCG, no baby." The hormone most pregnancy tests search for is a clear indicator of whether a fetus is growing in the uterus. None was ever found in her system.

Cynthia slams her fist into the table, jarring the silverware, but doesn't raise her voice. "That's invasion of privacy. I'll have your medical licenses for violating HIPAA laws."

I slide the envelope across the table. "Our hospital's standard protocol is to analyze fetal DNA for genetic markers if one of the parents has a known genetic anomaly. My family has a history of heart defects. As the stated father, it is entirely within my rights to receive a copy of that report to protect my future children. It's due diligence." Paternity testing was no longer an option, but Bud reminded me that wasn't the only test they would have performed on Cynthia's blood. "It is your OB's responsibility to inform me if that test never occurred. I repeat, why did you lie? Do you make it a habit of lying to the people you claim to love?"

She removes the document from the envelope. Her eyes skim back and forth across the official letter from her obstetrician. Her hands look like claws as she rips the page to shreds. "I refuse to be part of this conversation any longer." She snatches her purse and knocks our waitress to the ground in her haste to stand.

Glass shatters. Water soaks the waitress' white button-down uniform.

"Are you okay?" Nathan slides out of the booth and checks the waitress for injuries.

Cynthia huffs and runs out of the restaurant as fast as her heels can carry her. My shoulders relax and contentedness settles on my chest.

She was never going to admit she lied, but she doesn't understand medicine. I could have requested a paternity test or genetic testing at any time.

The possibility of being a dad blinded me long enough to allow Cynthia's lie to root. She knew I would be too hopeful to doubt her initially, giving her time to complete her lie.

If I had asked for the paternity test right away, I would have saved myself months of heartache. I would have still had trust issues, but I could have dealt with them sooner.

I wouldn't have made Bridgette endure the broken man she encountered on the beach that first night. I would have been worthy of her from the start because I would have trusted myself to love her the way she deserves.

When I think about babies now, I see little blonde-headed girls with smiles like sunflowers, and my heart stutters and races with the excitement of what life will hold with Bridgette by my side.

I told her I wasn't ready to propose, but that wasn't quite the truth. No one will ever take her place in my heart.

The waitress mumbles several choice expletives.

Nathan chuckles. "That about sums it up." He pulls her to her feet and brushes the hair from her face. Their eyes lock and something passes between them.

The manager appears at our table. "Is everything all right?"

The waitress jumps away from Nathan.

I shrug into my suit coat. "Your poor server was an innocent bystander in an ugly temper tantrum. I apologize." I pull my wallet from my back pocket and grab a wad of cash. "This should cover the time we spent at the table, your dry cleaning, and a little something extra for the inconvenience. I'm so sorry."

The waitress darts a glance between me and the manager, then takes the money. "I accept your apology. Please don't bring her back."

"No worries there," I say.

Nathan and I leave the restaurant. I lean against the brick façade, rubbing my face. "Not quite closure, but it's something."

Nathan shoves his hands in his pockets. "Genetic testing was a good tactic. What else can I do?"

"I need everyone to know the truth." I'm a fool if I think Cynthia will slink away quietly.

"I'm not one for gossip, dude."

"I know. That's why you're perfect. If you hear someone talking about me and Cynthia, will you set the record straight? I wouldn't be surprised if she makes a scene when I'm back on Monday." All the more reason I need Nathan to pave the way over the next few days.

"Yeah, I can do that."

If you chart gossip on a graph, it has an exponential growth curve. I need enough people talking about her horrible lies for my story to catch fire and clear my name.

Too many women in our practice have dealt with the true emotional wounds of a miscarriage for her to pander to peoples' sympathies using it as her bait to catch me.

If she had half a heart, she would have known better.

If she had half a heart, she would have cared about me more than the letters behind my name, and we never would have been in this situation in the first place.

Nathan holds his hand out. "See you bright and early."

"Thanks again."

He steps back toward the restaurant.

"Forget something?"

He winks. "Our waitress's phone number."

"Good luck." To both of them.

He smooths his coat and checks his appearance in the window. "I'm too good to need luck."

Chapter 35

Keegan

My office is empty, but it feels good to relax in my desk chair. I run my hands down the leather armrests and stare at my degrees on the wall. A refreshing calm settles in my chest. Cynthia would never admit her lies, but I'm glad I confronted her.

It doesn't matter what she said about me. If I can get Nathan, my rival, to believe me and stand up for me, that's more than enough to quell my anxiety.

"Knock, knock." Bud steps into my office. "I didn't expect to see you for a couple more days."

"Hey, boss. I wasn't planning to come in, but ..."

He runs his hand along the doorframe. "There's something about this place that you can't get anywhere else."

"That's the truth." This is where I thrive. Some people go to church to find sanctuary. I come here. The antiseptic smell, polished linoleum floors, and constant hum of activity are unlike anywhere else I've ever been.

Except Bridgette loves Bubee. She's built deep friendships in the three short weeks she's been in town. What right do I have to take her away from them?

Bud settles into the chair across from my desk. "What's going on in that head of yours? You have a strange expression on your face."

"I have some big decisions to make."

"Is this about …"

"Cynthia and her miscarriage rumors?"

"I wasn't sure if we were speaking those words out loud."

"It's fine. She's not Voldemort. Silence doesn't make it go away." I brace my elbows on my desk and steeple my fingers under my chin. "Nathan and I met with her this evening."

"And?"

"She continues to deny her lies."

"I wish there was something I could do to help."

"Unfortunately, she didn't break any hospital rules, so we can't get her fired. Nathan's going to help set the record straight, but I know it'll take time."

"Can you work with people talking about you?"

I hold my hand out at shoulder level. "I'm steady. I don't care what she did anymore. I hate that she ruined my reputation and the emotional roller coaster I've been on for the last few months, but I can't fix the past."

Just like Turner can't make a Dotty forgive him, I can't go back in time and prevent younger me from asking Cynthia out on that first date. I probably wouldn't listen anyway.

"You're still making that face."

I rock back in my chair. "I love this hospital. I love my colleagues. You're an amazing boss."

"But?"

"But I don't know if I belong here anymore."

"Why is that?"

Bud's been my mentor for years and supported me through this entire process with Cynthia, so I trust him.

At the same time, I can't make any decisions until I know if Bridgette wants to stay in Bubee. She said she did when she yelled at Dotty, but will that change if she doesn't win Jake's restaurant?

We can make a home here in Dallas, but the vibe is so different from Bubee. I'm not confident she'll like it. I don't doubt she'll settle in, make friends, but I don't want to put her through that if I don't have to.

"Are you operating on the fifteenth or should I give the slot to another surgeon?"

"I'll be there. I have responsibilities to my patients, and I honor my commitments."

Bud tips his head and stares at me. "Never thought homesickness would pull you away from here."

"I'm just as surprised as you are." Jake's class was a refuge. It wasn't supposed to be anything more. Then Bridgette upended my entire world.

"Do I need to interview for your replacement?"

I lean my elbows on my desk. "I have a proposition to run by you."

"I'm listening."

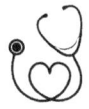

Bridgette

I miss Keegan. He's only been gone a couple of days, but Daisy's house doesn't have the same glow as when he's here. Turner comes down the stairs from his old bedroom and gives me one of his big smiles. "Mornin'." The word has an extended drawl to it.

"Your accent is taking over already. Next thing I know, you'll be saying *y'all* and *fixin' to get 'em ready.*"

He pours himself a cup of coffee. "I'm glad you remembered to pack your sass."

"Never leave home without it. Are you ready for the party?"

"Not really, but I can't hide in my parents' house forever. People know I'm here. I should make an appearance if just to quiet the gossips."

"Georgi warned me Dotty never misses one of Amanda's parties." We haven't seen her in the five days since she stormed out of Daisy's kitchen. Georgi says she's fuming and has called me every name in the book, but I don't care. Turner is happier than I've ever seen him. This is his place. These are his people. He deserves to be here as much as she does.

He settles next to me at the kitchen table. "I can be civil."

"Can she?"

"That is not my concern."

"I don't believe you. Will you tell me what happened on her wedding day?" My nosiness can't help but get the better of me.

I've let him be since he arrived, but I know there's more to the story than the bits and pieces I gleaned from the letters. Those details are only what Turner felt drawn to write, not the complete picture.

He scrunches a crooked eye in my direction. "Does it matter?"

"It matters to me." I settle into my chair like this is story time before bed.

"Why don't you whip up some scones while I tell the tale?"

I wiggle my butt in my comfortable chair. "I don't want to get up."

He continues to blink placidly.

This is not a battle I will win. "Oh, blackmail, I knew I learned it somewhere."

I grab a mixing bowl from the cabinet next to the stove and get to work. "What flavor would you like?"

"What are my choices?"

"Considering Daisy stocks her kitchen better than Hannah, you can pretty much have whatever you want."

"Cranberry?"

"She's got frozen cranberries." He always requests cranberry. He claimed they were for the non-existent grandson. Pretty sure they were his favorite. I snag the bag from the freezer.

"What about pineapple?"

"Cranberry and pineapple. That's a weird combination."

"I'm not asking you to combine them. I'm asking if she has pineapple."

"Hmm, let me check." I search the pantry, freezer, and refrigerator and find dried mango and passion fruit. I hold up the bags. "This will satisfy that tropical itch."

"Perfect."

I slice my knife through the bags, dump the dried fruit into a bowl, and sprinkle it with flour so the pieces don't stick together. "So, how did you find out about the wedding?"

"Even though I had stopped sending my letters, my mama continued to write. She was surprised how quickly Dotty had agreed to marry August, wondered at a pregnancy rushing things, but said Dotty's parents were over the moon that their daughter was going to be a Buchanan."

"That must have hurt." I measure ingredients and add them to the bowl.

"I borrowed the keys to my platoonmate's car and drove nonstop to get back here."

"Did you even think to ask for leave?" It's a trifle, but if he'd asked, he would have saved himself at least half the heartache.

He chuckles and runs his fingers along his chin. "About the time I crossed the Alabama state line, but by then it was too late to turn back."

"What happened when you got here?" I hand him the bowl to stir while I get the powdered sugar for the glaze.

"I went straight to Dotty's parents' house. Climbed in her bedroom window like I used to."

"And?"

His gaze drifts to the table. "In her wedding dress, she was the most beautiful thing I'd ever seen. She looked born to be a bride."

"What did you say?"

"Lots of dumb things."

"Details, Turner. I need details." I take the mixed batter from him and portion it.

"I told her I loved her, that I was sorry I hadn't sent my letters. I tried to give her the stack, to prove I hadn't forgotten about her, but she didn't want them. She was too mad by then. She threw them at my head."

My heart breaks all over for him. To stand in her room, seeing her in a dress he'd imagined her walking toward him wearing. I can't imagine the sadness he must have felt. "You begged her to run away with you."

He draws a finger down the space between his nose and his cheek. "Cried like a baby beggin'."

"She refused." She chose the man who treated her like a partner. That's the strength I see in Camille and Liam's marriage.

Love is important, but it's not everything.

If Keegan and I hope to build a strong future with a solid relationship, we need to learn to rely on each other too. Like him trusting me to get him to the hospital after the deck collapsed and me trusting him to fix everything with Cynthia without me.

Trust and intimacy take time. Time I'm willing to devote to us.

Turner spins his coffee cup, continuing his story. "Dotty called me a bunch of names that I will not repeat but were all true. She told me I had broken her heart, and she knew August never would, so she chose him."

"She's stubborn." I slide the scones into the oven.

"It was my fault. I know that. She made the right choice. August was always a better man than me."

"That's not true. You're a wonderful man. Look at all you've done for me."

"That's sweet, if false. I've done more wrong in my life than I've done right."

"You're not a twenty-year-old kid anymore. Everyone's allowed to make mistakes."

"I never could have given her the grand life she deserved. Daisy told me August took her on a world tour for her fiftieth birthday. She'd always wanted to see New Zealand. I never could have taken her."

"Why does everybody think big houses and fancy trips are the key to happiness? Happiness comes from being with the people you love. It doesn't matter where you are."

"Is that your way of saying you're moving to Dallas?"

"Do you think I should?"

I've made up my mind, but I appreciate Turner's opinions and points of view. He's wiser than I am, so maybe he has insight I haven't considered.

"Don't make the same mistakes I did. Is Keegan the one?"

"Yes." Unequivocally, with my entire heart, he's the man I want to spend the rest of my life with.

Turner's eyes latch onto mine. They shimmer with hidden emotion. "Hold on tight, kiddo and never let go."

"What about you? What are you going to do?" Now that Texas is home again, he can come and go as he pleases.

He blinks and takes a lazy sip of coffee. "I can be convinced to spend Christmas in Dallas or come back here, whichever you choose, but I can't give up Minnesota winters."

The oven beeps. "That's not what I'm asking. What are you going to do about Dotty? Do you want to reconcile?"

"It would be nice for her not to hate me, but for anything more, I don't know."

I rest my hip against the counter and cross my arms over my chest. "Why didn't you ever get married?"

Plenty of women in Emerald Bay would have happily retired his bachelor card, but he never even went on a date. He seemed so settled in his little bookstore bubble. He wasn't necessarily happy, but he wasn't sad. The only time I ever saw a fissure in his veneer was the night he gave me Jake's class. He hid his loneliness behind other tasks. Only in retrospect can I see how obvious it was.

Turner shakes his head. "I never put my heart back together. It would have been unfair to promise something broken to someone else."

"You still love Dotty, don't you?"

He shakes his head. "I loved what we were and what we could have been."

"That's not a no." I hand him a plate with his scone. "I hope she'll listen to you."

"I've already apologized. What else can I do?"

"Grand gesture?" I slice a bite. The tart mango and sweet passion fruit waltz across my tongue. I love scones.

"Any ideas?"

"No, but we can probably come up with something between the two of us."

Daisy's shoes clip-clop down the hall. "Smells good. What are you making?"

"Mango-passion fruit scones."

"Wonderful. I bought the fruit on a whim and never figured out what to do with it. Thank you for cleaning out my pantry."

"Turner and I were just talking." He shakes his head like he doesn't want me to share our plan with Daisy, but I forge ahead anyway. Who better than her best friend to tell us the secret door to Dotty's heart? "Turner wants to do a grand gesture for Dotty to prove he's sorry and would like to spend time with her to earn her forgiveness. Any suggestions?"

Daisy scowls. "Not this again. Didn't you learn your lesson the first time?"

He scoops an extra-large bite into his mouth and glares at me. "Apparently not."

"What would help her see how sorry he is?"

She taps her lips. "Her heartache is not something you can fix with flowers or chocolate."

"That's why we're doing a grand gesture. What was the grand gesture in that novel you finished last week?"

Her cheeks glow pink.

I brace my chin on my elbow and lean in. "Oh, it must have been good if you're blushing. Tell us."

"I'm not going to repeat it in front of my brother."

My eyebrows wiggle. "Bodice ripping?"

Turner shoves his fingers in his ears. "Lalalalala!"

"Come on, you two. No one knows Dotty better than you. We've got to come up with something."

Turner draws a triangle with his fingernail on the table. "Do you still have *Gypsy*?"

"Of course." Daisy serves herself a scone. "That boat was the last thing I had to remind me of our good times."

"Sailing was your thing, wasn't it?" I ask.

"Dotty loves the ocean. What about the shack?"

"The deck collapsed, but the rest of the building is intact."

I tell him the story of Keegan rescuing me and injuring his arm. The omission of his profession and how we've managed to work everything out. The G version, at least, because I'm not a kiss-and-tell kind of woman.

"We could rebuild it. That would be a pretty awesome grand gesture." And I wouldn't mind having a secret hideaway to drag Keegan to when we need a break.

"Do you think we can make it happen?" Turner asks.

"I know an orthopedic surgeon who's good with his hands."

Turner drags his hand down his face. "I hope that's not a euphemism."

"Oh, shush. You're good with your hands too. It's probably just been a while."

As we nibble our scones, we figure out how to rebuild the shack and kidnap Dotty for the day once the project is complete. I can spearhead the operation while Turner's back in Emerald Bay.

Stomach full of scone, I collapse on Daisy's porch swing and hand our notes to Turner. "This is a good grand gesture. I think she'll appreciate the effort you put into it."

"Only time will tell."

"Speaking of time, it's time I got to Amanda's house to help her prep for the party. I'll see you guys there later?"

Daisy pats my hand. "Wouldn't miss it."

I just hope Georgi's wrong, and I don't end up knee-deep in crawfish heads.

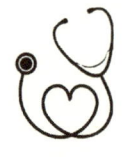

Chapter 36

Bridgette

Amanda's family lives on a ranch fifteen miles north of Bubee. Cows moo in the pastures, corn stalks sway in the breeze, and a smattering of wildflowers decorate the yard. Kids chase each other with water guns as I add toasted ham-and-cheese sandwiches to the serving platters.

Not a crawfish in sight.

Declan arrives early as well with two bottles of whiskey from his siblings' distillery. Amanda points to the table under a forty-foot oak tree threaded with white lights and hip bumps her husband. "Drinks over there, darling. Gary, get the beer out of the fridge in the garage."

He kisses her cheek and follows directions.

Slowly the rest of our classmates trickle in with their contributions to our potluck. Cheesy creamed corn, mustardy potato salad, spicy baked beans, bacony cornbread, crunchy green salad, sweet watermelon wedges, and decadent brownies overflow the tables.

SMITTEN WITH THE ORTHOPEDIC SURGEON   341

After my last drinking experience with Declan, I stick to lemonade and mingle among my friends. It doesn't feel right to celebrate the end of our class without Keegan here, but what he's doing in Dallas is more important than keeping me company today.

Jake, Turner, and Daisy arrive, and we fill our plates, settling into the table next to Amanda's kitchen garden. Georgi waves when she arrives. Four men I've never seen before flank Nora, Tipsy, and Dotty. I assume the oldest is Tipsy's dad, based on the angular noses and sparkly green eyes.

Dotty hovers on the opposite side of the yard ignoring our table.

"She's not even going to come say hi?" I ask Daisy.

"Dotty has a lot to think about. Don't rush her. That'll just make things worse." Truth resonates in Daisy's words.

Our grand gesture will take weeks. Weeks I'm not sure I have in Bubee. I'll know more when Keegan comes back, but until then I keep my seat and let the sun warm my shoulders. I'm wearing the same dress I wore the night I met Keegan, to help me feel closer to him.

When Dotty glances my direction, I offer her a friendly smile and little wave. Her eyebrows draw together, but she raises her hand in acknowledgment.

It's something.

Healing and forgiveness aren't quick processes. If they are, it's only because the pain inflicted isn't deep.

Turner wounded Dotty's soul. She feels judged, trivialized, and discarded by him. It doesn't matter if those weren't the heart behind his actions. We can never guess how people will react when we act out of our fears and they react out of theirs.

But we can offer kindness and humanity, validate their concerns, and learn from our mistakes.

I send up a little prayer for Dotty's heart to soften toward Turner.

Georgi throws her leg over the bench next to me. "This is yummy." She tips her head toward Declan. "So is he."

"He's leaving, so don't get too excited," I say.

She waggles her eyebrows. "How did your coffee date go with Dr. Sullivan?"

I dip my head so no one can see the heat racing to my cheeks. "Fine."

"Yay!" Georgi throws her arm around my shoulders. "You're officially a Bubble!"

Daisy rolls her eyes. "We are not Bubbles. We are Bubians."

Georgi's nose wrinkles. "That sounds like Barbarians, and I refuse to be a marauding vigilante. Besides, what's wrong with being Bubbles?"

Tipsy skulks to our table and taps Georgi on the shoulder. "Harry sent me to tell you to get him a drink."

Georgi yanks her down to our bench. "Your lazy brother can get himself a drink."

"Daddy wants one too, and Miss Amanda won't give me what they want. You know what they're like if they don't get what their way."

"Today is not the day to pick fights." Jake stands from the other side of Tipsy. "I'll take care of them."

Georgi gives him an appreciative smile. "Thanks, Jake. Will you ask Amanda to water them down please?"

He pats her shoulder and winks. "Already on it."

It's not my business to ask questions, curious though I am. I can guess based on Tipsy's hunched body language. Alcoholism has a way of infecting everyone.

Georgi steals a bite of my baked beans. "Is Jake announcing his winner today?"

"He didn't say."

"But it's the last day." She shovels more into her mouth.

"Of class, but he may want to speak to the winner privately. He wasn't forthcoming about the competition in the first place, so maybe he'll keep his successor a secret until ownership changes hands." Part of me was tempted to interrogate him when he arrived with Turner and Daisy. I can't plan the next step of my life without knowing which city I'll live in.

"When's Keegan back?"

"Next weekend." Seven more days.

"Is the plan for him to commute back and forth every weekend?"

"We haven't talked about it."

She gives me a side eye. "So you might not be a Bubble after all?"

I shrug. "Kind of depends on Jake's decision."

It's silly, but I want to run Jake's restaurant and I want to be with Keegan.

Does that make me selfish?

I will never be content unless I am feeding people. The more lives I help, the better. What better way to do that than with a restaurant like Jake's?

Georgi springs from the table. "Let me see what I can find out."

"Georgi, don't." I grab her wrist. "Jake will give his restaurant to whoever he thinks is the strongest candidate when he's ready. Today is about celebrating." I drain the rest of my glass. "Refill time."

"You have more patience than I do."

"It's taken me a while to learn to sit back and not stress over the things I can't control, but it's worth it." I spread my arms. "Look where we are. This place is beautiful and serene. Don't destroy that with questions Jake may not be ready to answer." I stride toward the bar.

"Grab me a sweet tea while you're at it?" Georgi calls.

"Of course."

Tyler, Brant, and Axel stand with Gary at the bar. I clink the ice in my cup. "Lemonade, please, and a sweet tea for Georgi."

Axel rests his forearm on the edge of the bar. "Who do you think is going to win?" I stare at Gary, so my eyes don't roll.

Didn't I just have this conversation? Can't anyone come up with something else to talk about? Sports, weather, life on Mars, anything?

"I don't know. Jake's not giving out any hints," I say.

Brant's eyes run from the top of my updo to the bottom of my peep toe shoes and back up. "We all know who's going to win. Only one of us is sleeping with the assistant."

My mouth drops open. "Excuse me?"

Axel fists his hand next to his mouth. "Dude, why would you say something like that?"

Brant sips his drink. I can't tell if it's whiskey or iced tea. I'm assuming whiskey based on his comment. "We woulda had better odds if Sullivan was a chick."

"My relationship with Keegan has nothing to do with Jake's decision."

Brant leans close. Yeah, he's been drinking whiskey. "You can tell yourself that, but we all know the truth. If you win, it's only because of Jake's friendship with your boyfriend. We saw how you burned that chicken, can't trim a brisket, or pull the silver skin from a rack of ribs."

He laughs into his glass as he takes another sip.

Nothing he said is wrong. I'm not the best chef. I burn things, and my flavors are off sometimes. If Jake wants perfection from a successor, I am not the obvious choice.

Considering Jake didn't tell us how we're being graded, it's logical to conclude that if I win, it will be because Jake loves Keegan and wants to make him happy.

But I am flippin' fantastic when I need to be. I'm learning and willing to take risks in search of perfection.

Brant's accusation ignores a lot about Jake's character. He could sell the restaurant and retire comfortably. Except, he doesn't do things to curry favor with others. He never *had* to teach his masterclass or offer the restaurant as a prize to one of us.

Jake's concerned more about the restaurant's future than the digits in his bank account balance. He values people and commitment. Those are things I value as well.

A flashback of Graham talking about Willa illuminates my mind. I never got to talk to her. Graham wouldn't give anyone I know her phone number, and it's one of my deepest regrets. When I get back to Emerald Bay to pack up my stuff, the first thing I'm doing is finding her parents to get the number.

Brant is so like Graham. He's scared and intimidated and likely thinks lashing out at me will make him feel better about himself.

If I've learned anything being here, from seeing what Keegan went through to earn respect that should have been a given, I know I can't be silent.

"Brant, I'm sorry that me being me threatens you. It was never my intention to make you feel insecure. I don't know why Jake decided to pass his legacy along the way he did, but I promise, if he chooses me, I'll do everything in my power to maintain the great reputation he's built. If he chooses you, I will loudly applaud you from the sidelines. We aren't rivals. We are teammates. When one of us succeeds, we all succeed. Good luck." I take my cups from Gary and walk back to my table with my head held high.

Brant's issues are about him, not me. I hope he learns that bullying and demeaning people isn't a positive, productive, or kind way to live his life.

When I approached the table, Turner stands and leads them in a round of applause. Georgi whoops and whistles a sharp shriek in the air. "That's my girl. Sweet as honey and sharp as a knife."

Jake follows Georgi's whistle with one of his own. "Since it seems there is some strife related to the naming of my successor, let's get this business out of the way." He turns to Amanda's oldest son. "Lawrence, may I have a drum roll please?"

The boy tosses his long bangs out of his eyes and pounds his fists on the wooden table.

"Y'all have done amazing jobs over the last three weeks. I appreciate your commitment and the time you dedicated to learning my calling. I've watched you work independently and in groups. A lifetime of experience has taught me that the best leaders are not the people who know everything, but those who are willing to ask for help, take risks, and learn from their mistakes. To that end, I've decided I'm leaving my legacy to two of you. Bridgette and Amanda will you please stand."

Amanda steps next to me and we clasp hands.

Jake raises his glass. "Ladies, you are two of the finest people I've had the privilege to know. Bridgette, your creativity is infectious, keep it up. Amanda, you were right, Jake's BBQ needs a catering arm and you are a force to be reckoned with. I would like you to take over Jake's BBQ and make it yours."

Cheers erupt from the crowd.

Tyler lifts his glass. "Three cheers for Bridgette and Amanda, the new proprietresses of Jake's BBQ. Now, please fix his awful dessert menu."

I bite my lip to control my smile. "We can do that." I lean against the table and catch Daisy's eye. "I hear you have a Bayou Goo Pie recipe that rivals my peach cobbler."

Georgi clings to Daisy's arm. "Please, please, please, give her the recipe. I'll bring you flat whites every day for a year if you do."

Daisy blushes. "Deal!"

"Yes." Georgi fist bumps Tipsy.

The loud chorus of celebration takes over the yard, except for Brant, who looks like he wants to crawl under the table in embarrassment.

I get it. He was excited about the possibility of having a well-respected, profitable restaurant dumped in his lap.

Gary lifts Amanda off her feet and spins her as he kisses every inch of her face.

Keegan should be here.

I reinforce my smile, but I doubt it reaches my eyes. Georgi shakes me. "Why aren't you happier?"

"What if Keegan doesn't want to move back?"

"Honey, that boy is in love with you. He'll be wherever you are."

"Shouldn't the same be said for me? If I love him, shouldn't I move to Dallas?"

"Let's think about that later." She pushes my lemonade into my hand. "Right now, we toast to your epic future. To Bridgette and Amanda." She clinks her glass against mine and presses the cup to her lips.

A chorus of "Here, here!" and "Congratulations" follows me around the rest of the afternoon.

I want to be excited. I was for a few minutes until I saw Gary and Amanda celebrating. The effervescent feeling deflated out of my chest. An uncomfortable twisting hollows my belly.

I wanted this. I asked for it. But now that I have it, I don't know what to do with it. I need to talk to Keegan face-to-face to figure out the unknowns.

I'm hiding on Amanda's front stoop when Dotty finds me. "You're staying?" she asks.

"Keegan and I need to talk, but yeah, it looks like it." That's probably more honesty than she expected, but that's what you're always going to get with me.

She harrumphs and sits next to me. "Well, in that case. I owe you an apology."

"I accept."

Her forehead creases. "I didn't apologize yet."

I wrap my arm around her shoulders. "You apologize for being a mean, angry, hurt, heartbroken, plate-smashing, finger-pointing—"

"Yes, yes, yes. All those things. You were right. I was raised to value other people's opinions quite highly, and maybe I let that get the better of me. Turner hurt me, and it's easier to hold that anger than forgive him."

"It's okay. Habits are hard to break. If it weren't for solving the mystery of why Turner ran away from Bubee, I would be in the same position as you are. It's hard to not care what people think of us or to interpret their actions as judgments on who we are. Especially when they are people whose opinions we cherish. But we need to make sure we silence the voices of the people who don't matter."

"Quite philosophical."

I nod to Turner, sitting with his sister and half my barbecue class. He's demonstratively telling a story that has everyone holding their stomachs and wiping tears of laughter from their cheeks.

"I had a good teacher. No one else could get me to debate Faust or Machiavelli for hours, then suggest a good steamy romance to cleanse my brain." I stand and extend my hand to her. "Would you like to join us?"

"I would. Thank you."

Chapter 37

Keegan

Cicadas sing in the bushes surrounding Gran's gazebo. I weave my fingers through Bridgette's. "Congratulations, Sunflower." I kiss her knuckles. "I missed you so much this week."

"What was it like being back in the hospital?"

"Calming. I pinned a humerus fracture for a kid shooting to earn a spot on A&M's football team. Add in a couple dozen knee replacements and a smattering of rotator cuff repairs, and I felt like the old me."

The relief on a patient's face when their pain is gone is what I live for, but I hated how lonely my apartment felt.

Bridgette and I chatted while I was gone, but it's not the same as snuggling under the stars.

"And the other thing?" she asks.

"The truth is slowly spreading. When people talk about me, sympathy fills their expressions instead of revulsion."

"The hospital is home again." There's something about her voice I can't place. Is she scared?

"It is."

"That leaves us with a hard decision." She spins so she's sitting cross-legged next to me. "Did Jake tell you he was going to pick me?"

"No. He kept telling me he wanted to give it to Declan."

"He would never stay in Texas. It's too hot."

I tuck a strand of hair behind her ear. "I bet you could convince him."

"Me?"

"I'm not the only one who fell in love with you at first sight."

She shoves my shoulder. "You did not."

I tug her into my lap. "Maybe not the way I love you now, but it was the beginning. I knew you were special. Unique."

She searches my eyes and sucks in a deep breath. "Dallas or Bubee?"

"I have a suggestion, but I need you to hear me out before you answer."

She taps the button on my shirt. "That makes me nervous."

"Me too." I trail kisses along the edge of her jaw.

"I'm not going to be able to listen if you distract me."

I add another layer of kisses to the shell of her ear. "As a busy business owner, you have to learn to multitask."

Her hand presses against my chest. "Do you want me to multitask making out with you and doing something else?"

"Well ... when you put it that way." I kiss the inside of her wrist. "What if we split our time between here and Dallas?"

"But—"

I press my finger to her lips. "I asked you to hear me out, please."

She nips the end of my finger.

"Amanda's wedding business is busiest in the spring and the fall, so she'll have less time to devote to Jake's. What if we spend May thru July and September thru November here running Jake's, and the rest of the time in Dallas."

"Will the hospital let you do that?"

"Bud says if I can find someone to fill the operating room time slots, we can swing it. Nathan wants to expand his practice, so if you're okay with it, I was going to ask him to be my partner."

"I thought you hated Nathan."

One of only a million little things that have changed in the last month. I could never have confronted Cynthia without Nathan by my side. "He's a good guy. I trust him to have our best interests at heart."

"That sounds like a great compromise. Are you going to help me barbecue?"

"Some, but the hospital here needs an ortho, so I'll split my time."

"And what do I do all day while you chop people apart in Dallas?"

I shake her shoulders. "What is it with people making me sound like a serial killer?"

She giggles and taps my chin. "That doesn't answer my question."

"What would you like to do?"

"I don't know. I have to think about it, but I hate the idea of sitting on my butt at home all day."

"There are endless opportunities for an ambitious woman to make her mark on that town. Besides, being in Dallas doesn't prevent you from being part of the team at Jake's. You can work remotely."

Georgi pops her head between us. "Or he could knock you up. That will keep you plenty busy."

I shove her face out of the way. "Gees, Georgi. Way to ruin a moment." She's like an annoying sister sometimes.

She flutters her fingers toward my groin. "What? Everyone's thinking it."

Bridgette swings her legs off my thighs. "What are you doing here?"

"Dotty had me bring her over to see Turner."

"Those two are worse than horny teenagers."

Over the last week, Bridgette's caught them making out in the gazebo, Georgi's car, under the pier during sangria night, and at Daisy's dining table.

I'm happy for them. It makes fixing the shack less of a priority for all of us, but still ... privacy is important.

"They give you two a run for your money in the PDA department." Georgi props her chin on the railing. "So, Dr. Love, what are your intentions for my girl here?"

Bridgette leans next to Georgi's ear. "Daisy made Bayou Goo. If you hurry, I'm sure she'll let you lick the bowl."

"Bye, y'all. Don't do anything I wouldn't do."

Bridgette rubs the bridge of her nose. "She's something else."

"She does have a point, though."

"Besides the one on the tip of her nose?"

"We skipped so many of the *get to know you* conversations. I know I love you and you love me, but what about the rest of it? You freaked out before when we talked about me proposing."

"It's too soon."

"Do you want to get married? Are we doing the committed-life-partner thing or the big-white-wedding thing?"

She twists her mouth and glances out to sea. "Both my best friends eloped without me. I don't want to do that to the people we love, but I don't need the expense or spectacle of an elaborate party either. Something small on the beach would be enough for me." She rests her forehead against mine. "When we decide the time is right."

"How will we know?"

"I'm not sure."

I reach into my pocket and pull out a canary yellow, heart-shaped diamond ring. "I think the time is right. Will you marry me?"

She scrambles off my lap. "You are such a liar."

"What?" That's not the reaction I expected. Where's the joyous jumping up and down?

She smacks my shoulder. "You just agreed it's too soon."

"That was before I knew what kind of relationship you wanted. Now I know, so I think we're ready."

She paces the gazebo. "I haven't met your parents. You haven't met mine."

I grab her hand and slide the ring over the tip of her finger. "If you say yes, everyone you love will be here in an hour for dinner. If not, it's going to be the most awkward dinner party Daisy's ever thrown."

Turner helped me arrange bringing her parents and best friends here to celebrate this weekend. It wasn't easy keeping everything a secret, but we did it. By the shimmer in her eyes, I think it was the right decision.

"You did that? You flew them down here?"

Family and friends are everything to Bridgette. I don't know if she's ever met a person who didn't become a friend within five minutes of their first conversation.

She's gravity. She's my sunflower.

I slide the ring the rest of the way onto her finger, cup her face, and kiss her softly. "Sunflower, I love you. You are my world. I want to spoil you and show you how loved and cherished you are every day. I can't be the man I want to be without you by my side. Please say yes. Be my forever."

"Yes. Yes. Forever yes!" She launches herself into my arms and kisses me with an intensity that leaves me breathless.

Every heartache and hard day was worth it because it brought me here to her.

Epilogue

Georgi

EVEN THOUGH JAKE'S BBQ is technically closed for Keegan and Bridgette's private event, it's packed. Wall to wall, sand bar to sand bar. The entire town—plus half of Minnesota—dressed up and turned out for Bridgette and Keegan's "small" beachside wedding, whether they were invited or not.

It doesn't suck to be loved.

It explains why Dr. Jerk-Face-Sugar-Free-Sanchez is standing at the bar laughing with Keegan.

Bridgette wraps her arm around my waist. "If you stare at Theo any harder, the back of his head might explode. Is that what you're going for?"

I point from my eyes to his head. "Do you think that would work? How did Cyclops get his laser eyes?"

"Sorry, I don't speak X-Men."

"No, I'm sorry. I shouldn't be pouting at your wedding." Bridgette has become one of my best friends. She doesn't mind my strange idiosyncrasies or random references to supernatural creatures. It's a bummer she and Keegan are only here six months out of the year. There's always hope that will change. Rachel said he's upping his hours at Third Coast Regional and had lunch with Dr. Crumb Bum Thompson the other day.

Bridgette snags a glass of bubbly from a passing waiter. "No worries. Talking to you allows me to escape Turner and Dotty making out by the cake table. Those two need to get a room already."

"They have a room. They just don't like using it."

We both wrinkle our noses. "Eww."

"Did Keegan tell you where you're going on your honeymoon yet?" I ask.

She drops her head back and growls. "No. I have snooped everywhere I can think of. There's nothing on his phone or in his e-mail. Daisy's not talking, and neither are my parents or Turner."

I bump her hip. "You'll have fun, I promise."

"You know?"

"I helped him plan it. You're welcome."

If I could plan a dream honeymoon, it wouldn't be what Keegan and I planned for Bridgette, but that's the point. It's perfect for her, and I love that I got to be a part of it.

"Can you tell me how to pack then? Because he won't. I've got one suitcase full of snow gear and one full of bikinis. If we're going to Hawaii, I don't want to schlep my parka across the continent, but he's not helping."

I mime zipping my lips shut.

"I'll send Theo over here to talk to you if you don't answer me."

"Are he and Keegan like friends now or something?"

"Or something. They talk about the boats a lot, and Keegan is trying to convince him to buy part of Willard Island and designate it a bird sanctuary."

"Why would he want to build a bird sanctuary?" I may not know much about Theo—how to protect myself from his smoldering chocolate eyes, I'm still working on that skill—but I don't think birds are his thing.

"Your guess is as good as mine. I usually tune out at that point in the conversation."

The speakers squeak. "We need the bride to the dance floor."

"Duty calls." She gives me a parting hug and weaves into the crowd.

I follow behind her fluffing her skirt. It's what any good bridesmaid would do.

Bridgette gasps. I step around her to see what's wrong.

But nothing's wrong.

Everything is perfect.

Keegan's standing on a picnic table in the middle of a dance floor. "Hello, wife. I owe you a dance." He stomps on the table with his cowboy boot.

She presses trembling fingers to her lips. "You remembered."

My heart melts. Tears spring to my friend's eyes, and her radiant smile makes *me* glow. I nudge her forward. "Get up there."

Her friends from Minnesota lift her onto the table. "I thought you didn't dance on tables," she says to her husband.

"I just needed a good reason."

An Imagine Dragons ballad serenades the group as Dr. and Mrs. Sullivan sway to the beat above our heads.

I feel *him* at my elbow, heat radiating from Theo's body before he speaks. His lips are so close to my ear, goosebumps erupt down both my arms. "You look beautiful tonight, Georgi."

"Good evening, Dr. Sanchez. Glad you could ditch your entourage for the party."

He slides his pinky along mine, palm up. "May I have this dance?"

The gooey, glowy feeling hardens in my belly. I tuck my hand around my stomach. "No."

"How about the next one?"

"My dance card's full."

"What do I have to do to get you to spend time with me?"

I turn so we are nose to nose. "That's not going to happen." I keep my eyes locked on his, so they don't drift down to his full mouth and sinfully dazzling smile.

Don't fall for it again.

He scrapes his bottom teeth across the edge of his upper lip, and my stupid eyes follow. He toys with the bow at my hip. "Why not?"

"You know why." Unfortunately, my words come out as a breathy sigh.

Being this close to him is dangerous.

Theo's five o'clock shadow amplifies the sharp chiseled angle of his jaw. His broad shoulders project a strength and security I want to sink into.

If I'm not careful, I'll get lost in the deep brown of his eyes like I did the first day I met him. When I thought he liked me, let him kiss me, and wasted too much time daydreaming about his lips on mine.

I won't let that happen again.

This is reality. I'm not a fairytale princess about to be miraculously whisked from my lowly life of poverty into an enchanted castle.

"I need you to leave me alone." I tell my feet to step back. They don't respond.

He stops playing with the flower, and his hand settles fully on the small of my back. "But I don't want to."

"Are all anesthesiologists as full of themselves as you are? I'm not going to be the stupid local girl who falls into your arms. I don't do swoony."

He tsks. "It is my mission to convince you otherwise because I know you're not stupid. You are brilliant. Breathtaking. Delightfully enigmatic. And ... you enjoy our Saturday night conversations as much as I do."

"I do not."

His thumb rubs methodical, intoxicating circles along my spine, and I have to scream at my knees to stay locked. "Princess, I watch you for at least five minutes before I walk into the coffee shop."

"Your point?" My skin needs to stop buzzing.

His eyes caress my cheeks. "You fix your hair and make-up before I come in every week."

I swallow the inconvenient lump in my throat. "No, I don't."

"Just give it time. I'll convince you I'm not the monster you think I am."

"Doubtful."

His lips whisper against my ear. "Then why is your hand curling into the front of my shirt? I like your warm hand on my skin."

I snatch my hand back. When did that happen? How did I lift my arm without even realizing it?

He lifts my hand to his mouth and kisses the inside of my wrist. "No offense to Bridgette, but you are the most beautiful woman in this room. You've melted my heart of stone, and someday I hope to return the favor."

Why do I want his words to be true? You'd think I would have learned my lesson the first time.

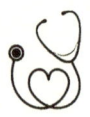

Bridgette has no idea what Keegan and Georgi planned for her honeymoon. That's because they need YOU to help them finalize the details. Scan the QR code to participate in a "Choose Your Own Adventure" style one-of-a-kind bonus epilogue.

QR code for Bonus Epilogue

**Participation does not require you to sign up for Daphne's VIP reader group. You will receive an email to kick off the experience and then be given the opportunity to join The Darlings reader group if you want to.

I won't flood your inbox with emails you don't want. My goal is to entertain and delight and nothing is less delightful than SPAM.**

Stuck with the Anesthesiologist

Don't miss book 2 in the Third Coast Medical Romance Series

I FELL IN LOVE with Georgiana Montgomery in one night and destroyed her faith in me the next.

I've spent the last year trying to right the epic screw up of our second date, but Georgi's made up her mind about me. I'm too shallow, egotistical, and unlovable to forgive.

But Georgi is the only one I can turn to when my sister shows up at our family's mega yacht anxiety ridden and contemplating abandoning her bid for the Olympic dive team.

Georgi's uncle kicked her out of their trailer and, as underhanded as it is, I'll use the opportunity to help the two women I love the most in the world. Her heart of gold will help calm my sister's nerves and fix the second biggest failure in my life, and I can give Georgi a home ... even temporarily.

Maybe being stuck with this anesthesiologist will finally let me prove to Georgi what I've known all along: we are soulmates and true love can be a fairy tale.

Treat yourself to Georgi and Theo's billionaire small town romance, the next book in the Third Coast Medical Romance Series, today.

Afterword

Dear Darling Reader,

Bridgette and Keegan's happily ever after didn't start out the way it ended.

When I first envisioned their story, Bridgette was a smaller personality. She hid behind her friends, was insecure, and pretty mopey. Love was going to pull her out of her shell and help her find her strength.

But the more time I spent with her, I realized she wasn't the kind of woman I wanted to hang out with for the six-ish hours it takes to read a book, let alone the five months it takes me to craft a novel. I knew in my heart of hearts, *joyless* wasn't who Bridgette actually was.

It took a spur of the moment Taylor Swift concert and helping my oldest wrestle with social issues after they broke their leg to land on why.

Jerry McGuire got it wrong.

Love does not complete us. We don't need to have a significant other to find the best version of ourselves.

We were each created to be our authentic selves without reservation or limitation.

That's where old Bridgette got it wrong. She based her self-worth on whether or not the cute guy in the barbecue class liked her.

As you've read, Keegan had a mountain of issues to solve. He was in no place to solve Bridgette's as well. She needed to have an inner strength drive her to take risks with her heart and allow herself to be vulnerable. Only then could she learn that the opinions of others don't matter if they compromise who you are and what you stand for.

This is a lesson I am constantly relearning. I'll get it for a while, then something will send me into a doubt spiral and I'll wonder if I'm worthy, if I'm enough, or if I've screwed everything up (again.)

My hope and wish for you is that reading Bridgette and Keegan's story has 1) entertained you, but also 2) allowed you to check in with your self-worth.

Do you give other voices more credit than they deserve?

Do you love who you are while striving to take steps toward the version of yourself you hope to be in five years?

Darling, in you there is no flaw. Own who you are. Love yourself. Ignore the voices that don't matter.

Thank you for spending time with me and my characters.

Best Wishes and Happy Reading,

Daphne

About Daphne

Lover of baking and running, Daphne spends her days imagining ways to mend broken hearts for happily ever afters. She currently resides in Texas, but was raised in Las Vegas (yes, that Vegas) and has the stories to prove it. Her kids make her a little crazy, as does her husband, but she wouldn't want to explore this beautiful world without them.

Visit her at www.DaphneDyer.com, Facebook at Author Daphne Dyer or Instagram at Author Daphne Dyer.